The Castle Doctrine

Daniel Faust, Book Six

by Craig Schaefer

D1328551

Cover Design by James T. Egan of Bookfly Design LLC.
Author Photo ©2014 by Karen Forsythe Photography
Craig Schaefer / The Castle Doctrine
ISBN 978-1-944806-03-3

The Daniel Faust Series

Prologue

Jace Brubaker didn't believe that a man's home was his castle. His home was a squalid roach trap back in Tucson, littered with cigarette butts and photographs of the kid he hadn't seen in five years. His castle, though, that was the open road. He ruled his kingdom from the leather bucket seat of a copper-painted Freightliner Coronado, six hundred horsepower of thundering steel with bright chrome stacks and a raised sleeper cab. Jace was one of a dying breed: a genuine owner-operator who held the slip to his rig, free and clear. After twenty years of long-hauling for a company that never spelled his name right on the paychecks, saving and scrimping every last penny to buy the Coronado, he had more or less resolved to blow his brains out behind the wheel before he'd ever call another man boss.

The work took him from New York City to the San Francisco Bay, snow to sunshine as the contracts shifted with the seasons, and that was just the way he liked it. You could be anyone you wanted out on the road, with nobody to question you. Sometimes he could even get a truck-stop waitress to call him "Jace the Ace," a nickname nobody had ever called him back home, but he steadfastly swore they all did. Tonight he was rolling up I-80 west just outside of Des Moines, hauling a forty-foot refrigerated trailer with a chugging, leaky compressor that occasionally drooled wisps of silver smoke into the tangerine sky. The trees along the highway stretched out skeletal fingers, nestling in blankets of rusty red and orange. Halloween weather.

Halloween was still three weeks away, but the big dusty sign for the Long Sun Truck Stop had a line of gaudy plastic pumpkins dangling along one side, strung like a tacky earring. A cardboard skeleton waved from the diner window as Jace eased his semi into the parking lot. His wheels rumbled on loose gravel, brand-new air brakes bringing him to a stop with barely a whisper. Jace gave the steering wheel an affectionate pat and checked himself in the rearview. Two days of stubble, could do with a shave and a splash of cologne, but he figured he wasn't unfit for human company just yet. He adjusted his white baseball cap—emblazoned with a black ace of spades, just like the driver's-side door—and hopped down from the cab.

Jace gave the semitrailer a once-over as he strolled on by, checking the tires, smiling at the cartoon pig on the side. This week's cargo was frozen sides of beef. The pig, dressed in an apron and chef's hat, beamed down at him and offered up a plate of steaming steaks. "Lombardi Meats," read the script beneath, "Come Meet our Meat!"

A steak sounded good right about then. After ten hours on the road with nothing but a weigh station to break his stride, he would have settled for burnt hamburger. *Might not have a choice,* he thought, navigating the lot and making his way toward the diner. Eating at a strange truck stop was like playing culinary Russian roulette. You might get a five-star meal, served up by some short-order cook who should be working in a big-league restaurant but never found his way. Or you might get heartburn and a bad case of the runs. Jace kept a bottle of Pepto in his glove box and took his chances.

Wiping his boots on a crusty welcome mat, he could have been anywhere in America. Dirty linoleum, yellow vinyl booths, the rattle of aluminum pans, and the smell of eggs and black coffee. A diner was pretty much a diner anywhere you went. Jace sidled up to the counter and sat back on a stool, picking up a laminated menu that might have been printed sometime back in the seventies. He didn't know why he bothered; in a place like this, there was only one way to guarantee a decent meal.

"What's good today?" he asked the waitress, who had probably been working there since around the time the menus were printed.

"If you don't mind breakfast for supper, can't go wrong with the corned beef hash."

"Sounds good. Set me up with the hash and a couple of eggs, sunny side up. And a coffee, thanks."

As she scribbled his order down, hooking the scrap of paper up behind the counter on a clothespin for the cook, the man sitting two stools down glanced his way. "A wise choice," he said with a genteel smile, gesturing at the same order on his own plate.

The guy was a weird sight for a truck stop. Older than the usual crowd, with dusky skin that almost looked dusty under the cheap fluorescent lights. Dust on his suit, too, a twill number with leather patches on the elbows like an old-time college professor, and a yellow bow tie with tiny brown dots.

"Good to hear," Jace said, returning the smile. "You traveling far?"

"Oh, yes. All the way to the West Coast. Going to visit an old friend." His smile grew, baring yellowed teeth. "Ecko's the name. Damien Ecko, at your service. Formerly the proprietor of D. Ecko and Company Jewelers. Alas, my fortunes took an unexpected turn. Had to close up shop."

"I hear ya. This damn economy, man, it's killing everybody. I'm Jace. Jace the Ace, that's what my friends call me."

Ecko ran the tip of his tongue over his teeth, as if tasting the name.

"Jace the Ace. Ah, like your cap. A fine appellation." He nodded to the window. "Saw you pull in. Is that a *refrigerated* truck?"

"The trailer is, yeah. She's a beauty. Keeps the meat so fresh you'd swear it was from right next door. You know, most people don't realize how far away their food gets trucked in from. Your average city is about three days from starvation if the trucks ever stop running."

Jace had picked up that fact from a *Reader's Digest* article, and he was very proud of it. Damien's eyes opened wider, acknowledging his expertise.

"You perform an invaluable service, good sir. Ah, to ride the open road on eighteen wheels. It must be majestic."

Jace shrugged, almost bashful. "Well, it's a living. What are you driving?"

Ecko sipped his coffee and sighed. "Sadly, nothing at all. My car broke down two miles up the road. An acquaintance of mine in Nevada owes me a good deal of money, but I have to collect it in person. So, for the moment, I find myself reliant on the kindness of strangers."

As the waitress brought over his plate, eggs steaming and the hash glittering with salt, Jace gave his dining companion a long, measuring look. He wasn't in the habit of taking on passengers; he liked making small talk here and there, but out on the highway he preferred his radio for company. Still, he didn't like the idea of leaving the old guy stranded in the middle of nowhere, not with night settling in and bringing the midwestern autumn cold with it. He just knew if he left, he'd pick up the paper tomorrow and read something about the cops finding the guy frozen and stiff at the side of the road. No, he couldn't have that on his conscience.

"Tell you what," Jace said, "I'm driving as far as Omaha tonight. If you want to ride with me, that'll get you a little closer to where you're going."

"You," Ecko told him, "are a hero and a gentleman. A most unexpected lifesaver."

They finished their meals and set out side by side. Night had fallen now, turning the parking lot into a corral of slumbering mammoths. Big steel, silent in the dark.

At the edge of the lot, the cab's nose facing a vacant and weed-choked field next to the truck stop, Jace hopped up into the throne of his rolling castle. He leaned over and pushed open the passenger-side door. The old guy was spry for his age, clambering up and inside, pulling on the seatbelt and adjusting his bow tie.

"Y'okay with country music?" Jace asked him.

"I'm partial to the opera," Ecko replied, "but country's fine. I believe the rules of the road state that a driver's authority over his own radio should never be questioned."

"We're gonna get along just fine," Jace said and slid the key into the ignition.

"Indeed. There is just...one thing, though."

"Yeah? What's that?"

The semi's engine rumbled to life, like the deep-throated purr of a lion. The headlights clicked on, washing the field in blinding halogen, turning night to day.

There were people in the field.

Twenty, maybe thirty of them, standing motionless in the headlights' glare. All of them turned toward the truck. All of them stared up at Jace. His short-lived surprise changed to confusion—and then to a cold, creeping fear that knotted his guts.

Some of the people wore paper hospital gowns, standing barefoot in the weeds. Others were stark naked, untouched by the autumn chill, and their chests bore the Y-shaped stitches of an autopsy. A woman looked up at Jace with wide, hungry eyes, as if she wanted to say something. But she couldn't, not without a lower jaw, her mouth a wet red ruin. A man beside her was missing the top of his skull, the bone sliced away with surgical precision to bare the rotted gray meat of his brain.

"We need to bring my friends along, too," Ecko said. "It's all right. They can ride in the back."

1.

My life wasn't exactly a riches-to-rags story. I never did manage the "riches" part. Still, I'd been somebody once. I had a home, cash in my pocket, and just enough security and comfort to take it all for granted.

Now I didn't even have a name.

As far as the government was concerned, Daniel Faust died in a prison riot. I'd burned my last lifeline, my final get-out-of-jail-free card, and killed my old identity just like I'd killed the warden of Eisenberg Correctional: at close range and without mercy. Now I was free and clear. Free to answer one burning question.

What do you do when you lose it all?

I guess if you're me, you find yourself in an alley in East Las Vegas, on a stretch of bad road you don't see in the tourist brochures. The Delaney brothers were in town, straight out of Belfast, flush with cash from a bank job. One wild night at the Medici had separated these two fools from their money, and now they had a quick, fat score in mind. They needed a hired wand. I needed operating capital. Needed it badly enough to consider working with the Delaney brothers, anyway.

"Y'gonna light him on fire?" Scottie asked, looming over me like a wall made of blubber with his face stuffed into an olive ski mask.

"I am not," I said for the fourth time, "lighting anybody on fire."

"Stop pesterin' the man," growled Sean—older, a grizzled

scarecrow with a body and teeth straight out of a "don't do meth" poster—"and take that bloody mask off. It ain't time yet."

"So when's it gonna be time?"

"It's time," I answered for Sean, "when you let me concentrate for five seconds."

"Mikki just lit people on fire," Scottie said. No idea who he was talking about. Didn't care. He caught Sean's glare and finally shut up.

I crouched on an oil-stained patch of asphalt, holding my open palms over a cracked clay bowl stained the color of rust, where the remnants of a half-smoked cigar nestled in a puddle of white ashes. Symbols painted in ash ringed the bowl at north, west, south, and east, winding glyphs in a forgotten language. The sorcerers who invented this spell had to reckon directions by the sun and the moon. I used a digital compass. I lit a second cigar—a Dominican Carrillo, with gold leaf writing on ink-black bands—and puffed it to life. A woody, hickory taste filled my mouth, painting over the bitter aftertaste of smoke.

Or maybe the bitterness came from realizing I was pushing forty, homeless, broke, and about to rob a liquor store. Yeah. I was going places.

I exhaled my resentment and it billowed past my lips, transformed into smoke. It emerged as whispered words, a slow and soft chant in a language only dead men remembered. Ashes rained down to feed the bowl. Silky smoke twisted up to feed the night sky. Words fed the world, soothing it, seducing it into bending to my will. Just a little, here and there. A tiny quiver at the edges of reality, a narrow stage where I could stand and issue my decree. Sometimes, with the shadows lit like neon in my second sight and the winds of magic churning around me, I had a sudden sense of history. As if I could see all the sorcerers who had come before me, standing in a long and unbroken chain stretching out across time.

Conjurers and philosopher kings. Victorian showmen and hermetic artists, builders and keepers of the Promethean fire. All the way back to the oldest shamans in the oldest caves, the first humans to interrogate the universe and come away with secrets earned through pain and blood.

And then there was me. I wondered if they could see me, too.

The smoke and the words struck a bargain with the universe. The ashes gave that bargain a place to rest. My penknife, whipping across my arm, stinging like a rattlesnake bite, offered the payment. Droplets of my blood tumbled from the shallow cut like a scattered handful of garnets, splashing over the glyphs one by one. North, west, south, east. I'd snuffed the cigar, but the smoke still streamed from my parted lips like a gossamer rope. Then I spoke the last word of the chant and the smoke faded, leaving me with the taste of dirty hickory on the roof of my mouth.

"Wait for my signal," I said, ripping open a Band-Aid and slapping it over my cut. I pulled on a pair of leather driving gloves. Then I dug my fingers into the bowl, scooping out a handful of ash.

I took a walk, right across the barren street, to the only place on the block that wasn't closed for the night or boarded up: Larry's World of Liquor. The name shouted down from a strobing marquee, ringed by bulbs that flashed like the gate to a carnival. It smelled a little like a carnival, too, the odor of stale beer and salty peanuts hanging in the stagnant air. Keeping my fingers curled and the ashes tucked away, I pretended to go shopping, scouting the aisles for civilians. We'd picked a good time: the balding cashier and I had the place all to ourselves. He sat on a stool, idly reading a gossip magazine, one hand never far from the shotgun we knew he had stashed behind the counter. I grabbed a bottle of gin and walked on up, just another customer, just another night.

He stood and reached for the bottle, leaning closer to my side of the counter. I brought up my hand, palm open, and *blew*. The ashes hit his face like buckshot. His eyes rolled back and he collapsed, hitting the grimy tiled floor, a puppet with its strings cut. I gave a big wave to the plate-glass windows and hopped the counter.

Scottie and Sean burst in, Scottie playing pack mule with a rucksack full of tools jangling on his shoulder. Sean flipped the Open sign, locked the front door, and hustled over to take a look at the fallen clerk.

"He dead?" he asked me.

I was bent over the console behind the counter, the controls for the security cameras. "No. Sleeping. He'll be out cold until sunrise, and when he wakes up he won't remember anything from the last twelve hours or so."

I yanked the tape from the console—an old VHS-style clunker—and ran a magnet over the cassette. We killed the lights, shutting the store down, and then Sean and I dragged the clerk into the back room while Scottie set up his tools. Larry's World of Liquor wasn't a random hit. The proprietor—I never found out if his name really was Larry—had a bad habit of storing the shop's cash in a safe all week long, letting it pile up, then bringing it to the bank with an armed guard every Saturday morning.

Today was Friday.

For his lack of smarts elsewhere, Scottie was a virtuoso box-man. I watched the street, keeping an eye out, while he pulled on a welder's mask and went to work on the safe with a thermal lance. Even on the far side of the store I could feel the heat, simmering against my cheek like the noonday sun. The fading screech of the lance and Scottie's whoop of joy told me the box had cracked. I turned from the empty street and joined them behind the counter to see what was waiting beyond the half-melted steel door. Stacks and stacks of rubber-banded bills nestled in the safe, alongside pyramids of rolled coins. We bagged the bills, left the coins, and cleaned out the cash register for good measure. No idea how much the take was, not yet—you never count until the job is done. On our way to the door, Sean snatched a bottle of Hennessy, holding it up like a trophy.

"Ya oughta grab yerself something, Dan. It's all on the house tonight!"

I shrugged and picked up a bottle of Veuve Clicquot. Champagne for celebrating a clean getaway seemed like the thing to do. All the same, even after we met up at a dive pool hall a quarter-mile away, sequestered in a booth in the back to split up the take and go our separate ways, I left the bottle unopened. Just wasn't in the mood.

*   *   *

Technically I didn't go home. I hadn't had one since my last apartment burned down around my ears. I'd been relying on the kindness and the couches of my extended family ever since, mostly crashing at Bentley and Corman's cramped garret over the Scrivener's Nook. They were long asleep by the time I crept inside, cupping my keys tight to keep them from jingling as I padded across the vintage shag carpet and into the kitchen. Legs of a remaindered wooden chair scraped across yellowed tile. Their bedroom door up the hall was closed, so I clicked on the overhead light, put my purloined bottle of bubbly in the fridge, and sat at the cluttered kitchen table to get a little work done.

Everything was just where I'd left it: a small stack of books from the back-room archives, with moldering covers and names like *Studies in Esoteric Wisdom* and *Myth-Cycles of Preclassical Civilizations*. And my slowly growing stack of notes, the papers festooned with circles and lines and sharp, accusing arrows like something out of a paranoid's fever dream.

I wasn't paranoid. There really was somebody out to get me.

I'd had a vision behind bars, a shamanic nightmare courtesy of some enchanted prison wine. A walk through the burning streets of a ruined world, the Vegas Strip shattered in the aftermath of a brutal war. That's where I met Cassandra, the old bag lady who called herself a prophet. This wasn't our Earth, she told me; it was "the world next door." And the guy who'd burned it all down—sometimes called the man with the Cheshire smile, sometimes just the Enemy—was here in my backyard and getting ready for an encore performance.

Normally I'd take a hallucination like that with a full shaker of salt, but too many details checked out. Like Buddy, the brain-fried psychic who said he was Cassandra's twin and knew too many things he shouldn't have. Then there was Ms. Fleiss. I'd pulled a heist for her back in Chicago, stealing an Aztec dagger from a necromancer named Damien Ecko. Turned out she was working for the Enemy all along, and they buried me behind bars under a bogus conviction and a hell of a powerful curse to keep me there.

From what I'd pieced together, they needed somebody called "the Thief" dead, and at the same time, they still wanted the guy around for whatever they'd been planning. So they worked some substitutional sorcery, gave *me* the title of the Thief, then sent assassins to take me out. A symbolic blood sacrifice. What was it all for? If I knew that, I wouldn't have been up until dawn every night for over a week now, poring through Bentley and Corman's grimoires and searching for something, anything, to make sense of this mess.

I knew this much, though, knew it down in my gut: the man with the Cheshire smile was real. He was out there. And whatever he and Fleiss were cooking up, it was bad news for all of us.

2.

"Again?" asked the faded, frail voice from the kitchen doorway.

Bentley stared at me, his aged face etched with sleeplessness, the hem of his cashmere robe wavering around his stockinged feet. I felt like a recovering alcoholic who'd just been caught with a bottle of Jack Daniel's pressed to his lips.

"It's...important," was all I managed to say after a moment of mental fumbling, gesturing to an open book I was too exhausted to read. "Somewhere in these books, there's an answer. Or a clue. Something to go on."

"Daniel—"

"That curse he hit me with, distorting everyone's sense of time, implanting memories of a trial that never happened—he changed my life's *history*, Bentley. No magician alive should have been able to pull off a stunt like that. We don't even know if the Enemy is human, if he's a demon. We don't know where he is, what kind of resources he has—"

"*Daniel*," Bentley said, his voice schoolteacher-sharp.

I fell silent. He walked over and pulled back the other chair, sitting down across from me.

"You've been through a lot," he said, gentler now. "We all have. And I'm not discounting the threat at hand, but I'm starting to think this is becoming a bad habit. And I'm not sure you're entirely aware of it."

"Aware of what? Bentley, this is a crisis situation."

"It is *always* a crisis. Daniel, ever since you took that job investigating that poor girl's death in the storm tunnels, you've been pinballing from one emergency to another. You're not stopping to catch your breath, you're not taking care of yourself, and Cormie and I are getting worried."

I shook my head, not getting it.

"What are you talking about? I'm taking care of myself just fine."

His fingers rapped the page of notes between us.

"As happy as we are to have you here, your current situation says otherwise. You lost your apartment months ago. Have you done *anything* to try and find a new home for yourself? And pushing yourself to exhaustion every single night and sleeping most of the day isn't doing your health any favors. I almost wonder..."

He trailed off. I looked him in the eye.

"What?"

"I almost wonder," he said, "if your new obsession is that important to you, or if living in crisis mode is simply a convenient distraction from having to decide what you *want* to do with your life."

Up until that moment, I'd been going a hundred miles an hour. Now I felt like my transmission had just dropped out, spilling broken metal all over the highway. Jolting to a brick-wall stop.

Bentley reached out, put his hand over mine, and gently squeezed.

"That's...that's fair," I said. I was out of words at the moment. *That's fair* was the best I could manage as I stood back and took a good hard look at myself.

"Jennifer told me she offered you a seat on the New Commission."

"And I told her I'd work security for them, when they need it, but that's it." My brows furrowed. "I spent way too long as an errand boy for Nicky Agnelli. I don't want to *become* him. Besides, I figured you'd be happy I wasn't out there playing gangster."

"I think," he said, "I'd just be happy if you aspired to something more than this."

I sighed. Nodded. Picked up my notes and tucked them inside the front cover of a book, stowing them away for the night.

"I'll work on it," I told him. "And I'm not just saying that, all right? Tomorrow I'm going to see Paolo about my new papers. Once that's squared away, I can start...rebuilding, I guess. I'll figure it out."

His chair squeaked as he pushed it back, and he gave me a patient smile.

"That's all we ask. Good night, Daniel."

He puttered back to the bedroom, and I clicked off the kitchen lights on my way to the threadbare couch. I glanced back at the refrigerator, suddenly thirsty for a drink, and thought about the bottle of champagne.

No. That would keep. Call it motivation to do something worth celebrating.

*   *   *

The next morning found me in another winning stretch of town, a street lined with foreclosures and For Rent signs taped to boarded-up windows. That and the big bubbly sign for the Love Connection, emblazoned with hot-pink triple Xs. With my Barracuda impounded by the cops—and it wasn't like I could ask for it back, seeing as I was dead and all—Corman had rented a car for me in the meantime. It was a tiny two-door Chevy Spark hatchback painted a garish neon green that almost glowed in the dark. As I pulled up to the curb outside the friendly neighborhood porn boutique, I wondered if Corman had chosen it out of frugality or just because he thought it was funny to watch me drive a lime on wheels.

The wire-rack aisles, laden with DVDs offering every sexual escapade imaginable and a few I'd never heard of, were empty as the Nevada desert. Customers weren't exactly banging down the door to get in, though to be fair, Paolo didn't do a lot of advertising; the porn gig was just a front for his real career, a thriving backroom business that operated on an appointment basis only. I found him kicking back behind the counter, watching a video on his phone. From the muffled grunts and groans erupting from the tinny speaker, I figured he was sampling his own merchandise.

"Is that the new Jane Austen adaptation?" I asked, leaning against the counter. "I've heard good things."

He jumped and fumbled at his phone, killing the sound. He jammed it into his pocket and stood up, red-faced.

"Yeah," he said. "Great, uh, great acting. I love the classics. So, you got what I need?"

I crossed his palm with a stack of green. It was my entire take from last night's job plus a little extra. Paolo didn't work cheap, but this was the very definition of a good investment. He locked up the shop and took me in back, where he'd converted a small, concrete-walled stockroom into his personal studio. Three different printers shared table space with a twenty-seven-inch iMac and an artist's digital tablet, not far from a stool with a blue canvas backdrop and a digital camera on a tripod, like you might find at a DMV. He rubbed his hands and fired up the computer, gesturing for me to have a seat on the stool.

"Okay," he said, "I've already got a good chunk of your papers lined up. One big question: what's your new name gonna be?"

My old alter ego was Peter Greyson, a solid citizen with a bulletproof paper trail and a decent-to-middling credit history. I'd had Greyson's ID on me when I got busted. That left good old Pete nothing but ashes on the wind now, and I sure couldn't operate under my real name. I was legally a corpse, but my vitals, my mug shot, and my prints were filed on the federal ViCAP database. One inquiry in the wrong direction and I'd go from "dead and forgotten" to "alive and wanted in the worst way."

"Paul Emerson," I told him. Paul had been my cellmate at Eisenberg Correctional, and Emerson was an undercover Department of Corrections officer who'd needed a helping hand. Neither of them made it out of the Iceberg alive. I figured they'd earned a tip of the hat.

Paolo double-checked the spelling and fiddled with Photoshop. "That works. What's he do for a living?"

I shrugged. "I don't know."

He looked my way, tilting his head.

"Just make something up. If you weren't you—if you could be anything you wanted to be—what would it be?"

I had to think about that. And I kept thinking. A bottomless well of possibilities, and I came up bone-dry.

"Don't worry about it," Paolo said. "I'll make him an accountant. Nobody wants to talk to an accountant about his job anyway."

I watched an imaginary man come to life one piece at a time, born from pixels and laminated paper. Paul Emerson sprouted a high school diploma, then a degree in accounting from a decent midwestern college, pausing to get his driver's license and social security number on the way. He passed the CPA exam with flying colors, and his business cards—listing a dummy address and the number on my burner phone—sported crisp black type on cream.

The hours slid by, and Paolo kept working while I ran out to grab us some burgers from the fast-food joint down the street. By the time the sun started to shimmer down a late-afternoon desert sky, he'd finished painting the final strokes on his human canvas. Paul Emerson was respectable, boring, and immediately forgettable: the perfect life to hide my chaos inside, like a nesting doll with fireworks in its belly.

"You're gonna have to work on his credit," Paolo told me while I filled a brand-new wallet with Emerson's artfully aged papers. "Build it up slow, just like last time. First thing you should do is get him a bank account, and establish an activity trail. Put some cash in, keep it there, and start using his debit card for groceries and such."

"I know the drill," I said, checking the time on my phone. Building a solid cover didn't end when the printer cooled down. It was going to take months, maybe years to make Emerson's identity bulletproof, just like I'd already done for Peter Greyson. I was starting from square one, all over again.

The bank would wait until tomorrow. It was already getting late, and I had an appointment to keep. I said my goodbyes and headed outside. In the gathering dusk, my rental looked even more like a lime on wheels. My disdain wasn't what stopped me with one hand on the door handle, though; it was the rattle and hiss of a can of spray paint, coming from the alley alongside Paolo's shop. I didn't think Paolo would care about somebody tagging his wall, but I figured I should check it out anyway, make sure it was just a kid or a wannabe graffiti artist instead of a gangbanger claiming territory rights.

It was an artist, all right.

A painting eight feet high and half as wide adorned the bare brick wall, scarlet and mad. An impression of hooked claws and vast, staring eyes, perfectly round. A flurry of bloody feathers. And beside it, the artist was putting on his finishing touches: a message, painted in screaming, jagged letters.

THE OWL LIVES.

The can of spray paint tumbled from the artist's shaking hand, rolling across the dirty concrete to rattle against four of its empty cousins. The man was in his late forties, almost bald with a ring of tufted hair, and dressed in a three-piece suit with his tie loose and dangling. Sweat plastered his ruddy cheeks as he turned to face me, his lips twitching. He threw up one hand and pointed a finger at his design.

"Did you see it?" he demanded.

I shook my head, mute.

"Did you *see* her?" He clutched his scalp, his bloodshot eyes rolling back. "Did you dream the dream? I did. I dreamed the dream. Last night. It got into my *head*. It won't leave, not until I spread the good word."

This whole situation had the tang of bad craziness. I took a slow step back, toward the mouth of the alley.

"There was a wise owl, who flew from her oak," the man

groaned, "we all turn to ashes, the wheel broke. Her soul is hunting, for her and hers. She's got a promise to keep."

"That's real nice, guy," I said, holding up my empty hands as I made my exit. "I'm happy for you, really."

"The Owl is coming," he bellowed at my back as I hustled to my car, suddenly thankful for my lime-green sanctuary. "She's coming, and God's gonna bleed! *God's gonna bleed!*"

3.

I drove up a block, pulled over just long enough to shoot a quick text to Paolo—*crazy guy in your alley, steer clear*—and kept moving. I usually felt like I was armpits-deep in whatever latest madness had descended upon Las Vegas. There was something weirdly reassuring in the knowledge that my city could happily lose its damn mind *without* it being my fault once in a while. Everybody had their own crazy to deal with.

Mine, tonight, came in the form of a nondescript door and a small blue neon arrow, just off the Vegas Strip. I walked past the line out front, ignoring the crowd as I made my way toward a bouncer in dark glasses and a black muscle shirt. He gave me one look and unhooked the velvet rope, drawing a chorus of groans from the pretty pack of twentysomethings waiting to get inside.

Membership has its privileges.

The bass hit me like a boxer's fists, hammering my heart and my brain with a machine-gun flurry. Winter was jumping tonight. The nightclub bathed in aquamarine light as ice-white stars tumbled on wall-mounted LED screens in time to the rhythm. The heat stole my breath, the kind of heat you only get from hundreds of bodies packed together and moving to a simmering beat. I was glad I didn't have to find Caitlin in the mob. We had dinner plans just as soon as she finished a meeting, and the conference room at Winter was carefully hidden from the public eye. As I wound my way through the crowd, I caught a snatch of shouted conversation.

"Did you see? Taylor Swift is here!"

"Dude, that wasn't her. That didn't even look like her."

"It was *totally* her!"

My face scrunched like I'd just bit down on a lemon. There were two possibilities, as I saw them. Either a world-famous pop star had decided to pay a visit to a nightclub secretly owned and operated by the powers of hell, or Caitlin had a surprise visitor who, I strongly suspected, got off on being confused for said pop star. And had a thing for wreaking havoc in people's lives, mine included.

Down an access corridor lit by pipes of frosty neon, a solid door with a keypad barred the way to Winter's second level. The door's guardian stood still and silent, a hulk wearing a gas mask and a black leather apron. The rusty blade of a machete dangled at his hip. As I approached, he turned without a word and keyed in the access code.

"Hey, is Taylor Swift here?"

The opaque lenses of the gas mask turned my way, and he uttered something like, "Mwuh?"

I sighed. "Nadine. Is Nadine here?"

The big guy shrugged. "Bwuguh."

I patted him on the shoulder as the door chunked open, swinging back to reveal a long and shadowy staircase.

"Thanks for the chat," I said. "It's been fun."

The blue and white neon turned to gold, set into black octagonal walls that evoked the feeling of a honeycomb. The bass tempo, sealed behind steel and stone, faded to a distant heartbeat that steered my steps through the maze beneath the dance floor. I'd been down here enough times to stop getting lost on my way to the conference room, winding through grottoes and black-walled chambers, past orgiastic piles of hungry flesh, hands grasping, touching, clawing, and tableaux of elaborately orchestrated torment. The moans and the gasps washed over me, a fervent accompaniment to the distant, driving beat. I kept my eyes straight ahead and my feet moving. I wasn't much of a voyeur, and honestly, getting distracted by seedy, anonymous sex when there might be an ancient lust demon on the premises sounded like the definition of a bad idea.

Past another octagonal hive room—this one with sheets of plastic tacked up on the walls, more plastic on the floor, and a scent like honey in the air—and down a dead-end corridor, the conference room awaited. I wasn't alone. A woman stood sentry at the door, a tall Nordic goddess in black biker's leathers, her long blond hair done in a waist-length braid. The skin-tight pants or the strategically low zipper on her jacket might have distracted me if I hadn't caught a whiff of something darker than her outfit. She glowed in my second sight, her heart an onyx prism that sucked in the light and spat out shadows.

Incarnate demon. And not one I'd met before. Not a local. As I approached, slow, wary now, she got in my way and held up one palm to stop me.

"No admittance," she said, her words dripping with a thick Russian accent.

I could hear voices from behind the closed door, loud enough to catch the anger, too muffled for me to make out the words. I tilted my head, glancing past the woman's shoulder, trying to be nonchalant and keep the sudden, simmering anxiety in my stomach in check. Winter was neutral ground for delegates from the courts of hell, just like the Tiger's Garden was Switzerland for Vegas's magicians. Only problem: I was a magician, not a demon. The "neutral ground" rule didn't necessarily apply to me, and throwing down with an incarnate without preparing for the fight, especially with one you'd never encountered before, would be a great way to get your spine ripped out and your head used for a tetherball.

And with that lovely mental image, I gave her my friendliest smile and established my bona fides. "It's okay. I'm Faust. Daniel Faust. I'm with Caitlin."

"This one knows what you are." Her nose wrinkled. "No admittance."

I sighed. "You got a name?"

"Nyx."

The name rang a distant bell, but I couldn't remember where I'd heard it before. "Nyx, hi. Look, Caitlin's expecting me."

"She will expect you here, outside, when the meeting is finished. This one has her orders. No admittance to anyone, for any reason."

I took a step back, wondering just how badly I wanted to push it. Before I could decide, a sharp voice shouted from behind the door. Nadine.

"What do you mean, 'hands-off policy'?" she bellowed. "They *humiliated* my daughter!"

Nyx winced. I had to feel a little sympathetic. She must have been one of Nadine's bodyguards, part of her entourage from the Court of Night-Blooming Flowers. I couldn't imagine that was a fun job.

"Rough gig, huh?" I asked her.

"This one is honored by her calling and her duties," she replied.

"Yeah, but you gotta admit," I said with a nod to the door, "your boss is kind of an asshole."

Nyx stared at me. I felt the temperature drop, like the air around us had started to curdle.

Then the door flew open. Nadine stood on the threshold, dressed for a Fashion Week runway, looking back over her shoulder. "I don't *care*," she seethed, "you fix this, or I will. Come on, Nyx, we are *leaving*."

Nadine stomped out, saw me, and her eyes lit up. The next thing I knew I had my back to the wall, slammed against it so hard I nearly lost my breath, with her forearm barred across my chest and her lips inches from mine.

"*You*," she said. "You had a run-in with Harmony Black, didn't you?"

Now I wasn't breathing at all, focusing on my magical defenses, sparks of power struggling to shore up a wall of sandbags against the onslaught of her mind-bending touch. Tendrils of her jasmine perfume still slithered into my nose, into my mind, telling me to inhale. Breathe in. Breathe *her*.

"I-I did," I stammered. I couldn't think of lying to her. With her skin against mine, I literally couldn't comprehend the concept.

"And you want revenge, don't you? You want to kill her."

"No," I said, forcing the words out one at a time, "I really, really just want to stay the hell away from her, thanks."

The next thing out of Nadine's mouth was a strangled gulp. Caitlin was on her in a heartbeat, her eyes swirling orbs of molten copper as she grabbed Nadine by the throat, tore her away from me, and hoisted her up to her tiptoes.

"Apparently I have not been clear," Caitlin said, her faint Scottish burr tinged with irritation. "You do not touch my human. Ever."

Nyx hissed, her mouth suddenly lined with shark's teeth as she circled the two, getting behind Caitlin's back. I snapped my fingers, sharp, and a quartet of playing cards riffled from my hip pocket to my outstretched hand, fanning out like a sheaf of razors.

"*Ladies*," Royce said, dressed in cultured arrogance and black Armani as he strode out to join the impending fight. "And...gentleman. Please, respect the Cold Peace and the rules of hospitality. We are the elite of our courts. This is deeply undignified behavior and reflects poorly upon our princes."

Caitlin slowly lowered Nadine to the ground and let go of her throat. Nadine stepped to one side, rubbing at her neck, glaring daggers. Nyx still looked jumpy, and closer to Caitlin's back than I liked. I kept my card hand high. We froze that way, just for a moment. Then Nadine shot a glance at her sidekick.

"We're leaving. *Now*."

Deflated, Nyx's head drooped as she followed in Nadine's wake like a puppy on a leash. A razor-fanged, killing machine kind of puppy. Caitlin turned my way, her eyes back to their usual sea-glass green, and touched my shoulder.

"Are you all right?"

I pocketed my cards and gave what I hoped was a rakish, devil-may-care sort of shrug. "Sure. Day at the office."

"Sorry about that," Royce told Caitlin. "Honestly, I had no idea she was going to follow me here. *Somebody* thinks a bit too highly of her position."

"She is Prince Malphas's favorite," Caitlin observed.

"And I'm his hound. Our business is none of *her* business. At any rate, I should be going. A pleasure as always, Caitlin."

"Hell prevails."

"Indeed," he said, turning his back and walking up the corridor. As he vanished out of sight, swallowed by the darkness and gold neon, Caitlin slipped one arm around my hip. She leaned in, tilting her head, and our lips brushed.

"That was a curiously hesitant kiss," she murmured. "Care to try that again? Once more, with feeling?"

"Sorry, just...what was that all about, back there? About Harmony Black?"

"Court intrigues, pet. Royce's court and mine appear to have a common enemy in the shadows, which he was kind enough to come and warn me about."

"Great. What's she up to *now*? She's not coming back to Vegas, is she?"

Caitlin laughed and shook her head.

"I don't mean your dear Agent Black, no. The problem is a bit more...nuanced than that. Don't worry. This is nothing you need trouble yourself with. And as for Nadine, well, she's just a sore loser. As always. Now I don't know about you, but I'm famished."

"Then I guess it's a good thing I got reservations for us at that new Cantonese place," I said, my worries melting under the warmth of her smile. She took my arm.

"You *do* have your uses. That sounds absolutely—hold on, let me see who this is."

She eyed her phone, then took the call.

"Dances, how *are* you? Are we still on for—what's that? Certainly, one moment."

She switched the phone over to FaceTime and lowered it so we could both watch. The screen became a camera, focused on a wall of stainless steel lockers. And a close-up of a familiar face: Fredrika Vinter, fashion mogul and queen bee of the Chicago occult underground.

"*Dahling*," she said, "you look amazing. As always. When are you going to model at one of my shows? I'm not taking no for an answer. And oh good, my favorite thief is with you. My BFFs, we have a problem here. And by 'we' I mean mostly you."

"Hey, Freddie," I said. "What's up?"

She pulled the phone back and took a long, slow pan of the room. Those weren't lockers behind her. They were mortuary drawers. And they were empty. The morgue was a wasteland of knocked-over gurneys, shattered lab flasks, and scattered tools, ransacked from top to bottom.

"Corpses," Freddie said. "A whole bunch of them, that's what's up. As in, they *got* up, and walked right out of here."

4.

Freddie passed the phone to the man at her side. Thinning hair, a bulky turtleneck under his lab coat, deathly pale skin, and the hint of rouge on his cheeks. I recognized him: Herbert, one of my tablemates at a poker tournament I'd played the last time I was in Chicago.

"Ahem, yes," he said. "I arrived this morning to find my workplace quite violated, and the security video is harrowing in its stark portrayal of a nigh-unthinkable reality. The dead became restless and perambulated as one, formed in a line like...like..."

"Like a conga line," Freddie said. "But without the booze. Or the fun."

Herbert held up an unsteady finger. "There are only two scholars in this city who possess any expertise in the revivification of the dead. And since I am quite blameless in this matter..."

He didn't need to finish the thought. We all knew exactly who to pin this on.

"Damien Ecko," I said.

Herbert's head bobbed. "An appalling, blasphemous stench hangs over this grim display. No, this is not the bold moral clarity of western science but something fell, like the taboo non-Euclidean geometries of old Araby or worse, the mad-eyed, savage rites of blackest Afri—"

Freddie snatched the phone out of his hand.

"I'm sorry, brainiac here can't go thirty seconds today without saying something *super* racist." She glared at him. "Seriously, what is your problem? Do you have a *condition?*"

"It was merely an observation."

"I will *eat* you." Freddie turned back to the screen. "So yeah, Old Dusty came out of hiding just long enough to steal about twenty corpses. Either he's a closet Michael Jackson fan and he's filming a remake of *Thriller*, or he's headed your way and looking for payback."

"You sure he's coming here?" I asked. "I mean, as far as anybody outside our circle believes, I died at Eisenberg Correctional."

"Does he know that? A lot of people died in that riot. They weren't exactly putting up lists of names on every TV channel. He might not even know you were locked up in the first place."

She had a point. I was safe from the government and the law as long as I kept my head down, but that didn't mean anybody else had been fooled. Still, I couldn't help but dig my heels in. It wasn't so much that I couldn't believe Ecko was coming for revenge—he had every reason, seeing as our last encounter ended with him fleeing the wrath of two infernal courts, framed for a crime I'd committed—but I just didn't *want* to. I had tunnel vision, a tunnel with the Enemy waiting at the other end, and I couldn't let myself get distracted from the hunt. Not now.

"How do you know he's coming here?" I asked. "I mean, yeah, he's got it in for me, but there are demons from here to Miami hunting for his head right now. That's a hell of a risk."

"Let's just say he left a pretty bold clue behind."

The phone swung around, camera pointing to the far wall of the morgue. Letters, scrawled in flaky, dried blood by a corpse's unsteady hand, left a message: *"Faust. Lighten Your Heart."*

"'Lighten my heart'?" I asked. "The hell does that mean?"

The screen tilted back toward Freddie's face. "He apparently thinks you know. Anyway, my darlingist darlings, you'd best keep your eyes open. I'm looking forward to a vacation in Vegas as soon as I can tear myself away from work, and I'd like everyone to be alive when I make my dramatic entrance."

Caitlin's eyes were hard, intent. "Thank you, Dances. I'll keep you in the loop."

"Ta! Kisses."

The screen went black.

"Well." Caitlin lifted her chin. "This is excellent news."

"A psychotic necromancer is coming after me with a posse of zombies. How does that constitute 'excellent news'?"

"Because I have a running bet with Royce. If I kill Ecko first, he owes me dinner. Speaking of, shall we?"

My assent came out as a shrug. My appetite had withered on the vine. It wasn't that I didn't want to confront Ecko; after what he'd done, trapping my old buddy Coop inside his own rotting flesh, using his tortured soul as leverage over me, I intended to take him down hard. Just not *now*. There was too much at stake to let myself get sidetracked.

We stepped through the honeycombed galleries arm in arm. Pausing at one point on the edge of a gathered and silent crowd, so Caitlin could admire one bold exhibitionist's artistic technique with surgical needles. That didn't help my appetite either, but the artist's model didn't seem to be complaining. Much. That's about when, casually scanning the room as an excuse to look away, I noticed we were being followed.

Not that Juliette and Justine were hard to spot. Two identical platinum blondes tended to stand out in a crowd, especially when they were accustomed to grabbing the spotlight by force. They were cambion, hell-blooded, progeny of a demon from the Choir of Pride. Strangely subdued tonight, though, almost sheepish, as Caitlin and I moved on and they followed us like bashful shadows.

We got as far as the stairs before Caitlin and I shared a knowing glance and turned as one.

"What?" I asked.

Juliette cringed. Justine put her arm around her twin's shoulder, the two of them taking a timid left-foot step forward.

"We have to ask you something," Justine said.

"And it *sucks*," Juliette added.

Caitlin and I shared another glance. "Okay."

"Nicky skipped town," Justine said, "and he paid us a lot of money, but he'd usually, like, put it in a bank account for us, and we don't even know where it is because he always bought us everything."

"We are poor as *hell* now," Juliette added. "We can't be poor, Danny. We're too hot to be poor."

"You don't have any way of reaching him? None at all?" Caitlin asked. She tilted her head, curious, calculating.

"No. When the FBI raided the Gentlemen's Bet, he just *left*. And Danny, you're the only person besides Nicky who ever answers our phone calls. Nobody else realizes how amazing we are." Justine swallowed hard. "We need your help. We need...a jay. Oh. Bee."

"A job?" I asked.

The twins flinched at the word, as if I'd slapped them across the face.

"You're always stealing things," Juliette said. "We can steal things! We can be your steal-thing-helpers!"

"As...enchanted as I am by that mental image," I told them, "I'm kinda between jobs at the moment myself. Look, if anything comes up, I'll call you, okay?"

Justine bounced on her tiptoes. "You promise? Pinky swear? That means we can cut your pinky off if you don't do it."

"That is not what that means," I said.

Caitlin hooked one arm around my shoulder and steered me toward the stairs, waiting until her back was turned before she rolled her eyes. She held her silence until we were out on the street, feeling the cool desert night breeze as we strolled past the steadily growing line to get inside. I could hear her mental gears turning.

"Penny for your thoughts," I told her.

"Nicky fleeing the city to escape arrest, that's understandable. I'm sure he had some sort of contingency plan, should his luck ever run out. A quick getaway to some sunnier climes without an extradition treaty."

"Sure," I said. "Never known Nicky not to land on his feet. What about it?"

Caitlin's eyes squinted, just a bit, as she cast a glance back over her shoulder.

"So why didn't he take the twins with him?"

She had a point. As long as I'd known Nicky, Juliette and Justine had been his constant companions. Sure, he got as exasperated with them as the rest of us, at least once in a while, but they'd come up together. Started from nothing, and carved out an empire. I could look past the bad blood between Nicky and me, far enough to give him a little credit: even if he had to cut and run to save his own skin, leaving them behind just wasn't his style.

That mystery would have to keep for now. I hit the remote unlock for the car, my rolling lime letting out a deflated squawk from the curb. Caitlin turned toward the sound and paused.

"That's...what you're driving now, is it?"

"For now."

"Right." She took my arm and wheeled us around. "Other direction. Parking garage. We're taking my car."

Dinner was all right, I suppose. The food was perfect, the ambiance quiet and cool, the company pleasant. I didn't really taste the meal, though, and it took all my effort to keep my mind from drifting as we talked. I'd come up with a plan to dig up some information on the Enemy. A plan I didn't dare tell Caitlin about. Not Bentley, either. Not just because I was trying to take our last discussion to heart—failing, but trying—but because it meant putting my neck on the line.

I woke before dawn, roused from a shuddering sleep and nightmares I couldn't quite remember, like a warning on the tip of my tongue. I rolled off Bentley and Corman's couch, shaved, showered, made myself presentable, then packed a mini cooler for my trip. Some protein bars, bottles of water from the fridge—then another few bottles, just to be safe. I put on a checkered button-down shirt, the sleeves rolled up, and a clean but sturdy pair of jeans.

I was leaving town for the day. Driving into the desert, far from human eyes, to find the closest thing I knew to sacred ground. Sacred ground I had no guarantee of leaving alive.

5.

I drove toward the rising sun, its molten-metal glare turning the highway to a strip of steel in a bed of powdered bone. Weaving through the light traffic, pouring on the speed, and drifting back to a morning just like this one, seventeen years ago. The first and only time I'd made this pilgrimage before today.

I left the highway, not on a paved off-ramp so much as the suggestion of a dirt road, veering off toward the swell of rust-red rocks on the horizon. No signposts, but there was a marker: a squat boulder on the roadside about two feet high, daubed with what looked like the image of a broken arrow in faded ocher paint. Another ten miles, with the Spark's wheels skidding in the rough and the engine whining, and the road stopped dead at a second, identical stone. End of the line. I cracked a bottle of water, guzzled it down, and got out with my mini cooler.

The desert air tasted like dried salt. A dying wind ruffled my shirt, and the sun beat down upon trackless Nevada sands. The highway was long out of sight, leaving me all alone, a nomad in the wasteland. I got my bearings, studied the stone, and began to walk.

An hour on foot, trudging through the sand, and my car was a distant memory too. I checked my cell phone. No signal. Vultures wheeled in the distance, circling a sky the color of warm slate. Even in October, the heat left my shirt plastered to my back, sweat running a tickling, gritty finger down my spine. At the third stone marker I paused just long enough to open another bottle of water, drinking as I walked.

Then the fourth, turning me in a fresh direction, toward the rising wall of rock. And the fifth, pointing the way down a narrow gap, the ground hard and tangled with dead scrub. I eased between the towering and jagged rocks, sunlight filtering down from far above, toward a dark opening in the stone. The mouth of a forgotten cave. The scent of fresh roses hung in the air, carried by a vapor I could only see when my eyes slipped out of focus. A vapor drifting from the cave like a plume of smoldering incense.

I steeled myself, my heart beginning to pound, my muscles fighting me as I approached the mouth of the cave. Just like they had seventeen years ago, when—spending my nights creeping through Bentley and Corman's backroom bookshelves, reading the texts they'd said were too advanced for me, too dangerous—I'd first read the legend of the Mourner of the Red Rocks.

Some said she was a survivor of a forgotten era, one of the elder races. Some said she was a spirit of the Paiute Indians, from a legend so old even they had forgotten it. Wherever she'd come from, she had been here before Vegas, before the first settlers from the east. Maybe before the desert and the towering, congealed-blood rocks that named her. The Mourner—never call her that to her face, never ask who she's mourning—knew secrets. The Mourner—remember your courtesies, show no fear or hesitation in her presence—might share them, if she felt so inclined.

Or you might join the others who had petitioned her and failed. The ones whose stripped and sandy bones littered the mouth of her cave, half-buried by time. More bones dangled on lengths of rotting rope like rattling wind chimes, a curtain of death marking the line between the outside world, the relative safety of the open desert, and her realm in the dark beneath.

I pushed through the curtain of bones, jaws and femurs clacking against one another, and stepped into the shadows.

The cave tunnel wound and turned down into the gloom, and

I felt my way with my palm pressed to cool, rough stone. Then, up ahead, the lonely glow of candlelight.

The candle rested upon a small, round table of knotty and dark-stained wood, the table's legs carved to resemble twists of petrified ivy wrapped around the boughs of a dead tree. Two high-backed chairs faced one another across the table, with a silver tea service on an ivory tray sitting between them. The Mourner wore white, from her heavy lace veil to the floor-length hem of her gown, her hands concealed under silken gloves.

Her fingers were too long for her hands. And as she reached for the silver teapot, they curled around the handle like boneless worms. She lifted her face, invisible behind the thick white lace, toward me.

"Daniel Faust." Her words emerged as a sibilant whisper. "You have returned to me."

"You remember me?" My voice uncertain.

I hovered at the edge of the candlelight. Her response was a slow, languid gesture to the empty chair. I sat down as she poured tea into a pair of silver cups. The steam carried the scent of dried flowers.

"I remember a young sorcerer, with no fear and great potential. And look at you now."

I didn't reach for the cup before me. Not until she did.

"I've been places," I said.

Her voice went cold. "You have been *nowhere*. You have done *nothing*. Is that why you return to me now? To ask for death, for disappointing me so dearly?"

I froze in my chair, the knotted wood hard against my back. That wasn't the reception I'd been expecting.

Part of me wanted to jump up and run for the exit. And part of me knew enough about the Mourner to realize I'd never make it out of this cave alive. She was faster than she looked. Much faster.

"I've...I've done a lot," I told her. "I saved the world once."

"And what is the value of a planet? I've seen planets born, seen them die, seen them born anew. This one, too, will die in its proper hour, and another will take its place. It is *lives* that interest me. I expected you to become a master of your art. A legend in the annals of sorcery. And what are you now? A beggar and a trickster, adrift and aimless. You are a boat with no oars and no rudder, a helpless pawn of the tides. You have allowed yourself to *rust*, Daniel Faust. And I *despise* rust."

I swallowed down the lump in my throat and shook my head.

"I might have...gotten sidetracked. Distracted a little. Hey, maybe my life doesn't fit some ideal road map, with goalposts and milestones. But whose does? Human lives are messy. We screw up, we make bad decisions. Then we pick ourselves up and try again. That's how it works."

"Do you even have a map? Do you have an ambition?"

"I do," I said. "I'm trying to stop a...I'm not sure what he is. He's called the Enemy, part of this legend, a prophecy I can't tie to anything in my books. I was hoping you'd know something—"

"*Silence*," the Mourner hissed. "Again, you miss the point. What is your ambition? You've been given a life. What do you aim to *do* with it?"

I slumped in the chair, grasping for something to say. She lifted her cup of tea, slipped it under her veil, and took a long, slurping sip. I left mine untouched.

"Once," she said, "I was a slave to an unworthy master. My ambition was freedom. And I became free, though the price was dear. Ambition is the fuel of triumph. The lever that moves worlds. What you insist is your goal is nothing more than a shroud over the empty hollow inside of you. So long as you keep running in place, you can lie to yourself and pretend you're traveling somewhere."

I threw up my hands. "Fine. You know what? Maybe you're right. Maybe I got lazy somewhere along the way. Maybe I just never got a handle on my life. And maybe I can change. Maybe I *want* to change, and I'm trying to figure out *how*. But right now, the Enemy is on the move, and I can't beat him alone."

"You don't need to defeat him at all," she replied. "I know the creature of which you speak. That isn't your fight. Walk away."

"He made it my fight."

"No. He made you a tool, which he then discarded. You were lucky to survive the experience. You won't survive it twice. You should consider the rest of your life a gift."

"My life," I told her, "isn't his gift to give."

"No. It's mine."

She folded her gloved hands on the table. Her boneless fingers rippled, bending backward, squirming in the fresh silence.

"I still see a shred of potential in you. Go forth and make something of it. If you don't, you won't have to come and see me again to meet your death. I'll come to *you*. Now go."

I pushed back my chair, just an inch, but I didn't rise. I knew I should. Knew I'd just survived a round of Russian roulette and here I was, spinning the chamber and putting the gun to my head one more time.

"Please," I said. "I came a long way to see you. I took my life and put it in your hands. Don't send me away with nothing. Tell me something about the Enemy, something I can use."

She nodded at my untouched cup.

"If you wish to stay, then drink your tea."

I picked up the silver cup. Felt its warmth, a trickle of steam rising from the ink-brown tea. If that's what it was. I knew the rules of sitting with the Mourner of the Red Rocks. Knew she could change the brew to rat poison on a whim. Or battery acid.

I wouldn't know unless I drank it. And she wouldn't speak another word until I did. The risk was the price you paid for knowledge. Her little game.

She was right. The last time we'd met, I had a world of potential ahead of me. I didn't know when I'd gone off the rails, or how, or why. Whoever I thought I'd grow up to be, a guy with no job, no cash, couch-surfing and scrounging to survive wasn't it. If I stayed, insisting on information she had no interest in giving me, would she kill me out of sheer irritation? Or would it show her that I still had some tenacity left, that I hadn't given up?

I pulled the trigger.

"Here's to your health." I put the cup to my lips and swallowed the liquid down. The tea, rich and hot, warmed my stomach and left an herbal aftertaste on my tongue.

"Still fearless," she replied, her voice carrying the hint of a smile behind her veil.

"Not fearless. Seventeen years ago, I was too young to know what I was risking. I'm old enough, now, that dying means something to me."

"But you drank nonetheless."

"Not fearless," I told her. "Just determined."

"Then have your reward for the risk," she said and raised her cup to mine.

6.

"**I** am versed in the language of time," she told me. "I see your *not-yet-maybe* stretching out before you, a tree of binary choices. Turn left, turn right. Say yes, say no. With every choice made, your life changes forever. Many of these branches lead to a permanent cessation of decisions. And soon."

"A cessation," I echoed.

"Dead ends. But even if you evade every snare in your path, make every right choice, and stride through the hurricane unscathed, I see your darkest hour on the other side of the storm. You will come to a point where all is lost, where your foe's fingers are wrapped around your throat."

"Sounds like a Tuesday," I told her. Fronting with bravado I didn't feel. The cave air felt clammy on my skin, hot-damp and prickling at the back of my neck.

"In that moment, as your last breath escapes you, remember one thing: a question. This question. Ask yourself, 'Where would you hide it?'"

I tilted my head at her. The teacup nestled in my palm, warm, still steaming, a tiny wisp of vapor rising up between us.

"Where would I hide *what*?"

She responded by taking a long, slow, slurping sip of tea. I could feel her smiling at me on the other side of the veil. She set her teacup down.

"Remember the question," she said, "and when the time is right, you'll know the answer."

"Great. A riddle. This isn't telling me where to find the Enemy."

"No. It's telling you how to survive the next four days. I think you'd agree that's a bit more important."

"And I'm not unappreciative," I said, "but how am I supposed to track this guy down if that's all I have to go on?"

"By being clever," she replied. "You have wit and guile. Use them. Or better yet, don't. The creature you hunt would destroy you without a second glance. You aren't ready to face him."

I set down my cup, pushed my chair back—its black iron legs scraping on the worn cavern floor—and stood.

"I'll find an angle. I always do."

"So eager to start another pointless war. So eager to leave another battle unfinished."

I paused, about to turn away. "What do you mean by that?"

"I can see your history trailing out behind you like ruins in your wake. Plans left unfulfilled, deeds left unfinished, schemes half-done and bleeding their complications out across the canvas of your life. You've skipped along from moment to moment, crisis to crisis, never cleaning up the damage you've left behind you. The pattern of your outer life mirrors the pattern of your heart. And until you change your ways, until you bring your life and your heart into accord, you will *never* be strong enough to face the Enemy."

She lifted her cup to me. And though I couldn't see her face behind the ivory veil, I could feel her gaze cutting through me like a scalpel. All that I was, exposed before her.

"Your free ride just ended," she said, "and the consequences you've escaped for so long have become wolves, circling your doorstep. Forget the Enemy. Abandon this pursuit. And cure your heart, if you hope to survive."

*   *   *

I left the Mourner's cave with more mysteries than I'd brought in with me. The noonday sun greeted me with a wave of arid heat and diamond picks for my eyes. I squinted, shrouding my brow with my hand until my vision adjusted to the light. Then I followed the first stone marker, spotting ghosts of my own footprints in the shifting desert sand.

She'd answered my questions with a riddle. *Where would I hide it?* It gave me something to think about on my way back to the car, though my long walk didn't bring me any closer to a solution. I couldn't drive off just yet: in my absence the windows had spent hours catching the sun, turning the car into a tiny green furnace. I opened the doors to let it air out for a minute. Close enough to civilization to get a signal, I checked my phone while I waited.

Four messages from Jennifer. Shit.

I hadn't *forgotten* that we'd made plans; I just hadn't remembered exactly how far the Mourner's cave was from the highway, and how long it would take me to get there and back again. As it stood, I about to be late for a meeting I really didn't want to miss.

"Sorry, sorry," I said, cradling the phone to my chin as I wheeled the Spark around and made for the highway. "I'm on my way right now."

"S'okay," she drawled, with a tone that told me I wasn't entirely forgiven. "They're runnin' late too, though I think they're just stalling to throw their weight around. Two can play that game. Where've you been, anyway?"

Jennifer, the sister I never had, was another person who didn't need to know I'd been drinking tea with the Mourner. I could imagine the lecture I'd get for taking that kind of risk: pretty much exactly like the one I'd get from Bentley and Corman, but with a lot more creatively foul language.

"Eh," I said, "just got a little tied up this morning."

"Ooh. You were with Caitlin."

"Huh? Why would you assume—" I paused. "Not *literally*, Jen."

She snickered. "Little slow on the uptake today. Better chug a mug of coffee and bring your A game, sugar, there's some plum weirdness afoot. I need you watching my back."

"On my way."

Not as directly as I hoped. My phone buzzed as I pulled out onto the highway, and I recognized the number at a glance. It wasn't a name I'd put in my address book, for his safety and for mine.

"Detective Kemper." I tucked the phone against my cheek and checked the rearview. "To what do I owe the pleasure?"

"The taphouse on East Charleston Boulevard. Get your ass over here. Now."

"Not that I wouldn't love to hang out, but I'm kind of in the middle of something—"

"Get over here," he said, "or I might just forget to keep my mouth shut about your miraculous resurrection."

I knew this was coming eventually. I'd needed Gary Kemper's help after my prison break, to shut down a civil war in the criminal underworld. We'd both come out ahead—me with my life and my freedom intact, him with a few juicy arrests—but now he had leverage over me in the worst way. One phone call to the feds—or worse, straight to Harmony Black—and I'd be a hunted man all over again.

"Food for thought, Gary: when you've got weight on some-body, you want to be real careful about how you use it. Go swing-ing that stick around too often, you might just hurt yourself."

"Or I might send you straight back to Eisenberg Correctional. Stow the tough-guy act, Faust. Your life is in my hands and we both know it. So when I tell you to be somewhere, you *do* it. East Charleston. One hour, or I start making phone calls."

He hung up. I set my phone in the cupholder, stared at the desert sky, and drove. This wasn't going to stand. I'd fought too hard, given too much to win my freedom back, just to spend the rest of my life as Gary Kemper's errand boy. Still, I couldn't be reckless: Kemper wasn't stupid. I was sure he'd set up a con-tingency, some envelope full of dirty secrets—including mine—that'd go to the authorities if he wound up missing. Besides, I've got a rule about not killing cops. By now I've broken most of my personal rules, one way or another, so I cling that much tighter to the ones I have left. For now, until I found a way to get my own leverage over him and return the favor, I could only play it one way. Straight and narrow.

The taphouse wasn't hard to spot, not with the line of squad cars out front and a couple of sad sacks in pressed uniforms holding back a curious crowd. I'd passed a trio of ambulances on the way over, their lights off and rolling slow, carrying passengers too late to save. Not hard to guess why, when I saw the river of broken glass outside the corner bar. The place had gone through a wood chipper. A twisted Budweiser sign hung limp as a corpse out a shattered window, the wall riddled with bullet holes. Not just one shooter, I guessed, and not armed with popguns either. The door, propped open with a bright orange construction cone, looked in on a tavern gutted by fire. More bodies lined up on the sidewalk outside, covered in starched white sheets, waiting for their free ride to the morgue.

I parked down the block and shouldered my way through the crowd. So many cell phones in the air, snapping pictures like paparazzi, you'd think they'd spotted a celebrity. *Great vacation photos*, I thought and tried to keep my face turned away from the cameras. The uniform held up a beefy hand to block my way, but Kemper—dressed in plainclothes and beet red in the face—hustled over to wave me through.

"It's okay, Officer," he said, "he's with me."

I waited until we'd slipped past the knot of people, his uniformed buddy out of earshot, before shooting a look in his direction. "I'm with you? Careful, Detective, you're going to ruin my street cred."

"You don't *have* any, dead man." He flung up a hand at the ragged tavern wall, the blown-out windows. "You know who owns this place?"

On paper, no, but that wasn't what he was asking. The taphouse was a front for Eddie Stone, one of the local luminaries who had been recruited for Jennifer's New Commission: the underworld council aiming to fill the power vacuum now that Nicky

Agnelli was on the run. I knew Eddie ran his business out of the back room: women, coke, a little of this and a little of that.

"Yeah," I told Kemper, not volunteering another word.

"So do I," he said. "Two hours ago, a couple of sedans rolled by. We've got a witness that says they opened up with a machine gun on the place. I'm not talking about a hand cannon. I mean they had a belt-fed M-sixty like it was fucking Vietnam. Then they tossed a couple of Molotovs through the front door, gunned down anybody who tried to make a run for it, and took off."

A limp hand stuck out from the corner of a coroner's sheet. The curled fingers charred black like overcooked sausages, nails cracked and broken.

"Eight dead," Kemper told me, "near as I can tell, all civilians. Barflies looking to get a head start on their cirrhosis."

"I hope you're not looking at me for this. Not my style."

Kemper jabbed his finger in my face.

"You told me you could fix the problem. You told me no civilians would get hurt. You gave me your *word*, Faust—"

"And I kept it. This wasn't the Calles, Gary. Trust me: the ones who wanted to join up with the Chicago Outfit aren't around anymore. Everybody who's left came to the bargaining table."

"Then it's their buddies." He nodded to the open door and the flame-washed carnage beyond. "One survivor got out alive, if you can call third-degree burns over half her body 'living.' She only got a partial number on one of the sedans, but she ID'd the style. The shooters had Illinois plates."

I looked from the bar to the bodies to the broken glass, working the angles like a pool hustler calculating a bank shot. A cold certainty set in, ice water trickling down my spine.

"Forget about the partial," I told him. "It's a dead end. Those plates were stolen."

"Huh? How do you figure?"

"Because the shooters aren't stupid, and they *wanted* to be seen. They planned this, all of it, in advance. They weren't trying to kill Eddie Stone and his boys. If they were even in the building, it would have been icing on the cake, but that wasn't what they were here to accomplish."

"Why?" Kemper shook his head. "What's the point?"

"It's a message. And what that message says is, 'Two cars with Illinois plates just shot up a New Commission front, in the middle of town, in broad daylight, and got away with it.'"

I took a long, hard look at the street. Eyeing every tinted window like there might be a gun on the other side, and a bullet with my name on it.

"The Chicago Outfit tried a soft takeover, making offers to the city's gangs and subverting the Calles from inside. We gave 'em a black eye for their trouble, so now they're doing things the hard way." I looked to Kemper. "I hope you're ready to put in some overtime, Detective. This was a declaration of war."

7.

If looks could kill, I would have joined the other bodies on the sidewalk. Kemper's voice dropped to a grating whisper as he moved in, close enough for me to smell his cheap aftershave.

"Fix this, Faust."

"Fix what? This has nothing to do with me. I'm not even part of the Commission—"

"Oh, like hell you aren't."

"When Nicky Agnelli was in charge," I said, "everybody thought I was working for him. Now he's gone and everybody thinks I want to *be* him. Is it that hard to imagine that maybe, just maybe, I want nothing to do with this mess?"

"Yeah," he told me. "It is. But you're not asking the important question here."

"Which is?"

Kemper stepped back. He took another long look at the shrouded bodies, shaking his head in disgust.

"The only reason I haven't done my sworn duty and turned you in is because you're useful to me. If you're telling the truth and you can't help me, that means you're not useful anymore. So tell me one thing, smart guy: why *shouldn't* I haul you out of here in handcuffs right this instant?"

He took my silence as an answer.

"Fix this," he said. "Whatever you've gotta do to calm things down and end this 'war' before it gets out of control, do it. Frankly, I don't give a damn if you assholes slaughter each other by the dozens, but *no more civilians*. If I've gotta clean up one more crime scene like this one, somebody's going down for it. Here's a hint: it's gonna be you."

I thought it over. Looking for a way out, and not finding one. In the end, I said the only thing I could say.

"I'll handle it."

*   *   *

You can find a little spot of paradise about three miles west of Vegas. A botanical garden in the desert sun. The Springs Preserve is over a hundred and fifty acres of walking trails, desert wetlands constructed in a storm-water basin, and bursts of color in the sand. Not my usual scene. When I'm looking for tranquility, I find my peace of mind in the beating heart of a bustling crowd under casino neons. Besides, I'd been a little uneasy around gardens ever since the Lauren Carmichael business. Thinking about plants for too long got me thinking about the Garden of Eden, and that left me stewing over all kinds of uncomfortable questions.

They never did find Lauren's body. Then again, they never found Meadow Brand's body either, but that's just because we picked a good spot to gun her down. Her bones were still out there somewhere, gleaming white and picked clean on the salt flats.

Jennifer met me in the parking lot. She'd dressed up for the occasion, swapping her usual T-shirt and jeans for tailored slacks and a breezy blazer in pastel blue. A little heavy for the weather, but it hid the bulge of her shoulder holster. Not a spot of red in her sharp, clear eyes. She'd gone at least a day without getting high on her own supply, which generally meant something important was going down.

"You're driving a lime," she told me.

"Protective camouflage. You know, I still can't get used to seeing you dressed like office management."

"Protective camouflage," she said. "Don't want these Triad boys to think I'm not taking 'em seriously. They already don't like me much."

In Nicky's absence, Jennifer had taken the initiative to forge the New Commission, a formal alliance to keep the Vegas underworld running smoothly—and just as importantly, to keep the city's big players from going at each other's throats. It was a gathering of equals, with Jennifer sitting as the chairperson just to keep things organized. Shangguan Jin, Red Pole of the local branch of the 14K Triad, thought that was a little too much authority for a woman to handle.

"Is this where they wanted to meet?" I asked. We walked while we talked, angling for the Desert Living Center. A cone of steel rose up ahead, like the skeleton of a cooling tower, catching the sun and shining bright. We stepped to one side as a forest-green cart hauling visitors chugged on past, remodeled to look like a vintage steam train.

"They wanted a meeting on their turf. I said, just as politely as I could muster, that wasn't happenin'. Until I know what they want, and why they can't bring it up in front of everybody at the next Commission meeting, getting together somewhere nice and public works just peachy for me. Besides, I'm stacking the deck a little bit."

She took out her phone and set it on speaker so I could listen in.

"Smile," Pixie's voice said, "you're on candid camera. I'm patched into the security grid all over the preserve—wherever you go, I'll have eyes on."

I held up three fingers and asked, "How many fingers am I holding up?"

"Three. Look behind you."

I glanced over my shoulder. The tiny, unobtrusive box of a security camera blinked from a pole at the edge of the parking lot. It swiveled back and forth, a mechanical wave.

"Now guess how many fingers I'm holding up," Pixie said. "By the way, nice ride. The color really pops."

"That reminds me: they impounded my car when I got busted.

Can you do some digging, maybe find out if it's being auctioned off?"

Jennifer arched an eyebrow. "Really? You're supposed to be playin' possum, sugar. A vintage Barracuda ain't exactly a low-profile ride."

"*Hemicuda*," I said. "And I love that car. *Caitlin* loves that car."

Pixie sighed. "I'll add it to your bill. On that note, I'm still checking into that lawyer for you."

When I cornered Eisenberg Correctional's warden, he tried to barter for his life. It didn't work. Still, I'd kept the business card he offered me, with the name of a law firm: Weishaupt and Associates. Warden Lancaster called that card a "golden ticket," claiming they'd hand me the world on a plate if I played ball and let him walk. Even after all I'd done to expose what was really going on behind Eisenberg's walls, after the initial explosion of outrage and a flurry of arrests, the story sank faster than a chunk of radioactive lead. Eisenberg was even back in business, shoveling all the blame on the dead warden's shoulders and promising a new era of ethical prison management. It was a carefully curated cover-up from start to finish, just like Lancaster had told me would happen.

Weishaupt and Associates had serious juice. They were a player, all right, but one with no connection to the occult underground or to the courts of hell for that matter. I liked knowing who my neighbors were, especially when they were throwing that kind of weight around.

"Any good news for me?" I asked Pixie.

"As far as I can tell, they've got no clients, no cases, and two of the 'lawyers' on their website are actors who pose for stock photographs. Oh, and their encryption would make the Department of Defense jealous. I'm working on it."

"Step carefully," I told her.

"Good thing you told me that, otherwise I would have been extra careless. I'll call you two back when your Triad buddies show up."

Jennifer pocketed her phone. We headed deeper into the preserve, past the museum campus and along trails bounded by tall walls of sandy rock and sprays of desert grass. Flowers bloomed in the colors of the Mojave, rust-red and lilac, and butterflies danced on a gust of dry, sweet wind.

"Amazin' what can live in the desert," Jennifer said. "Survivors always find a way."

"Speaking of survivors, one of Eddie Stone's places got hit this morning."

"I was the first person he called," she told me. "Being the city's eyes and ears is kinda my job now. Anyhow, we knew this was coming. Chicago wants what we got, and they ain't takin' no for an answer. So when are you gonna step up?"

I shrugged. "Thought that's what I was doing right now. You asked for backup. I came, didn't I?"

"That's a favor for a friend kinda thing. I'm not talking about friendship, Dan. I'm talking about business. There's a seat at the New Commission's table with your name on it. All you gotta do is say the word."

"Not interested."

She stopped dead in her tracks and wheeled around to face me, squaring her hands on her hips.

"And why the hell not? You could *run* this town. I'm talking about real money, real power, the opportunity of a damn lifetime. All you gotta do is take a chance, reach out and put your hands on it."

"I've never been much of a joiner. You know me, Jen. I do my own thing."

"Do you?" she asked me.

"Meaning?"

"Meaning I don't know what it is you *do* anymore. How long have we been friends?"

"Long time," I said.

"Long time. Seen some shit together. But here's the thing, Dan. I'm climbing this ladder, and I want to see you climbing right next to me. But I look back, and there you are, down on the ground, like you're comfortable there, sitting in a rut. I think that's your problem."

"What is?"

"You're *comfortable*," she said, pronouncing the word like it tasted rancid on her tongue. "Folks like you and me, we're outlaws. We were never meant to get comfortable."

We walked in silence, following the curving path past signs pointing to the hiking trails and the wetland preserve. I caught Jennifer giving the sign for the botanical garden a squinted eye.

"You too, huh?" I asked.

"Hell, after that Lauren business, I don't even like salad anymore," she said. "I half expect the lettuce to start talkin' to me."

We staked out a spot on an empty stretch of path, hemmed in by tall willows that rustled in the breeze. Jennifer used her sleeve to mop away a dab of sweat on her forehead, her jacket pulling back to flash her chromed .357.

"They're doing this on purpose, making us wait," she said. "Reckon they think they're putting me in my place."

"They don't know you very well."

"They do not. And if they wanna get catty, well, the Sun Yee On would *love* to get a foothold in Vegas. The Fourteen-K can either learn to play nice or I'll just start talking to their competition. I've been practicing my Mandarin. So far I only know how to ask where the bathroom is, but gimme a little time, I'll get it down."

I had to smile. "I thought you were just coordinating the New Commission, not calling the shots."

"People can think whatever they wanna think. You know how this game gets played: all you get in life is what you're willing to fight for. And anything you don't fight for, you're gonna lose, because somebody out there wants it more than you."

Jennifer's phone trilled. Pixie on the line.

"Good news and bad news," she said. "Good news is, your guests just arrived."

"And the bad?" Jennifer asked.

"When they agreed on a two-on-two meeting, they forgot how to do math. Jin is coming your way with six guys, and it looks like they're all carrying. They left another dozen behind: two men covering every way off the museum campus and every route between you and the parking lot. If you run now, you could probably navigate the hiking trails north and get through the preserve on foot, then go the long way around to find an access road."

Jennifer and I shared a glance. We didn't need to say anything; we knew each other too well. She made her decision, and I agreed to stand by her, with nothing more than a look.

"We're not runnin'," she told Pixie. "Call me if you spot anything else."

She hung up, one hand smoothing her blazer over her shoulder holster as if reassuring herself that the gun was still there.

"Think they're looking to appoint a new chairperson?" I asked. She shrugged and looked past me, checking the trail in both directions.

"I know they want me out, but if they're fixin' to kill me, this is a dumb way to do it. I expect that Jin—bless his heart—is gonna ask me to resign all peaceful-like."

"How's that gonna go, do you think?"

Jennifer pushed her shoulders back and flashed a cocky smile. Almost eager, like a cat about to pounce on a tangled ball of yarn.

"Badly," she said. "Real badly."

8.

They didn't keep us waiting much longer. Shangguan Jin led the way, old and stoop-shouldered with stringy white hair but the bright blue eyes of a twenty-year-old. His posse favored tailored suits, red neckties, and dime-sized silver lapel pins to mark their fealty to the Triad. Not everyday wear for most—they'd dressed up nice for the occasion, showing solidarity. Jin stood his ground about seven feet away from us, his boys clustering at his back. I took a step back, too, standing stoic at Jennifer's shoulder.

Jennifer broke the expectant silence. She offered a slight bow and said, "Thank you for coming, *dai lo*. I hope your driver didn't have any trouble finding the place."

A subtle dig at their lateness and, combined with the honorific, a deniable one. If it landed, it didn't show in Jin's expression. He returned the bow and said, "None."

Another silence. Jennifer spread her hands.

"You wanted to meet. So we're meeting. What's on your mind?"

"Chicago," he said.

"That's the number-one ticket on our next meeting's agenda," Jennifer said. "We've all got Chicago on the brain. So what couldn't wait?"

"They made us...an offer," Jin replied. Cagey, his bright eyes studying Jennifer's face. Taking it slow and weighing her every reaction.

I was more focused on his backup. They were all strapped—no

surprise there—but they kept their hands nice and empty, body language open. When a gang is planning to bushwhack you, inevitably *somebody* in the pack will show it: nervous tension, the anticipation of the kill showing in their face or their moves. Nothing like that here. Either these guys were consummate pros, or they really weren't looking for a fight.

"They made the Calles an offer, too," Jennifer said. "Didn't work out too good for the ones who said yes. You can find most of 'em buried in shallow graves in an old water park off Interstate Fifteen."

"Our offer was more generous. Their man came directly to me, in respect, not trying to subvert my society from within as they did with your...street friends."

"Keep talkin'," Jennifer said lightly.

"We would maintain our markets, our autonomy. Business would proceed as usual. All they request is a tribute. A simple offering, a small percentage of our income, so tiny we'd barely miss it. Not a heavy price to ensure a peaceful resolution."

"Big-box store," Jennifer said.

Jin tilted his head, squinting at her. "Hmm?"

"When I was a kid, back home in Kentucky, one of those big-box stores came to town. Best deals you'd ever seen. Then, slowly, one by one, all the old mom and pop stores—I mean, businesses that'd been staples in that town for five generations—closed up shop. They couldn't compete. Till finally, one day, the big box was the only store left for twenty miles around."

Jin's men murmured softly, casting glances at one another. Jin shook his head. "I don't see—"

"That was the day all the prices went up." Jennifer's eyes went as hard as her voice. "See, they knew what they were doing all along. Suckered us all in with deals that were too good to be true, until the competition was gone. Then they had us where they wanted us, bent right over a barrel. Nowhere to shop but the company store, nowhere to *work* but the company store. They destroyed that little town and turned a lot of people—good, honest, *proud* people—into beggars with their hats in their hands."

Jennifer gave the opposition a long, slow stare, talking as much to Jin's men as she was to their boss.

"Can't you see that's exactly what's happening here? Sure, the Outfit's gonna promise you the sun and the moon if it'll get you in their corner. The war ain't coming; it's here. It started this morning. Chicago just wants to keep you out of the way while they mop up anybody they can't twist. And as soon as they're done, as soon as the rest of us are dead and gone and you've got nobody to back you up, believe me, the prices are gonna go up. *Way* up. They'll squeeze you for everything you've got, and you won't be able to do a damn thing about it."

More scattered murmurs. The sounds of dissent in the ranks. Jin wrung his liver-spotted hands and took a hobbling step closer.

"Please, Madame Chairman, be reasonable about this. I came to you in confidence because they're willing to extend the same offer to you. Five percent. A simple five percent tithe. With your influence, you could convince the others. We could end this war before it truly begins."

Something smelled here, and it wasn't the earthy odor wafting over the artificial wetlands. I didn't know Shangguan Jin all that well—we weren't exactly drinking buddies—but I'd had enough encounters with him to peg his type. He didn't wear his arrogance on his sleeve so much as bristle with it, like a porcupine made of entitled ego. And one thing he didn't do was plead with a woman about anything, ever. He'd wasted no time raising a stink about her taking the Commission's chair.

"I'm sorry," Jennifer said, staring across the wavering reeds for a moment. "I was just daydreamin', thinking about the good old days. One night, me and my brothers got all liquored up, filled up some bottles with bootleg hooch and grabbed some rags and matches. And we burned that big-box store straight to the fucking ground. See, that's my philosophy: if somebody's dead set on turning you into a slave, you don't waste time negotiating with them. You just burn 'em down. Ends that nonsense *real* quick."

While she talked, I stretched out my senses. Psychic tendrils, like curling tentacles of purple mist in my mind's eye, wavered over the Triad men and darted in to lick with wet, sucker-lined tongues. Tasting thoughts and emotions, conveying their messages back to me in the form of symbols. Jin glowed darkly and tasted like peat moss. Like jungles, and fire, and fear sweat. I only knew two creatures in the world who resonated like that. And one of them, as far as I knew, was tending her restaurant back in Denver.

"Ms. Juniper," I said softly, casting a look at Jennifer, "perhaps our honored guest would understand you better if you spoke in his native tongue."

Our eyes locked, and she caught my meaning. She squared her shoulders, one hand within striking distance of her revolver, and turned to Jin.

"*Ce suo zai naer?*" she asked.

Jin stared at her. He blinked, lifting his chin ever so slightly. Some of his men chuckled, the others sharing confused glances.

"I don't—" he stumbled over his words. "Just speak English, your pronunciation is terrible."

"It's a simple question," Jennifer said. "*Ce suo zai naer?* No reason you shouldn't be able to answer it."

"Unless," I said, "he doesn't actually know a word of Chinese."

"Nonsense," Jin snapped. His jaw clenched, trembling. "You are wasting our time."

"Answer the question." I felt the cards in my hip pocket warming in anticipation, like a heating blanket pressed to my thigh. "Or would you prefer we asked it in Hindi...Kirmira?"

With his men at his back, none of them could see not-Jin's eyes shift from bright bird blue to tiger orange.

"I changed my mind," the Outfit's pet rakshasa ordered. "Kill them. Kill them both."

A flurry of guns whipped from under black jackets, but

nobody fired. Not as my cards leaped from my pocket in a whirl-wind, my index finger stirring and guiding them like an orchestra conductor while they circled me and Jennifer in a pasteboard tornado. Some of the gangsters stumbled back, wide-eyed, while a couple fixed their boss with confused gazes and kept their pistols down.

"That's not Shangguan Jin," I said, watching them through the shield of cards. "Ask him something. Something personal, some-thing only he would know. He won't be able to answer."

The gunman at Kirmira's shoulder, a big guy with a sweaty brow and a double chin, asked something in Mandarin. Kirmira didn't even turn his way. He was fixed on us, on me, his fiery glare burning with repressed rage. The gunman asked again, louder. Then he punctuated it by leveling his pistol at the back of Kirmira's head.

"I said," the gunman seethed, switching to English as the gun shook in his grip, "*what day is my birthday?*"

Kirmira let out a deep, resigned sigh.

"With all due respect," he said in his real voice, soft and tinged with an Indian accent, "fuck your birthday."

He exploded from the Jin disguise. Clothes ripped, bursting at the seams as his flesh bloated and bubbled and turned scaly green. His mouth stretched, skull snapping and resetting with a sound like crackling chicken bones. His head grew inhumanly wide, froglike, his eyes bulging. A foot-long purple tongue lashed the air as Kirmira squatted on half-human haunches ending in webbed and clawed feet. He leaped from the path, a ten-foot bound on muscles tailored for escape, splashing across the wet-land and fleeing north through the preserve. Shots crackled through the air, thudding into the inch-deep water around the glistening abomination and sending a flock of birds winging into the desert sky.

"Stop shooting," Jennifer shouted. "Stop *shooting*, dang it! You wanna bring the cops down on us?"

The whirlwind of cards landed in my outstretched hand, coming home. "He's gone. Forget about it. Who's second in command here?"

The guy with the double chin thumped his chest. "Chou Yong. White Paper Fan."

"Looks like you just got promoted," I said. "When's the last time you saw your boss, *before* this morning?"

"Last night." He stared out across the preserve at the disappearing blot of the leaping creature before it vanished from sight. "Dinner."

"And today?"

"He called me to pick him up," Yong said. "It was weird. Normally I come in and get him, hold the door open for him, all that jazz. He told me to wait in the car."

"Let's go," I said. "I've got a feeling we're about to find your real boss."

9.

The pickup spot was back in town, and we slipped out of the preserve past milling, confused tourist crowds. They'd heard the shots, but nobody expected gunfire in the middle of paradise. It helped that Pixie was proactive; by the time we called her, she'd already scrubbed the last hour's worth of security camera footage. The most the cops would find, if they even bothered looking once they showed up, was a few spent shell casings floating in shallow marsh water. No body, no blood.

I was pretty sure Kirmira could bleed, though. And I intended to find out.

Yong led the way to Best Foot Forward, a spa at the edge of a half-empty strip mall. Black magnetic letters on a yellow plastic sign advertised hot rock therapy, whirlpool massage, and pedicures by appointment. The front door, glass made opaque by a sheet of badly cut custom tinting, rattled stubbornly against my hand.

"You got a key?" I asked him. He shook his head.

The glass cracked under my elbow and speckled my sleeve with glittering shards. No time to do this the clean way, and I had a hunch the burglar alarm hadn't been turned on. I reached through the pit in the broken glass, flipped the latch, and let myself in.

A woman's body, maybe the receptionist, lay on a stretch of dusty red carpet. She was red, too, red from her neck to her belly with deep, ragged rents, her throat torn out. The aftermath of some savage animal's attack. Yong put his hand over his mouth, going pale, his other hand trembling as he aimed his gun at shadows. He said something in Mandarin. I didn't know the words, but I understood the question just fine. So did Jennifer.

"It's called a rakshasa," she said, stepping around him. "It can be anything it wants to be, but it mostly likes being a tiger."

"A *big* tiger," I said and took the lead. We made our way slowly up a narrow corridor, the air thick with the dirty-copper stench of spilled blood. Another body lay slumped over a massage table in a side room, the walls and the flickering overhead lights splashed scarlet. A fat black fly buzzed through the air, landing on his pale cheek and crawling across his earlobe.

Sometimes I hated being right. We found the real Shangguan Jin in back, half of him on one side of his office and the other half on the other. His spine jutted out from his torso like a curling tail of bone, the end splintered and gnawed down to a toothpick. I had to give Yong credit: he was sweating up a storm, his skin like wax paper, but he held his lunch down like a champ.

"I'm gonna guess the Outfit really did make him an offer to defect." I breathed through my mouth, the rotten-meat and spilled-bile stench shoving me out of the room one stubborn inch at a time. "And I'm gonna guess he said no."

Jennifer cupped her hand over her mouth and nose, standing in the doorway. "Sounds about right. Then Kirmira decided to improvise."

"Thankfully, he's not that good at it. When we met, I got the distinct impression that he's not leadership material. Angelo Mancuso and his pal treated him like a lackey, even mocked him right to his face, and Kirmira didn't say jack about it."

Jennifer frowned. "Think they've got something on him?"

I'd had enough of the local sights. I turned my back on Jin—both pieces of him—and led the way up the lightless hallway. Fresh air, even parking lot air and diesel fumes, sounded like a good idea right about then.

"Maybe." I thought it over. "But how do you blackmail a rakshasa? He can literally be anybody he wants to be."

"Ask your buddy in Denver, maybe?"

"Naavarasi is *not* my buddy. And I tried talking to her about Kirmira, back when she visited me in prison. No dice. She doesn't believe me. According to her, she's the last of her kind, and that's that."

The broken door swung open under my hand. A loose chunk of safety glass tumbled from its frame and jangled on the pavement at my feet. I squinted against the sudden sunlight and took deep, grateful breaths, a wave of nausea ebbing away on a gust of autumn wind.

"Well, I know what I saw," Jennifer said.

"And I know what I felt. Look, you've gotta gather up the rest of your Commission buddies and get them out of town. Have to figure Shangguan Jin was just the first stop on Kirmira's hit list."

"I am very confused," Yong said, standing behind us. He mopped his face with his blue silk handkerchief, looking miserable. We ignored him.

"I know," Jennifer said, pacing the parking lot. "This critter's hitting us like a bad flu. Gotta get everybody in quarantine until we figure out our next move. I'll bring everybody to my place and keep 'em locked down there."

"Out of town entirely would be safer. And work out a recognition code, some kind of verification phrase only you would know," I told her. "Kirmira's great at impersonating people, but he's sloppy. Doesn't do his homework."

"I don't believe I'm sayin' this, but I still kinda wish Naavarasi was here. I'm a firm believer in fighting fire with fire."

"Her help never comes for free," I said. "I'm already on the hook with her, favor for a favor. I don't want to owe her two, and I don't want *you* owing her a damn thing."

"That's my choice to make, Danny."

I dug out my phone, taking a step back. Then I nodded at

Yong. "We'll talk about it later. I've gotta make a quick call. While I'm doing that, talk to this guy before he has an aneurysm, okay?"

I hit the speed-dial. The phone trilled twelve times before anyone bothered to pick up, which didn't surprise me.

"Southern Tropics Import-Export," said the nasal voice on the other end of the line. "How may I direct your call?"

"Daniel Faust calling for Emma Loomis, please."

"*Certainly*, sir," said the receptionist from hell. "I can take a message and arrange for her to call you back by next Wednesday at the absolute earliest."

I watched the traffic rumble by, trucks and delivery vans kicking up clouds of smog, and counted to five under my breath.

"I really don't have time for the usual banter today," I told her, "so let me put it this way: I'm calling about one of Emma's personal investments. If you don't put me through to her right now, she's most likely going to *lose* said investment. If that happens, I'll be telling her it was your fault."

"One moment, sir," she said quickly. "Patching you through now."

"Thank y—" Too late, she was already gone, the line ringing to a new extension. I'd have to remember that trick.

"Daniel?" Emma asked. "I'm hearing rumblings of discord on the streets today. What's going on?"

"The Outfit's on the move, and the leader of the Fourteen-K is splattered all over his office. Looks like their pet shape-shifter has a list of targets. And seeing as you invited yourself to join the New Commission—"

"By right, as a representative of Prince Sitri's financial interests. I'm still offended that Jennifer didn't reach out to me."

"Yeah, well, that means you're on the hit list, too, so maybe work on mending that fence, okay? Look, I'm calling because these guys don't care about collateral damage. Hell, they're *hoping* for it. If you're a target, so is Melanie. Can you get her out of town for a while, maybe send her to see some relatives out of state or something?"

66

"Nonsense," she said. "The safest place for Melanie is right at my side. I won't let her out of my sight."

"Emma, these guys did a drive-by on a corner bar this morning. The civilians they didn't kill with bullets, they lit up with a Molotov. And those people weren't even connected to their target. It was just wrong place, wrong time. If they'll do that to innocent bystanders, think about—"

She cut me off, her voice sharp as a fillet knife.

"And if they come for us, thinking us easy prey, it'll be a delight to educate them. Melanie could use the experience."

I didn't answer right away. I was too busy connecting the dots, reading Emma's message loud and clear.

"You *want* her to get in a fight," I said.

"She's about to turn eighteen and hasn't even been blooded yet. That's fine, by *average* cambion standards, but Melanie is bound for greater things. She needs to learn to embrace her heritage."

Back when Melanie's dad was still alive, I'd had a front-row seat for his arguments with Emma. Ben wanted to raise her as a normal kid, human to the bone. Emma wanted to bring up their daughter the same way she'd been raised, even if only half of Melanie's blood was demonic.

Melanie's dad was dead now. Emma snapped his neck while he begged for his life. I had a front-row seat for that, too. To be fair, he had it coming.

"Maybe she needs room to make her own choices," I said. "She's been through a lot in the last few months. That's more weight than she should have to carry."

"I have a wonderful idea," Emma told me. "How about you mind your own business, and let me worry about how I raise my daughter. Sound good?"

I bit my tongue to keep a flurry of comebacks, each one more acid than the last, from escaping my lips. I hung up on her instead. Didn't have time for this right now. On the other side of the parking lot, Jennifer and Yong were having a walk-and-talk. He looked a little more grounded, the color back in his flabby cheeks. I joined them.

"Sorry," I said. "I had to try and be helpful."

"How'd that work out for you?" Jennifer asked.

"Not great."

"I'm gonna round up all the bosses and take a road trip," she said. "Can you ride shotgun? And I mean that literally. I'll loan you my shotgun. Once we get everybody squirreled away safe, we can plan our next move."

"Your next move is staying in hiding with the others. Look, it's not just the rakshasa. The Outfit's in town and they've got professional hitters, they've got firepower—"

Jennifer crossed her arms and glared at me. "So do we. More than they brought with 'em, I double-goddamn-guarantee that."

"Which means nothing if we don't know where they're hiding. They're an insurgency fighting a standing army; until we figure out where they're holed up, they can hit wherever they want, whenever they want. They're setting the rules of engagement."

"So what do you suggest we do about it, then?"

I'd been thinking about that. Thinking about any possible way to avoid volunteering myself for active duty in an army I wasn't a part of, too. And not finding a solution. It all came back to Gary Kemper. This wasn't my fight, wasn't my mess, but he'd decided it was. And as long as he could dime me out with a single phone call, putting me right back in the FBI's gunsights and making me a fugitive all over again, I had to keep him happy. That meant ending the war and cooling things down on the street. No more dead barflies, no more collateral damage. Once I managed that, it'd buy me a little breathing room, and time to work on a permanent solution to my Gary Kemper problem.

"I met Angelo Mancuso back in Chicago," I said. "This whole deal is his baby. He's looking to step up and prove himself to his old man. But that doesn't mean the old man signed off on it."

Jennifer put her hands on her hips. "You think he's going behind the don's back?"

"I think this whole war is some stupid, reckless bullshit insti-gated by a stupid, reckless punk with a trust fund. Angelo's a hothead who wants to play big shot. On the other hand, his dad Dominic has been running the Chicago underworld since the sev-enties. You don't keep the throne for over forty years by being sloppy. So...I'm gonna go talk to him."

"Talk to him," Jennifer echoed, her voice flat.

"I'm not on the Commission. I'm not a target."

"Maybe you're forgettin' how they framed you for murder."

"Okay, so I might have pissed Angelo off a little," I said. "Fair enough. But his dad's a businessman. He has to be. So I'll go, I'll be nice and friendly, and we'll talk business. If I can show him how far off the rails his kid's gone, he might yank Angelo's leash for us."

"Still rather put two bullets in him," Jennifer said.

"No argument here, but you heard what Angelo's soldiers pulled this morning. I was there, Jen. I saw the bodies lined up on the sidewalk. Civilians. And dead civilians are bad for busi-ness. Metro's on red alert, and they're gonna be crawling up *all* of our asses, looking to lock up anybody they can get their hands on. How about, before this bomb really goes off, you give me a chance to snip the fuse?"

Standing behind us, Yong cleared his throat.

"Sounds reasonable to me," he said.

I held up a finger. "Didn't ask you, but thanks for the vote of confidence."

"Fine." Jennifer relented with a frustrated sigh. "I'll round everybody up and find a cozy place to lay low in the meantime. You be careful out there. Just because you didn't take your seat on the Commission don't mean they won't assume otherwise."

"I know," I said. "I'm hip-deep in this mess. Whether I like it or not."

10.

Two hours later I was nestled in a blue vinyl seat on an American Airlines flight, traveling first class, winging it east over a blanket of white-silver clouds. Caitlin sat next to me, one leg primly crossed over the other while she tapped out emails on her phone. Bringing Caitlin along for the ride hadn't been my original plan. I'd just asked her if she could call Royce and guarantee I wouldn't have any trouble from the locals. The Court of Night-Blooming Flowers could get a little territorial even at the best of times.

"Nonsense," she told me. "Give me ten minutes to rearrange a few meetings, and I'll come with you. Yes, I could make a courtesy call, but Royce's protection only counts for so much these days. I think Nadine is angling for his job. And considering the encounter you just had with her and her daughter—"

I thought back to Nadine, visiting me at Eisenberg. How one of her lackeys had cut our reunion short, telling her that her kid was about to go on some kind of a hunt.

"I heard she had a daughter," I said, "I've never met her, though."

Caitlin tilted her head at me. "Of course you did. At Winter. You were talking to her when we left the conference room. It's very cute that you pretend you don't look at other women, but I'd think all that black leather would stick in your memory a bit."

I felt the blood drain from my cheeks.

"Oh. *Her*. Oh. Huh. I just assumed she was Nadine's body-guard or something."

"She is. Bodyguard, assassin, *quite* a skilled bounty hunter, and an elite member of the Order of Chainmen. Why?"

"I...might have called her mother an asshole."

Caitlin stared at me. She didn't need to say a word. Her look was eloquent enough, making me feel like a little kid with a bad report card.

"I," she finally said, "am definitely coming with you. You clearly need to be chaperoned for your own safety."

At least she upgraded our tickets. I wasn't a big fan of flying, but extra legroom and a glass of merlot—or three—went a long way toward easing my anxiety. Our plane glided down from a golden sunset, wings glowing like hammered brass in torchlight, and below I saw the lights of Chicago ignite like fireflies in the long shadows. Cars snaked along the ribbon of Lake Shore Drive, tiny as toys and jammed up solid, the city's commuters emptying out the town on their nightly exodus to the suburbs.

I spent most of the flight with my head back in Nevada. Remembering my pilgrimage to the Mourner of the Red Rocks and trying to make sense of her cryptic advice. That, and looking for an angle of attack. The Mourner's warnings aside, I wasn't going to stop hunting for the man with the Cheshire smile. *Couldn't* stop. I shelled out for the in-flight WiFi, wincing at the twenty-buck surcharge, just to give my brain something to do.

I had an email waiting, from an address I didn't recognize. Short and sweet, just a link and a message that read: "*Daniel. Care for some inspirational reading? — A Friend.*"

The link took me to a storefront page for a novel, released a week ago: *The Killing Floor* by Carolyn Saunders. I scrolled past the cover art, showing a grim-faced fantasy swordsman on the edge of an arctic plain, and read the synopsis.

Nobody has ever escaped from the Iceberg. It's a wizard's stronghold deep in the hinterlands of the frozen north, staffed by brutal guards and surrounded by trackless tundra. Framed for murder and snared in a deadly curse, Donatello Faustus lands behind bars with a target on his back—

"What the *shit?*" I blurted.

Caitlin looked my way. I turned my phone, letting her read the screen. One pert eyebrow slowly lifted. She took out her own phone and paid for the WiFi.

I bought the book and downloaded an e-reader app, skimming pages as fast as my fingertip could flick across the screen. Most of the book was harmless, just your average beach reading with a little gore and kinky sex to spice things up, but when the plot rolled around to the ordeals of "Donatello," I couldn't take my eyes off the screen. It was a pretty familiar story. After all, I'd lived it.

Donatello eyed the madman warily, and the potion in his trembling, outstretched hand. Could it really be magic? The man with the Cheshire smile had banished him to this prison, doomed him to rot forever. How could he pass up the chance, however slight, for an escape? He downed the potion, and the world swung dizzyingly around him as his stomach lurched.

He found himself outside once more, standing in a vision. A vision of the city of Mirenze, laid to waste, its bell towers and salmon rooftops in ruin...

The details were all over the map, like a story relayed through a game of telephone ten layers deep, but the broad strokes were all in place: my imprisonment at Eisenberg Correctional, meeting Buddy the Prophet, my first doomed attempt at an escape—the prison garage, in this version of the story, recast as a stable where the corrupt wizard-king kept his flying griffins. After that point the whole story went off the rails. Donatello Faustus, the master thief, went on to slay a dragon and bed a pair of leather-clad vampire vixens, both of which I was pretty sure didn't happen in real life.

"Even still," I murmured. "*What?*"

"Indeed," Caitlin replied, her voice dry. She'd downloaded some of Saunders's other books, speed-reading as we touched down on the O'Hare runway. Momentum pushed me forward against my seatbelt, my ears popping from the pressure as the brakes roared.

A brisk evening wind whistled down the access tunnel as we disembarked. Caitlin still had her phone out, hunting and pecking with slender fingertips as we walked. Out in the concourse, we grabbed a plastic table at the half-empty food court.

"This is flatly unacceptable," Caitlin said. "This *person* not only knows about the courts of hell, one of her novels explicitly refers to the Court of Jade Tears. Ruled by Prince 'Citron' instead of Sitri, but still."

"Check this out," I said, showing her my screen with a highlighted passage. "The Tiger's Garden. In her version, it's a tavern for medieval wizards, but she describes the damn place down to the carpeting. You just can't *do* that."

The occult underground had never been big on authority figures. Every now and then, some genius tried to start a Council of Magic or some other grandiose ruling body, and they generally wound up dead in an alley with portions of their own anatomy shoved down their throats. We only had one real rule, the one no sorcerer ever wanted to get caught breaking: just like Fight Club, the first rule of magic was that you kept your damn mouth shut about it. While she wasn't exactly shouting the truth from the rooftops, there were enough nuggets of fact buried in Saunders's books to get her in serious hot water.

With me, first and foremost, seeing as I was the involuntary star of her latest epic.

"All right," I said, "one crisis at a time. Let's do what we came to do, stop this gang war before it gets any worse, and then we'll track down our wayward author."

Caitlin pursed her lips, reluctantly putting her phone away. "Agreed. And how did you find out about this...story?"

"An anonymous tip. I'm gonna sic Pixie on it, see if she can trace the sender. Somebody wanted me to find out about this, but I'm not sure what they're trying to—"

I realized Caitlin was looking past me, over my shoulder. I

turned in my chair and followed her gaze. Mack and Zeke were marching straight for us, just a pair of ordinary college kids wearing pro-wrestling T-shirts and murder in their eyes. Mack had put on another ten pounds since the last time I saw him.

"No," I said, holding up my hand as they approached our table.

"But—" Mack started to say.

"No," I said. "We're busy. Zip it."

"You can't just—" Zeke said.

"No," Caitlin told him. "Leave."

"We're calling our boss." Mack bristled.

"Buh-bye," I told him. I waited until they'd stomped off, swallowed by the tourist crowds, to look at Caitlin. "Seriously, Mack needs to lay off the soft pretzels. I'm starting to worry about that kid."

"I assumed it was the cinnamon rolls. He had a dribble of frosting on his shirt. Shall we take our leave?"

"Definitely."

We jumped in a cab, riding against the nighttime flow, from the outskirts of the burbs into the concrete canyons of Chicago, rattling over bumpy pavement and swerving around construction cones. We sat under the rusty canopy of the elevated train tracks at an intersection. A train rattled past above our heads, trestles shaking, leaving us with the dentist-drill squeal of metal on stubborn metal. We got out of the cab two blocks from our final destination and walked the rest of the way; where we were headed, that was considered a general courtesy.

The parking lot was the same as always: Italian sports cars and Bondo-sprayed wrecks parked shoulder to shoulder under the pale glow of a fizzing sodium light. No security guards. They didn't need any. I knocked on the back door, knuckles rapping on cold and battered sheet metal. The door swung wide, and a thin man in a scarlet vest and a black tie greeted us with a carefully reserved smile as he looked us up and down.

"Hound of the Court of Jade Tears," Caitlin said, cutting him off before he could say a word, "and her consort. You'll let us in now."

The doorman's eyes went wide as he scurried out of our way. He beckoned us in with a sweep of his arm.

"Of course. Welcome, esteemed guests. Welcome to the Bast Club. Please observe our simple rules: speak no true names, lay hands on none without their invitation, and speak no secrets that are not yours to share."

Nice rules, in principle. In practice, more like shaky guidelines, enforced at random by the club's absentee landlord. As far as I knew, Management had never made a personal appearance. He preferred to work through proxies—like the shadows that wriggled and squirmed along the Victorian-era wallpaper, silhouettes of millipedes and crouching spiders that didn't line up with anything in the room. Caitlin and I walked arm in arm across a grainy hardwood floor cut to look like pieces in a massive jigsaw puzzle, stepping out into the main lounge.

It took me a second to get my bearings. At least the local magicians' hangout back home, the Tiger's Garden, had the tang of familiarity. A visit to the Garden was like a trip to the old neighborhood watering hole, all friendly faces and drinks mixed by a bartender who always knew exactly what you wanted. By contrast, walking into the Bast Club felt like taking a hit of bad acid. The air crackled with wild tangents of loose magic, dancing like DNA helixes in my second sight and playing bursts of static mingled with discordant chimes in my inner ears. I had to take a breath, steadying myself against Caitlin's arm, until the rush passed and I found my footing again.

Another rush was coming on fast, a burst of adrenaline on two legs cutting her way through a crowd of bloody-eyed cambion. Fredrika Vinter—Freddie to most, Dances to her close personal friends—cradled a martini glass in one hand and reached out with the other, cooing her delight. Her curly mane of fire-engine-red hair flopped over one shoulder of her silk dress, the fabric adorned with oversized and ruffled accents.

"*Darlings*," she said and pulled Caitlin into a hug. They kissed each other's cheeks, and then Freddie paused as she looked her over. "Dear, *who* are you wearing? Really, now."

Caitlin tilted her head, looking vaguely offended. "It's Prada."

"It should be me. The answer should always be me. I'm sending you a new wardrobe." Freddie looked my way. "And you brought my favorite thief! Old Dusty hasn't found you yet, I take it."

"He's gonna have to get in line," I told her. "As threats to life and limb go this week, Damien Ecko isn't even in the top five."

"I wish you'd take him more seriously," said the woman who approached us from the side, her long, oval face wrapped under a powder-blue headscarf.

"Doctor Khoury," I said, inclining my head as I looked her way. "Good to see you again."

"He is not to be underestimated." Halima turned to Caitlin. "Take it from those of us who have lived in his shadow for many, many years. His madness is that of the fox, not the rabid dog. Desperation will only amplify his cunning and his determination to survive."

Freddie tossed back her glass, drinking deep, then eyed the goblet like she wasn't sure where all the booze had gone.

"And on that cheery note," she said, "I need a refill. Let's grab that nook over there and get caught up."

Halima furrowed her brow, standing up on her toes to look over the heads of the milling crowd. "I think it's occupied."

"They're saving those seats for us," Freddie said. "They just don't know it yet. I'll explain it to them."

11.

Five minutes later we were seated on plush red velvet divans in a recessed nook, comfortable on the sidelines of the chaos. A waitress in a dress lined with bright copper buttons whirled past with a tray of drinks, and the first sip of Jack and Coke sliced through my nervous tension. I'd spent two weeks sidelined from life's little pleasures—alcohol and sex, mainly—after the concussion I'd earned trying to bust out of prison. Now that Doc Savoy had finally written me a clean bill of health, I was making up for lost time.

"Happy as I am to see you," Freddie told us, "I'm not sure Dusty's hometown is the best place to hide from him."

"Not hiding. We've just got bigger fish to fry." I paused, something occurring to me. "Did you show Halima the video from the morgue?"

"I have no desire to see such things," Halima said, her voice soft.

"It's just that, well, you know him pretty well, right?"

"An accurate statement."

"He wrote something on the wall," I told her, "and I'm not sure what he's trying to say. It was a message to me: 'lighten your heart.' Any idea what that means?"

Halima sighed, cradling a glass of club soda in her cupped hands.

"Damien still believes in the old gods of Egypt, though he's forsaken them—and they, if they exist, have forsaken him. It was once believed that the spirits of the dead stood before Djehuty, lord of wisdom, and their hearts were weighed on a scale against a single white feather. If your heart was as light as the feather, you'd be welcomed into the afterlife."

"And if not?" I asked.

"If not," she said, "you'd be thrown to Ammit, the eater of souls, to be devoured and consigned to eternal darkness. Damien is telling you to prepare yourself for judgment. And he is promising, by the strongest words he knows—the words of his heritage and his homeland—that he will not stop until he has sent you there."

"Cheerful," Freddie said, breaking the silence that descended upon the nook. She tossed back a swig of vodka. "Flag the waitress down. I'm going to need another of these in about five more minutes."

I contemplated my glass. "Look, Ecko's a problem, sure, but there's a lot more on the line right now. I need a sit-down with Dominic Mancuso. His kid's running riot all over Vegas. There's a detective in Metro who knows about my miraculous resurrection. If I don't cool this feud down before it boils over, it's my neck on the line."

"Not the kind of social circles I run in, darling," Freddie said. She glanced up to the light sconces, soft tongues of fire flickering behind frosted green glass. "I am an *artist*. That said, it *is* Columbus Day weekend. Not the shindig it used to be, but Chicago still throws quite the parade. And the elder Mancuso—in his capacity as the city's favorite philanthropist and entrepreneur—will be the grand marshal as usual."

"I was hoping for something a little more intimate."

"Then you want the pre-parade party. Tomorrow night. It's a private fiesta for the city's movers and shakers. The mayor, a few aldermen, the wealthier half of the chamber of commerce. In a word, boring. In two words, fucking boring. But if you can get past the front door, you've got a better-than-average chance of bending Dominic's ear. It's at the Willowbrook Ballroom; they rent the whole place out for the night so they can talk about...I don't know. Hedge funds? Whatever boring old men talk about. Security is tight, too. They don't want any reporters sneaking in and recording anything naughty."

"Sounds like our best bet," I said. "Any chance you've got a line on a guest list?"

Freddie downed her drink and waved her empty glass. "Amy. Amy, Amy, Amy. You are expressly *needed*."

I recognized the young woman, rail-thin in a pinstripe pantsuit and black silk blouse. Amy Xun had been a big help the last time I was in Chicago, though she was the one who came out ahead of all of us, walking off with the stolen prize at a poker tournament, her hands clean as the driven snow while we set up Ecko to take the fall for it. Coming out ahead in every deal was pretty much her thing. She favored me with the slightest bow of her head, her dark eyes sizing me up and quietly assessing the size of my wallet.

"Guest list for the Willowbrook Columbus Day party," Freddie told her. "Can you get it?"

Amy held up a finger. "Five minutes."

It took her two. She came back to the nook as silently as she'd left, cradling her phone and giving the screen an appraising glance.

"Yes," she said.

"And?" Freddie replied.

"I will trade it for the location of the gravestone of Goody Naughton."

Freddie rolled her eyes. "Want me to throw in the Holy Grail and the Shroud of Turin while you're at it? It's a guest list for a holiday party. Get real. I'll give you fifty bucks, cash."

"Five words," Amy said, regarding Freddie with an appraising eye, "of the true chant of the Polarian jeremiad."

Freddie sighed. "One word."

"Three."

"Three, and they come from any part of the chant I want."

Amy pursed her lips and thought it over.

"Deal," she said. She and Freddie stepped away from the nook, looking for a quiet corner to confer in the shadows.

Freddie came back just as my phone buzzed in my pocket. She gave me a faintly smug smile as she dropped onto the plush divan, cradling a fresh cosmo.

"She just texted you the list," Freddie said. "*Such* a drama queen. You're welcome, by the way."

Caitlin inched closer to the edge of her divan, a glass of Malbec resting on the curve of her knee. "Grateful as always. We'll repay the favor."

"Anything for my BFF. But I know that look: something else is making your world all topsy-turvy. Dish."

Soon enough, Freddie and Halima were sitting side by side on the couch, eyes wide as they read the screen of Caitlin's phone.

"Some of the details in these books." Halima fell silent for a moment, shaking her head. "You just can't *do* that."

"That's what I said," I told her.

Freddie's lip curled in a pout. "And yet, no mention of a glamorous and devastatingly witty fashion-designer-slash-socialite. Zero out of five stars, would not skim again."

"I'll be sure to mention that when we drop in on her."

Halima's eyes met mine. "I wouldn't advise it. Paying a visit, that is."

"Yeah? Why not?"

She handed the phone back to Caitlin.

"Consider," she said, "that a very powerful foe orchestrated your imprisonment and intended for you to die there. You escaped, throwing a pole into the spokes of his plan, and disappeared. Now an anonymous 'friend' points you toward a freshly published novel obviously designed to get your attention. You're being called out, Daniel. This feels like a trap."

"Sorry, Doc, but my curiosity isn't going to let me walk away from this."

"I know. Which is exactly why it feels like a trap. And at the very least, a dangerous distraction. Damien Ecko isn't going to wait patiently while you go hunting for strange authors."

"Like I said, he's gonna have to get in line."

Freddie stretched languidly, almost purring. "At least the next few days shouldn't be boring. So, Cait, seeing as the party isn't until tomorrow night, how about you and I *finally* go out and get a bite to eat together?"

My stomach rumbled in sympathy. "I could go for some dinner myself."

Freddie and Caitlin both looked my way. Freddie, visibly amused, batting her eyelashes at me, and Caitlin with a barely audible sigh. Freddie sidled onto the divan on my other side and leaned in close to whisper in my ear. In my peripheral vision, her face rippled and changed. A cheek charred black by arctic frostbite. A blue and half-lipless mouth, curled in a leering smile.

"You're always fun to have around," Freddie said, "but where we're going, you wouldn't care for the cuisine."

On my opposite side, Caitlin patted my knee and rose, still cradling her wineglass.

"I'll meet you back at the hotel, pet. Don't wait up."

Halima watched them go, arm in arm. She glanced my way.

"Do you like shawarma?" she asked. "I know a good spot, not far from here."

*　*　*

Shawarma it was. We sat across from each other in a booth in a little hole-in-the-wall restaurant down the block from the Bast Club. The brown vinyl bench was understuffed, and the hard coil of a spring jabbed into the small of my back as I looked over a paper menu speckled with suspicious stains. Slabs of meat sizzled behind the front counter, slowly turning on fat skewers and filling the air with a spicy, gingery aroma I could almost taste. We split an appetizer, a dish of hummus surrounded by lemon wedges and strips of beef like the spokes of a savory wheel. Halima squeezed one of the lemons with careful fingers, drizzling a glossy trail over the pureed chickpeas.

"Something I don't get," I said. "You and her."

"Hmm?" She looked up at me, uncertain.

"You're not...*like* a lot of people in the underground. You work a legit job, you stay away from the shady stuff, you're, ah—can't think of a word for it."

"A decent human being?"

"Ouch," I said. "I was gonna go with something like 'rigorously ethical,' but okay, that shoe fits."

"I try to hold myself to certain standards," Halima said. "I don't always succeed, but that's the nature of existence. We are flawed creations, faced with one choice: to fall further into our flaws, or strive for something better. *Inshallah*, I will continue to strive."

"So what's with you and Freddie? I mean, you two are tight."

"Best friends," she said. "Have been for years."

I dipped a strip of beef into the hummus. The flavor, rich and lemony and touched with a hint of cinnamon, made me think of olive groves in some Mediterranean paradise.

"You know what they're probably doing tonight, right?"

A tiny smile rose to Halima's lips, though her eyes held a trace of some distant sadness. She glanced over her shoulder, making sure nobody was close enough to overhear.

"Is that a delicate way of asking," she said, "if I'm aware that my dear friend dines on human flesh? And that she—along with your paramour, I might add—is hunting for a suitable victim at this very moment?"

"More or less."

Halima shrugged. "Dances has a condition which necessitates a very strict, very specific diet, once every month or so. I think gazelles are beautiful, but I don't fault a lion for eating them. Every creature has to survive in its own way. Besides, her methods of selection are quite rigorous. She hunts...other hunters. Predators. People who degrade the world by their very presence. It isn't ideal, but she makes the most of her situation. I notice you don't seem to be having ethical qualms over it."

"We've already established that I'm a lousy person. And Caitlin...Caitlin is Caitlin. She's gonna do what she's gonna do."

"What she's going to do," Halima said, "is mourn your passing, if you don't attend to your priorities. You're running in five places at once, while Damien Ecko moves in only one direction: toward you, as swift and as inerrant as an arrow dipped in cobra venom."

I rested my hands on the table. "Look, Doc, I realize you've got history with the guy and you're skittish. I know he's not a cream puff. Believe me, I've seen his zombies in action. But at the end of the day, he's just a necromancer with a tiny bag of tricks. I've faced bigger guys than him. They're all in the ground, and I'm still here."

"*Just* a necromancer," she said. "As one might say, *just* a nuclear weapon. You think you know what you're up against. You don't."

"Then enlighten me."

She didn't say a word until we ordered our entrees, her lips pursed in taciturn silence. I could hear the cogs of her brain turning, weighing her options, deciding which cards to show and which ones to hold close. I dug into my dinner, chicken shawarma wrapped in pita, the flour-speckled bread seared with golden grill marks. Her order—chicken kufta kabobs, lying in a nest of greasy wax paper—sat untouched.

"I'll start at the beginning, then," she told me. "Damien Ecko is just the latest of his many, many names. He changes them every few decades, discarding identities like soiled linens when he outlives them. His true first name is Kaemsekhem. *Prince* Kaemsekhem, of the Sixteenth Dynasty. And he is over thirty-six hundred years old."

12.

"**M**uch of Egypt's Sixteenth Dynasty has been lost to the mists of history," Halima told me, "and we have him to thank for it. I can tell you what I know: that the young prince had a talent for *heka*, the magical arts of his homeland, and a strong teacher. Djehutimesu, his father's court magician, took Damien under his wing. Djehutimesu was a master of his craft, and...hmm. Interesting. Something just occurred to me."

I tilted my head at her, my pita halfway to my mouth. "What?"

"He was a bit of a trickster, they say. An illusionist, with a scoundrel's reputation but essentially a good heart."

"Sounds like a fun guy."

"I'm sure he was," Halima said. "He was not, however, a good judge of character. He couldn't see the shadow inside of Damien, his insatiable need for more and more power. When he learned everything Djehutimesu could teach him, the prince turned his eye toward...darker paths of knowledge. Tell me, have you ever heard of a creature called the King of Worms?"

Heard of it? I'd met the thing, twice, on a trance-induced ride to the heart of madness. I'd stood at the foot of his colossal throne, gazing up at the moldering corpse in royal rags, and asked for a favor. Once out of rage. The second time, alone and trapped behind bars, I was just desperate for a weapon. Both times, the king had been happy to oblige. His gifts, he'd reminded me, were free for the taking.

That is, if you can call a psychic maggot squirming across your brain, leaving slug trails of toxic filth in its wake, a *gift*. I shuddered at the memory, my scalp crawling like a blanket of lice. I ran nervous fingers through my hair, reassuring myself, trying to pass it off as a casual gesture. The king wasn't a man, wasn't a demon. He was something different, *older*, steeped in insanity and corruption I didn't even have a frame of reference to understand.

"You have heard of it." Halima lifted her chin, squinting as she stared into my eyes. "No. More than heard. Oh, Daniel. What did you do?"

"My back was up against the wall," I told her. "I needed a little help."

"And that is how it always begins with his kind. Just a little. A little edge, a scrap of secrets, a helping hand when you need it most. And it's always free. Then you go back, again, and again, and you take a little more, and a little more—"

I set my pita down and folded my arms. I'd lost my appetite.

"I'm not going back. And yeah, I know how temptation works. I'm dating a demon, in case you didn't notice."

"Knowing and resisting are two different things. Damien, for instance, quickly became an apt pupil. The King of Worms taught him the art of necromancy. And inch by inch, with each new foul ritual he mastered, corruption overtook him. A rot from within that demanded he resort to extreme measures to preserve his own life."

"How extreme are we talking here?"

"He used his defiling magic upon himself. With sutures and salt and clay jars for his organs and an iron nose hook for scooping out his own brain."

Halima reached for her Styrofoam cup, sipping ginger ale through a fat, red-striped straw.

"In an act of supreme will and inconceivable suffering, Damien Ecko mummified himself," she said. "And then he brought himself back to life. He *is* one of his own undead creations. Just as strong, just as relentless, just as indestructible. More so, in fact, given the wards and amulets that shield him from harm."

I stared at her.

"You have got to be kidding me," I said. "He's a living mummy? Like, bandages and beetles and Boris Karloff?"

She nodded. "The man you see is not his true guise. He's cloaked himself in the semblance of life, using the illusions Djehutimesu taught him. He can't bear to see his true face, not now. Not after centuries of rot and vile magic have taken their toll. His first teacher, I might add, also became his first victim. Djehutimesu confronted his wayward student, trying to turn him back to righteousness. Damien swatted him like a fly."

"What happened next?"

"Hard to know," Halima said, "as our records of the Sixteenth Dynasty crumble at points. There was a plague, you see. A blistering pox that swept across the land, killing cattle and men alike, leaving them to rot and choke upon their own bile. Cities toppled and the throne fell as the corpses piled high."

"Ecko," I said.

"An offering to the King of Worms. Destroying his own people, along with the last scraps of his humanity. You know as well as I, Daniel, that nothing is truly free. Payment always comes due in the end."

We fell into an uneasy silence. I poked at my food, thinking back to my last encounter with Ecko, in a warehouse packed with his resurrected monsters. A glimmer of hope sparked in the back of my mind, spurred by the memory.

"Wait a second," I said. "This is good news. We've killed his creations before. About a dozen of the damn things, in fact. They're afraid of fire, they burn like Roman candles, and I know a vodou priestess who can drop the living dead as easy as snipping puppet strings. If he's like them, this'll be no sweat."

"*Like* them, but a higher order of being. He's no animal, going into a panic at the sight of an open flame. And he's had thirty-six hundred years to master the arts of sorcery. Beyond his own spells—and he's forgotten more about magic than you or I will ever learn—he's crafted traditional amulets of warding and sewn them underneath his skin. He has all the benefits of the undead, and none of the weaknesses."

"Help me out, Doc. If he's coming for me, I need a plan. There's got to be some way to take him down for good."

Halima bit down on her bottom lip, thinking it over. She tapped the tip of her straw.

"There is one way," she said. "Damien Ecko has a heart of stone, and I mean that quite literally. It's his amulet of animation, carved upon a fist-sized rock and sewn inside his chest where his human heart used to be. Destroy the stone and you destroy the man. But it's not that simple. If it were, I would have done it myself. His speed and strength are incredible. He doesn't sleep, ever. He can hear the buzzing of a fly's wings from a hundred paces away. The only way to get at his heart is to take him by surprise, and he *can't* be surprised. You'll be dead before you try."

"I don't know," I told her. "I can come up with some neat surprises when I put my mind to it."

After that, there wasn't much left to talk about. I took a cab to the Four Seasons. Then I lingered alone in a gloomy bedroom and listened to the steady, strong hum of the air conditioner, waiting for Caitlin. I drifted off to sleep, only stirring at the sound of the shower running, alarm clock glowing 2:47 in the dark. She slipped between the sheets, molding the curve of her warm body against mine, and I drifted away again until the sunrise.

*   *   *

We spent the morning with a couple of caramel macchiatos and the party guest list, looking up the who's who of the local political scene. I had a plan for getting into that ballroom, but the target had to be just right. Nobody who traveled with heavy security, nobody who would raise any alarms if they went missing for a few hours. In other words, we needed the least-important important people in the room.

"These two." I circled the last couple of candidates. "Connor

Townsend and his wife Lois. He's an investment manager who dabbles in philanthropy, and a big investor in the mayor's reelection campaign. Looks like that's the only reason they snared an invite: they're cash machines on legs."

"All right," Caitlin said, "and what do we do next?"

"Didn't Freddie say she was going to fix you up with a fresh wardrobe? Might want to give her a call. We've gotta look presentable for the party."

She looked more than presentable. Caitlin eyed herself in a floor-length mirror, sheathed in a light cream gown that hugged her curves like snakeskin and shimmered as she turned left and then right. I was a little less fashionable, dressed in a shabby chauffeur's outfit we rented from a costume store on the other side of town. A squared blue cap sat flat on my head, the brim smelling like old marinara sauce, and a starchy black tie coiled tight as a noose around my throat. I'd rented a tuxedo, too, but for now it stayed safe in its plastic dry-cleaning shroud.

The next thing I needed was a gun. I figured hunting one down would take most of the afternoon, but Freddie slipped her hand into her purse and obliged me with hers: a slim nickel-plated .22 with a snub nose.

"I'm going to need that back," she told me.

I turned the pistol over in my hand, the metal cool and light as a feather. "Wait, why do *you* carry a piece? I figured you could do more damage without one."

"*Dahling.*" She rolled her eyes. "There's a time to use a scalpel, and a time to use a sledgehammer. There is also, every now and then, a time to use a gun. Variety is the spice of life."

Next we needed a limo.

We cruised the north-side suburbs in a rental car, getting the lay of the land. We were in Winnetka, a patch of prime real estate lined with shady trees and brick mansions, and I pulled into the driveway of a shuttered house with a For Sale sign on the neatly trimmed lawn. I pulled the sign up by its steel roots, walked around back, and tossed it into the yard. A fat black plastic key box dangled from the front doorknob, sealed with a combination lock. While Caitlin played lookout and shielded me from the road, I swiveled all four combination wheels to zero.

"Time me," I said.

A thin lockpick slid between the edge of the box and the first wheel, nestling like it belonged there. I thumbed the wheel slowly, one digit at a time, waiting until I felt the inner reel drop. Then I jimmied my pick between the next two wheels and repeated the process. Once all four wheels had been set, I bumped them three numbers ahead, gave the lock a hard pull, and the box popped open to reveal the house key nestled inside.

"Two minutes and forty-eight seconds," Caitlin said. "You can do better than that."

"Next time," I told her, and we let ourselves inside. The house had been detailed, every inch swept clean and the polished furniture posed for photographs in the crisp afternoon light. It was antiseptic in a way no lived-in house could manage. Nice place, but we weren't staying. I used my burner phone and called for livery service. Half an hour later, a white stretch limo rolled up to the curb.

I walked to the car as the driver stepped out. His initial smile wavered as he looked me up and down, taking in my cheap chauffeur costume. He wasn't sure what to make of me. Even less when I pulled the .22 and jabbed it into his gut.

"Don't do anything stupid, and I don't have to use this," I told him. "C'mon, let's talk inside."

I marched him into the unfinished basement, zip-tied his hands and ankles, and sat him down on the cold concrete floor with his back to the drywall. I patted him down and took his phone and his car keys.

"Sorry, pal, but I need your wheels. Just for a couple of hours, then I'll call nine-one-one and let them know where to find you. Tell me something: you get paid hourly, or are you on salary?"

"Salary," he stammered, looking shell-shocked. "Plus...plus tips."

"How much is an average tip? Twenty bucks?"

His head bobbed. "U-usually. About that."

"I've got a great idea," I said. "When the cops show up, how about you tell 'em you didn't get a good look at us? See, that serves two purposes. First, if you don't talk, I don't have to come back and shut you up the hard way."

I unfurled a rumpled hundred-dollar bill and held it up in front of him. Then I stuffed it into his shirt pocket.

"Second," I said, "if you don't talk, you don't have to mention the Benjamin I just gave you. Sound good? A hundred bucks for sitting around and doing nothing for a couple of hours?"

He nodded, fast. I patted him on the shoulder and headed upstairs, leaving his phone on the kitchen counter.

"All set?" Caitlin asked.

"All set. Let's go pick up Mr. and Mrs. Townsend."

13.

I'd never been behind the wheel of a stretch limousine before. It handled like a beached whale, swaying and over-steering as I pulled away from the curb and tried to keep it steady.

"Everything all right up there?" Caitlin asked. She sat in the back, looking regal, talking to me through the open partition.

"No problem. After driving a prison bus, this is a piece of cake."

"Didn't you *crash* the prison bus?"

I met her eyes in the rearview mirror and wrinkled my nose.

"In my defense," I said, "people were shooting at me."

She flicked her fingers at me, lifting her chin in mock disdain.

"Eyes on the road, driver."

"Yes, ma'am," I said and set the dashboard GPS. Right about then, a second limousine from another service would be on its way to pick up the Townsends and ferry them to the party. I had to get there first.

The Townsend house was ten minutes away, a two-story colonial at the end of a short private drive. They must have been waiting—they emerged from the house as I pulled up out front, both of them dressed to the nines. She wore an ocean's worth of pearls, and he made sure to flash his Versace chronograph watch as he straightened his bow tie, a calculated move he must have been practicing in the mirror. I got out, all smiles, and opened the limo's back door for them.

"You're not our usual driver," she said, more conversational than worried.

"He's got the night off," I told her. "Don't worry, I'll take good care of you."

They slid into the backseat only to find Caitlin sitting across from them, the borrowed .22 nestled in her hand. She crossed her legs and aimed the gun with casual grace.

"We're going to need your invitations," she said. "Also your clothes."

I shut the door and got back behind the wheel.

They protested halfway to the party. Finally, exasperated, Caitlin turned to talk to me through the partition.

"Your plan isn't working. Shall I just murder them both?"

"Sure," I said, "go for it."

Now they cooperated. Caitlin snatched the invitations—elegant calligraphy on thick stock, and embossed with a gold-leaf seal depicting Columbus's ships—and waited patiently while they undressed. She rolled down the window just long enough to toss their clothes, evening finery billowing out along a quiet suburban street. She kept the pearls and the watch. I focused on the road, feeling the limo wobble while she zip-tied their hands and ankles.

"Comfy?" Caitlin asked them.

"Why?" he blurted. "Why are you doing this?"

"Because while I have no qualms about bloodshed, my lover is a bit soft when it comes to the execution of 'innocent' bystanders. I'm sure you're guilty of *something*—in fact, I know you are, both of your souls are tarnished as old brass—but apparently that's just not good enough. So you're only suffering a bit of indignity instead. Be thankful. You know, some people enjoy this sort of thing."

The end of the line was in Willow Springs, about twenty miles southwest of downtown. The ballroom resembled an old-world hunting lodge, sturdy brick and dun-shingled roof topped with an iron weather vane, ringed by flowerbeds and lampposts. The marquee out front looked like a throwback to the fifties, a vintage font spelling out the ballroom's original name, "*willow-brook*," on an oblong rust-red sign.

The party was already jumping. A line of limos and town cars inched their way up the front drive in a serpentine conga, under the watchful eye of suburban cops who had been enlisted to guide traffic. I rolled slowly past a hard-eyed officer, the brim of my cap pulled down, our hostages out of sight behind the smoked-glass windows. When it was finally our turn at bat, I put the car in park and jumped out, keeping my head low as I hustled around to open the back door for Caitlin. She favored me with a feline smile, holding Mrs. Townsend's invitation between her scarlet fingernails.

"Be back promptly at ten," she told me, "and don't dawdle. I won't tolerate dawdling, driver."

"Yes, ma'am," I said, trying not to roll my eyes. She was enjoying this too much. I hopped back behind the wheel, and a bored cop's windmilling light sticks guided me across the parking lot. I slid between two parked limousines, sleek black walls pinning us in, and killed the engine. I tossed my cap onto the passenger-side floor, tugged off my jacket, and reached for the dry-cleaning bag folded neatly on the leather seat at my side.

"Here's how this works," I told the couple on the other side of the partition, "even if I gagged you, it wouldn't be hard for you to thump around and make enough noise to get somebody's attention. Another driver, a parking-lot attendant, somebody would come and rescue you. On the other hand...well, if you're embarrassed now, just think of all the things that might happen if the wrong person found you two like this."

In the middle of changing into my rented tux, French cuffs billowing, I paused. I held up my phone, stuck it through the partition, and snapped a few quick photographs.

"Not to mention these photos getting leaked onto the Internet. You wouldn't want that. Especially since the angles I shot look less like 'hostage' and more like 'sex game gone wrong.' People do tend to misinterpret things in the worst way, don't they? Now, rich folks like yourselves, I'm guessing you've got a helper monkey on the payroll—somebody you trust to handle untidy business."

"My lawyer," he snapped, glaring at me.

"Good. Give me his number."

I tapped it in, saving it on my phone, then went back to changing my clothes. Five minutes of awkward fumbling around in the driver's seat, bumping my elbow on the steering wheel, before I arched my back to shimmy into the pleated dress pants. My new outfit was the color of fresh-churned cream, matching Caitlin's gown. The bow tie was the last part, and the hardest. My hands might as well have been meat hooks as I struggled to get the knot just right.

"Seriously," I said, "how do people wear these things? Okay, here's the deal: you two stay nice and quiet, and in a couple of hours, I call your lawyer buddy. He swoops in to save the day, and nobody has to know that any of this ever happened. Sound good?"

I interpreted their sullen silence as a yes. I held up my invitation and gave them a farewell salute, stepping out of the limo.

I caught a glimpse of myself in the tinted windows. Transformation complete, from a hapless driver in a cheap suit to a hard-charging businessman in an expensive tux. I reached up to adjust my tie, imitating Townsend's move from memory and flashing my stolen watch.

Stepping in front of a rolling limo, projecting equal measures of arrogance and irritation, I ignored the driver's horn and kept walking. All the way to the front steps, where a pair of big-shouldered guys in black suits were checking invites. I offered mine up and held my breath. This was the moment of truth. If they actually knew what Connor Townsend looked like, I was about to be caught red-handed. If not...

"Thank you, sir." He handed the invitation back with an empty smile. "Please enjoy your evening."

A small brass band played in the grand ballroom under Spanish glass chandeliers with swirling filigrees. The light shone off the polished parquet floor, the oaken slats shifting from light to dark and reminding me of a vintage bowling alley. The jazz played strong—an old Charlie Parker tune, if I remembered my education from Bentley's vinyl collection—but not many couples were dancing. This was one-quarter party, three-quarters networking opportunity, and Chicago's business luminaries rubbed shoulders with aldermen and political fixers over dirty martinis. Some milled about in small groups, talking in low voices, while others camped at the white-draped tables ringing the dance floor. I found Caitlin over by the open bar, sipping a glass of pale rose wine as she eavesdropped on a nearby conversation.

"This has been fun," she murmured as I sidled close. "You should pose as my servant more often. So, today we've committed three kidnappings *and* grand theft auto. What's next?"

"Hopefully a reasonable, polite conversation followed by a clean getaway." I craned my neck, looking for the man in charge.

"That doesn't sound terribly entertaining."

"No, but it's the option that gets Detective Kemper off my back, at least long enough to buy me some breathing room. All I have to do is convince Chicago to call off their goons. Dominic Mancuso's no dummy, not like his kid. He'll listen to reason."

I spotted the elder Mancuso, looking just like the photo on his charity website, in a knot of conversation with the mayor and a few hangers-on. Even if I didn't recognize him, I'd know he was the top dog in a heartbeat. He might have been pushing seventy, but his steel-gray eyes hadn't lost one ounce of fire. Every movement, every slow sweep of his hand as he spoke, every reserved nod of his head and cutting glance projected purpose and control. Control of himself, control of the room, the center of the conversation even when he did nothing but listen. This was a man who had spent a lifetime learning to get exactly what he wanted, when he wanted it, and "no" wasn't in his vocabulary.

Might have to teach him a new word tonight, I thought and

weighed my options. This wasn't a conversation to have in public, and Dominic wasn't traveling alone. I spotted a pair of silent bruisers keeping watch at a respectful distance, wearing neatly tailored jackets over their shoulder holsters, and another pair standing guard by the ballroom doors. Then I saw my shot: Dominic broke from the pack and headed up a short hallway, under a sign marked Restrooms. Two of his boys followed him. I took one last look, counted to ten under my breath, and then I followed him too.

One of his bodyguards waited right outside the men's room door, hands folded before him, standing at parade rest. I kept it casual, playing my role, and stepped past him as he gave me the once-over. Inside, Dominic's second escort stood his post in the corner, next to a row of closed toilet stalls and a trio of urinals. I strolled to the opposite side of the narrow room and pretended to check my hair in the mirror.

Dominic finished his business and stood at the sink beside me, pumping a trickle of soap and scrubbing his liver-spotted hands under the tap. I swallowed, my throat suddenly dry as desert sand. I had one shot to get this right, one chance to make the sale and stop a bloodbath. More important, one chance to keep Gary Kemper from blowing my cover and tossing me right back in prison, this time for good.

I took a deep breath and turned to face him.

14.

"**M**r. Mancuso, sir," I said. "May I have a moment of your time?"

He barely glanced my way, grunting out a "Hmm?"

"My name is Daniel Faust. I was hoping to talk to you about a sensitive matter—"

"I know who you are," he said, still washing his hands. "Clocked you the second you walked in. I was wondering when you were gonna grow the balls to come over and say something."

I blinked. "I...assumed you wouldn't want anyone to overhear anything about your business. Your real business, I mean."

Dominic snorted. He turned off the tap and flicked his wet hands at the sink, droplets of water spattering the bottom of the mirror. He finally turned my way, looking me up and down. In the mirror, I saw his bodyguard tense up. Not reaching for his piece, not yet, but getting ready for it.

I was ready, too. My deck of cards grew warm against my hip, tingling with nervous electricity.

"Son," Dominic said, "one way or another, I own every man in that room. If they're not indebted to my family, or my family business, they're indebted to someone who is. And they might play dumb because it makes 'em feel better, but each and every one of them knows exactly who I am and what I do. I could walk out there, pick some schmuck at random, and blow his brains all over the dance floor. Know what they'd do about it? Nothing. I wouldn't even have to tell anybody to clean it up. It would just *happen*. Welcome to Chicago."

He walked past me, turning his back like I wasn't even there, and grabbed a couple of paper towels from the dispenser.

"Okay," I said, "well, if we're going to be blunt, let's try this: I'm here about your son. Angelo is starting a war between your organization and the Las Vegas underworld."

Dominic rubbed his hands dry, tossing away the wadded-up towels and tugging down a couple more.

"And? I'm aware."

"You...sanctioned this?"

"Back in the seventies, our family had a gripe with the Detroit Combination. My old man put me in charge of the beatdown. It was a test to see if I could handle myself, handle my men on the street. We got the job done. Fought 'em until they cried uncle, at least." Dominic looked my way. "Just between you and me, Angelo's a pansy, but I'm hoping this toughens him up like it did me. Every father wants to see his son outshine him. Or in Angelo's case, at least not be a goddamn embarrassment."

"Look, you might think we're easy pickings with Nicky Agnelli gone, but that's not the case. You don't want this fight."

"Right." Dominic's lips curled in a sneer. "Your 'New Commission,' with some pothead split-tail in charge. Think you're powerful? Let me teach you something about power, right here and now."

He looked to his bodyguard and nodded to the door.

"You. Hit the bricks. I need the room."

Without a word, his only protection walked out through the bathroom door, leaving us alone together. Dominic spread his hands, taking in the room around us.

"Look at that. Here we are. Me with no guys, no gun, no nothing. Now tell me something, Faust. Do I look scared to you?"

He didn't. If anything, the old man looked more confident than ever. He met my eyes, his steel gaze utterly defiant.

"Maybe you should be," I told him.

"Because you could cast a curse on me? Like I said, I know who you are. I know you're a freak. Why even bother? I'm seventy-six years old. I've got emphysema and diabetes and god knows what else. You could just strangle me with your bare hands. I couldn't stop you. And yet I'm not scared. Why is that, Faust? Can you tell me? You got any clue?"

I shook my head, suddenly mute. He took a step forward, closing the distance between us as his voice dropped to a growl.

"Because I am a man of power. A man of power fears nothing, because he's already accounted for every possibility, every angle, every outcome. I could end your life with a whisper, or just burn everyone you love and leave you alive to suffer. You think you're something special, with your 'magic' and your little deck of cards, and your tricks. But that's not *real* power. You've never even seen real power. Not until now. Here you are, holding the advantage, armed, every opportunity to kill me...but I'm the one in control. And you know it."

"I came here out of respect," I told him, keeping my voice steady as I fought to hold his gaze. "I came in the hopes of stopping a massacre. Call off your dogs, Dominic. Rein your son in. If you don't, he'll be coming home in a casket."

Dominic nodded back over his shoulder. "You notice, when I told my guy to give us some privacy, he didn't gripe about it. Didn't hesitate, either. Didn't question me. Absolute obedience. That's what I demand from each and every one of my men, and that's what I get. They trust me. I'm the shogun, and they're my samurai, ready to die as soon as I give the order. *That* is respect. Threatening my son's life? Have you heard a goddamn word I've said? I gave Angelo the green light on you, your buddies, and your entire city, to see if he can man up and earn his place in this family. If he can't, then I don't give a rat's ass *what* you do to him. If he fails, he's no son of mine. So go for it. Do your worst, because you're handing me a favor. He wipes you vermin out and takes the city, or you kill him and save me years of frustration. Either way, I win. Survival of the fittest. That's what this world is all about."

I inched closer to him, our toes almost bumping on the tile floor as my anger simmered. A low, steady fire in the pit of my stomach, threatening to boil over.

"I don't think you realize just how *fit* we are. This is your last chance. Call it off."

Dominic smirked. "You're chicken feed. So you've got some street gangs, some cut-rate thugs, and a handful of freaks. We've got more men, more guns, and more experience. And I don't like working with your kind, but we've even got you outmatched in the freak department."

"Your shape-shifter? Yeah, we know all about that. You got some good early licks in, when you had surprise on your side, but he won't be a problem much longer."

"What? Tony the Tiger?" Dominic said. "Oh, no, he's just my kid's house pet. I've got something even better than that. See for yourself."

He whistled. We weren't alone after all. And as one of the stall doors swung open, I saw the source of Dominic's confidence. All seven feet of him, three hundred pounds of rock-hard muscle squeezed into a tailored black suit. He looked my way, the overhead lights gleaming across his razor-nicked scalp and prison-ink neck tattoos, and bared his teeth like a shark spotting his first meal of the day.

"This is Koschei," Dominic said. "I believe you two have met."

The last time I crossed paths with Koschei the Deathless, he was on the payroll of a coke dealer out in LA. A coke dealer I was trying to rip off, so the meeting didn't go too well. We electrocuted him. It didn't stick. Then Caitlin snapped his neck. That didn't work either. Finally, we fed him into a wood chipper.

Some people just don't know when to quit.

He took two running steps, faster than he looked, and hoisted me up by the lapels of my rented tux. Then I was weightless, flying like a skydiver who forgot to pack a parachute. My back slammed against the bathroom door hard enough to knock the breath from my lungs and I just kept going, through the door and hitting the bodyguard standing right outside. We went down in a tangle of bodies. As I tried to clear my head, jolts of pain shooting down my spine like I'd been pounded with a ball-peen hammer, I saw Koschei steaming toward me, a runaway train.

I reached into the stunned bodyguard's jacket and snatched the nine-millimeter from his holster. The ballroom erupted in screams as I opened fire, shooting Koschei three times in the chest. The slugs tore his dress shirt and clung to his unbroken, bloodless skin like medals of honor. Grinning now, he swatted the piece from my grip and got one hand around my throat, the other around one leg, lifting me like I was a rag doll. He took a running start, swung back, and then heaved. I tumbled in the air and crash-landed into a banquet table, rolling, hitting the hardwood floor and bringing a rain of broken wineglasses and burgundy-stained tablecloth down with me.

The gunshots had sparked a stampede, partygoers pounding across the dance floor in all directions, shrieking as they crammed the doorway at every exit. I had blood and Bordeaux on my tux, one shoulder torn at the seams, one arm sliced up from a shard of broken glass. The biting sting was the only thing cutting through my reeling head fog, and I was seeing double. Either that or Koschei had suddenly sprouted an identical twin, both of them standing over me in triumph. He bent down, reaching for my throat again—and then Caitlin hit him from the side, ramming him like a linebacker and sending him sprawling.

They squared off on the empty dance floor. He snarled silently, slowly circling, his oversized hands strangling the air in anticipation. Caitlin held him in her cool gaze, studying, planning.

"Care for a rematch?" she asked him.

She kicked off her high heels one at a time, sending them spinning across the polished floor. Then she reached down with both hands and tore the hem of her evening gown a few inches along one leg, shredding the fabric, giving her more room to maneuver.

"I assure you," she said, "I am *quite* happy to oblige."

15.

Koschei roared as he charged at Caitlin, his boots pounding a war-drum beat on the dance floor. Caitlin caught him by the elbow and heaved him off his feet, flipping him over her shoulder and slamming him down hard on his back. She swept one bare foot high, bringing it down in a kick with the sound of a whistling ax, and he rolled out of the way just in time. The parquet floor splintered under her heel. Clambering to his feet, Koschei put his fists together and hit her in the stomach with the force of a sledgehammer, sending her staggering back.

An ordinary human couldn't do much against an incarnate demon like Caitlin, but the giant Russian was anything but ordinary. The last time they'd squared off he broke her arm as easily as snapping a twig, and he would have done a lot worse if Jennifer and I hadn't been there. Still groggy, blood trickling down my sliced-up arm, I staggered to my feet and looked for a way to help.

They were in close now, trading hits in a ballet of violence. Koschei grunted as Caitlin spun on one heel and lashed out, hitting him with a rib-splintering kick. He threw a pile-driver punch, aiming for her jaw; her scarlet hair whipped the air as she ducked backward, his fist missing her by a fraction of an inch. Dominic stood at the edge of the dance floor, flanked by a few of his thugs. They lined up and drew steel, taking aim at me and Caitlin.

"They're too close," one said, his pistol bobbing helplessly. "I can't get a clear shot."

Dominic glowered at him and snatched the gun out of his hand.

"Idiot. Koschei's immune to bullets." Dominic squinted one eye closed as he sighted down the barrel. "Shoot *through* him."

I flung out my hand and sent a royal delegation of playing cards winging through the air. Four kings jumped between us and the gunfire, dropping dead with four bullets in their faces. The distraction bought Caitlin the split second she needed to take Koschei off guard. She grabbed his wrist, spun him around, and wrenched it behind his back until his howl of pain rang out over the wet *pop* of splintering bone.

"Caitlin!" I edged backward toward the ballroom door, throwing up more cards to catch another hail of bullets. "Time to *leave*."

"Next time," she growled in Koschei's ear. She shoved him toward the gunmen and joined the retreat, both of us running for the door with death on our heels. We raced through the abandoned foyer and burst out into the cool night air. The parking lot was a tangled mess, a hundred panicked guests all trying to fight their way out at once, a cacophony of jolting brakes and squealing horns. The wail of sirens rose in the distance, coming in fast.

"Forget the limo," I said. "We'll never get it out of here before the cops lock this place down."

We ran on foot, skirting the lot and hitting the sidewalk. No destination but *away*. Once we got clear of Dominic's thugs and the local police—who probably answered to someone on Dominic's payroll anyway—we could figure out our next move.

A battered old Datsun with an NPR bumper sticker rumbled up to the curb. Halima behind the wheel, and Freddie riding shotgun. The window rolled down.

"Say the words," Freddie told Halima.

"I'm not saying it."

Freddie waved a checkbook at her. "One thousand dollar donation to the Field Museum, right here and now, but you have to say the words."

Halima let out a weary sigh and looked our way.

"Come with me if you want to live," she said.

Freddie squealed with delight as we piled into the backseat. The Datsun lurched away from the curb, fading into traffic, leaving the chaos and the cops behind us. Scribbling out a check, Freddie turned in her seat and gave us a once-over.

"We figured you might run into a little trouble, so we decided to come and be helpful."

"*I* thought we were going to the movies," Halima said, "until you insisted I circle the block for half an hour."

"I needed you to drive. My Ferrari only has two seats. I'm assuming the negotiations didn't go your way, Dan. Hate to break it to you, but you're not getting the cleaning deposit back on that tux." Freddie gaped at Caitlin. "Where are your shoes? And the *dress*! You tore the *dress*!"

"The party was wilder than we anticipated," Caitlin said.

Freddie rubbed her chin, her brow furrowed. "Honestly? The side slit isn't bad. No, you know what? Next version, I'm incorporating that into the design. Just...less raggedy and battle-damaged."

"Thanks for the ride," I said to Halima.

She met my eyes in the rearview mirror. "I assume this means a peaceful solution is impossible?"

"Did my best. Turns out Angelo Mancuso hasn't gone rogue. His old man *wants* him to pick a fight, to see if he's tough enough to lead the family. He doesn't even care if his kid lives or dies; it's some sick survival-of-the-fittest bullshit."

"When a man abandons his humanity and chooses to live as a beast," Halima mused, "it should not be surprising that he views life and death just as a beast does. What will you do now?"

"Get a change of clothes, find some bandages for my arm, and figure out plan B on the flight back home. Gotta shut this down fast, or Gary Kemper's gonna throw me to the wolves. If they won't talk peace...I guess we give 'em the fight they're asking for."

"Well, while you were spilling perfectly good wine all over

your tuxedo, Halima and I were solving a mystery." Freddie looked to Halima. "Go ahead, tell them what we found."

"Right. What *we* found. Trying to locate the elusive Carolyn Saunders was difficult at first. Her novels are all self-published, and her 'company' is a bogus address."

I shrugged. "Makes sense. If I was writing dirt about the real occult underground and selling it as pulp fiction, I'd be in hiding, too. Lots of sorcerers would take a shot at her just on general principle."

"Well, then I did a little digging. Turns out, until she suddenly quit her job and became a virtual recluse about five years ago, she taught history and literature at a local college. She once released an archaeological study through the Oriental Institute of the University of Chicago, which, by good fortune, is also *my* very occasional publisher. And I have friends on the staff."

"Prepare to be awed." Freddie reached over the seat and pushed a yellow Post-it note into my open palm. "My beloved BFF made a few phone calls, and answers were granted. This is the address where Saunders gets her annual royalty checks from the OI. Google Maps says it's a ranch house in the boonies a few miles outside Bloomington. Bloomington, Illinois, not Bloomington, Indiana. It's south of here, maybe a two-hour drive."

I stared down at the neatly written address. I had a tough decision to make.

The four of us walked through the lobby of the Four Seasons, Caitlin shoeless and her dress torn, me bloodied, wine-drenched and bedraggled, drawing eyes from a few late-night tourists. Security got between us and the elevators, and I warded them off with a wave of my key card.

"It's okay, guys, we're guests. Hey, send some bandages up to my room? And a bottle of bourbon. On second thought, make it two bottles."

At least my cuts were shallow, mostly clotted by the time I locked myself in the bathroom, stripped down, and turned on the shower. I studied my body in a cloud of billowing steam as the mirror slowly fogged and turned me into a winter ghost. Fresh bruises on my arms, my back. A pulled muscle that treated me to a whip crack of pain every time I bent my left shoulder too far, but nothing I couldn't live with. I stood under the shower's spray, letting the hot water pulse against my tender skin until I felt human again. Mostly, though, I tried to work the angles and figure out my next move.

Damien Ecko was out there somewhere, hunting for me. That was a problem, but one I could put on the back burner. As long as I stayed underground, he could hunt all he wanted. My best move was to figure out a way to find him *first*, and set the terms of battle. That could wait, though. It was going to have to, with the Chicago Outfit on the rampage.

Gary Kemper said he'd give me up to the FBI, making me a fugitive all over again. And I believed him. We weren't exactly the best of friends before this whole mess started, considering I'd blackmailed him once, and I was only breathing free air because—for now—he'd decided I was more useful on the loose than I was behind bars. My best bet was to dig up something just as lethal to dangle over his head in case he dimed me out, keeping the peace with the threat of mutually assured destruction. That was going to take time, though, time I didn't have.

So that left Angelo and his crew. Shut 'em down fast, stop any more civilians from eating a bullet, and get Kemper off my back. Seemed like the obvious choice, the only right answer.

Almost.

Because I'd been handed the home address of a woman who knew way too much about my life, and who had put it in a book for the world to read. A woman who knew about the man with the Cheshire smile. Carolyn Saunders was my one lead, my one clue to tracking down the Enemy. I thought back to my kitchen-table conversation with Bentley, his fear that I was getting obsessed. I'd promised him I'd rein it in, that I'd get my head right and my priorities in line.

But Carolyn was a two-hour drive from here. One shining lead, dangling right in my face, so close I could touch it.

I already knew what I was going to do. It just took me the rest of the shower to talk myself into it. You can justify any bad idea if you really work at it. Halima and Freddie were still in the hotel room, talking while Caitlin and Freddie shared glasses of bourbon. Freddie poured a third glass and held it out to me as I emerged from the bathroom, thankful for a fresh change of clothes.

"You clean up nicely," she told me. "Here, drink. You probably need this."

I probably did. I savored the smoky tang and sat on the edge of the bed.

"I'm going to see Carolyn," I said. "Cait, can you go back to Vegas and maybe watch over Jennifer until I catch up with you? I'll see if there's an airport near Bloomington. Maybe I can fly back from there and save some time."

"Alone?" Caitlin frowned. "We *did* discuss the possibility of a trap, did we not?"

"I'll be careful. Look, the Outfit is on the move, and Jen needs backup. And now that we know Koschei's alive, she's in even more danger. It's not like that giant psycho forgot what the three of us did to him. I'd feel better if she had a guardian angel until I got back."

Caitlin arched an eyebrow. "Guardian what now?"

"Figure of speech. Sorry."

"I thought you promised Jennifer you'd be at her Commission meeting."

I winced. "She's in safer hands with you anyway. I'll only be a few hours behind you, I promise. This is just...this is just something I have to do, okay?"

"Think carefully," Halima said. "This woman, whoever she is, whatever she knows, can wait. Meeting her is likely to bring even more problems to your doorstep, and that's assuming this isn't a trap. Can you really afford to buy more trouble right now?"

I wanted to say I didn't have a choice, but we both knew that'd be a lie.

16.

We took Caitlin to O'Hare and put her on the next flight west, and then I made my way down to the rent-a-car kiosks. My new Paul Emerson persona was getting a workout. So far, no red flags, and nobody took a second glance at my new ID. Budget set me up with a shiny new Elantra and a GPS that pointed me toward the nearest on-ramp, the screen sketching out a long ride ahead.

The strobing white lines lulled me, fatigue sinking bone deep as the road hypnosis set in. I pulled into a convenience store for a big cardboard cup of black coffee, then got right back on the road. I was in no shape to be driving—no shape to do anything but sleep, truth be told—but I forced myself to push through it. I'd left the city lights behind, plunging into rural Illinois, and it felt like the world had turned into a vast, flat and endless plain. Soil and cornfields and the occasional hamlet, rusting away in the moonlight.

Whoever he is, whatever he is, I told myself, *the Enemy's not sleeping right now. Neither am I. Just keep going.*

I twisted the radio dial until I found a hard rock station and turned up the volume, squealing guitars carrying me through the still hours of the night.

The first shimmering rays of dawn, breaking over a cornfield, brought me to Carolyn Saunders's doorstep. She lived on the edge of farm country, in a ramshackle ranch house with faded gray clapboard siding and ginger lace curtains in the windows. A massive weeping willow squatted in her front yard, its drooping boughs casting a moss-green canopy over her gravel driveway. I pulled in behind a rusty Toyota pickup truck, turned off the engine, and studied the house.

If this was an elaborate trap, a clue planted by the Enemy to lure me out of hiding, he'd have no idea when or if I'd follow up on it. I doubted Ms. Fleiss and her goons were sitting in the living room, twiddling their thumbs and waiting for me to show up. *On the other hand*, I thought, *a few pounds of Semtex and a pressure trigger on every door and window would turn this place into a nice little bomb. They could rig the house to blow and go on their merry way.*

I took slow, deep breaths, stretching out my senses. Psychic tendrils, like violet sea anemone, wriggled out and stroked the walls, the windows, feeling for wards or signs of magic. Little glimmers, here and there. My senses bounced off a pentacle of cold iron, nailed up just inside the front door. A sprig of dried herbs, wound in rune-inlaid ribbon, deeper inside the house. Little enchantments, kitchen witchcraft to ward off misfortune. I'm not sure how well they worked. After all, I was still here.

Nothing left to do but introduce myself. I strolled up the front walk, keeping my eyes on the windows and watching for an ambush, and pressed the doorbell. A shrill buzzing echoed from inside the house. Then silence.

Deadbolts clicked and a chain rattled. The door opened, just a crack. The woman on the other side was in her mid-sixties, with a sleep-lined face and tangled, stringy white hair. She wore a fuzzy pink bathrobe and worn, tartan-patterned slippers. She didn't say anything.

"Carolyn Saunders? I'm Daniel Faust. I think you've been trying to get my attention."

She rolled her eyes.

"No shit," she said. "You couldn't wait until I took a shower and had breakfast, maybe? Lucky for you, I'm a morning person. Well, come in already."

Her living room was cluttered with keepsakes and mementos,

photographs of tropical vacations in kitschy frames, tiny crystal figurines. An old, leaning wooden bookcase, stuffed with fat and faded paperback novels. A threadbare sofa draped in a flowered quilt. She led me through an open arch into her kitchen, where unwashed dishes piled high in a tub sink. She plugged in the coffeemaker and pulled down a pair of mismatched mugs from an overhead cupboard.

"I'd apologize for the house being a mess," she said, "but I don't think either of us cares. Cream and sugar?"

"Black is fine. So, not to be rude, but..."

"But you want to know how I found out all about you and your stint in Eisenberg Correctional."

"And why you wrote about it," I said. "That too."

"Second question first: like you said, I wanted to get your attention." She started the coffee and turned, resting one hand on her hip. "You weren't exactly easy to find *before* you faked your own death. I didn't have any way to reach you. So I took a half-finished manuscript, slapped in my own version of your story, and hoped you'd stumble across it. It was a shot in the dark, I admit, but it was the only plan I could think of."

"So...you didn't send that anonymous email telling me to read it?"

"Honey, if I had your damn email address, I wouldn't have written the book. I've got better things to do with my time. Still, it got you here."

"So how did you know about me in the first place? About any of this?"

"Easy," she said, "Buddy told me."

Now it made sense. Now I understood why her novel recounted everything that happened to me in Eisenberg, up until the first failed escape attempt. I got caught. Buddy didn't. He hadn't been there to see what happened after that—or to tell Carolyn the story—which was why the fictional me ended up slaying dragons while the real me was getting blasted with a fire hose in solitary.

"You're the one," I told her. "You're the one the voices were telling him he had to see."

"Nope, just a side stop on the road, to bring me up to speed. We know each other from way back. Way, *way* back." She gave me a rueful smile. "I'm the Scribe. That's Scribe with a capital S, but you can call me Carolyn. Buddy and I have a most distinct role in this sad drama. His job is to see the doom that's coming, though nobody will heed his warnings until it's far too late. My job is to write the story when it's all over. A cautionary tale that will help no one, and change nothing. My previous incarnations, I'm told, had a habit of drinking themselves to death. Can't imagine why. When I found out what I really was, a few years back, I went a little nutty for a bit. I'm better now."

"You're gonna have to start at the beginning," I said. "I don't even *know* what you are."

A burbling hiss rose from the dusty coffeemaker. She lifted the glass carafe and poured it out, filling the two mugs, taking hers black like mine. She passed me a mug and raised hers in a wry salute.

"I'm a fictional character," she said, "in the very first story ever told. And now you are too, which is why I needed to talk to you. Hate to break it to you, dear, but you're up to your neck in this shit. And it only gets deeper from here."

"The Thief." I blew across the brim of my cup, scattering a curlicue of steam. "Buddy—well, his sister, in a vision, she explained it to me. Sort of. She said the Enemy swapped me for him. That he needed the Thief dead, but he also had plans for the guy, so he pulled me in to take his place."

"And I'm still working out how he did that trick, but yes. The good news is, it's probably temporary. The bad news is, you need to cling to that title as long as you possibly can. The future of this planet may depend on it. Come on. I want to show you something."

She led me to her den, where a vintage PC with a bulky monitor sat on the edge of a rickety desk. Sticky notes and graph paper covered every surface, and stacks of reference books piled high in teetering stacks. She walked to the back wall, took hold of the wooden paneling, and gave it a tug. The paneling popped free and she shoved it aside to reveal a hidden nook.

"This is where I do my homework," she said.

The room was just big enough for the two of us, a walk-in closet lined with corkboard, looking like a conspiracy theorist's wet dream. Photographs and newspaper clippings, printouts and receipts, tacked up and connected by a sprawling spiderweb of colored yarn. A few of the clippings hit close to home, like an article about the collapse of the Carmichael-Sterling Group and the FBI raid at the Enclave Casino. And a piece charting the downfall of Ausar Biomedical twenty years ago, after a wave of birth defects linked to their Viridithol fertility treatment. Carolyn followed my gaze and nodded.

"Oh yeah," she said, "you've been in the middle of this mess since day one. Pretty good for an outsider. Probably why the Enemy took an interest in you."

I ran my finger along a length of violet string, connecting the Ausar article to a yellowed clipping about a drug cartel massacre in a remote Mexican village. *Eden Tendril here*, Carolyn had scribbled in the margins with a faded red marker. *Xerxes mercenaries, using deniable cover?*

"I stepped into somebody else's war," I murmured, following the lines. "This woman, Lauren Carmichael, she was looking to become a god. A couple of creatures I'd never seen before—we called them the smoke-faced men—were using her as a pawn in a long con. Promising to make her queen of the world, when they really just wanted to burn it all down."

"Fortunately for us, neither side succeeded. And do you know where these 'smoke-faced men' came from?"

I nodded. "I met a man named Bob Payton. Former Ausar scientist. His team had cracked the barriers of space and time, learned to see into other places, other *worlds*. They'd found a gateway to...someplace terrible."

"The Garden of Eden," Carolyn said, her voice a near whisper.

"Payton knew the Eden experiments were getting out of hand. So he used their research to open a doorway to another Earth. An Earth burned to a cinder, with a black sun and a rotten moon. See, he was looking for the antithesis of life, the perfect antibody for Eden's power. What he got was the smoke-faced men."

Carolyn nodded, sipping her coffee as she stared at the tangled web of string and clippings.

"Oh, he got more than that. There's a name for that black-sun Earth, Daniel. It's called the Pessundation. It's a prison. A prison built to hold one, and only one convict: the man with the Cheshire smile. The smoke-faced men were his jailers. Payton, well-intentioned idiot that he was, unleashed a far greater evil than the one he was fighting. He set the Enemy loose on our world. Fortunately, in a weakened state. Once the Enemy finds the key to his lost power, he'll be unstoppable. And we will all, sad to say, be utterly fucked."

"So we just have to find it first," I said. "What's the key?"

Carolyn gave me a lingering, humorless smile.

"*You* are."

17.

"There are other worlds than this," Carolyn told me. "You've seen glimpses of them. Many are just like ours, so close you could accidentally visit them and never notice, save for the tiniest details. Others are radical diversions, parallels where evolution took a different tack or history veered off its path. And the First Story visits each world in turn. I've counted thirteen characters so far, including myself. When we die, we don't go to any heaven or hell. No final destination for us. We reincarnate, on some far-flung parallel Earth, with our memories burned clean."

"Then what happens?" I asked.

"Then we do it all over again. Our lives are shaped by the Story. When it was spoken into existence, we were created. And so, one way or another, no matter how hard we try, we repeat. We dance the dance, go through the motions. The Killer is murdered by his protégé. The Drifter freezes to death at the edge of a lonely road. The Salesman is imprisoned by a tyrant, his hands and tongue cut out. The Witch and her Knight burn in each other's arms. The Prophet dies alone and in ruin, having seen all of his warnings ignored."

"I gotta ask," I said. "What kind of fucked-up story *is* this?"

"I believe it was a cautionary tale. A morality play to teach you what you ought not do. But it's a tale woven by a storyteller who's been dead for a million years, for an audience that doesn't exist. All that remains is us. Cursed to repeat the cycle again, and again, and again." She sipped her coffee. "I need to Irish this up. How about you?"

"A little early, but I won't say no."

She came back with a half-empty bottle of Glenlivet, pouring a generous dollop of whiskey into each of our cups. She waved the bottle at her net of colored string, the endless clippings.

"The story always ends with the Enemy, and the Paladin. Sometimes it's a grand affair, the armies of light and darkness clashing, horns blaring, banners and dragons and unicorns, all that bullshit. Sometimes it's a knife fight in a rainy back alley, with the loser lying dead in the gutter. If the Paladin wins, that's it. Story's over until the last of us dies, and we start the next go-around on some other unsuspecting planet. If the Enemy wins, he gets to run the place for a while. Do some remodeling. Plagues, nightmares made flesh, torment and misery for everyone. He gets off on it."

"And there's no way to break the cycle?"

"Someone tried," Carolyn said. "This is all rumor and conjecture, understand, but it's what I've been able to piece together. An alliance of mages rose up against the Enemy. They'd found a way to steal his power, to render him harmless as a shadow and cast him into the Pessundation. And good riddance to the son of a bitch. Thing is, he saw it coming. He knew he couldn't stop them from winning, so he took the long view. He used their technique to drain his *own* magic before they could do it to him. He hid it in a reliquary, gave it to his most trusted servant, and sent her across the wheel of worlds. To wait for his return, no matter how long it might take, and find him."

"Her," I echoed. "I'm guessing that's Ms. Fleiss."

Carolyn nodded. "That was the Enemy's plan. To bide his time, escape when he could, and reunite with Fleiss. She'd hand him the reliquary and he could return to his full strength. Perhaps stronger, if he'd learned some new tricks along the way. It's not as simple as opening it up and bathing in his old magic, though.

He couldn't risk it being stolen while he was away. So he sealed it, with locks only he could open."

"What kind of locks?"

Carolyn reached out, tracing one of the colored threads. Following it from point to point, scrap to scrap, a pattern only her eyes could see.

"He's changing things. Using his influence and what little energy he has to...rewrite the world, you might say. He's already directly interfered in a few of my fellow characters' lives, altering the usual course of events. I believe that with every revision, with every twist in the tale, another lock pops and a little more of his power returns. Which brings us to you. The real Thief, a cat burglar named Marcel Deschamps, is working for the Enemy."

Her roving finger landed on another newspaper clipping. A private-museum heist in Dubai, where the intruder had carved his way in through a window on the seventy-second floor.

"He's been stealing some interesting things. Aztec relics, mostly, and a curious sideline: have you ever heard of a man named Howard Canton? Canton the Magnificent?"

It rang a distant bell, but I shook my head.

"He was a stage magician in the forties," she said. "Mostly forgotten today. Also, quite the skilled occultist. He concealed his affinity for *real* magic behind his sleight of hand. I believe you know a thing or two about that."

"I'm not the first guy to work that angle," I told her.

"The Enemy has been gobbling up anything and everything to do with Canton's career. Vintage posters, props from his stage act." Her finger trailed along a stretch of pink string to a still image from a security-camera feed. An auction, with Fleiss sitting front and center in the first row. "This was taken at Sotheby's London last week. Canton's top hat was up for bid. The price ran to a cool million."

"They paid a million dollars," I said, "for a *hat*?"

"Tried to. Fleiss lost the auction; she was outbid by a stage magician with a private museum. I assume you've heard of David Gosselin?"

My lips puckered like I'd bit down on a lemon wedge. "Sure. Made the White House disappear on live television. Owns his own island in the Caribbean. I've heard of him."

Carolyn tilted her head, catching my expression.

"Just *heard* of him?"

"We've met," I said. "He made a move on my ex-girlfriend, who was not my ex at the time. There may have been...an exchange of harsh language."

"Charming. So, that's all I know on that subject. The Enemy is obsessed with the Aztecs and Canton memorabilia, but I can't begin to guess why. Could be connected, could be two different aims. The most interesting thing I've found, regarding the Canton archives, is a scrap of rumor about his stage wand. They say he used it for ritual work, and it was inlaid with bone on both tips. *Human* bone."

"He was a necromancer?"

"An illusionist. On one end—if the story is true, mind you—the bone came from the mummy of an ancient Egyptian trickster by the name of Djehutimesu."

Damien Ecko's teacher. We have a saying in the magical world: there's no such thing as coincidences. And hearing the name of the same dead sorcerer from Halima's lips two days ago, then Carolyn's now, rang every alarm bell in sight. One name stretching out like a bridge across time to tie two threats together, by way of a stage magician from the forties. It felt like part of some vast pattern I couldn't make sense of, not yet. I could see all the puzzle pieces, just not how they fit.

"And the other end?" I asked.

"Allegedly, a chip from the skull of Harry Houdini."

I frowned. "That can't be right. Houdini wasn't involved in the occult underground. Hell, the guy was a professional skeptic. He'd travel around debunking fakers and exposing their methods."

"It balances, doesn't it? The power to weave illusions, and the power to banish them. Lies and truth. I can imagine any number of things the Enemy could do with that wand, none of them good. It's a moot point, though. Nobody knows where it went. Just about all of Canton's stage kit is accounted for, in private collections or on the open market, except for the wand."

"So if I rounded all this stuff up," I said, getting the idea, "that'd slow the Enemy down, right? Throw a wrench into whatever he's planning to do with it?"

"*You* need to stay as far away from the Enemy as possible, which brings me back to my point, and the entire reason I wanted to talk to you. Remember those locks I mentioned? His old power, waiting to be claimed? Safe to assume that changing the Thief's ending—ensuring he, or *you* in this case, died in prison—is one of the keys. Except you didn't die. You're the Thief now, Daniel, and as long as you escape the fate he had planned for you, that lock will *never* open. The Enemy may still win in the end, but he'll never return to his full power so long as you stay hidden and safe."

Given everything else Carolyn had said about the story, the litany of torments and disasters awaiting its cursed characters, a sneaking suspicion occurred to me. "So what's the Thief's original ending? How is he supposed to die?"

Her gaze darted away, then back again, quick as a hummingbird's wings. She didn't quite meet my eyes when she replied.

"I'm not sure. But you'll be fine, as long as you stay in hiding."

Lying is like any other skill: you have to do it a lot if you want to be any good at it. She was a rank amateur. I let it slide, for now.

"What about the real Thief, what'd you say his name is, Deschamps? Can't I...give the title back to him somehow?"

"I wish I knew how. As far as I can tell, killing him *might* do the trick. He'd reincarnate in some other world, reborn as the Thief again. In theory."

"Uh-huh. And wouldn't that screw with the Enemy's plans even worse?"

Carolyn gave me an uncomfortable shrug, pursing her lips. "You have to understand, this is all conjecture. I think I know what *might* happen. Or I could be wrong. Kill Deschamps and you might be stuck in the Thief's shoes for all eternity, as trapped as the rest of us. There's only one thing I know with absolute certainty: right now, your survival is a thorn in the Enemy's side. The best thing you can do, for yourself and for this entire world, is to hide and stay out of his way."

"Run and hide. Seems that's what everyone is telling me to do."

"It's wise advice."

"It's bullshit," I said. "This guy's aiming to wipe out the entire universe, one Earth at a time, and you think I'm gonna sit on my hands? I could help if you people would just *let* me. What about you? Aren't you afraid he's going to come after you next?"

Carolyn snorted. She poured a second dollop of whiskey into her mug—more booze than coffee now—and drank it down.

"I'm told he generally lets the Scribe live until the very end. It's an ego thing. Who else is going to write the story of his great triumph?" Her gaze went distant, her voice wistful. "All those books, written by other mes. Scattered across countless dead worlds, lost and unread forever. I wonder if any of them were any good."

"So is there *any* upside to being the Thief? Do I get...special powers, or anything?"

"You should be very good at stealing things."

"I was *already* good at stealing things."

"Well then," she said, "I guess you got screwed, honey. Welcome to my life."

18.

I left Carolyn Saunders to her cynicism and her Irish coffee. She'd told me what I needed to know: namely, that the Enemy had a good reason to see me dead, and he wasn't going to stop coming after me. Fine. I had every intention of returning the favor. More than that, though, Carolyn had given me a lead. If the Enemy was after all of Howard Canton's stage gear, I didn't think being outbid in an auction would slow him down. That hat was sitting in David Gosselin's private museum, just waiting to be stolen.

His private museum, about fifteen minutes outside Las Vegas.

I doubted getting my hands on some dead magician's top hat would strike a crippling blow against the Enemy's plans, but it was *something*. I needed to throw a punch, to get a little payback for burying me in Eisenberg and turning my life upside down. For now, I'd take what I could get. Besides, if the thing had any residual enchantment from Canton's heyday, maybe I could figure out what was so important about it.

So, I thought, *time for a little heist. At least I'm back in my element.*

I turned on my phone as we landed at McCarran Airport. Three messages from Jennifer. That wasn't good. Shuffling in lockstep off the crowded plane, I gave her a call.

"Really could have used you at the Commission meeting, sugar."

"Sorry," I said, "I had some business to follow up on. I just got back in town."

"Caitlin filled me in. Negotiations didn't go so good, huh?"

"That's an understatement. She tell you about Koschei?"

"I was a little hazy on that part," she drawled. "That's the same Koschei we fed to a wood chipper back in LA?"

"Same guy. Apparently, he got better. What happened at the meeting?"

She sighed. "Well, had our first walkout. Little Shawn and the Playboy Killers decided they'd be better off on their own."

"They flipping sides?"

"Not saying they are, not saying they aren't. I'd give it pretty good odds, though. Forget 'em, they're punks. Meanwhile, my big plan to send everybody into hiding was a non-starter. Nobody wants to put their business on hold. Oh, and after insisting up and down that she have a seat at the table, your girl Emma didn't even bother showing up."

"She's not *my* girl, Jen."

"She's Prince Sitri's accountant. Remind me, which one of us is dating a demon? Face it, Danny, you're pretty much hell's ambassador to the Vegas underworld these days. Nobody else has an inside line like you do."

"Not a job I asked for." I hustled down the access tunnel and emerged into the terminal. Slot machines rattled and jangled in thick banks down the middle of the concourse, welcoming me home as they sucked the last bits of spare change from tourists' pockets. "Still, that's not like her. Did you try calling?"

"Sure, I tried." She didn't even pretend to be enthusiastic. "Got her voicemail."

"I'm gonna swing by her place, just to be safe. You want to grab dinner later, maybe?"

"Already made plans. Sorry."

I didn't need a translator to interpret her tone. I'd chosen chasing a lead on the Enemy over covering her back, and we both knew it. It didn't matter that I'd only been delayed a few hours, didn't matter that I'd sent Caitlin to watch over her. I wanted to get defensive, get angry, tell myself she'd have done the exact same thing if she were in my shoes. Thing was, I knew she wouldn't have.

I'd make it up to her. I jumped into my lime-green Spark, paid the equivalent of a college tuition to get out of airport parking, and headed for Summerlin. It was near sunset by the time I rolled up on Emma's quiet little suburban tract, neat rows of tan stucco houses, manicured lawns, and minivans. Her freshly washed Caravan was parked in the driveway, sporting a "My Daughter is an Honor Student at Palo Verde High School" bumper sticker.

The front door to the house hung open, swinging in the afternoon breeze, its twisted lock dangling from splintered wood.

My wheels slammed against the curb. I threw the car into park and jumped out running, racing up the front walk and hitting the broken door shoulder first as I barreled into the living room. Details hit me like drumbeats, snapshots of information seared across my mind's eye. Their glass table, shattered. A cell phone in a slim pearl case abandoned in the debris, screen flashing with an incoming call as it rattled in a bed of broken shards. A slow, heavy, rhythmic thumping sound up the hall, somewhere to my right.

"Emma!" I shouted. "*Melanie!*"

A high-pitched scream echoed through the house, muffled behind a closed door. The thumping grew louder, more fervent. I ran toward the sound, reckless, rounded the corner and froze. A dead man stood in the hall, hammering his raw fists on a closet door. He was dressed in ragged denim, with a baseball cap bearing the ace of spades perched on his pale brow. His head lolled back to bare the gaping, crusty hole where his throat had once been. A rasping, mournful hiss whistled from the dead man's lungs as he slowly turned, fixing his sightless eyes on me.

"Melanie," I called out as I took a defensive step backward, "can you hear me?"

"Dan! We're in the closet—Mom's hurt!"

"Just—just stay right there." I backpedaled as the zombie lurched toward me, his outstretched hands clawing at the air. "I'll take care of it."

A fine notion, as soon as I figured out how. I'd seen Ecko's creations in action back in Chicago. One had ripped off a man's jaw as easily as a child snapping a wishbone. Another had punched a hole through its victim's chest. These things were slug-slow and clumsy, but if they got their hands on you, it was all over. I jogged backward, keeping its attention on me and away from the battered closet door.

The hall was too tight to maneuver. I backed up into the living room while the dead man shambled my way, ducking away from another clumsy lunge as he grabbed at me. My fingers dipped into my pocket, a pair of cards jumping to my fingertips, and my hand swept out to send them flying like razor-edged hornets. One card hit him in the shoulder, burying itself half an inch into necrotic skin and muscle, gouging a bloodless wound. The second card went straight for his left eye. It ruptured like a rotten egg, the card flopping as it dangled from his eye socket, watery goo running down his cheek. The thing didn't even react. No pain, no hesitation, just the endless whistling moan from his ravaged throat.

I looked around, frantic, searching for an edge. Then I found one: the long, cherry-red stick of a fireplace lighter, sitting on the living-room mantel. I darted around the dead man, my shoes crunching on shattered glass, and snatched it up. I held the lighter out before me like a magic wand, triumphantly pulled the trigger—and watched a tiny, quarter-inch flame spark at the tip. Not good enough.

The creature groaned and lunged at me, stumbling forward, faster than I thought he could move. I threw myself to one side, hit the carpet, and rolled, wincing as chips of broken glass dug into my shoulder. I came up in a crouch and jumped backward, his clutching hands flailing at my face.

"Melanie," I shouted, "do you have any hairspray?"

"What?" she called back.

"*Hairspray!* Now would be good, please!"

I ran circles around the dead man, keeping him turning, stumbling, confused, as running feet pounded up the hallway. Melanie stood on the other side of the room, the creature between us. In the stress of the moment, she wasn't even trying to pass for human. The teenager's demon blood expressed itself with egg-yolk eyes and a web of veins, blue as her mop of neon-dyed hair, that spread across her cheeks like the pattern on a butterfly's wings. She held up a slender black can of L'Oreal.

"Like this?" she said.

"Perfect, toss it!"

The can sailed in an arc over the dead man's head. I snatched it out of the air, aimed the can and the lighter, and pulled both triggers.

The spray touched the dancing flame and erupted, billowing, a wave of heat that sucked the air from my lungs. My makeshift flamethrower blasted the creature dead-on and lit him up like a torch. He flailed wildly, staggering across the living room and leaving gouts of burning carpet with every thudding step, blindly careening into the wall. I kept the pressure on, hitting him with burst after burst, until he collapsed in a motionless heap. The can fell from my singed fingertips, and I stomped out a patch of smoldering carpet near my foot. The living room filled with gray smoke and the stench of rotten meat on a barbecue spit.

Melanie darted into the kitchen, racing back with a fire extinguisher clutched in both hands. As the burning patches of carpet slowly spread, the flames greedy to grow, she washed the smoking body in a torrent of icy foam.

"I've got this," I said, taking the extinguisher from her. "Go get your mom."

I hoped I had this. I coughed into my shirtsleeve, feeling like a fist of smoke was squeezing my lungs as I battled the fire. The extinguisher squealed and kicked in my hands, white mist pushing back the blaze one inch at a time. As I put out the worst of it, smoke clearing to reveal a motionless and charred corpse, Melanie helped Emma hobble to the front door. Emma was limping, one arm around Melanie's shoulders and the other dangling useless at her side, snapped in two places. Exposed, white bone glinted at her wrist, her hand encrusted with blood.

"I'll get her to the car," Melanie said, but I waved a hand to stop her.

"Can't go outside like that." The extinguisher kicked in my hand again, killing another patch of burning carpet.

"What? Why?" She paused, catching a glimpse of her face in the mirror by the door. "Shit, shit, *shit*."

Emma's eyes were heavy-lidded, her skin pale. She rested her forehead on her daughter's shoulder.

"Deep breaths," Emma said.

Melanie closed her eyes. Deep breaths through her nose, out through her mouth, as the butterfly tattoo of veins slowly faded. I was almost done putting out the fire when the extinguisher rattled and died, kicking out a sad wisp of white mist. I tossed it aside, grabbed a cushion from the sofa, and beat out the last of the flames. The living room was a wasteland. Broken glass, charred carpet, a door-sized chunk of wall scorched black and the paint bubbling, and the gnarled corpse of a dead man. The smoky stench clung to everything, the air thick with an oily haze. I dropped the cushion, wiped a few specks of glass from my sleeve, and surveyed the damage.

"Well," Emma murmured, her voice slurring, "it *was* a lovely house. I guess we're remodeling. Melanie, dear, I've lost a lot of blood. A hospital would be appropriate, I think."

We put her in the backseat of the Spark and I hit the gas. Summerlin Hospital Medical Center was five minutes away. I pulled up outside the ER, tires squealing, and Melanie ran in to get some help. A team of orderlies laid Emma on a rolling gurney and rushed her inside. As they wheeled her away, her eyelids slowly drifted shut.

19.

Hospital time is the dark twin to casino time. Both move at their own pace, untouched by the world outside the walls, playing tricks on you and skewing your vision. Hospital time runs slow. I watched the minutes tick by on the old clock in the waiting room, thick black hands under a plastic bubble. Then I'd look away, make small talk with Melanie, try to read a random crumpled magazine, only to find myself right back where I'd started. The minute hand was carved from stone, the hour hand a glacier.

"He just seemed like a harmless old man," Melanie told me, her voice a library whisper. "He came to the door and said his car broke down, asked if he could borrow a phone to call for help."

"Let me guess," I said. "Old suit, probably a bow tie? Dark complexion, gray hair?"

She nodded. "It took him a second when I gave him my phone. I thought maybe he didn't know how to use one. Then I realized he was looking at my name. 'The Loomis family,' he said. 'Just wanted to be sure I had the right house.' And that's when...that's when..."

Her bottom lip curled. Her eyes shifted, catching the harsh fluorescent lights, her irises starting to yellow and blur. I put my arm around her shoulder and pulled her close.

"It's okay," I told her. "You don't have to talk about it now."

We waited in silence under the motionless hands of the clock.

A young doctor in emerald scrubs emerged through a swinging door. Melanie jumped to her feet, and I was right behind her.

"She's going to be all right," he said. "It was touch and go there for a bit—she lost a lot of blood—but your mom is one hell of a fighter."

Melanie let out her held breath, her clenched shoulders relaxing as she gasped a sigh of relief. I felt relieved, too, but for a different reason. Emma was a hijacker, the kind of demon that could only get a foothold in our world by possessing a human body. I didn't have a good history with hijackers. Emma was a rare exception, since the body she'd commandeered was brain-dead: an heiress on life support who made a "miraculous recovery." If she'd been forced to abandon her damaged host and jump into an unwilling victim, our generally amiable relationship would have gotten...complicated.

"We need to keep her overnight," the doctor told us, "maybe a couple of days, and she'll need physical therapy for her arm. Recovery's not going to be easy, but I think she'll eventually get her full range of motion back. She's awake. Would you like to see her?"

He ushered us into a private room that smelled like faded flowers and rubbing alcohol. Emma's arm was in a suspended cast, along with one leg, her chest wrapped in bandages. Monitors beeped softly around her bed, her broken body nestled in a web of tubes and wires. Emma's head lolled on the stiff, starch-white pillow, her good hand curled around the control button for her morphine drip. Her sleepy eyes lit up when she saw her daughter.

The doctor left us alone, and I shut the door behind him.

"I am so proud of you," Emma told Melanie.

"I was *useless* back there," Melanie said.

"You were not. You did everything right." She looked my way. "Hilarious, the surprise on that bastard's face. He thought he was facing a couple of *humans*. Then his dead puppet hit me from behind. I got a good lick in, though. Melanie, did you bring it?"

She nodded and handed me a folded square of tissue paper. I gently opened it to unveil the treasure inside. It was a tiny amulet, carved to resemble a falcon with unfurled wings, painted blue and glazed like ceramic pottery. Egyptian hieroglyphs adorned the back of the amulet, glittering with latent magic. Scraps of withered sinew, like rotted beef jerky, clung to the stone.

"The old man tried to grab Melanie," Emma said. "When I shoved him back, I felt these strange lumps under his chest. So I grabbed one, twisted, and *tore*. You should have heard him scream. He fell back, but his puppet kept coming, and that's when it latched onto my arm. Melanie dragged me into the hall closet before it could finish the job."

"And he just...left?" I asked.

"Oh, he was furious. I heard in the hallway, making a phone call to 'Mr. Mancuso.'"

"*Angelo* Mancuso?"

Emma gave a tired shrug. "Who else? He said that Mancuso should have warned him what he was up against, that he needed special ritual items to 'permanently deal with someone like me,' and he would have brought them if he'd known. I think that was the plan: leaving his zombie to keep us penned in while he ran and fetched his gear. From the tone of his voice on the other end, I don't think Angelo had any idea what he was talking about."

I paced the room, making the connections, putting it all together. Only one answer fit.

"Damien Ecko is working for the Outfit," I said aloud. I brought them up to speed fast, sketching out the broad strokes of my first encounter with Ecko in Chicago, from the heist at his jewelry store to the frame job that left a bounty from two infernal courts on his head.

"So *that's* the human Caitlin was talking about," Emma said. "Apparently she and Royce have a bet going on."

"Ecko hooking up with Angelo makes sense. Damien wants me dead in the worst way, but he can't find me. The Outfit probably offered him a trade: he helps with their hit list, wiping out the New Commission one member at a time, and they help track me down. They're a double threat, but you just gave us the edge we need."

"What's that?"

I held up the amulet. "Like attracts like. And this has been buried under Ecko's skin—literally a part of him—for about thirty-six hundred years."

"You're going to use a tracking spell," Emma said, reading my mind.

"You got it. Finding him is going to be a piece of cake—and wherever he's holed up, Angelo and the rest of his goons are probably right there with him. We can wipe them all out at the same time."

And, I didn't bother adding, get Detective Kemper off my back and buy a little room to maneuver.

"Excellent," Emma said. "One of you, get me a phone. I'm calling in some private security to see me through the night. Tomorrow morning, I'm checking out, regardless of what the doctor says. I don't know if this Ecko person can actually harm me, but I don't like the sound of being 'permanently dealt with.' Daniel, I'm giving you the address of a safe house, operated by Southern Tropics. Take Melanie there, if you would, please."

"Mom," Melanie said, "I should be here with you. I don't need to go to a safe house."

"Yes, you do." Emma looked my way. "I hate to admit it, but you were right earlier. I want her packed away someplace safe until this situation is properly managed."

I took the address down, idly wondering just how much real estate Prince Sitri's corporate front actually owned. Melanie gave her mother a gentle, careful hug and followed me outside. It was full dark now, hospital lights cutting through the shadows, while a medevac helicopter thrummed over our heads and slowly settled onto a rooftop landing pad. Melanie walked fast, keeping her jaw clenched, her arms tight against her sides.

"Everything's going to be fine," I told her.

She spun and punched me in the shoulder. "You *asshole*," she snapped.

"What? Hey, news flash, I just saved your lives back there."

Melanie hit me again, punching me in the chest, driving me back a step.

"You fucking irresponsible *asshole*. This is *your fault*."

"The Outfit targeted your mom because she joined the New Commission. I warned her—"

"If Damien Ecko wasn't in town looking for you, he wouldn't have joined forces with those guys. And he wouldn't have come to our house, and my mom wouldn't be lying in a *hospital bed* right now. You picked a fight with him back in Chicago. You robbed his store, and then you framed him for a crime he didn't commit. Neither of which I really care about, except for one little problem: you let him go. I mean, are you fucking *surprised* he's obsessed with you? You picked a fight, you didn't finish it, and my mom got hurt because of it. Because of you and your half-assed bullshit."

I thought back to my encounter with the Mourner of the Red Rocks. "*You've skipped along from moment to moment, crisis to crisis,*" she'd told me, "*never cleaning up the damage you've left behind you.*"

It wasn't the first time I'd left dangerous men in my wake. I thought back to the Lauren Carmichael business. There was Angus Caine and the remnants of his Xerxes mercenary team. The mad scientists, Nedry and Clark. Hell, one of the smoke-faced men was still out there somewhere. I'd crossed swords with all of them, given them good reasons to want me dead, and skipped along on my merry way. Practically daring them to come after me and mine.

Damien Ecko was just the first person to take me up on it.

The Mourner warned me that my free ride was over. I understood what she meant now, but I didn't get the message fast enough to save Emma from a trip to the hospital. She'd gotten lucky. At best, Ecko would have trapped her in a soul bottle and buried it in a shallow grave. At worst...I didn't want to think about it. At the root of it all, one inescapable truth: I was the one who brought him here.

"You're right," I told Melanie. I shook my head. "You're right. It's my fault. And I'm sorry. I'm sorry your mom got hurt. I'm sorry your house got trashed. I can't...I can't undo any of this, but I'll do whatever I can to make things right. I promise."

Her head sagged low. She turned her back and trudged through the parking lot. I followed, just not too close.

"I felt so helpless," she said. "Squeezed in that closet, Mom bleeding out, that...*thing* pounding on the door. I mean, my blood makes me a little stronger than a normal human, a little faster. That doesn't amount to a whole lot, does it?"

"Don't sell yourself short. He doesn't look it, but Ecko's kind of a heavyweight. Anyway, muscle and speed are just tools. What matters isn't what you've got, it's how you use it." I tapped the side of my head. "You were quick up here, where it counted, both times: saving your mom, then helping me take that zombie down. A lot of people would have frozen up, been too scared to move. You kept your cool."

She let out a nervous laugh. "I didn't feel cool."

"Trust me. You were pretty cool."

The Spark squawked, locks clicking as we approached. We got in the car and I double-checked the address Emma had given me.

"Do you really have to take me there?" Melanie asked.

"You'll be safe with Emma's people. It's just for a night. What's wrong?"

Melanie sighed. "I just...I mean, Caitlin's great, I love Caitlin, but the other people my mom works with...I just don't like most of them. And they don't like me. Mom always says there should be this natural bond, because they're 'my people' and we 'share a common blood,' but I don't *feel* it, you know? Most of them are creeps."

I clicked on the headlights, backed out of the parking spot, and slowly rolled toward the exit.

"How old are you now?" I asked her.

"I turn eighteen next month. Why?"

I was about to give Emma a brand-new reason to be pissed at me, but that was all right.

"I think that's plenty old enough to decide who *you* want to hang out with," I said. "And when it comes to who 'your people' are, blood doesn't even come into the picture. Family runs deeper than that."

The safe house was left. I turned right instead.

We got to the Scrivener's Nook just as Bentley was closing up. He puttered to the bookshop door, unlocking it and waving us inside.

"Hey," I said, "you remember Melanie, right?"

"But of course. A delight to see you again, young lady." He offered her a gentlemanly bow, then glanced back over his shoulder. "Cormie! Cormie, we have a guest."

"Melanie's house got hit by the Outfit; looks like Damien Ecko's working for Angelo now. We need to stash her someplace for the night. I was thinking, well, you're not on the Outfit's hit list, and Ecko doesn't know you exist. That makes your apartment the safest place in Vegas right now. Would that be okay?"

Corman lumbered from the back room, tipping an invisible hat. "Of course she's welcome to stay with us. Any time. But, uh, we only got the one couch, kiddo."

"Don't worry, I've got a lot of work ahead of me. Probably gonna be an all-nighter." I looked to Melanie. "So is this cool with you? Better than the safe house?"

For the first time all night, Melanie flashed a smile, equal parts happiness and relief.

"Better than all right," she said.

20.

While Corman tidied up and Melanie prowled the shelves, looking for something to read, I took Bentley aside. I showed him the glazed amulet, Emma's trophy from her fight.

"Straight from Damien Ecko's body," I told him. "Think this is a good enough anchor for a tracking spell?"

"I think you'd be hard-pressed to find a better one. Going to use the back room?"

"If you don't mind."

"Lock up when you're done," he said. "We'll be upstairs."

"Thanks. And hey, thanks for looking after Melanie tonight. The kid's had a rough few months."

Bentley waved my concerns away. "Think nothing of it. She's a delightful young woman."

"I just think she could use some positive role models in her life right now."

He chuckled. "Cormie and I? Positive role models? I think you're stretching the definition a bit, son."

"Hey, I turned out all right. Mostly. Everything's relative."

Once the shop was locked up, the lights were doused, and the three of them had decamped for the apartment on the second floor, I was left alone with my thoughts. A pervasive quiet filled the store, no sound but the murmur of occasional traffic outside and a distant, nearly inaudible hum from the television upstairs.

The back room had everything I needed. The private shelves where Bentley and Corman kept their personal books of magic, leather-bound grimoires stretching from the 1750s to the 1950s; an old, battered sea chest filled with candles, chalk, and all the tools of the magician's trade; and a nice, wide stretch of bare concrete floor to work on. I knew exactly what I was looking for, a ritual from Morgenstern's *Book of the Salamander's Egg*. I lit a tall, white beeswax candle and worked by its warm glow, flipping through gilt-edged pages until I found the right chapter.

Etching the seal of art took time. Two concentric circles, six feet across, drawn in luminous orange on the cool concrete. I taped a long piece of string to the middle of the floor and wrapped the other around my stick of chalk, a makeshift compass to guide my hand. Inside the larger circle, an inscription in Hebrew, every letter perfectly spaced. Outside the outer ring I drew planetary seals symbolizing Mercury, Saturn, Jupiter. And between them, runes of calling, of finding, of coveting and claiming.

I had a piece of Damien Ecko in my hip pocket. I wanted the rest of him.

When it comes to magic, distraction is the devil. You have to work with absolute concentration, absolute focus. Sometimes it felt like half of my apprenticeship with Bentley and Corman was learning how to turn my mind into a steel trap, to stay locked on target through any kind of disturbance.

Tonight, though, I couldn't hold my focus. One little thought poked at the back of my mind, jabbing with every step I took like a pebble in my shoe. I kept circling back to my talk with Carolyn Saunders and learning about the Enemy's weird fixation on some forties-era stage magician. Ms. Fleiss had missed her shot at Canton the Magnificent's top hat, beaten by my old "pal" David at the auction, but she didn't strike me as a graceful loser. And the Thief—the *real* Thief, a man who climbed the side of a Dubai skyscraper for a heist—was on her payroll. I figured it was a matter of days before he paid a visit to David's private museum and snared that hat. Maybe a matter of hours.

I didn't even know what they wanted the damn thing for. I just knew that they wanted it. Which meant I wanted them *not* to have it.

I pushed the thought out of my mind. It came right back, bobbing in front of me like a carrot on a stick. I focused on my breathing as I sat in the heart of the ritual circle, spreading out a rumpled map of Clark County. I'd tied a length of twine around the falcon amulet, turning the glossy blue stone into a makeshift pendulum. It dangled from my fingertips, inches above the middle of the map, swaying like a cobra's head as I spoke the ritual words. A chant in tangled, bastard Latin, spilling from my lips in a whispered and serpentine rhythm.

The pendulum should have moved. It should have tugged at my fingers, pointing the way on the map, showing me where Ecko was hiding. Instead, it just rocked back and forth, useless. I tried again, taking a few deep breaths to center myself. Nothing.

I knew finding Ecko and ending him had to be my top priority. All the same, I couldn't get that damn magician's top hat out of my mind. The Enemy's target was fifteen minutes from where I was sitting, and I was in the perfect position to deny it to him.

So I'd scratch the itch. One quick heist, a little smash and grab, and that would be that. Then I could focus on my Ecko problem and make another go at tracking him down.

David Gosselin had built his private museum in an old factory building on the edge of town. I'd never been inside, but I knew what to expect: hardcore security, probably a Polymath alarm system, and some magical wards for good measure. A short con would be the easiest way in. Get him to voluntarily open the place up, and sneak past while he was distracted. Bentley and Corman were always my go-to accomplices for that kind of job...but after my kitchen-table talk with Bentley, and his worries about my obsession, asking them for help wasn't an option.

I called Caitlin. When she picked up, her voice was muffled by the throb of electronic dance music.

"Daniel," she shouted over the bass, "Emma called me from

the hospital. Is Melanie still with you? Are you taking her to the safe house?"

"Um, in a manner of speaking. Hey, I was wondering if you were busy tonight. I've got a thing, and I could use another pair of hands."

"What? Hold on, I can't hear you."

I heard a door swinging shut. The music dropped to a low roar.

"That's better," she said. "Jennifer and I are having an evening out on the town. Or doing a good job pretending to, while she checks on her people."

So those were the "plans" I wasn't invited in on. "She still pissed at me?"

"I wouldn't put it that strongly. She's just...disappointed."

I winced. I'd rather she was angry.

"She'll be fine. Just make sure she knows you're here for her, hmm? It's been a stressful week for everyone." Caitlin paused. "So what did you need help with?"

I couldn't ask. I'd already let Jennifer down once, blowing off her meeting so I could chase a lead on the Enemy. I could just imagine how well "I need to break up your evening so Caitlin can help me with *another* lead" would go over.

"It's nothing," I said. "You two have a great night out, and be safe. I'll catch you tomorrow, okay?"

Who else could I reach out to? Mama Margaux was a strong hand when it came to magic, but pulling cons wasn't really her thing. Pixie had some fierce social-engineering skills, but she worked best with a phone or a computer screen, and this was a purely physical job. Naavarasi could do it, but she was out in Denver, and besides, I didn't need to owe her any more favors. I didn't have anybody left to call.

Wait. I did. I didn't *want* to, but I did.

"Danny!" Justine squealed as she picked up the phone. "My sister and I were just talking about you!"

"No we weren't," Juliette said in the background. "We were talking about fudge."

"Close enough," Justine said.

I cleared my throat. "So, any chance you two are still looking for work?"

"Payment first. We want a new cherry-red Porsche, a pony named Buttercup, and ten bars of gold bullion. Also, you must henceforth refer to us in public as your immortal, benevolent, and adored queens."

"I'll write you a check for five hundred bucks, you have to wait a week to cash it, and you can keep anything you steal on the job. Also, I will tell people that I find your company not entirely intolerable."

"You drive a hard bargain, but you talked us into it. Deal!"

*   *   *

I had a grudging respect for David Gosselin. He'd worked his way up from nothing, starting with a good smile and the old cup-and-ball routine, parlaying it into television shows and sold-out theaters. He had a knack for real magic, too—he used to be a fixture at the Tiger's Garden back when I was still Bentley and Corman's apprentice—but as far as I knew he'd earned his millions the honest way with showmanship, innovation, and a hell of a lot of hard work.

I was still going to rob him blind, but hey, if I didn't, somebody else would.

His late show got out a little after eleven. Juliette and Justine were right where I wanted them, hanging out with a small mob of autograph hounds in the alley behind the Crown Theater, poured into little black cocktail dresses and done up to the nines. The perfect bait, assuming they didn't get distracted and wander off before the job was done. Or forget what the job was in the first place. Or get bored and start murdering people. There were a lot of "ifs" in play here.

I sat behind the wheel of the Spark, in the shadow of a broken streetlight, and watched from a safe distance. Applause rose up as the backstage door whistled open and David strode out to greet his fans. He wore painted-on black silk trousers and a ruffled white poet's shirt with billowing lace sleeves. It wasn't his outfit I hated, it was that he actually, somehow, made it look good. The twins were on him like a pair of magnets. I couldn't hear a word, but they were giving off all the right body language, and David responded in kind. He worked the crowd, signing autographs and shaking hands, but he stayed close to them as the thinning audience trickled away.

I fired up the engine and took a slow cruise around the corner, the perfect spot to watch David invite Juliette and Justine into the back of his limo. The limousine's brake lights flared red as it rumbled out of the parking lot, and I followed at a safe distance. Now came the real test: I'd told the twins to ask David for a tour of his private museum. I wove through the night traffic, following the limo onto the highway, aiming for the outskirts of Vegas.

When we reached our destination, I let out a breath I didn't know I'd been holding. By some miracle, the twins had remembered their lines. The limo stopped short outside an old factory building, red brick with steel crenellations along the roof like an urban castle. The museum was for private showings only; there were no signs out front, nothing to hint at the treasures hidden inside. I parked the Spark out on the street, just up the block, and slid low behind the wheel.

David walked to the factory door, sandwiched between the twins as they clung to his arms, and led them inside. His limo rolled out, leaving the front unguarded. Time to get to work.

21.

David had locked the front door behind him, but I wasn't concerned about locks. It was the alarm system that worried me, and as long as he was giving his new friends the grand tour, that'd be safely deactivated. I crouched under a sodium light and worked fast, thumbing through my waterproof sleeve of lock-picks, tugging out a tension rake and a pick with a spade-shaped tip. The tumblers fought me, rolling over with little steel mule-kicks, but soon the pins fell into perfect order and let out that satisfying *click*. The well-oiled door opened without a whisper, and I slipped inside.

In his private sanctum David had created a museum, a show-room, a love letter to the history of stage magic. Vintage posters in underlit frames hearkened back to the greats of the stage: Thurston, Carter, Blackstone. Painted portraits from the roaring twenties depicted somber-faced magicians in evening attire with cartoonish imps perched on their shoulders, whispering secrets in their ears. David had collected mechanical automatons and ven-triloquist's dummies, posing them in high-backed chairs or clus-tered around trick tables. Tall dividers broke the open floor up into small galleries, each one dedicated to a particular magician or classic illusion.

I kept low, creeping my way from divider to divider, ears perked, checking every angle. High above my head, starlight streamed down through long glass skylights, while electric lights made to look like Victorian-style gas lamps cast a cold, soft glow across the pristine hardwood floor. I heard David and the twins just up ahead, around the next bend.

"And this is my pride and joy," he told them. "The world's largest collection of Houdini memorabilia. This tank is the original water-torture escape, first used in 1914—"

A clanging noise, like someone pounding his fist against sheet metal, echoed across the factory floor.

"What's this?" Justine asked.

"Another classic escape. Houdini would climb into this iron milk jug, and his assistant would padlock the lid from the outside. They'd put a sheet over the jug, and five minutes later, he'd emerge—free as a bird, with the padlocks magically undone."

"I bet *you* can't do that trick," Juliette chirped.

I headed in the other direction, prowling the galleries for any mention of Howard Canton's name. Then I found it. A tiny nook lit by footlights, and a faded poster of Canton the Magnificent. He'd been painted in a dramatic pose, waving his bone-tipped wand and an open hand at a hovering, sleeping woman, as if commanding her to rise. "*SEE the Unthinkable!*" the poster proclaimed in a lurid font. "*WITNESS the Miracles and Mysteries of Magic from Seven Continents!*"

Beside the frame, resting on a mahogany plinth and posed to catch the light, rested the only other piece of Canton memorabilia: a black top hat, identical to the one he wore on his poster.

"Nice hat," I murmured, gently lifting it by the silky brim. "Not sure I'd pay a million bucks for it, but—"

My fingertips tingled on the brim, feeling a shiver of long-dormant magic, and my eyes slipped out of focus. In my second sight, layered upon the blurry world like a transparent film, the hat glowed a soft, pulsing violet. Runes, carved of shimmering gold, rippled around it like a spool of ticker tape before vanishing with a crackling hiss. I wasn't sure if they were a warning or a welcome. I held the hat gingerly, like it was a vial of nitroglycerin, and traced my steps backward to find the twins.

I heard metallic echoes and muffled shouts. When I rounded

the bend, Justine and Juliette were alone, casting disparaging glances at a four-foot-tall iron jug. The lid of the jug, clamped down under three heavy padlocks, thumped relentlessly.

"I *knew* he couldn't do the trick," Juliette said.

"Magic is boring," Justine said. "Can we leave now?"

The lights died, fizzing out as the factory plunged into darkness. Someone had killed the power, and it wasn't us.

"Yes. Yes, we can," I said, navigating by murky starlight from the glass skylights. I led the way toward the museum door—then froze, ducking around a divider and pulling the twins with me.

Ms. Fleiss's high heels clicked on the polished wood. She was wrapped in a floor-length trench coat, purple leather glistening like snakeskin, her eyes hidden behind onyx-dark glasses. She wasn't alone. A four-man squad in black balaclavas and urban camouflage spread out behind her, flashlights flashing on the muzzles of their sleek submachine guns.

I'd been prepared for an encounter with the Thief. Hoping for one, honestly. A run-in with Fleiss and a heavily armed hit squad wasn't a risk I'd planned for. I sprinted back to the Houdini exhibit as quietly as I could and put my face against the edge of the iron jug's lid as it thumped and rattled.

"David," I hissed, "David, shut up. Stop making noise."

His eyes squinted at me through the narrow crack. "Daniel?"

"Listen, you're being robbed."

"No *shit* I'm being robbed! By *you!*"

"No, not by—" I paused. "Well, okay, you *are* being robbed by me, but there's also some very nasty people here with some very big guns. So please, for your own sake, stay down and keep quiet."

"When I get out of here," he snarled, "I'm gonna kick your ass."

"Just do it *quietly*. Shh."

I slipped away from the exhibit, meeting up with the twins, the three of us staying just ahead of the encroaching bootsteps and sweeping lights. On my left side, Juliette's eyes rippled, spidery black veins rising like the curves of a tribal tattoo along her neck and one shoulder. On my right, Justine flashed rotten, jagged fangs, bouncing with anticipation.

"Party time now?" she asked me.

I waved my hand, sharp. "Not looking for a fight here. Let's slip around them and get out quietly."

We crept from divider to divider, exhibit to exhibit, staying low. On the other side of a display, a wall of faded iron keys and padlocks, I heard one of the gunmen speak.

"It's not here, ma'am."

"It's here," Fleiss replied. "I know it is. I *feel* it. Keep looking. And take the poster. He'll want that too."

We had almost made it, ten feet from the door, when a flashlight swung around and strobed across my face. I was blind, hot diamonds in my eyes, and one of the twins hauled me to the floor a split second before the submachine gun unleashed a three-round burst. Bullets tore into a display case, and a cascade of broken glass and vintage iron keys went raining to the floor in a musical clatter.

I rolled left, came up in a crouch, and reached for my cards. Four aces spread in my fingertips like a brace of throwing knives as boots rushed our way. Justine hit the first gunman in a running tackle, the two of them rolling across the hardwood, her shark teeth clamping down on his throat until his strangled scream ended in the crunch of cartilage. Juliette took the high ground, leaping on top of the nearest divider. She ran along it, arms out to her sides, and dove like a hawk to bowl over another two hitters. The fourth gunman came from the other direction, his muzzle sweeping my way and pinning me in the flashlight's glare. I whipped all four cards toward him. The flashlight shattered and died. He died with it, slamming against the wall and slumping to the floor, his eyes rolling back as blood dripped from the neck of his balaclava.

Ms. Fleiss stepped around the corner, casual as a Sunday stroll. Her brows furrowed.

"You," she said, "are a deviation from the plan. You should have died in Eisenberg."

"Sorry. Dying's not something I'm good at."

"We'll have to work harder."

"Not tonight," I said. "You know, I'm glad you're here, come to think of it. You can deliver a message to your boss for me."

"Which is?"

I flicked a card from my deck and sent it flying, a magic-charged hornet with a killing sting.

She caught it.

Fleiss plucked the card out of the air like it had been moving in slow motion. It twisted in her fingers—then melted, turning black and withering until all that remained was a tiny lump of congealed rot. She tossed it to the floor, her lip curling in mild disdain.

"I have walked upon worlds," she said, her tone conversational, "where children wielded greater magic than this. And I have stood proudly at my lord's side while he *ate* those worlds. Still, credit where credit is due, by local standards you're not entirely untalented. I'm sure you're quite proud of your little tricks. Would you like to see one of mine?"

Her jaw snapped. Distending, bone and muscle tearing then reknitting as her skull buckled, stretching backward, like an Easter Island idol. Her glasses fused with her flesh, giving her eyes of obsidian that reflected my horrified face in stereo. Her arms drooped from the sleeves of her coat, stretching inhumanly long, bending with a crack as each arm sprouted a second elbow, then a third, her elongated limbs wriggling like fleshy centipedes. Her fingernails fell out. They tumbled to the floor around her feet, and in their place, black iron claws forced their way out of her bloody fingertips one jutting inch at a time.

I watched, petrified. All I could manage was a whisper: "What *are* you?"

Her spine buckled as her legs grew and widened. The hunch-backed creature towered over me, leering, her head bobbing on a boneless, rubbery neck.

"Some call me the Mother of Nightmares," she hissed. "Now, I'm curious. Let's find out what *you're* afraid of."

She thundered toward me like a stampeding rhino and clamped her clawed hands on the sides of my head, her onyx-eyed face dropping nose to nose with mine. I could feel her now, a cold wet oil torrent trying to force its way into my mind. She inhaled my breath, tasting it, licking her cracked lips while I fought a psychic war. Fleiss hammered against my mental defenses like a hurricane on a sheet-metal shack, my walls slowly caving, about to give and let the torrent in.

Then she staggered back with a frustrated bellow as Justine hit her with a spinning kick, her foot slamming into the creature's bloated, rubbery gut. I felt her power recede as her hands ripped away, freeing me from my paralysis. I jogged backward, firing off card after card, shouting for the twins to run to the car. Fleiss batted the cards away as fast as I could hurl them. They weren't hurting her, but now she was a rhino in a cloud of stinging gnats, more focused on protecting herself than coming after me. I kept up the onslaught until my shoulder bumped the door. Then I turned and ran.

The car was out front, the twins already inside and waiting for me. A frustrated shriek tore the air at my back as I jumped behind the wheel, throwing the car into gear and stomping the gas. We squealed out of the parking lot, lurching over a pothole as we swerved onto the street.

"What *was* that?" Justine asked, sitting in the passenger seat.

"Something...I don't know. Not from this planet, I don't think. Not from anything *like* this planet. Hold on, I'm getting us out of here."

I turned left at the first intersection. Up ahead, a dangling and lonely light above a four-way junction flickered from red to green. I kept our speed up, coasting on through.

Then came the blare of a horn and the wash of headlights as a dump truck screamed through the red light, coming in from the side, and smashed into us at full throttle.

22.

Blood-streaked glass tumbled past me in slow motion. I saw the impact, the aftermath, timed to each jackhammer beat of my heart. The passenger-side door buckled, broken metal impaling Justine, the window glass slicing her face to ribbons as her spine shattered. Juliette wasn't wearing her seatbelt. The collision threw her as the tiny car rolled, and I heard her neck snap as the impact folded her like a broken doll. The pavement shot up to greet me and—

—I was running from the museum, the car waiting outside and ready to go. Fleiss's angry bellow split the air behind me. I jumped into the driver's seat and hit the gas.

"What *was* that?" Justine asked, sitting in the passenger seat.

"I don't —" I paused, shaking my head. "Wait. Hold on, this isn't right."

I came to the first intersection. Left—no. Left was wrong. Bad choice. I turned right.

I coasted through the next intersection, green lights all the way to safety. Then came the scream of the air horn as the dump truck T-boned us, turning the world into bloody glass and a wash of white-hot agony. I watched Justine die, then Juliette, sharing the rolling, crumpled steel with their mutilated bodies. I blacked out—

—I ran from the museum, the car waiting outside, ready to go.

"What *was* that?" Justine asked, sitting in the passenger seat.

I slammed on the brakes.

The car's engine hummed as we stood at the first intersection. I held the steering wheel in a death grip, staring straight ahead. Juliette bounced in the seat behind me, craning her neck to look behind us.

"Come *on*," she said, "what are you waiting for? That thing will catch us if we don't *move!*"

"There's no right choice," I murmured to myself. "Whichever direction I pick, it's the wrong one."

"You have to decide," Justine told me.

Not Justine anymore.

Coop sat in the passenger seat. My old buddy, the best safe-cracker west of the Rockies, looking just the way he did the last time I saw him. Dead, shot in the heart, with his eyes glassy white and his mouth sewn shut with mortician's thread. The thread ripped as he forced his jaw open, the skin of his lips tearing and oozing trickles of blood down his chin.

"You have to decide, Dan."

"What happened to you in Chicago was my fault," I told him. "Every time I try to make a play for something better in my life, every time I reach for a big score, I make the wrong choice. I skip away free, and it's the people I care about who take the hit."

In the backseat, Spengler leaned forward. I hadn't seen the big man since the day he died screaming on his living room floor, tortured and killed by Lauren Carmichael's followers. One shattered arm flopped onto my shoulder, his guts spilling out over his lap.

"You're not wrong, you know," he told me with a jovial smile.

I stood on an empty plain. Cracked, dry earth under my feet, a rumbling storm on the horizon staining the sky black. Corpses littered the ground, the aftermath of a battle.

Bentley. Corman. Jennifer. Mama Margaux. Pixie. Caitlin. My family of choice, my circle of trust. All of them laid out in a ring around me. Brutalized and broken. All of them with their dead eyes wide open, staring at me in silent accusation.

"This is what happens," I said to myself. "It's better not to try. Better to stay where I am. Tread water. I can tread water forever."

Lightning crackled in the distance. A peal of thunder echoed from the gathering clouds, growing higher in pitch, sounding more and more like a—

Voice. A hand shaking my shoulder.

"Come *on*, Danny!" Justine shouted in my ear. My stomach lurched as the world swung back into focus. Fleiss was down on the museum floor, knocked flat and dazed, slowly pushing herself back to her feet. Juliette grunted as she hauled down one of the display partitions, sending it crashing onto the creature's head and burying her under cracked wood and vintage art. As Fleiss clawed her way from the rubble, Justine snatched up one of the fallen gunmen's weapons and let it rip, emptying the magazine into Fleiss's gut. Black ichor spattered and the creature staggered back with her face twisted in fury. I followed Justine's lead, grabbing the fallen top hat in one hand and a submachine gun in the other. I took aim and hit Fleiss with short, tight bursts, concentrating my fire. She flailed her arms, bellowing. Then she turned, her dagger-like claws ripping at the open air beside her.

She tore a hole in the world.

Reality frayed, splitting aside to reveal a gaping, howling void. An endless and starless night. Fleiss curled her hand around the edges of the tear, forcing it wider. As the faint scent of roses drifted through the museum, the creature turned my way and spoke a single word.

"*Soon.*"

Fleiss dove through the hole and it whipped shut at her back, vanishing in a heartbeat.

Justine stumbled beside me, panting for breath. "What," she said, "*was* that?"

"A problem," I told her.

*　*　*

The car wasn't waiting right out front this time. It was exactly where I'd parked it, out on the street, just up the block. I set Canton's hat in the backseat, resting atop a pile of submachine guns. The twins wanted the firepower, and I didn't ask why.

I came to the first intersection in the road, and stopped.

"Light's green," Juliette told me.

Freed from Fleiss's grip, her torrent of visions felt like a vivid dream now. I wasn't afraid that I was still in her grasp. I just wanted to understand what I'd seen. She'd sent me on a roller-coaster ride straight to the core of my own battered mind, and I'd found fear, all right. Not fear of death, or things that go bump in the night. Fear of failure and the fallout. I'd always seen life as one long, running gamble: you rolled the dice every time you got out of bed and anted up with every decision you made. Normally, I did okay.

Then I'd laid all my chips on the wrong bet, and Coop and his nephew paid the price. Just like I'd been too slow when I went up against Lauren Carmichael, made the wrong play, and watched Spengler die right next to me. Something had gone out of me over the last few months. Not a quick snuff of the flame, but a slow, chilling frost that settled into my bones and made the easy way look like the only way.

Easier not to take care of myself and get back on my own two feet, letting what should have been a short-term stay turn into permanent couch surfing at Bentley and Corman's place. Easier to stand on the sidelines while Jennifer did all the work of forging the New Commission by herself, and easier not to reach for some-thing bigger than I'd ever had by taking my seat at the table. Easier to obsess about the Enemy, a hazy and far-off fight, than to roll up my sleeves, take down Ecko, and clean up my own backyard.

No more.

I had a choice to make, here and now. Keep going the way I'd been going, the safe and easy road all the way to the grave, or step up and face my fears head-on.

"I'm turning here," I said out loud.

"Fine." Juliette waved a confused hand at me. "Do it. Nobody's stopping you."

I stepped on the gas.

"You're goddamn right," I told her.

I hadn't lost everything in Eisenberg. I'd been given a gift. A brand-new start. My old life was dead, and I was a phoenix rising from the ashes, with the chance to do anything, be anything. The man with the Cheshire smile hadn't broken me. He'd done me a favor.

Someday I'd get the opportunity to pay him back. I'd write my thank-you note on a bullet.

I dropped the twins off at a roach motel with hourly rates, a stone's throw from the airport. Not the glamorous digs I was expecting. Juliette sighed, looking up at the grimy windows. "They threw us out of Nicky's penthouse at the Metropolitan. Apparently you have to pay money to live there. I told them we were the hottest people in the hotel and they should be paying *us* to stay there because we make everything awesome, but some people just don't listen to reason."

"But we have guns now," Justine added, hefting one of the weapons.

I wrote them a check. Alone with my thoughts and an old magician's top hat, chasing dawn, I was too sleepy to plan my next move. I figured I'd swing by the Strip, find a cheap room, and crash for a few hours. Still, something nagged at me. Nicky. Caitlin and I both thought it was weird that he'd flee from the feds but not take the twins with him. I knew what kind of a man Nicky Agnelli was: egotistical, venal, cruel, and occasionally murderous, but if there was anyone in the world he felt genuine, bone-deep loyalty toward, it was the twins. So why would he skip town and leave his partners in crime to live in squalor?

"Because he's still here," I said and pulled a U-turn at the next intersection.

In a city with no shortage of dive bars and strip clubs, the Gentlemen's Bet had never been on anybody's top-ten list. Down on a seedy stretch of warehouses and vacant lots, it mostly catered to long-haul truckers, a few local barflies, and the occasional low-rent bachelor party. Now it didn't cater to anybody; the yellow police tape over the front door saw to that. My car was the only one in the lot. I walked past the dead neon and the crimson-painted runner of Astroturf out front and skirted the building. A fence ringed the back, penning in an overstuffed and reeking Dumpster. I clambered up the fence, pulling myself over, dropping down to the broken asphalt on the other side.

The back door was locked. I tugged out my picks and got through it in a minute flat, letting myself inside.

The house lights glowed across the vacant club, turned down low, casting the stage in lonely shadows. I ran a finger along the mirrored bar, coming away with a few grains of dust. Then I walked around and surveyed the rows of bottom-shelf booze. The bartender's caddy had gone rancid, the lemons and limes sprouting moldy fuzz. Not many options for a good cocktail. Still, I dug around past the cheap liquor and came up with half a bottle of Jack Daniel's. The premium stuff, single-barrel aged. I set it on the bar next to a pair of water-spotted glasses.

"You gonna come out?" I asked the empty room. "Or am I drinking alone tonight?"

The door to the manager's office creaked open. Slowly, uncertain, almost sheepish, a shadow emerged from the back hallway.

"How'd you know?" Nicky asked me.

"Because I know you." I popped the bottle, catching the rich aroma of Tennessee whiskey. "Grab a stool. Let's have a chat."

23.

The King of Las Vegas had tumbled from his throne, and from the looks of him, he'd landed hard. Nicky's tailored shirt was spotted with damp stains, cuff links gone and his sleeves sloppily rolled up. His matted hair, once movie-star sculpted, hadn't seen a comb or a shower in a week. Bristle covered his cheeks, too long to be roguish, too short for a beard.

I poured a splash of whiskey into each glass and slid one his way. "Probably shouldn't be pouring for you, since I suspect you already drank half the shelf, but what the hell."

He lifted the glass in a tired, shaking hand. I saluted, knocking my glass against his.

"I fucked up, Dan. Got blindsided. I was looking left when I shoulda been looking right."

"Happens to the best of us." The whiskey tingled on my lips. "I was just in prison myself."

"I heard about that. The Outfit set you up. Used you to get at me."

"Planted all the evidence in my trunk. Everything the feds needed to come at both of us, full force." I paused. "Damn, I miss that car. I'm driving a Spark now. Looks like a goddamn lime on wheels."

Nicky grunted out a chuckle.

"So what have you been doing, besides hiding in here and murdering your liver?"

He ran his fingers through his greasy hair. "Looking for a way out. The bastards burned me down, Dan. My businesses, my bank accounts, all that real estate out in Eldorado, the helicopter...the feds impounded everything. 'Evidence.' Even the stuff I had in a shell trust. The stuff I stashed under an assumed name. They must have been watching me for *years*. They had a dossier on me a mile thick. I was so sure, *so* damn sure I was made of Teflon. That as long as I greased all the right palms and covered my tracks, I'd be on top of the game forever. Now what's this I'm hearing about Jennifer taking over?"

"Not taking over," I said, then paused. "Well, yeah, she kinda is, but it's more of a 'first among equals' deal. Somebody had to rally the troops."

"I'm surprised it wasn't you."

I shrugged. "Didn't think I wanted that kind of power. It's a trade-off: you get the big money, the big prizes, and the big risk right along with it. Play your cards wrong, you can go from the top of the world to...well, here."

"You said 'didn't.' Past tense."

He held out his glass. I poured another dollop of Jack for both of us.

"I made some bad decisions," I told him. "Got knocked down. And instead of standing right back up, I laid there and took it. Laid there so long I fooled myself into thinking that's where I belonged."

"You played yourself," he said.

"Now I understand what everybody's been telling me. I got a clean slate when I broke out of Eisenberg. A new start. What I do with it, where I go, that's all up to me. So now I'm thinking about the future. Making some hard choices about what I want, and what I'll do to get it. By the way, I hung out with the twins tonight. You wanna tell me why they think you skipped town without 'em?"

"You kidding me?" He ran a weary hand over his stubbly cheeks. "*Look* at me. I'm a loser, Dan. They're better off without me."

"You call holing up in a roach motel by the airport 'better off'?"

He frowned. "Son of a bitch. My place at the Met was paid up five months in advance."

"Apparently management decided not to honor that arrangement."

"They've got money, though. I opened a bank account for 'em ages ago, and I kept it flush. None of that was in my name. The feds shouldn't have been able to touch it."

"Did you ever make sure," I asked him, "that Juliette and Justine actually know how banks work?"

His shoulders slumped. "Knew I forgot something."

"They're a little hazy on the concept of money in general."

"Those girls." He sipped his whiskey. "The three of us came up from nothing. I was just a runny-nosed punk without a pot to piss in when they met me. They showed me, y'know—they showed me I could make something of myself. That I could *be* somebody. How can I face them now, huh? How can I let them see me like this?"

I took a long look around the room. The faded lights, the tarnished mirrors, dust motes in the dark.

"The Nicky I used to work for, he never sweated over setbacks. He'd take a hit, every now and then, but it didn't slow him down. He always had a plan to get back on top."

"This is a little more than a setback, Dan."

"Is it? You said it yourself: you came up from nothing. So here you are, back at nothing again. How did you become the King of Las Vegas? Was it dumb luck or hard work?"

"I put in the work," he said.

"Yeah, you did. So you can do it again. I thought I lost everything when I landed behind bars. Tonight I realized it was just the kick in the ass I needed. I'm lighter now. That makes me leaner. Faster. This isn't the end of my road. It's the start of a comeback. And if I can do it, you can do it too." I raised my glass. "Here's to the phoenix."

As he lifted his glass, a little of the old fire came back into his eyes.

"To the phoenix." He tossed back a swig of whiskey, nodding to himself. "I got one move I haven't made yet. One shot at getting my feet back under me. But I can't do it alone."

"Yeah?"

"Yeah." He rapped his fingernails on the mirrored bar. "The feds might not have taken everything. I had a safe-deposit box at this credit union on West Sahara, under a cover name."

"What's in the box?"

"Clean cash. Fat stacks of it. Enough to bankroll me for a while. Enough money to start making *more* money, you get my drift? Thing is, I can't get near it. I tried once. I think the feds might be watching the place, waiting to see if I try to pick it up. I circled the parking lot and got a real hinky feeling about some of the customers, so I took off before anybody spotted me. Course, I could be wrong. It was just a feeling I had."

I knew what he meant. Spend enough time in the underworld and you start growing a sixth sense for danger. Ignoring those bad vibrations was a good way to end up in jail or a shallow grave.

"So they might be looking to grab anybody who opens that box," I said.

"Might be, yeah."

Of course, they'd be outside the vault room. So if somebody went in to open a *different* box...I played the angles in my mind, sorting out the rough sketch of a plan. It could work.

"For old times' sake," I told him, "and a finder's fee, I'll go get your money. But you have to do something for me first."

"What's that?"

"I assume the FBI tapped the lines in here. You got a clean phone on you?"

"Sure."

"Then take it out of your pocket, get your shit together, and call the twins," I said. "You need them, and they need you."

He finished his drink, long and slow, and set the empty glass down on the bar.

"Yeah," he said. "When you're right, you're right. Okay. I'll do it."

"Good man."

He stepped into his office to make the call. I lingered, alone behind the bar, sipping my whiskey and contemplating the empty club. He was all smiles when he came back, wearing his relief on his face.

"It's cool," he said. "They're on their way over. Thanks, Dan. I mean it."

"Thank me with a cut from that safe-deposit box. I've got expenses."

I stifled a yawn behind my hand. No windows in the club, but the clock behind the bar told me the morning sun wasn't too far away. I had come to that moment of truth every veteran drinker has faced at least once: the place where you either pack it in, sleep through the morning, and salvage what remains of the day, or throw good sense to the wind and pull an all-nighter. My choice was obvious; the adrenaline rush from the museum was long gone and I was coasting on fumes.

"I gotta crash for a few hours," I told Nicky. "I can barely see straight, and the booze isn't helping."

He chuckled. "Weak. You used to be able to drink with one hand and shoot with the other, twenty-four hours a day."

"I *used* to not be nearly forty years old."

"I'm a couple years older than you are."

"You've got demon blood," I said. "We mere humans are made of frailer stuff. You got a cot in here, somewhere I can rest my head for a few?"

"Yeah, it's—" He froze as a loud knocking echoed at the front door. Silent, Nicky nodded downward. I followed his eyes to the blue-metal .45 sitting on a low shelf behind the bar. I picked up the revolver and we padded to the door, flanking it. On a quiet three-count, I aimed down the sights and Nicky yanked the door open.

Standing on the scarlet runner, Justine blinked at me. "Normally *I'm* the one who shoots people at the front door."

I lowered the gun. Nicky pulled her into a tight hug. "Goddamn, it's good to see you. Where's your sister?"

"In the car." Justine bounced on her heels. "We gotta go, *now*. We saw a police cruiser circling the block."

I sighed. "They probably spotted my car in the lot and wanna know why it's there, since this place is supposed to be a crime scene. Okay, let's split up and clear out. Nicky, I'll call you when I wake up, and we'll work out our next move with the safe-deposit box."

A warning klaxon rang out through the fog in my tipsy, sleep-deprived brain. Not surprising: some lucky beat cop could make his career if he picked this exact moment to look our way, catching a fugitive crime boss and a supposedly dead prison escapee in his headlights. I mostly just thought it was weird to see one of the twins without her sister in tow. As I walked ahead of Nicky and Justine, stepping out into the lot, I realized I'd never actually seen the twins more than ten feet apart.

That's when a hand clamped over my nose and mouth, holding a white handkerchief drenched in a pungent chemical brew. A sharp smell like rubbing alcohol flooded my sinuses, and my vision doubled, tripled, then faded to black. The .45 tumbled from my limp fingers, clattering on the pavement. I was right behind it.

24.

I wasn't sure how long I'd been out. My senses returned in scattered, random bursts, the world defying me to make sense of it. I felt a burning sensation against my back, then realized it was actually bitter cold. Heard a distant, rhythmic thudding, like somebody working out his frustrations on a punching bag. Voices, garbled and slow, swam in and out of my ears on tides of nausea.

My vision blurred back into focus. Concrete cinder-block walls all around me. Bare metal supports above, and a single light bulb dangling over my head. I was naked. Strapped to a metal folding chair with my arms behind my back. Loops of duct tape clasped my crossed wrists and fixed each calf to the chair, forcing my knees apart.

I was in a garage, I thought, some kind of auto body shop. A back office, bare-bones furniture and a pin-up calendar from five years ago tacked up on a corkboard, Miss June posing in a bikini on the hood of a T-Bird. Through the open door I looked out to a shadowy loading bay where nightingale-blue car lifts stood rusting and abandoned over an oil-stained concrete floor. Cast in a narrow bar of stray light from a boarded-over window, a body dangled from one of the lifts by bound wrists. His feet swung an inch above the floor.

Not just a body. Nicky. His battered face looked my way, a strip of duct tape plastered over his mouth, while a couple of guys in cheap suits worked him over. A beefy fist thudded into his gut, drawing a wheezing grunt.

They hadn't started in on me yet, but my situation wasn't looking any brighter. Not when I glanced to my left and saw the tools laid out on the desk. A claw hammer. A hacksaw and a pair of stainless-steel pliers. A box of nails and a canister of black pepper. A scalpel. A soldering iron, plugged in and ready to go. Everything precisely posed to ensure I'd see it as soon as I woke up.

Footsteps heralded a new arrival. I would have recognized his arrogant, frat-boy sneer anywhere. Angelo Mancuso stood over me like an art collector surveying an expensive piece he'd just bought. I knew the slob in the Hawaiian shirt on his left, too: Sal, his bodyguard, who I'd met back in Chicago. The man on the right I'd only seen from a distance. He'd been one of the Outfit thugs I framed in a marijuana sting right after my prison break, while I was trying to rescue Jennifer. Apparently the charges hadn't stuck. He was a wispy blond with high thick cheekbones and a recessed, tiny chin, like his face was a half-inflated balloon tethered to a scrawny neck.

I tugged at my bonds. No good. Had to try anyway.

"You know," I told Angelo, "usually when I find myself tied up and naked, somebody at least buys me dinner first."

Angelo and Sal snickered. "This guy," Angelo said. "I love this guy. This one's got a sense of humor."

The man on his right fixed me with an unblinking stare. "That's usually the first thing to go."

"Really, guys, don't take this the wrong way, but none of you are my type." I batted my eyes at Angelo. "You strike me as a selfish lover. And I only like men who cuddle."

The man on the right stepped around to the desk, sorting through the tools. Placing and arranging them according to some inscrutable torturer's feng shui.

"Patient demonstrates the use of dismissive quips as a guard against his fear and vulnerability," he murmured to himself. "A shield of false bravado. Not unexpected. Easily remedied."

Angelo looked back over his shoulder, where his guys were using Nicky as a human punching bag. "I gotta thank you. We've been combing the damn city looking for Nicky. See, the feds didn't know about his backup burner. But we did. We had that thing tapped for a month, but he barely *used* it, and when he did we could never get a fix on where he was hiding out."

"So you overheard the call and sent Kirmira, disguised as Justine, to draw him out."

"Yeah, you were a bonus. Don't feel bad: if you got past Tony the Tiger, there were another five guys hiding behind the cars, and three more out back behind the club. You two didn't stand a chance."

"Sounds like you thought of everything. Except you fucked up, Angelo."

"How do you figure that?"

"Because now the twins know Nicky's in town. And they'll know, when they get to the club, that he's been kidnapped. Justine and Juliette aren't just hitters. They're demon-blooded threshing machines, and they got an armload of brand-new guns tonight."

Angelo barked out a laugh and spread his hands wide.

"And? Let 'em look! This garage is on the other side of town, it's been boarded up for five years, and the only neighbors are a vacant lot and a couple of foreclosures. They ain't gonna find you. Not in time to do anything, anyway. Lemme introduce you to a buddy of mine. This guy here? We call him the Doctor."

When Jennifer was abducted, the Outfit had flown in their very own torture specialist to wring her dry. I'd impersonated him, playing the part to get close and cut her loose.

Now I was face-to-face with the real thing.

"We know just about everything," Angelo explained. "Who's a part of this 'New Commission,' what they own, who their guys are. Some of your guys are our guys now."

I remembered Jennifer telling me about the meeting and the sudden defection. "Little Shawn and his crew."

"Yeah, they've been helpful. Not as helpful as you're gonna be, though. We've still got some questions, and you're gonna fill in the blanks."

"You assume I *have* the answers."

"I will determine if you do, or if you don't," the Doctor said. "It will be unfortunate for you if you don't."

Angelo snorted. "Pretty unfortunate either way. You should have accepted our job offer in Chicago, Faust. Hell, you even ended up helping us take out Nicky, just like I wanted you to. How's that for ironic? You could be living the good life right now. Instead, by the time the Doc is done with you...well, let's just say it ain't gonna be an open-casket funeral."

He turned to leave. I bit down on a surge of panic. I needed to keep him here, keep him talking. Every second I could buy, staving off the inevitable, was more time for the twins to track us down and come to the rescue.

"You're forgetting one thing," I said. "Damien Ecko."

Angelo paused, glancing back at me. "What about him?"

"He's working for you, isn't he? Helping out with the hit list."

He shrugged. "He's had his uses."

"Because of me. Ecko isn't a mercenary. The only reason he'd work for the Outfit is if you promised to help him find me. I'm right, aren't I?"

"I might have made some promises to that effect. So what? The guy is a fuckin' loon. Nobody's gonna find whatever's left of your body. When we're all done wiping your buddies out and planting our flag in Vegas, it'll be 'oh, so sorry, guess Faust wasn't here after all, he must have skipped town.' How's he gonna know any different?"

"You're underestimating him," I said. "He's obsessed with getting revenge against me. If he finds out that you denied him his moment of triumph—and he *will* find out—you'll be next in line. You don't want that."

Angelo put his hand to his chest. "I'm touched by your concern for my well-being. That said, I think I'll take my chances.

C'mon, Sal, let's leave the Doc to do his thing. I just ate lunch, I can't watch this shit."

"You're making a mistake—" I shouted, but the door swung shut. Leaving me trapped in the tiny office, alone with the Doctor.

He stood before me. Looking me up and down, silent, tapping his finger against his chin. Like a sculptor with a fresh block of marble, deciding the perfect place to chisel the first cut.

"I'm not going to ask you any questions," he told me as he walked around to the back of my chair.

He took hold of my left hand, grabbed my little finger, and snapped it in two places.

"Yet."

The pain hit me like a bucket of boiling water. Lancing up my hand, my wrist, straight to my spine. I howled through gritted teeth, wheezing, rocking back and forth as far as my bonds would let me.

He waited until I could breathe again.

Then he broke my ring finger, bending it backward until the bone snapped. Leaving it dangling like that, claw-hooked backward and limp, as my swallowed scream came out as a high-pitched, keening groan. I thrashed against the tape, my head flailing and the folding chair's legs thumping against bare concrete.

He let go of my hand and walked around me. He pulled over a second folding chair from the corner and sat down across from me, almost knee to knee, waiting patiently as I struggled to find my breath.

"I was army, before I went into the freelance market." His voice was sedate, a patient schoolteacher explaining a complex lesson. "Intelligence. My stint in Iraq was an important turning point in my career. That's where I learned a fascinating truth."

I hissed between my teeth, jaw clenched. My fingers felt like they were pressed to a hot stove and I couldn't pull them away. I met his gaze, but I couldn't find the breath to speak.

"It is a common belief," he said, "that torture doesn't work. That it's an exercise in empty cruelty, as the subject will simply tell the torturer anything they want to hear. That they're as likely to lie as tell the truth—*more* likely, in fact. Anything to make the pain stop. And this is, I can confirm from extensive firsthand experience, one hundred percent true."

He held up a finger.

"But! This presupposes an environment where the subject is otherwise treated as a viable human being, a life that will continue beyond the interrogation itself. That there is an expectation of eventual release or, depending on the government in question, that the subject can be reformed or remolded into a model citizen. So one imposes arbitrary limits. Waterboard, but not *too* much. Employ sleep deprivation and sensory-bombardment techniques, but not to the point of total psychological destruction. *Say* you're going to throw a man's child to a pack of feral dogs and force him to watch...but don't actually *do* it. I developed an alternative regimen. Which, unfortunately, led to my aforementioned freelance career. My superiors in the military were, how do I put this? Not pleased with my scientific rigor."

"You're a fucking whackjob," I grunted. "I don't even know what you want from me."

His eyes lit up. "Exactly! That's phase one."

He reached for the desk and picked up a cordless drill. The titanium bit whirred to life as he squeezed the trigger, gleaming like a white-hot brand. Its shrill, grating whine filled my ears.

"This is phase two," he said and pointed the drill at my left eye.

25.

I bucked wildly in the chair, flailing against the duct tape, desperate to get away as the whining bit inched closer and closer to my face. The Doctor stood up and put his free hand behind my head, gripping my hair and holding me still. The whirling bit loomed large now, the overhead light glinting off its tip.

"This drill is designed for professional construction work. The bit, a high-quality one, can drive through a two-by-four as if it were butter. In a moment, it will rupture your left eye. The cornea will go first. Caught on the tip, shredding, twisting, the bit's construction effectively tearing it away. The rotation of the bit will cause the remainder of your eye to collapse. The intraocular fluids, normally kept in a pressurized state, will burst like a water balloon."

"Just tell me what you want to know!" I fought against his hand, feeling a clump of hair rip out at the roots with a fresh burst of pain, but I couldn't get loose. "What's the point of torturing me if you haven't asked any *questions?*"

He let go of my hair and lowered the drill. The bit whined to a stop.

"And there," he said, "is the genius of my method."

He placed the drill back on the table and set a small gray box beside it. A digital timer, with bright red numbers. He turned the timer, making sure I could read it.

"The seed of any subject's defiance in the face of torture," he explained, "is hope. The hope of earning release, of survival, or simply of enduring an interrogation without being permanently disfigured. I have learned that the ideal way of extracting information is to start by removing these distractions. Please listen carefully, as my process depends on you fully understanding this part."

He set the timer for ten minutes but didn't start the countdown. The LED numbers flashed, expectant.

"I'm going to check on my other patient. I will return in precisely ten minutes. When I do, I will subject you to extensive and irreparable mutilations. We will begin with your permanent disfigurement, the surgical removal of your nose and lips. Then I will employ the drill to remove your left eye, exactly as promised, before moving on to both of your kneecaps—"

"Why?" I shouted at him. "What's the *point*?"

He gave me a tiny smile. "The point is, that when I have finished my list of alterations—I was only getting started before you rudely interrupted me—you, as you understand yourself, will no longer exist. All that remains will be a broken and bleeding lump of tissue that vaguely resembles a human being. And then, truly without hope, truly destroyed, you will tell me anything I want to know. And you will not lie, for you will no longer have any reason to. You will no longer have a life to save."

He tapped the button on the timer. The glowing numbers flicked to 9:59.

"See you in ten minutes," he said and stepped out of the room. He closed the door behind him, leaving me alone with the clock.

Bentley and Corman had taught me escapology and magic hand in hand. The point wasn't to learn how to shiv a pair of handcuffs or slip out of a knotted rope, though both of those had come in handy more than once in my life. The point was to master the one skill that both arts demanded: focus under fire.

"*Folks see a stopwatch and they start to panic,*" Corman had told me. "*It turns into a guillotine hanging over their heads. Then they rush, they get sloppy, then they screw up. Always remember, kiddo: every predicament is a puzzle. The clock isn't your enemy; it's just another piece of information. Take a deep breath, look around, and break everything down.*"

Four deep breaths. That's what I calculated I could spare. A slow five-count in, a slow five-count out. I faced my aching hand and my fear and stepped through it, past it, gently pushing away my emotions. I needed cold reason now. Cold reason and a weapon.

The timer was a mind game, that was obvious—but it didn't mean the Doctor wasn't coming back to do everything he'd promised and then some. He just wanted me good and terrified before he got to work. Had to assume his threats were genuine. Second assumption: the cavalry wasn't coming. No reason to assume Angelo was lying about how remote we were, and if the twins had some way of tracking Nicky down, they would have known he was still in Vegas in the first place.

Magic. My cards, gone. No tools, nothing I could use, and no hands to work with. Even my impromptu magic needed a surface to work on, a drawn sigil, *something*. Without any gear, the best I could do was call a spark to my fingertips and let it tumble to the oil-stained floor. As the timer ticked down, I studied my bonds. No chance of snapping the duct tape with brute strength. If I could get to a cutting edge, though...I looked down at the chair. Folding chair. That was good. Folding chairs *moved*. My hands were tied behind me at the wrist, poking through the open back of the aluminum chair but not taped to the frame itself.

I rose slowly and curled the fingers of my good hand around the back of the chair. Half-standing, half-crouched, I tugged at the frame. My back ached as the chair started to buckle on its hinges, its frame straightening out and the seat vanishing from under me. Then it was done. I stood on my own feet, the chair folded perfectly straight behind my legs. I lifted my bound wrists and rested them over the back of the chair. Six minutes and forty-two seconds on the clock.

I couldn't walk, but I could hobble, making my way to the desk one clumsy, shuffling, swinging step at a time. If I turned my back to the desk, I figured I had just enough range to reach back and grab something to cut myself loose. The scalpel. I lined myself up and swung myself around, working blind and the chair digging into my back as I groped behind me. My fingers closed over the scalpel's hilt. Carefully, like threading a needle, I turned it in my fingertips and lined up the blade with the middle of the tape binding my wrists.

The scalpel slipped. It cut into the meat of my palm, drawing blood, and the sudden shock made my fingers twitch. The blade tumbled to the floor, lying beside my bare foot.

I tried to crouch, as far as my bonds and the chair would let me. My fingertips clutched at empty air, straining, but it was no good. I couldn't reach the blade. I straightened my back, ignoring the blood dribbling down my fingers, and took another look at the desk. The timer clicked down to five minutes and twenty-seven seconds. Almost half my time gone, and all I'd managed to do was stand up.

I dismissed the hacksaw: too big, too awkward to work with in this position. Nothing else offered a good cutting edge. Then my eyes fell upon my last, solitary hope.

The soldering iron.

I took a deep breath, turned my back to the desk, and felt for it. My good fingers closed around the tool's plastic shaft—about the size of a fat Magic Marker, with a metal tip on the end—and tugged it from its charging stand. That cost me thirty seconds. Another half-minute to carefully swivel it around, getting the tip lined up with the duct tape around my wrists.

This was my last shot. If I dropped it, if I let go, I might as well sit down and wait to die. I clicked it on with my thumb and spent another thirty seconds waiting for the device to heat up. Then I took a deep breath, steeling myself, and pressed the tip against the duct tape.

The tape sizzled, rippling with flame. I couldn't see it but I could smell it, the air filling with the sharp metallic tang of an electrical fire. And then I felt it, as the burning tape clung to my bare skin and the tip of the iron bumped against my wrist.

I threw my head back and clamped my jaw shut, fighting with everything I had. Struggling not to scream, battling every instinct to drop the iron as the white-hot tip seared a ragged line along my skin. The muscles of my neck stood out like steel cords, my eyes squeezed shut and brimming with tears as I forced the iron down one agonizing quarter-inch at a time.

The tape parted. My hands snapped free and I tossed the iron onto the desk, tore off the smoldering, severed tape, and gasped for breath. My stomach churned as I surveyed the damage. Two fingers, hooked and dangling limp like broken claws, and the insides of my wrists marred with lobster-red burns and blisters. Scraps of charred tape clung to my skin, and the tip of the iron had drawn a ravaged line along my wrist like a suicide's razor. I needed medical attention, fast. But first I needed to survive.

Two minutes and eight seconds on the clock.

I crouched down, snatched up the fallen scalpel, and went to work on the tape around my calves. The folding chair fell free and I caught it, a heartbeat from clanging against the floor. Couldn't risk drawing attention now. That door would swing open soon enough, and I needed every second I had left to get ready.

I had my choice of weapons. Hammers, hacksaws, pliers. Nothing so elegant as a playing card or a pistol. Only a savage killed with tools like these.

That was all right. As the timer counted down and I stood alone, naked, bleeding and burned and waiting for my executioner, I was feeling pretty goddamn savage myself.

26.

The timer hit zero. I crouched, like a wounded panther waiting to pounce, and waited.

The door swung wide. One of Angelo's goons behind it, not even looking my way as he talked to somebody over his shoulder. "Yeah, the Doc just says to—"

I hit him with my shoulder, knocking him against the door, and ripped the hacksaw blade across his throat. His eyes went wide as he collapsed, blood spilling from the ragged wound in a gurgling torrent. His buddy was right behind him. I dropped the saw, grabbed the hammer with my good hand, and as he rounded the corner, brought the claw end down on the crown of his head. The steel prongs punched through his skull, digging in an inch deep, then wrenched free with a crackle of shattered bone. I flipped the hammer in my grip, raised it high, and hit him with the business end until he fell to the floor. Then I kept hitting him, until his feet had finally stopped twitching and my arm was tired.

Both of the dead men were strapped. I tossed the hammer aside and took their guns, a snub-nosed .32 and a black matte nine-millimeter Beretta. My bad hand throbbed, serving up a fresh jolt of bone-deep pain with every move I made, but the Doctor had made one mistake: he didn't break my trigger finger.

"The hell are you guys doing in there?" Angelo called out.

I answered him with bullets as I burst through the doorway, striding out across the concrete expanse with both guns raised high. Angelo and a pair of his soldiers dove behind a clutter of old oil drums as slugs sparked off the rusting lifts, ricocheting across the dusty garage. Sal and the Doctor were over by the side door, open to show the weed-choked vacant lot outside, the two of them smoking cigarettes. They ducked out the doorway, the Doctor running while Sal stood just outside the doorframe and pulled his revolver.

The two-gun theatrics bought me time to find cover. I put my back to a fat steel lift and dropped the empty .32, gripping the Beretta in my good hand. One of Angelo's guys poked his head up. I stepped out, took careful aim, and dropped him with a bullet in the face before ducking back behind the pillar.

"Got one for you, too, Angelo!" I called out. A hail of return fire pinged off the steel, one bullet slashing the air an inch from my cheek. I figured I had about three shots left. Had to make each one count.

The hitter on the floor was howling as he clutched his ruined face. Then I heard another gunshot, and sudden silence.

"Mercy bullet?" I shouted. "Hope you saved one for yourself. Because when I get my hands on you, you are sure as *fuck* dying slow."

Sal snapped off a few rounds from the doorway and cupped his hand to his mouth. "Boss! C'mon, I'll cover you! Let's just *go*. It ain't worth it!"

Angelo and his last soldier standing broke cover, racing to the side door while Sal unloaded his revolver at me. Throwing a hailstorm of lead that kept me pinned down for two crucial seconds. I popped up the instant he spent his last round, emptying my magazine at Angelo's back, but all I hit was a chunk of concrete in the lot outside. I heard someone leaning on a car horn, probably the Doctor, and then the screech of tires.

I stumbled over to Nicky's side, where he dangled naked from the fork of a car lift like a side of raw beef. They'd done a number on him. Just fists, but with one eye swollen shut, his nose pulped, and his chest a patchwork quilt of deep black bruises, he wasn't going to be entering any beauty pageants. I tore the strip of duct tape from his lips. His good eye struggled to focus on me.

"Danny," he croaked, "you look like shit."

"You're welcome," I told him, then went to find the scalpel. He tumbled into my arms as I cut him down, too weak to stand, and I gently rested him on the concrete floor.

"I thought I was good at *giving* a beatdown," he said, letting out a laugh that turned into a hacking cough. "Turns out I'm a pro at taking 'em, too. I'm a man of countless talents."

"Wait here a sec. I'm gonna get our clothes and some wheels, in that order."

Our clothes weren't hard to find, dumped in a pile in the back corner with the contents of our pockets scattered around them. I got dressed fast, careful with my fingers as I buttoned my shirt. I poked my head out the side door, suddenly thankful for fresh air and sunlight. Angelo hadn't lied: we were somewhere in no-man's-land, a street lined with boarded-up foreclosures and empty asphalt, not a taxi or a bus line in sight. The Outfit had left us an accidental present, though. They'd only taken one car. The other, a sleek silver Mercedes, sat parked out front. I ran back inside and patted down the dead men, finally coming up with a ring of keys.

Nicky couldn't walk on his own. I helped him pull his clothes on, both of us looking like we'd woken up in a Dumpster, and he leaned against me as we staggered to the car together. I laid him down in the backseat, keeping him out of sight; he was still a federal fugitive, and the last thing I needed was to get pulled over by some sharp-eyed cop.

"Hang tight," I said, then gritted my teeth as I tried to hold the steering wheel, my wrists feeling like they'd been shredded by a cheese grater. "I'm taking us to Doc Savoy's."

Doc Savoy was the best off-the-books medical practitioner in Vegas. Technically he had a veterinary degree, not an MD, and he earned his civilian money working as a mortician, but he had decades of hands-on experience and he could patch up pretty much anything that ailed you. His "clinic," the Rosewood Funeral Home, was the criminal equivalent of a Red Cross hospital: even when the city's sets went to war, nobody touched Doc, and nobody started trouble within three blocks of his place. He never took sides and never asked questions.

But as I turned onto his street and saw the flashing lights up ahead, the black smoke billowing into the clean October sky, I knew things were different now. I felt like I'd swallowed a rock, feeling its weight down in the pit of my stomach.

"Keep your head down," I told Nicky.

"Why? What's up?"

I slowly rolled past a line of squad cars. Two fire trucks barricaded the parking lot. Teams trained hoses at a roaring blaze as the funeral home burned to the ground.

Cops held back a small crowd of rubberneckers, another waving a line of cars toward an impromptu detour, away from the fire. I spotted a familiar face in the chaos: Gary Kemper, stalking past the fire trucks and barking at somebody on his phone. I pulled over on the opposite side of the street and told Nicky to hang tight.

The detective turned on his heel as I jogged up to him, hanging up his phone without another word to the person on the other end. His gaze shot from my face to my mangled hand. "The hell have you been up to?" he demanded.

"Is he okay? Savoy. Is he okay?"

"He's fine." Gary nodded toward the blaze. "Somebody firebombed the place, but he and his assistant got out the back door."

"Somebody," I echoed.

"Let's get on the same page," he told me. "Yeah, we know 'Doc' Savoy's real business. Have for years, but we figured he's doing more good than harm and it wouldn't be worth the time to put together a case on him. I've got him in protective custody now. These Chicago thugs don't have a lot of regard for anyone who tries to stay neutral, do they? And what are you doing, Faust? I told you this shit needs to end. It's not ending, it's *escalating*."

And it was about to get a whole lot worse, but I didn't say that out loud.

"I need a favor," I told him.

He blinked at me. "Excuse me?"

Showing was better than explaining. I led him across the street, back to the Mercedes, and pointed to the back window. He leaned in and his jaw dropped open.

"No. Uh-uh. *No.* Faust—"

"He needs a doctor, and he needs one *now.* Doc Savoy isn't here, so that means a legit hospital. You need to help him get checked in without setting off any red flags."

"You want me to help *Nicky Agnelli* get a freakin' checkup? Do you even know how many charges he's facing? I should cuff him right now. Hell, I should cuff you both."

"And if you do, he still has to go to an emergency room. Except I just saved him from the Outfit, and they'd love to get him back. The second the news of Nicky getting busted hits the radio, it's not just the feds who'll know about it. Chicago's got ears everywhere. Do you really think these animals are gonna draw the line at shooting up a hospital full of innocent people?"

Gary chewed his bottom lip, looking for a way out. "So we keep it local. I'll pull a detail from Metro to stand guard, and a total news blackout until he's stable enough to be transferred to a secure facility."

"Detective, these people are everywhere. They've got informants and insiders. They're running wiretaps. This is a criminal organization with millions of dollars at their disposal. You gonna tell me you really, one hundred percent, trust *all* your brothers in blue? Look me in the eye when you say it."

His gaze dropped.

"I've got some...suspicions," he told me. "I mean, every squad room's got a couple of guys on the take, the kind of cops who'll look the other way for *little* things, but..."

"But you think some of your colleagues might be getting their marching orders from Angelo Mancuso."

He gave me a weak shrug. "I can't prove anything. Yet. But yeah, the city's not safe for anybody right now."

"Then you know what you have to do." I pointed at the car window. "I think he's bleeding internally. He's going to die if you don't help. And I don't think you're the kind of man who would stand back and let that happen."

"*Damn* it." He ran his fingers through his hair and let out a heavy sigh. "All right. Follow my car. Let's do this."

27.

We were halfway to Sunrise Hospital when Nicky went into a seizure. He thrashed on the backseat, spasming fingers clawing at the blood-smeared leather, his jaw clacking but no sound coming out.

"Hold on," I told him, weaving through traffic behind Gary's unmarked police car and leaning on the gas. "We're almost there. Just *hold on.*"

We screeched to a stop outside the ER. I jumped out and waved my arms at Gary. "He's seizing!"

Gary spun and sprinted to the doors, holding up his detective shield. "Metro," he shouted, "we got a code blue out here!"

A crash team raced to the Mercedes, lifting Nicky out and laying him down on a rolling gurney. Gary and I followed them inside, the afternoon heat stolen away by the gust of air conditioning and the mingled aroma of antiseptics and bleach. He led the way through the crowd in the waiting room, softly asking an attendant for the nurse in charge.

"I'm Detective Kemper," he told her. "The guy who just came through on the crash cart, and this guy here—I need 'em both checked in as John Does."

The older woman, dressed in lilac scrubs, furrowed her brow. "That's not something we normally do, Detective. We at least have to get insurance information—"

"I get that, I really do, but here's the thing: they're assault victims. Got jumped by a gang just a couple of blocks from here. The perps took their wallets and ID, meaning they know these guys' names, and I'm worried they might come looking to finish what they started." He lowered his voice. "Sooner they're taken care of and shipped outta here, safer it is for everybody, get my drift?"

Her eyes widened as she glanced to the sliding glass doors, then to the crowd of people waiting for treatment. She looked my way. "I...think we can manage something. A room just opened up. Why don't you come with me?"

Having a room ready didn't mean having a doctor to go along with it. I sat in a windowless cell with teal wallpaper, about the size of a walk-in closet, dressed in a paper gown and dangling my legs over the edge of a padded examination table. The bubble clock on the wall, second hand crawling and minute hand refusing to budge, made me think of Emma. Nicky was the second person in my orbit who had landed in a hospital bed because of Angelo Mancuso. There wasn't going to be a third.

Eventually the wooden door swung open and another nurse, a man in his early twenties with a peach-fuzz mustache and emerald-green scrubs, came in to sort me out. Splinting my fingers was only marginally less painful than breaking them in the first place. Then came the slow, laborious torture of cleaning the burns on my inner wrists, scrubbing the twists of scorched duct tape from my lobster-red skin. He coated them in an ointment that smelled like mint and felt like a coat of fresh snow, before wrapping my forearms in strips of tan gauze.

"What about the other guy?" I asked while he was working on me. "The one I came in with, any idea how he's doing?"

"Still in the operating room, as far as I know." He secured the gauze in place with a tiny metal clasp. "Now, we need to see about keeping you overnight for observation. I'm worried about infection—"

"Nope," I said, tugging off the paper gown, my good hand already reaching for my shirt. "I'm checking out, thanks."

"Sir, you have serious burn damage to your wrists. This isn't like a mild burn from touching a hot pan, okay? You could be facing all kinds of health complications. If nothing else, if you don't get long-term treatment and possibly reconstructive surgery, you're looking at extensive, permanent scar tissue."

I looked down at my wrapped wrists as I pulled on my shirt. Feeling them throb like I'd plunged them into a bucket of ice water. I'd gotten hurt because I'd been careless, shortsighted. Because it had taken me too long to get my head right and realize what I needed to be doing in the first place.

"I earned these wounds," I told the nurse. "Let 'em scar."

Jennifer was my priority now. I had to meet up with her, get right with her, and come up with a battle plan. As I emerged from the ER waiting room and into the fading light of the late afternoon, though, I had a voicemail waiting for me. Caitlin.

"Hey," I said, calling her back, "sorry I've been out of touch. Had a run-in with the Outfit. What's going on?"

"Ecko. We found out where he's been hiding."

"Gimme an address. I'm on my way."

* * *

I called Jennifer on the road. She wasn't picking up—I tried not to worry, which just made me worry more—so I left a message to bring her up to speed. My second call was to the twins.

"Danny!" Justine chirped. "Where are you? Where's Nicky? We've been looking all *over*."

"We got bushwhacked. Nicky's hurt pretty bad. You two need to get over to Sunrise Hospital right now, okay? Look for a detective named Gary Kemper, he'll help you out."

The Gentlemen's Bet was on the way. I pulled into the parking lot and swapped the stolen Mercedes with my rental car. Canton's top hat still sat in the backseat, the black silk brim murmuring hints of a mystery I couldn't begin to unravel.

The address Caitlin had given me was on West Dorrell, a modest apartment complex across the street from a strip mall. Down in the lobby, floored with imitation black speckled marble that made me think of a bowling alley, Caitlin sat on a padded gray vinyl bench by the elevators. The woman beside her, weeping into her hands and held tight in one of Caitlin's arms, wore a rumpled pantsuit with a damp sleeve. A snakeskin attaché case leaned against one of her feet, forgotten. Caitlin's gaze darted to my splinted fingers, but she didn't ask. Not the time for it.

"I was only gone for three days," the woman sobbed. "I should have been here."

"And if you had been here, you'd have likely suffered the same fate." Caitlin's arm was soft, reassuring, but her eyes were hard as chiseled stone as she beckoned me over with her other hand. "Daniel, this is Rebecca. Her husband, Alfred, was one of my prince's subjects."

I glanced over my shoulder, making sure we were alone in the lobby. "Cambion?"

She nodded, sharp. "She returned from a business trip, only to discover that Damien Ecko had moved into her lodgings. He had evidently been making his home here for a few days now."

"He killed him," Rebecca whispered. "Why did he do that? He never hurt anybody. We kept a low profile. We followed the *rules*—"

"Shh," Caitlin said, stroking her hair. "Sometimes there isn't a reason."

I tilted my head at Rebecca, studying her with all of my senses. Nothing special about her, human, no trace of magic in her veins, just another civilian sucked into the crossfire.

"What I don't understand," I told her, "is why he let you live."

"He said...he said he'd just gotten a call from his friends, giving him his next assignment, so he had to leave in a hurry. Then he asked what I'd do if he let me live. I said I wouldn't call the police, I promised—and he...he *laughed* at me. He said he knew about the hound, and calling the real police would probably do more good."

I looked to Caitlin, a question in my eyes.

"Cambion living within my prince's borders," she said, "and mixed couples, all have my card. In the event of an emergency, they know they're to call *me*, not the local authorities."

"He said he wanted me to make the call." Rebecca swallowed

hard, steadying herself. "He wanted the hound to see what he'd done, because that way she'd pass a message on to someone named Faust."

My skin crawled. I already knew the answer, but I had to ask the question.

"What was the message?"

She looked up at me with wet, red eyes, her cheeks stained with tears.

"He wrote it on the wall," she said. "I...I watched him leave. He had a truck."

"A pickup truck?" I asked.

She shook her head. "N-no. A big—a big truck. A semi, with a trailer. I watched from my window. I couldn't move. I couldn't *move*—"

Caitlin pulled her close and murmured in her ear. Her other hand reached out, jangling a ring of keys at me. She tossed them over and I snatched them out of the air.

"Now listen to me," Caitlin told Rebecca, counting out a stack of crisp hundred-dollar bills and pressing them into her trembling hand. "We will take care of everything. You are to find a hotel—a nice one—and get yourself a room for the night. Buy any clothes or toiletries you need on the way. Stay put, and I'll call you in the morning."

"But...but Alfred's body—"

"Will be dealt with. As will his killer. Your union with your husband made you a part of our court, Rebecca. Alfred can't protect you anymore, so Prince Sitri will. Your silence, your loyalty, and your obedience will earn you great rewards. We'll take care of you now. Do you understand?"

Rebecca nodded, silent.

"Good," Caitlin said. "Hell prevails."

Rebecca's gaze dropped to her feet. "Hell prevails," she whispered.

Caitlin patted her cheek. "Go."

Rebecca fumbled for her attaché and stumbled out of the

lobby. Caitlin didn't say another word. She just tapped the elevator button, her back straight as an iron rod, as I stood beside her. The brushed-steel doors rumbled open. She pressed the button for the third floor. The doors closed, penning us in.

"Are you all right?" I asked her.

Caitlin spun and threw her fist against the elevator wall. It hit with the sound of a cannon, steel buckling as the cage jolted on its tethers. She turned, facing the doors again, and took a deep breath.

"No," she said calmly, "I am not 'all right.'"

Every instinct told me it was a good idea to keep my mouth shut right about then. Instead, I put my hand on the small of her back.

"Did you know him?"

"We crossed paths occasionally. Not the point. Daniel...I am charged with the protection of my people. I am my father's left hand on Earth. This world is a hostile and frightening place, and they count on me, they *trust* me, to shepherd them. I swore an oath of duty to keep them safe. And today Damien Ecko made a liar out of me."

The elevator chimed as the doors rolled open. We stepped out into a stubby hallway lit by dim, dusty overheads, the walls lined in bubble-patterned wallpaper that might have been fashionable in the sixties. Brass numbers clung to weathered oak doors. Caitlin glanced left, then right, leading the way up the hall as she hunted for the right apartment.

"Here we are," she said, stopping at 332. "You might want to prepare yourself. I suspect this will be...unpleasant."

I turned the key in the lock, and we stepped into Damien Ecko's house of horrors.

28.

I'd smelled something faint out in the hallway, something like the odor of garbage left out on a hot, sunny day. As the door swung wide, the full force of it choked the breath from my throat. The stench of human decomposition, of rotting meat and leaking bile, a body coming apart under the teeth of nature. Flies were everywhere. I batted one away from my face as we stepped inside, the fat black insect buzzing past my ear. I put one hand over my mouth and struggled to keep my stomach from revolting.

Broken furniture, a shattered coffee table, a framed picture of Rebecca and a smiling man lying in the debris. All the signs of a home invasion—Ecko had forced his way in and gone ten rounds with Alfred, bouncing him off every piece of furniture in the cozy living room. I wanted to imagine Alfred had died in the fight, but I knew he hadn't been that lucky. And there, painted on the wall above a couch with shredded upholstery, waited Ecko's message.

"*Faust. Lighten Your Heart.*"

Caitlin wrinkled her nose as she took in the wreckage, shutting the door behind us. Then she looked at the wall, and I felt the temperature drop.

"I know," I told her. "He's here because of me. It's not your fault this guy got killed. It's mine."

She walked past me.

"It's not about blame," she said. "It's about duty."

We found Alfred in the bedroom. He'd been roped to the bed, spread-eagle, his corpse left pale and bloodless. His arms and legs were a road map of cuts, some fresher than others, skin stained with rivulets of crusted blood.

"He tortured him," Caitlin said.

I frowned. This whole scene wasn't adding up. Killing a cambion to get Caitlin's attention—knowing his insane "message" would get back to me through her—that made sense. But not a damn thing else did.

"I don't think that was the idea," I said. My stomach churned, but I forced myself to get closer. A maggot squirmed from one of the cuts, flopping onto the flower-patterned bedspread. The curiously dry bedspread.

"What would you call this, then?" she asked, pointing to the body.

"I'm not sure yet. Okay, let's do some detective work. Start with the victim. Why him?"

"You know why. Ecko knows about the courts of hell. He *certainly* knows Royce and I—and the entire Order of Chainmen—are hunting for his head, and he knows you and I are connected. Easy enough way to get your attention."

"Sure, but why *this* guy? Who is he?"

Caitlin shrugged. "He worked for Southern Tropics. Under Emma, in the accounting department. No one of note. Why?"

"Can you get access to his personal info? His bank accounts? Travel history?"

She folded her arms across her chest. "Easily. We keep close tabs on our people, even more than usual since the Redemption Choir incident."

"Ecko doesn't have access to that kind of information. There's no way he could know that some Joe Nobody in a midrange apartment is a halfblood in disguise. He was *given* Alfred's name. Check him out. I'll bet you a dinner at Le Cirque that you'll find a Chicago connection in his background."

Caitlin stepped outside of the apartment to make the call, leaving me alone with the dead. I lifted one of Alfred's heavy, clammy arms, studying the faint splotching underneath, then let it fall limp. I was no medical examiner, but I'd seen enough corpses to learn a thing or two. He hadn't been dead all that long. Not enough lividity, the bruising from blood draining to the body's lowest point of gravity, and the few maggots in his wounds were tiny, newborn.

So Ecko had been holing up here since he arrived in Vegas. Keeping Alfred alive until it was time to leave. Cutting on him every now and then, but not with the gusto of a serious sadist. That kind of casual, pointless cruelty didn't fit. Why not do what he'd done to Coop and turn him into an undead slave, another weapon in his arsenal? Bleeding the guy and murdering him felt like a waste of resources. Ecko was crazy, but he wasn't wasteful.

Caitlin poked her head into the bedroom, holding up her phone. "Until Prince Malphas closed the borders and started his pogrom against the local cambion, Alfred was a frequent visitor to the Midwest. He was also quite the gambling addict. Racked up considerable charges at a horse track in Arlington, not far from Chicago."

"And I bet you found some questionable deposits, too," I said. "Like he was taking loans from the kind of guys who break your legs when you can't pay up."

"It appears I owe you dinner," Caitlin said, "though I doubt either of us will have an appetite anytime soon. So, Alfred was in debt to the Chicago mob. They looked into his background and discovered his demonic heritage. Then Angelo Mancuso gave his name and address to Ecko."

"Right, so that's half the puzzle. But not the *important* half. You know what I keep thinking about? The neighbors. This is a big building, lots of folks around. Nobody heard any screaming while Ecko was bleeding this guy?" I pointed to the nearly pristine bedspread. "That's what this is. Not torture. See where the blood trails on his skin stop? Ecko wanted his blood. He was collecting it. Bottling it, maybe. He kept Alfred alive—and pumping blood—until the very end."

Caitlin's eyes narrowed like a cobra's. "To what purpose?"

"That's the million-dollar question. Hold on. I've got a hunch."

I closed my eyes, pushing away the stench and the carnage around me, ignoring the faint tickling sensation of plump flies landing on my skin, buzzing around my ears. I reached out with my psychic senses, glowing violet tendrils licking at the air. I'd had a strange sensation since I walked into the apartment. The world outside the door had suddenly felt muffled, like I'd stepped into a soundproof room. Or a casket.

I opened my eyes. Glanced to my left. Clothes lay scattered across the thin beige carpet, a wardrobe's worth of men's and women's outfits piled in wrinkled heaps. Then I took two quick strides to the bedroom closet, grabbed hold of the wooden knobs, and shoved back the accordion doors.

In the back of the empty closet, a sigil painted in blood covered the plaster wall. It resembled the Egyptian Eye of Horus, with a ragged X blotting it out. The lines of the X were scrawled in a savage, angry hand, yet somehow still precise. A ring of hieroglyphs surrounded the symbol, each one defaced or partially destroyed in a different way.

"The forgotten god," I murmured, "by his name you shall know him not."

"What's that?" Caitlin tilted her head at me.

I gestured at the sigil. "I've seen these glyphs before. Back when we first met, I borrowed an old relic from Bentley and Corman's collection. It's an amulet called the Black Eye. The story goes, it's a holdover from an old Egyptian cult, dedicated to a god who wanted to be forgotten forever. When you wear the Eye, it cuts you off. Severs you from the flow of magic. As far as the universe is concerned, you just...don't exist. I used it to keep Nicky's seer from spying on me while I was working to set you free."

"So this is the trinket, writ large," she mused as she studied the sigil. "Large enough to cloak the area around him, or at least this room and anyone in it, giving him a safe place to make his lair for a few days."

"Ecko's over three thousand years old. Hell, he might have *invented* this spell. This explains it. I tried a tracking ritual, but it didn't work. I thought it was *my* fault it failed. No wonder I couldn't draw a bead on him; he's practically been invisible since the second he rolled into town."

Caitlin stepped into the closet. She drew a finger across the sigil's face, rust-red flakes peeling away from the ivory plaster. She stared at her fingertip with disdain, flicking the flakes away.

"Cambion blood," she said, "is a bit more potent than a human's."

I nodded. "More gas for the engine, if blood magic is your thing. He might not even be able to work this trick with human blood. Oh. Oh shit, Cait—"

"I know." She strode out into the living room, pulling up her speed-dial list as she stood in the wreckage. "He'll need a new base of operations now, and when Alfred's blood runs out, another cambion to drain. I'll have to relocate every local halfblood on my registry and move them into safe houses for the duration. That, and call in the cleaners to take care of this mess."

My hunt wasn't over yet. Rebecca said Ecko had gotten a call, another name on the Outfit's hit list. I followed Caitlin into the living room and prowled through the wreckage.

"Doc Savoy's place just got hit," I told her, "but they used a Molotov. Not Ecko's style. He must be after somebody else."

"Another member of Jennifer's council, no doubt. You've warned her?" Caitlin turned away from me, lifting the phone to her ear. "It's me. Execute a Code Indigo for Las Vegas and outlying, a ten-mile radius. I want all cambion relocated to the Los Angeles safe house. Also, mobilize a cleaning team to my location..."

I fell into my thoughts, picking through the broken furniture and searching for a clue. The Outfit's hit list was getting smaller by the hour. Shangguan Jin was dead; Little Shawn and his gang had defected. The hit on Emma had failed, but by now she'd be a hundred miles underground, out of their reach. Going after Doc

Savoy was the orange in a basket of apples; he wasn't a member of the New Commission. He was absolutely neutral when it came to the Vegas underworld—and absolutely vital.

Maybe that's the idea, I thought, stepping into the kitchen nook. *Cut us off at the knees, take out the people we depend on. If Gary is right, and they're actively recruiting crooked cops, that'd make a lot of sense. Undermine enough of our resources and the Outfit could make it impossible for us to operate in Vegas.*

The fight hadn't spread to the kitchen. It was relatively unscathed, if messy, with junk mail piling up next to a greasy box from some no-name pizza joint.

So who fits the same category as Savoy? Neutral pros, specialists, who'll work with anyone who pays?

There was me, of course, but that was a given. Anybody who needed a safe cracked knew to call Coop, but Coop died in Chicago. Then there was—

I pulled out my phone and hit the autodial for the Love Connection. As soon as I heard a click, the words spilled from my lips on a torrent of held breath.

"Paolo, listen, it's Dan. Lock up and get out of there, *right now*. The Outfit might be sending hitters your way. Head to the East Coast for a few days. I'll call you as soon as it's safe to come home."

No response. Not even the sound of breathing.

"Paolo?"

A soft, amused chuckle rippled over the line.

"Hello, Mr. Faust," Damien Ecko said.

29.

Another dry chuckle filled the silence.

"It's been a while," Ecko said. "I was beginning to think you were avoiding me."

"Let him go, Damien. The only reason you're helping the Outfit is because you want a throwdown with *me*. Let him go, and I'll give you what you want."

"Oh, are we on a first-name basis now?" he said, his voice sharp. "Very well, *Daniel*, I want my life back, my shop back, the bounty lifted from my head, and my reputation restored. Can you do that for me? Can you wave a magic wand and repair all that you destroyed?"

"I don't know. Can you bring my buddy Coop back to life?"

"I had nothing to do with that. Your ill-chosen and traitorous partner shot him. I merely came upon his dying body and put it to good use. You seem determined to paint yourself as some sort of righteous avenger. May I remind you that *you* invaded my home, destroyed my pet, broke into my safe, and stole my belongings? Then, just to add insult to injury, you framed me as a thief. I am the *victim* here, *Daniel*."

"Just tell me what you want. Leave Paolo out of this. You don't have to play the Outfit's errand boy anymore. If you want a fight, I'm ready to oblige."

Ecko's laughter was a harsh, braying sound, like the throaty rasp of a hyena.

"What I want...I've given that a great deal of thought. Originally, I wanted you to make a full confession. An admission before the courts of hell that you framed me for the theft of the Judas coin. Removing the death sentence from my shoulders, and placing it where it rightfully belongs."

"Lighten my heart," I said.

"Indeed. But then I got to thinking. They won't let me go, will they? They'll come up with some reason to keep the hunt going, no matter what."

"You attacked a pair of hounds," I told him. "Doesn't matter if it was self-defense. You go down for that. That's hell's law. I can't help you."

"So. There we are. I have survived upon this Earth for thousands of years, peerless in magic and skill, but now...now I see the last sands in my hourglass finally running down. I might survive for another year, another decade, another century if I'm lucky, but eventually they'll corner me. Hell doesn't forget. Nor does it forgive. So in the time I have left, I've resolved to turn my hand to pleasant work."

"Yeah?" I asked. "Like what?"

The response was a sharp, shrill scream of pain. Not Ecko's. As the cry devolved into muffled whimpers, Ecko put the phone back to his lips.

"Hurting you," he said.

"Damn it, let him *go!*" I gripped the phone with white knuckles, my hand shaking. "This is between you and me. You wanted me, you've fucking *got* me. Just name the time and the place."

"No," he mused, "I don't think so. Murdering you would be a trivial act, barely requiring exertion on my part. It will be far more satisfying to destroy you *before* I end your life. This man is important to you? That's all the motivation I need to do this."

Paolo's scream felt like a bullet in my heart. He shrieked until his breath ran out.

"You brought this upon yourself," Ecko said. "And upon this man, and upon every other life I tear to ribbons before I finally deign to kill you. You started this fight."

196

And in that moment, I realized two things. First, he was right. I'd taken the job, the heist at Ecko's jewelry store, because I needed some quick cash. No noble cause, no better reason than that. I'd started this feud, and all the death, all the chaos that spiraled out from it was on my head alone. Then I'd committed a far worse sin: I underestimated him. I'd done my usual song and dance, the trickster pulling off the impossible and vanishing into the night, never thinking about the consequences farther down the road. And just like the Mourner of the Red Rocks had warned me, my free ride was over.

The second thing I realized was *I didn't care*. I didn't care who had started this fight, I didn't care who the original victim was, and I didn't have time for guilt when there was work to be done. Life wasn't about right and wrong. Life was about me and mine. Forget the forces of hell—the second Ecko used my friends against me, first with Coop and now Paolo, he'd written his own death sentence.

"Sure, I started it," I told him. "And now I'll finish it. Get ready. I'm coming for you."

Caitlin was still on the phone, working out the logistics of making Alfred's body disappear, as I swept from the kitchen. She caught the look in my eyes, and nothing needed to be said. She raised two fingers in a silent benediction, a battle blessing, and sent me on my way.

* * *

The Spark's engine whined as I pushed it to the redline, threading the needle up the highway. I cursed under my breath, one eye on the rearview and watching for cops, as I tried to call Jennifer again. She finally picked up, half a ring before it would have gone to voicemail.

"Hey, sugar," she said, sounding breathless, "got your message. Sorry I've been incognito, hell of a busy day. Outfit boys rolled on that strip club where the Bishops hang out. They pulled a drive-by on the parking lot. Coulda been a lot worse, but Eddie Stone's got a couple of bandannas to hang on the memorial wall. I've been working overtime trying to convince 'em not to bail on us."

"Damien Ecko's got Paolo."

"Right *now*? Shit. Where at?"

"His store, unless he's already moved him. I'm ten minutes away."

"I'm fifteen. All right, I'll load for bear and meet you. Don't do anything reckless till I get there."

Fat chance of that. I thought about Paolo, but all I could see was Coop, after Ecko had gotten done with him. A broken, half-alive creature with milky eyes and sewn lips.

I screeched to a dead stop outside the Love Connection, lurching against the seatbelt as my front wheels bumped the curb. I left the car running, jumped out, and hit the front door with my shoulder, bursting into the store. My eyes squinted in the gloom, the overhead lights shattered and the thin, dirty carpet littered with shards of broken bulbs. They crunched under my feet as I prowled the aisles, slow now, my heart thudding in my ears as I made my way toward the back room. I stood before the door, squared my shoulders, and flung it open.

Ecko was gone. Paolo wasn't. He sprawled on the bare concrete floor next to the smashed remains of his computer gear, his clothes and his flesh torn from a dozen cuts. Fresh blood leaked out around him like an oil spill, filling the dry air with its coppery stench.

His jaw opened, twitching, as his eyes struggled to focus on me. I raced over to him and dropped to one knee at his side as I yanked out my phone and dialed 911.

"I didn't...didn't tell him shit," Paolo croaked.

"Don't try to talk, just stay still," I said. "Hello? Yeah, my friend is hurt. We need an ambulance, fast—"

"He told me...told me he had a soft spot for artists, so he'd let me live."

Paolo held up his trembling hands, gloved in sheaths of congealing blood. On his right, where his fingers used to be, were nothing but ragged stumps gnawed down to the bone. On his other hand, Ecko had only left him his index finger and his thumb. The fingers twitched, hooking like a lobster's claw.

"He'd let me live," Paolo wheezed, and I realized the retching sounds rasping from his throat were an attempt at laughter. He slumped against me, his head against my shoulder, and his eyes drifted shut. Still alive, but fading fast.

Jennifer and her crew were first on the scene. The store filled up with Cinco Calles in brown bandannas, hard-eyed bangers toting machine pistols. They made the hardware disappear when the ambulance arrived, parting like waves to let the paramedics rush out with Paolo on a stretcher. I stood out on the sidewalk and watched the ambulance go. It veered around the corner, out of sight, but I could still hear the siren wailing in the distance. I didn't go back inside. Needed some fresh air. I sat down on the curb.

Jennifer came out alone. I could feel her standing behind me, silent. Then she dropped down on the curb beside me and rested her elbows on the ripped knees of her faded blue jeans. I fumbled for words.

"I'm sorry," I told her. "I wasn't there when you needed me."

"You're here now," she said.

"Yeah. I'm here now."

Jennifer glanced at my splinted fingers. The edges of the gauze binding my wrists and forearms poked out from under the wrinkled sleeves of my shirt. "Got into a scrap, huh?"

"Could have been worse. You should have seen Nicky."

"I called the hospital," she said. "Don't ask me why. Morbid curiosity, maybe. Took some bluffin', but I eventually got a loose-lipped orderly to tell me the 'John Doe' who came in for surgery pulled through. I guess Nicky's still around. Hope he doesn't want his city back. Finders keepers, it's mine now."

"Ours," I said.

She looked at me. One eyebrow lifted, a curious tilt of her head.

"Nicky told me once," I said, "back when the feds were rustling the bushes, about the castle doctrine. You familiar with the concept?"

"Sure." She nodded. "Somebody invades your home, you got the right to blow 'em away."

"He phrased it as more of a...moral imperative. If you don't fight for your home, if you don't fight for what you've got, *with* everything you've got, you deserve to lose it." I felt lead weights on my shoulders weighing me down as I took a deep breath and let it out in a tired sigh. "When I say I wasn't there when you needed me, I don't just mean the meeting I blew off so I could go chasing another clue. All this time, while a hurricane was coming our way, you were putting up sandbags and building a wall while I stood on the sidelines. Staying neutral, thinking I was untouchable, playing it safe. Playing it safe just got Paolo fucking *mutilated*, and that's on me, because I let it happen. No more. I'm done playing it safe."

"Still got a seat for you on the New Commission," she said. "If you want it."

I offered her my good hand.

"I'm all in," I said. We shook on it.

She pushed herself to her feet. "Well, let's rally the troops. Lotta work to be done. Can you fight with your hand like that?"

"Not going to be throwing any punches, but I can pull a trigger just fine. Don't suppose you've got any prescription-strength painkillers on you?"

"C'mon back to my place, I'll hook you up with some Tylenol Three." She smiled, then glanced over at the lime-green Spark. "Let's take my car, though, huh? You can't drive that thing in my neighborhood. I mean, you can, but...you shouldn't."

I grabbed Canton's top hat and tossed it into the backseat of Jennifer's Prius, climbing in on the passenger side. She got behind the wheel and shot a look over her shoulder.

"What's that?"

"Million-dollar top hat," I said. "Beyond that, no clue. The Enemy wants it, though. And the magician who wore that hat back in the forties had a wand with a chip of bone in it, taken from the body of Damien Ecko's first teacher."

"Heck of a coincidence," she said, "if I believed in coincidences."

"Exactly. I don't know, there's some magic clinging to the thing, but I couldn't tell you what it actually does."

"Have you tried wearing it?"

I blinked.

"Well...yeah, of course I did. First thing I tried."

"Liar." Jennifer smirked, pulling on her blue-tinted Lennon glasses as we rounded a corner, driving toward the setting sun. It felt good. On the move, riding with an old friend, making a plan of attack. Maybe everything would work out fine.

Then the strobe of harsh lights in the rearview mirror, from the unmarked police car on our bumper, told me how wrong I was.

30.

A shock of adrenaline hit my veins, telling me it was time for fight or flight. Then I realized the smart play was "none of the above," and forced myself to sit tight while my heart pounded a staccato beat. Your average cop would have no reason to recognize me, much less be looking for me now that I was legally dead. That said, if they ran us in, I was finished. One look at my fingerprints and alarm bells would be flashing from here to Quantico. Jennifer slowed down, pulling toward the side of the road, her lips pursed in a tight and bloodless line. She passed me her chromed .357. I slipped it into the glove compartment, safety off and the grip turned my way so I could get at it fast if I needed to.

They kept us waiting. Eventually, the doors on the sedan behind us swung open, and a couple of men in cheap department-store suits came swaggering our way. Jennifer squinted at the side mirror.

"Vespucci and Ames," she said, her voice low. "They shouldn't be rousting me. They already got their envelope for the month."

I knew them by reputation. They were both vice detectives of the "selectively deaf and blind" variety, willing to look the other way if you slipped them some green and didn't make a nuisance of yourself. A couple of bottom feeders out for a slice of whatever they could get. Vespucci didn't bother pulling his checkered jacket back into place when a gust of hot wind pushed it back, baring his shoulder holster. His partner, in an Afro and shades, stood behind him with his arms crossed and his caterpillar-thick brows furrowed. Jennifer rolled her window down.

"I don't suppose I was speedin'," she said.

"Do we look like fucking traffic cops?" Vespucci asked her. "You're a problem, you know that? We're up to our necks in bull-shit, and you just keep shoveling it on."

"Me?" Jennifer said. "What'd I do?"

"Oh, I don't know, started a goddamn gang war? The brass is all over us. Climbin' up our asses, demanding we squash this thing. I ain't seen my kids since the day before yesterday. I'm sleeping under my desk."

"And if they're all over us," Ames said, "they're all over *you*. We got orders to bring you in."

Jennifer scowled at him. "On what charges?"

"On two counts of who-gives-a-fuck," Vespucci said, "and one count of you're-a-pain-in-our-asses in the first degree. It's protective custody. You've been identified as a 'likely factor in the current state of unrest,' and the brass wants you off the streets until everything blows over."

"That's the deal," Ames added. "You get three hots and a cot, and a room all your own. With bars on the window. As soon as the natives stop banging the war drums, we'll cut you loose."

Jennifer shook her head. "This is *bullshit*. What am I paying you two for, if you can't cover my back with Metro? How am I sup-posed to end this fight if you pull me *out* of it?"

"This *is* us covering your back," Vespucci said. "The brass wanted us to find some actual charges to bust you on, or make up a few. We talked 'em down to protective custody. You telling me you can't steer your little army of bangers from inside a cell?"

"You gonna let me keep my phone?"

The detectives shared a look. Vespucci let out a long-suffering sigh.

"Come along peacefully, don't start any shit," he said, "and I promise we'll 'forget' to search you. Deal?"

Jennifer leaned my way. Her voice dropped to a low murmur.

"Take the car over to my place by the airport. Gabriel should be there—tell him what's up. He'll rally the rest of the Calles, and I'll call you both once I get settled."

"You sure about this?" I asked her.

"Not even a little, but they've got a point. Lot harder for Chicago to take a shot at me this way, and I can still help from inside. Don't you worry, I'll be out in two shakes of a lamb's tail."

They led her over to their car. Uncuffed, but they still put her in the backseat like a perp. I had an ugly feeling, watching them cruise away toward the nearest on-ramp. A feeling that only got uglier as my phone buzzed against my hip. A call from Gary Kemper.

"Is this good news?" I asked.

"Opposite of that. Listen," he dropped his voice. He sounded muffled, as if he was cupping one hand over the phone. "I can't talk too loud. I'm at the precinct. It's not safe here. Word came down the grapevine, words I wasn't supposed to hear, get me? You've been green-lit. You and all your buddies."

"Green-lit by *who?*"

"By the powers that be. Let's just say the Mancuso family is writing a very large and generous check to the mayor's reelection campaign. Whoever you think you've got in your pocket? You don't."

"Your theory," I said as I clambered behind the steering wheel, "about cops on the take, switching sides to work for Chicago—"

"It's not a theory. Chicago just outbid your ass. They're in. Your people are out. They're protected from on high. Your buddies *aren't.*"

I stomped on the gas, tires squealing, the car lurching out into traffic as horns blared behind me. I leaned into the wheel, squinting at the horizon as the sun shimmered down and turned the highway into a branding iron.

"And these dirty cops. Would Vespucci and Ames be among them?"

"Can't prove it, but I'd bet two weeks' pay. Hell, I'd bet a month's. Those two are pirates."

"Thank you," I said. I cradled the phone against my shoulder, both hands on the wheel, swerving hard to sweep around the side of a lumbering semi and dart ahead.

"Faust? What are you doing? What are you gonna do?"

"If I don't tell you," I said, "you don't have to deny anything later."

I hung up on him and tossed the phone onto the empty seat beside me. The screen lit up, buzzing as he called back. I ignored it. The dusty white sedan was just up ahead, Jennifer sitting oblivious in the back while they carted her off to her doom.

I'd told her I was going all in. That I was ready to get off the sidelines and fight for my city. Now I had to prove it. There were certain lines I'd never crossed, the sketchy code that let me look myself in the mirror every morning. Never killing an innocent man, that was one of my rules—and I'd broken that one behind the walls of Eisenberg Correctional to survive.

Not killing cops, that was another part of the code. Then again, that rule was mostly intended for the honest ones.

The sedan took an off-ramp nowhere near a precinct house. They turned onto an industrial corridor lined with squat gray slabs of concrete and half-empty parking lots, an occasional delivery truck rumbling along the narrow strip of asphalt. The detectives apparently hadn't noticed they'd sprouted a tail, or that the car behind them was still moving at highway speed and bearing down on them fast. I scooped up the phone and called Jennifer.

"Yeah, sugar?"

"Hey, Jen. Don't react, just listen. Those two are bent, and not in our direction. They're taking you for a one-way ride. Is your seatbelt on?"

"Always," she said, her voice carefully even. "Safety first."

"Good. Brace yourself, okay?"

"See you soon," she replied.

I swung the wheel left, closing the gap, then veered hard to the right. Bumpers slammed with a screech of buckling metal, the sedan fishtailing wildly as I jolted against the seatbelt and a lance of pain shot down my neck. Behind the wheel, Ames recovered fast, wild-eyed and gesturing to his partner as he hit the gas. I was ready for round two. I pulled out of my lane, then jumped back behind them as a semi rolled by in the other direction, air horn blaring. As soon as we were clear, I swerved alongside the sedan, lining up the nose of the Prius with their crumpled bumper, and swung the car like a batter out for a home run.

The sedan spun out, tires smoking and leaving black streaks on the road, and I jolted to a stop right next to it. One hand clicked the seatbelt release. The other reached for the glove compartment and grabbed Jennifer's gun. I felt the heft of the .357, the cool chrome heavy against my palm as I threw open the door and jumped out. Ames came up from the battered sedan with an automatic in his hand, taking aim. The .357 boomed like a cannon and his head snapped backward, blood and broken bits of skull spattering the sedan's roof as he slumped to the pavement.

Vespucci popped up on the other side of the car. I got off two shots, one going wide and the other catching him in the shoulder. He grunted and clutched his wound as his piece clattered to the ground. He crouched low, fumbling for the fallen gun while I sprinted around the back of the sedan. I stomped on his hand then kicked his pistol under the car, just out of reach.

The detective's face had gone pale. Scarlet lines trickled out between his clenched fingers. He stared up at me in disbelief.

"Jesus, you just...you *killed* him. You can't do that. We're *protected*."

"Not by me." I opened the back door, letting Jennifer out. "Not *from* me. You should have worn your Kevlar vest to work, Detective. Safer that way."

I put the barrel of the .357 to his forehead, pressing hard enough to leave a ring-shaped welt.

"Of course, it wouldn't protect you from a headshot. Now, I've got a few questions. Let's start with this: where were you really taking her?"

"Fuck you," he spat.

Jennifer sighed, casually walking over to crouch beside him. "Aw, sugar, this one's just being ornery. Pain'll do that to a critter. Let's see how bad you winged him."

She tugged back the shoulder of his bloodstained jacket and dug her fingers into the ragged wound. Vespucci howled, his feet thrashing against the broken street. She pulled her hand away and wiped her bloody fingers in his hair.

"That ain't so bad," she told him. "Looks like a clean through-and-through. Reckon it could get worse any second now, though. A *lot* worse."

"Cobalt," he stammered. "We were told to take you to the Cobalt Lounge."

Jennifer gave me the side-eye. "Little Shawn's place. Playboy Killers turf."

"Told by who?" I asked him.

He let out a sputtering laugh. "The powers that be, man. The powers that be. Don't you get it? It ain't just a couple of cops on the take. Mancuso's making deals with everyone from the mayor's office on down. City hall had to make a choice, decide on the lesser of two evils, and they chose Chicago. You got no friends, not anymore. You show your face in a precinct house or a lockup, you're dead. Walk into a municipal building, you're dead. You call for a goddamn mailman and you're gonna get a delivery of lead. It's obvious who's gonna win this fight. We're all just falling in line behind the big dog."

"You made a bad bet," Jennifer said. "How much did they pay you to hand me over?"

"There's a standing bounty. Five Gs for any member of the New Commission who won't change sides. Ten for you."

"Hope you got your money up front."

"Cobalt," I said. "Is Angelo there?"

Vespucci coughed. "Nnh—no. He doesn't bunk with the

plebes. Him and his inner circle are somewhere on the Strip, no idea where, swear to God. But Little Shawn is playing host to the rest of his 'delegation.' Buncha soldiers hanging out in the VIP rooms, waiting for orders."

"How many?"

"Fifteen? Twenty? I didn't count. Plus Little Shawn's gang. More heat than you can handle. Listen, listen, Jennifer, we always had a good, you know, a good working relationship, right? This wasn't personal."

She patted his good shoulder and stood, dusting off her hands.

"You just tried to take me on a one-way ride, darlin'. Hard not to feel a little miffed about that."

Vespucci's gaze swung my way. Staring up the barrel of the .357.

"C'mon, man," he whimpered. "You gotta let me go. I got a *family*—"

"So do I," I told him.

Then I pulled the trigger.

31.

We left the two bodies where they fell, bleeding out alongside the wreckage of their sedan. The Prius's hood was crumpled and leaking wisps of steam, but it was still drivable. The engine faintly rattled as we hopped in and fled the scene of the crime.

Jennifer gripped the wheel, scowling as she stared dead ahead. "The *nerve* of some people. Thinkin' he could pull a stunt like that, then skate. You okay?"

I rolled my left shoulder, wincing. "Little banged up, no big deal. How about you?"

"I'm too pissed off to see straight. Okay, so we found the army, just not the general. We gotta shut this circus down fast and teach a few people who really runs this town."

"Sounds like a call for grossly disproportionate violence," I said. "Sorry about your car, by the way."

"Aw, it's fine. I was thinking about getting one of them Teslas, anyway. Goin' full electric. Better for the environment, y'know?"

We stashed the car at Jennifer's place, a stone's throw from McCarran Airport. She'd bought up an entire tenement block slated for demolition and converted it into an urban fortress. Spotters in Calles colors watched the streets in every direction with high-powered binoculars, the side roads blocked off with rusted-out cars, funneling any would-be invaders into a killing box. I didn't see the snipers in the windows, covering us as we rolled into the courtyard, but I felt their crosshairs on my face.

Gabriel lumbered out to meet us. He was the big man in the

Calles and a big man all around, three hundred pounds and change draped in a tent-sized Lakers jersey. He broke into a relieved smile, pulling Jennifer into a hug. Then he clasped my fist, yanked me close, and thumped my back.

"Good to see you two in one piece." His voice, melodic, almost high-pitched, didn't match his massive frame. "Word just came down from Eddie Stone and the Bishops. Couple of *pendejos* with badges snatched their number-two guy right off the street. They found him in an alley, carved up like a turkey."

"We got a police problem," Jennifer said. "Scratch that, we got an everything problem. Good news is, we found out where Chicago's hitters are holing up."

Gabriel clapped his hands. "Sweet deal. Let's mount up and blaze these chumps, get this shit over with before suppertime."

"They've got numbers," I said. "Their guys, plus Little Shawn's entire crew. More importantly, Angelo isn't there. We can kill his soldiers all day long, but he'll just call for reinforcements. To kill this beast, we've gotta lop the head off."

"We need a meeting," Jennifer said. "Every loyal member of the Commission we've got left. All hands on deck."

Gabriel shook his head. His fingers stroked his sculpted goatee.

"That ain't gonna be easy, mama. Way things are now, these fools ain't setting foot on the street without at least ten dudes backing 'em up. Hell, I wouldn't leave without five myself. That many people in one place is gonna draw the bad kind of attention."

I racked my brain thinking of places we could gather and still keep a low profile. The Silk Ranch, Emma's rehabbed brothel, was an obvious choice: outside the city, far from prying eyes. *Too* far, though. It was a long and winding drive into the desert, miles outside the Clark County limits, and we didn't have that kind of time. Besides, Emma had probably figured out I hadn't taken her daughter to the safe house by now, which wasn't going to put me on her list of favorite people. I kept thinking; there had to be a place where we could meet in secrecy.

Or did there? Maybe it was my contrarian streak, but my thoughts started to run in the opposite direction.

"Vespucci said Angelo and his inner circle are hiding out on the Strip."

"Yeah?" Jennifer said. "What about it?"

"Forget hiding. I think it's time for a show of strength."

*   *   *

"Margaritaville," Jennifer stared at the model seaplane dangling from the rafters, the faux palm trees and long tropical bar. "We're holding a meeting of the Vegas underworld, and you rented out Margaritaville."

"You're damn right," I said.

To be fair, it wasn't my first choice, but finding a place that would cater a private party on short notice wasn't easy. We stood at the heart of the Strip, with a balcony overlooking the bumper-to-bumper traffic on Las Vegas Boulevard. The place had history; it felt like a hundred years ago, but this was where my family had come together to prepare for our first showdown with Lauren Carmichael and her corporate cult. Now here we were all over again, drafting battle plans.

Gabriel brought a pack of Calles soldiers, decked out in bandannas and street gear. "You want they should dress like civvies?" he had asked me. "Keep it low profile?"

"Colors," I told him. "Let everybody know who they're representing. Low profile will make us look weak, like we're hiding from the Outfit. Screw that. Let's get *loud*."

Speaking of loud, I heard the Blood Eagles delegation before I saw them, a dozen custom Harleys rumbling down the boulevard in tight formation. Riding heavy iron and carrying it too, packing heat under their leathers. Winslow led his men into the restaurant past the increasingly nervous waitstaff. The grizzled biker, built like a lumberjack, squeezed my hand in a vise grip and slapped my arm.

"Camping out in the open, daring those Chicago pricks to take a shot at us?" he said. "Brother, we almost bailed on this mafia bullshit altogether, but this is our kind of fun."

"Stick around." Jennifer threw her arm around his burly shoulders. "Fun ain't even started yet."

Eddie Stone made the scene with a posse of Bishops in blue and black. He flashed a gold-toothed smile and kissed Jennifer's hand. A few unsteady glances shot across the restaurant—the Bishops and the Calles had been feuding before Jennifer squashed that beef—but the mood lightened up once I announced we'd paid for an open bar. More bangers filled up the room, sporting red and white to represent the Fine Upstanding Crew.

At least for now, Chou Yong had taken up the reins of the local 14K in the wake of his boss's death. He looked more composed than the last time I'd seen him; he and his fellow Triads dressed in tailored black suits, red neckties, and brass lapel pins. The Inagawa-kai, on the other hand, didn't bother with uniforms. The yakuza dressed sharp, like fashion models out for a night on the town, sleeve tattoos poking out from beneath stylish cuffs.

An unexpected face was the last to arrive, her scarlet hair worn in a French braid and tossed over one shoulder. Caitlin's fingers trailed across the back of my neck, sending a tingle down my spine.

"Emma's in no shape to travel," she explained, "but she was absolutely insistent that Southern Tropics have a representative on hand. So here I am. Incidentally, she's a bit miffed at you right now. And by 'miffed' I mean if you weren't my consort, she'd most likely feed you your own spleen."

"C'mon, Cait, Melanie is safer with Bentley and Corman than she would be anywhere else. The kid's almost eighteen. She needs to make her own choices."

"I happen to agree. Emma and Melanie have a great deal to work out together, I think. That said, for the sake of my friendship with Emma, and the well-being of your internal organs, do me a favor and *don't* get in the middle of it."

"All right, all right, I'll stop being helpful."

She favored me with a smile. "That's all I ask."

The bartender was sweating bullets. I ordered a margarita and tipped him a folded twenty. The lime and salt was savory, a wash of tartness on my tongue. I surveyed the crowded restaurant while I drank. Uniting this lot, all under one roof, and convincing them to work together was an accomplishment. Keeping the peace was a bigger one. I couldn't take any credit for that—Jennifer had done all the hard work. Tonight, though? Tonight was all on my shoulders.

"You about ready?" Jennifer asked me.

"Ready as I'm going to be."

Jennifer pulled the manager aside and handed her a small wad of cash.

"Do me a favor, hon. We need to have a candid discussion with our fellow partygoers. How about you take your whole staff outside on an extended smoke break? We won't break nothin' while you're gone, I promise."

She didn't need to be told twice. Once the civilians had cleared out, Jennifer gave me the thumbs-up.

"Excuse me," I called out. "Can I have your attention, please?"

Barely anybody looked my way, my voice lost in the din of conversation. Then Jennifer put her fingers to her lips and let out an ear-piercing whistle. A hush fell over the room.

"*Thank* you." She patted my back. "He's gonna say something. Do me a favor and listen up."

Every eye looked my way. Waiting, expectant. I tossed back a swallow from my margarita glass and cleared my throat.

"Chicago thinks they've already got us beat," I said. "And why wouldn't they? They're hitting us where we live, and hitting hard. They've got the mayor's office on their side, the cops in their pocket, and they're ready and willing to throw their own guys into the meat grinder by the dozens if that's what it takes to run us out of Vegas."

I spread my open hands wide.

"I say, let's oblige them. I picked this place for the meeting—right in the heart of the action, right in front of the world—to send a message. That this is *our city*. And starting tonight, we're taking it back."

A sea of hard-eyed stares. A few whispers, people jostling shoulders and nodding my way.

"We know that the bulk of the Outfit's forces are scattered through Little Shawn's territory. Most of them holing up at the Cobalt Lounge. Taking out Angelo Mancuso's soldiers won't end this war—he'll just call up more from Chicago—but that'll buy us some time to regroup. Now, I've put together a plan of attack. If we all work together and play our parts, we should be able to—"

A chair clattered back. One of the Bishops stood up, a lanky kid with a smirk. "Yo, who the fuck *is* this dude?"

And just like that, he took command of the room. He laughed, sizing me up as he gestured my way.

"Seriously, man. Comin' in here, calling shots, acting like somebody appointed you General Patton or some shit. Who *are* you?"

I had a plan. Past tense. It was a pretty good one, too. But as I took in the room, the temperature going ice cold and resentful murmurs simmering, I realized I'd made a serious mistake. I was used to working with my family, my crew. People who knew and trusted each other with their lives. Most of this room didn't know me beyond a name and a whisper, and I was demanding their respect when I hadn't done anything to earn it.

"You want to know who I am?" I asked him. "You really want to know?"

He folded his arms, looking a little nervous, but he didn't sit down.

"Yeah. I wanna know. I think we all wanna know."

"I'll tell you, then. I'm the guy."

I cast a slow gaze across the restaurant, making sure I had everybody's attention.

"I'm the guy who's going to walk into the Cobalt Lounge, all alone, no backup, and put a bullet in Little Shawn's head."

32.

The kid from the Bishops sat down, shoved back into his chair by the weight of my boast. Hard looks turned to surprise, curiosity, eagerness. Up front, one of the Calles sitting next to Gabriel leaned in and muttered, "This motherfucker is *loco*."

Gabriel grinned. "*Yeah* he is. Just watch, he'll do it, too."

I felt like I was out on the schoolyard, swearing to my classmates that I was going to seduce a teacher or fist-fight the principal. I'd bought a little grudging admiration just by making the claim. Of course, the problem with big talk is that you have to follow it up with big deeds, or all that admiration vanishes into thin air.

So. I'd pledged to walk into a gang stronghold, all by myself, and assassinate a traitor. Oh, and come out alive and in one piece afterward. That part was important too. Great idea. I would have felt more confident if I had any clue how I was going to pull it off. For now I rolled with the momentum, working the crowd.

"Now that we've established who I am to your complete satisfaction, maybe I can keep going? Yeah? Thank you. Let's talk about who *you* are. I'm looking around this room, and you know what I *don't* see? A single weak link. Individually, every crew represented in this room is the best of the best. Together? We're unstoppable."

I set my drink down and walked the floor in front of the bar, heads swiveling to follow me.

"The Outfit knows that. That's why they've been picking at

us, trying to kill us or turn us one by one and break this alliance apart. So I say we show them what a united front looks like. Tomorrow we do recon. Tomorrow night, come sunset, we ride. And we give them such a bloodbath that they'll wish they'd never *heard* of Las Vegas. We'll chase Angelo and his boys all the way back to Chicago, kick in *their* front door, and burn the place down around their ears."

Winslow raised his bottle of beer and shouted, "Let's kick some ass!"

That drew a rowdy cheer from his brothers-in-arms. The righteous glee turned viral, rippling across the room, bangers throwing up hand signs, hooting, stomping their feet. As I drank in the raucous energy, basking in the chaos, I could almost believe we were going to win. I waited until they simmered down to lay out the plan—or at least the parts that could still be salvaged, now that I'd volunteered for a suicide mission.

As the meeting broke up, Jennifer and Caitlin cornered me.

"You're the guy, huh?" Jennifer's voice was dry as sawdust. "The guy who's going to walk onto Little Shawn's turf and take him out in front of his buddies, all by yourself."

"Honestly." Caitlin bristled. "Did you pause to think, at all, before you opened your mouth?"

"I can honestly say I spent at least three seconds thinking about it. Maybe four. Look, I've spent my entire career either working under Nicky Agnelli's thumb or freelancing on the weirder fringes of the underworld. Jen, these guys *know* you. By comparison I'm practically an outsider. I had to give them a reason to respect me, so they'd fall in line."

Jennifer sighed. "You're not wrong, but I think we coulda found an easier way."

"Could we have done it tonight, here and now? Time is not on our side."

"So," Caitlin asked, "how are you going to pull off this impossible feat?"

I shrugged. "Cheat, obviously."

"Obviously," they said in unison, sharing a sidelong glance.

Winslow swaggered by, nursing a fresh bottle, and I waved to catch his attention.

"Hey, any chance you could open up the arsenal for me?" I asked. "I'm going to need a little extra firepower."

"You and half the room. Come by the garage tomorrow morning. I'll hook you up. And, ah—cash only, champ."

Jennifer put her arm around my shoulder.

"Put it on my tab," she told him. "Anything for...*the guy*."

Winslow snickered and walked away. I leaned my head against Jennifer's arm.

"Assuming I survive tomorrow night, I'm not living that down anytime soon, am I?"

"You'll be fine." Caitlin arched one eyebrow, her voice deadpan. "No obstacle is insurmountable...for *the guy*."

* * *

Bone-tired, pride only slightly more bruised than usual, I trudged up the steps to the second-floor garret over the Scrivener's Nook. I figured their couch was still taken, but I wanted to check on everybody before I found a place to crash for the night. Corman answered the door, a quizzical look on his face.

"Hey, kiddo. I got a call from David Gosselin. He's trying to find you. Sounded pretty pissed off."

"I can explain that."

He glanced down, to the top hat cradled in my hands.

"He said you stole his hat and he wants it back. Said that hat cost him a million bucks."

"He should have taken better care of it, then," I said.

"See, that's what I told him."

He waved me inside. Over on the threadbare couch, in front of a fat old box TV tuned to CNN, Bentley and Melanie sat side by side.

"All right," Bentley was saying, "now here's the crucial move. When you take the card back from me, palm it like I showed you, and put it on the *bottom* of the deck, face up."

Melanie held a deck in her hands—Bicycle Dragon Backs, just like mine—and palmed the top card. Crude technique, but the kid had a little raw talent.

"Like this?"

"Perfect," Bentley said, smiling proudly.

"What is this?" I wandered across the cluttered living room. "You taking on a new apprentice?"

"Mm, after how the last one turned out, I'm not sure that's a good idea." Bentley winked.

"I guess my mom's pretty pissed at both of us," Melanie told me. "Sorry."

"Hey, let me worry about me. Not your fault." I held up the hat. "So, I've got a mystery for my two favorite magical scholars. This hat belonged to a showman-slash-sorcerer named Howard Canton."

Bentley sat up straight, eyes wide. "Canton the Magnificent? He's a legend. An underrated one, but his stage technique and his occult work were both leagues ahead of their time."

"Well, a lot of bad guys—I mean, worse ones than us—are looking for this hat. And it's got some weird secondhand connection to Damien Ecko, too. Apparently Canton's wand was crafted with a bit of bone from Ecko's first teacher. No such thing as coincidences, etcetera. I can sense some old magic clinging to the hat, but I've got no idea what it does or what it's for."

Corman shambled into the kitchen nook, rummaging in the fridge. He looked back at me over the refrigerator door. "Did you try wearing it?"

"Of *course* I—" I stopped, sighed, and put the hat on. I waved my hands theatrically. "Ta-da! Presto. Abracadabra."

Nothing, not even a tingle. Bentley tilted his head at me, while Melanie put her hand over her mouth to conceal a smirk.

"As fond as I am of the classics," Bentley said, "there may be a reason those went out of style."

"You look like a total dork," Melanie added.

"Yeah," I said, taking off the hat, "but not a mystically enlightened dork."

Corman cracked open a bottle of Bud and leaned against the doorway. "Leave it with us for a couple of days. We'll do some digging, see what we can figure out. Speaking of Ecko..."

"He's lying low. Turns out he's got a technique for going invisible. Not literally, but as far as tracking spells go, he might as well be on the other side of the world. Thing is, he needs a special ingredient, and Caitlin's making sure he can't get any more of the stuff. So it's only a matter of time before I can use that amulet Emma ripped out of his chest to track him down and finish this."

"What does he need?" Melanie asked.

"A certain...kind of blood."

She caught my meaning and her smile faded. "Oh."

"Hey, you're safe. No worries, okay? Ecko doesn't know about this place, or my connection to Bentley and Corman. No reason he'd even think to come here."

The sound of splintering wood spun me around as a rotting fist punched a hole through the apartment's front door.

The door blasted open. The creature that lurched in, one crooked arm clutching at the air, had been a living woman once. I wasn't sure what had taken her life—a car accident, maybe—but it had left her corpse a ravaged, twisted ruin. Her nearly severed jaw dangled on a ropy tendon, one crushed shoulder hunched forward, raw bone jutting from the split skin of her hip. Her injuries didn't slow her down or steal any of her supernatural strength—Ecko could command the dead to serve him no matter what shape they were in.

"Behind me!" I shouted as the dead woman limped into the living room. I wasn't sure what I was going to do, though. My cards were useless against Ecko's puppets, I didn't have a gun, and Bentley and Corman weren't the kind of people who stockpiled weapons in their home.

The silken brim of the top hat, almost forgotten in my hand, pulsed. The zombie's head snapped my way, sightless eyes homing in on it.

A shiver of magic rippled from the hat. It felt like I'd brushed up against something old and powerful, some alien sentience, and it had responded in kind. Allowing me to feel what it felt. Whatever was inside the hat *recognized* Ecko's handiwork. And hated it, hated it with enough passion to ignite a dying sun. The feeling was mutual.

A rasping hiss escaped the dead woman's throat like steam from a boiling kettle as she staggered toward me.

"Cormie," Bentley called out. "Bedroom closet! Get my ritual box from the top shelf!"

As the creature moved in on me, clearing the doorway, Corman darted past it and raced up the hall. I heard the closet door slam open. Gnarled fingers clawed for me, swiping the air as I stumbled, fell, and scrambled backward on my hands to escape.

Melanie swooped in. Her eyes were blobs of runny yellow and pus white, face alight with blue butterfly-wing veins, and she threw a punch at the base of the zombie's spine. Bones crackled as the dead woman wheezed, spun, and flung a brutal open-handed slap that caught Melanie across the cheek. Melanie grunted and fell, hitting the sofa, tumbling down and thumping her forehead against the shag carpet. She groaned and pressed her hands to her face.

She'd bought me time to get back on my feet, just as Corman burst into the living room with an overstuffed shoe box in his arms. Bentley scurried to meet him, tossing the lid to the floor and rummaging through the box while I played matador with the zombie. I waved the hat in the creature's face, keeping it focused on me, leading it in a slow, deadly dance around the room.

Bentley held up a glass vial, filled with brick dust and something that sparkled like shavings of silver under a hot desert sun. He crouched down beside the wall, tapping out the powder and drawing a four-foot line on the carpet.

"A derivative of marrowgoode powder, mixed with Mama

Margaux's spirit-warding dust," he murmured. "Potent against spirits and lower forms of the infernal, and *should* have the same effect on the risen dead, at least from an alchemical standpoint, assuming Paracelsus's Constant is correct and Heinrich Agrippa wasn't a *complete* quack—"

I ducked under a frantic swing, broken fingernails jabbing for my eyes. "Bentley! A little help here, please?"

"Right, right—try to lead it over the line of dust!"

I jogged sideways, waving the hat, taunting the dead woman. She lunged toward me—and stopped short at the line of dust, as if she'd run headlong into an invisible wall. The creature's face twisted in confusion.

Behind it, Melanie groaned as she pushed herself up on her elbows. Unable to get at me, the zombie spun and focused its attention on fresh prey.

33.

Melanie was still stunned from the hit and the fall, her hair sticky, matted, a trickle of blood leaking down her neck. She didn't see the dead woman shambling her way. She wasn't going to get up in time.

I ran between her and the zombie, grabbing Melanie by the shoulder and hoisting her to her feet. I felt the dead woman's fetid breath on the back of my neck, heard her rattling wheeze as she reached for me—

—and the thing went down in a heap of snapping bones as Corman tackled it head-on, throwing himself into the fight. He hit the floor alongside it, rolling clear and scrambling on hands and knees to get away as the infuriated creature thrashed and kicked. Corman gasped, getting up on one knee, both hands clutching the small of his back.

Bentley crouched over the carpet a few feet away, intent on his work as he drew a second line in glittering dust. "Almost done!" he shouted.

I waved the hat to catch the dead woman's attention, bringing her toward me again, while Melanie darted over to help Corman back to his feet.

"Okay," Bentley told me, "bring her back over this way. Careful! Don't scuff the lines with your shoes."

Easier said than done. I backpedaled as fast as I could, neck craned to watch the floor behind me. Bentley had drawn a corral of dust, extending from one wall, then making a hard turn, three sides of a box. I led the zombie into the heart of the trap. She bumped the invisible wall again and turned, just as Bentley poured out the final line behind her and sealed her in.

The dead woman staggered, bumping forward, stumbling back, arms scrabbling at a barrier she couldn't touch. Penned in, at least for the moment. I raced over to Corman and Melanie.

"Are you two okay?"

Melanie winced, pressing her fingers to the back of her head. They came away wet. "I think I'm all right. It's just bleeding a lot."

"We have a first aid kit in the bathroom." Bentley gently took her by the shoulder and steered her past the flailing zombie, up the hall. Corman clutched his hands against the small of his back, taking deep breaths with his eyes squeezed shut.

"Take it from me, kiddo, don't get old. Getting old *sucks*."

"Hell of a tackle, though."

"Yeah, and I'm gonna be paying for it. My back ain't as strong as it used to be."

"Anything I can do?"

He nodded. "Bring me the heating pad from the hall closet. And my beer."

I got Corman more or less comfortable on the couch, but my thoughts were racing, miles away. How had Ecko found this place? He was getting his intel from the Outfit, and they didn't know about Bentley and Corman, so how did he? Exhausted as I was, fixing this mess wouldn't wait—and that started with finding a permanent solution for the furious dead woman trapped in the living room.

"I'm gonna run downstairs," I told Corman. "Need to see if the coast is clear. We've gotta get the three of you someplace safe for a few days. Just until I deal with Ecko."

I jogged down the stairs. The street-side door at the bottom had suffered the same fate as the one above. Ecko's pet had smashed her way through, littering the foyer with shards of broken glass. I pushed open the door and stepped out onto the sidewalk, tasting something funny on the night air. The scent of frankincense, and some exotic herbal oil.

A shadow lunged from the alley, and withered hands clamped down on my throat with crushing strength. An autopsy patient in a blood-smeared hospital gown, his cranium sawed open. Black flies nestled on the exposed, rotten gray meat of his brain, laying their eggs. The fingers clenched, cutting off my air, dropping me to my knees as scarlet flecks flooded my blurring vision. My throat strained. I felt the cartilage about to buckle like a cardboard tube under the dead man's merciless grip.

Then a dark hand landed on his shoulder and a voice barked, "Baron says *sit*."

Something gusted past me, like a ghost on gossamer wings, and the walking corpse crumpled lifeless to the pavement.

I coughed, wheezing, rubbing my sore throat. Mama Margaux—a pillbox cap perched on her cornrows, the neckline of her midnight-blue dress laden with copper and pewter amulets—held out a hand and pulled me to my feet.

"That evil man's in town, leadin' a parade of the dead, and I'm not the first person you call?" She shook her head at me. "*Ou se yon moun sot.*"

I didn't speak Creole, but the tone of her voice was all the translation I needed. Once I caught my breath, I spread my hands helplessly.

"I've...I mean...it's been a *really* busy couple of days."

Margaux crossed her arms and stared me down.

"Mm-*hmm.*"

"Look, just...hold the door, or what's left of it, okay? Can't leave this thing out on the street."

I got my arms under the corpse's shoulders, trying to ignore the stench of rot, the flies that swarmed my face, and lugged the dead weight into the vestibule one aching foot at a time.

"There's another one in the apartment," I told her. "It's penned in, but still moving."

"On it," she said, sauntering up the stairs ahead of me.

Once the dead woman had been laid to her final rest, left in her pen of dust where she'd fallen, we all clustered in the tiny kitchen nook while Bentley put on a pot of coffee.

"One thing I don't get," I said after bringing Margaux up to speed. "How did you know Damien Ecko was in town?"

She looked at me like I'd asked why water is wet.

"The *loa* told me. That man is an abomination. The things he does are an abomination. They want him"—she snapped her fingers twice, whipping her hand back and forth—"*gone*. Just haven't been able to find him, not for lack of trying."

"He's got a spell for that. His ingredients are running out, though. He'll have to surface soon. Surface or leave town, and I don't think that's an option."

"Thought as much. So then I tried my hand at finding his creations. They give off a...a stench. They must be invisible at his side. Can't find the nest. But when he sends them out on errands, they light up the city if you've got the nose to sniff 'em out."

"Glad you did," I said. "What's bothering me is that he found *this* place. I don't know how he pulled it off."

Margaux knitted her brows. "You said you had something of his?"

I handed her the blue-glazed amulet, wrapped up tight. She unfolded the tissue and scowled at the stone Emma had torn from Ecko's chest.

"You were gonna track him with this?"

"That was the idea. It's been buried under his skin for a few thousand years. It's basically part of his body. You can't ask for a better sympathetic link. Like attracts like."

She handed it back to me.

"Uh-huh. Which is how he found *you*. You said it yourself; this is a part of his body. He's using that link. Wherever you carry that little stone, he knows."

"So he followed me here, put two and two together, and put a target around your necks." I slumped back against the kitchen counter. "This was my fault. Damn. I'm sorry."

"Nonsense," Bentley said. "I suggested you try it, and the risk didn't even occur to me. I think we can share the blame evenly."

Melanie curled her bottom lip. She stared at the amulet like it was radioactive.

"And besides, if my mom hadn't given it to you, if he'd followed her to that hospital room..." She left the rest unspoken.

I tapped my fingernail against the stone falcon's wing.

"All right. So now we know. And that's good, because Ecko doesn't *know* we know."

Bentley gave me a worried look. "You're not throwing it away?"

"Hell no. As long as I'm not going someplace we can't let Ecko know about, like the Tiger's Garden or Caitlin's penthouse, this sucker is staying right in my pocket. I want him to think I'm oblivious, and he can track me down whenever he wants."

"Risky play," Corman said.

"Risky, but this is how we'll draw that bastard out of hiding. There's one other thing I need." I looked Bentley's way. "I have to borrow the Black Eye."

"That...wretched *thing* is downstairs, in storage. I'll dig it out for you."

"Thanks. Ecko's got a way to go invisible whenever he wants and slip under the radar. Now I will, too. You three need to get clear for a while. Corman, do you still have that timeshare in Orlando?"

"Unfortunately," he grumbled, shooting a look at Bentley.

"Well, go soak up the Florida sun for a few days. Visit Epcot Center or something. I'll call you as soon as Ecko's been dealt with. Melanie, you need to go be with your mom and her people right now. They'll be able to keep you safe until this blows over."

"I'd really, *really* rather not."

"I know," I told her. "But she's worried about you, and she loves you. Look at it this way: making your own choices is only half of what it means to be an adult."

She gave me a dubious look. "What's the other half?"

"Doing stupid shit you hate. For some people, it's putting up with a crappy nine-to-five job. For others, it's going head-on against a three-thousand-year-old necromancer who mummified himself. For you, it's putting up with your mom's obnoxious coworkers for a couple of days."

"When you put it that way," she said.

"Right? Bentley and Corman can drop you off on their way to the airport. Obviously I can't follow either of you, since I've got Ecko breathing down the back of my neck. Shoot me a text when you get where you're going, so I know you're safe."

Bentley handed Melanie a deck of cards.

"Besides," he told her, "you need time to practice that palming technique. Get it perfect, and I promise—next time we meet, I'll teach you the oil-and-water routine."

Her face lit up, and she clutched the deck like a talisman.

"What about my part?" Margaux asked.

"You? You're my secret weapon, my ace in the hole. Which means I need to stay far, far away from you until it's go time, so Ecko can't use me to hunt you down. Just wait for my call."

I didn't like isolating myself from my family and friends, but it was the safest choice. Well, safest for everyone but me. I thought about Nicky and Paolo, both of them languishing in different hospital rooms, one a victim of the Outfit's greed and another the victim of Ecko's vengeance. I wanted to check in on them, but we were well past visiting hours and the lump of blue stone in my pocket felt like a lead weight against my hip. Anywhere I went from this point forward, Ecko could—and would—be following. I couldn't expose anyone else to that kind of danger.

But soon he'd run out of cambion blood. And with his tarnished soul bared to the winds of magic, and mine hidden under the shroud of the Black Eye, it would be time to turn the tables.

34.

I spent the night in a cheap room at the Karnak, halfway up the black-glass pyramid. Ecko knew I did, too, thanks to the blue amulet snug in its nest of tissue on the nightstand. When I finally slept, I slept light. It wasn't like he could bring a platoon of zombies into a casino—at least, I didn't think he was *that* crazy—but nothing was stopping him from paying me a personal visit.

Calculated risk. I figured he wanted to hurt me more than he wanted to kill me, at least for now. And since that meant going after the people I cared about, I had to gamble that he'd hold back, bide his time until I gave him another target.

I was on the move before dawn. Out on the highway and rolling south, toward the outskirts of Vegas. I pulled over a few blocks before my destination and walked the rest of the way, leaving Ecko's amulet in the car.

The end of the line was the Sunset Garage, standing in the shadow of an overpass. Dead neon rimmed the pillar-mounted sign out front, the faded plastic showing a vintage Studebaker under a glowing sun. Down on the street, where the air smelled like diesel and dust, a pair of mastiffs in spiked collars snarled and hurled themselves against a barbed-wire fence.

Inside the open garage bay, a few of Winslow's Blood Eagles performed surgery on the open belly of a Harley Fat Boy, power tools whining over the tinny guitar rock that blared from a radio on a cluttered shelf. Winslow looked over from a machine lathe and gave me a tired wave.

"Early bird gets the best worms," he told me. I followed him to a tarp in the corner of the garage. He hauled it aside, then tugged a rope tied to a ring in the floor. A panel groaned back to expose a ladder that plunged down into the dark below.

Winslow's real business was in the cellar. He clicked on an industrial light, the fat bulb dangling in an orange plastic cage, and shed a hot glow across the wire racks that ringed the concrete walls. It was a gunslinger's paradise, everything from six-shooters to sleek assault rifles modified for full-auto rock and roll. Winslow spread his hands wide, inviting me to browse.

"You in the mood for an expert opinion?" he asked me.

"Always."

"Well, my first opinion is, you're a goddamn lunatic."

"Duly noted," I said.

"But if you're really gonna walk onto Little Shawn's home turf and take him out, I'm thinking you wanna go with the shock-and-awe approach. Hit the room loud and nasty, get the job done before they even see you coming, and leave any survivors pissing their pants."

"Sounds like a plan." I looked to one empty corner of the cellar. "Don't suppose you've still got that old flamethrower lying around?"

Winslow gave me an odd look. "Funny, I had that damn thing forever, just collecting dust. Sold it yesterday, to a brand-new client. Weird chick."

A sneaking suspicion tugged at the back of my brain. A curious itch I couldn't help but scratch.

"This 'weird chick,' she wasn't a blonde with short, mussy hair, was she? Wearing a black suit and a man's necktie?"

"Yeah," Winslow said. "How'd you know?"

So Harmony Black was in town. And now she had a Vietnam-era backpack flamethrower. Great.

"Just a hunch. You know she's a federal agent, right?"

He snorted. "Not yesterday, she wasn't. She wasn't looking to put anybody under arrest. *Underground*, more like."

Nothing to do with me, I told myself, using it as a mantra to push my worries aside. I hoped I was right. Studying the weapons kept my mind busy, my thoughts drifting back to Damien Ecko. I remembered Halima's warning, telling me there was only one sure way to bring the necromancer down. "Got a funny question for you."

"Pardon me if I don't laugh," Winslow said. "I've got a notoriously deficient sense of humor. Comes from a bad childhood."

"If I needed to blow up a chunk of stone, roughly the size of a human heart, and I was probably only going to have time to get a single shot off...you got anything that can handle that?"

"A chunk of stone the size of a human heart," he echoed. "No, I'm not even gonna ask. But sure, easy. Got a fifty cal that'll put a fist-sized hole in an up-armored engine block, if you're a good enough shot. Stone ain't no thing at all. Can you do it at range?"

I shook my head. "I wish, but I have a feeling this is going to be up close and personal."

He thought about it, rubbing the stubble on his weathered cheeks, then nodded.

"I know just what you need. An oldie but a goodie."

The weapon he chose, gingerly taking it down from the rack and passing it over to me, looked like something a stagecoach guard would tote in an old western. A sawed-off shotgun, its varnished maple stock inlaid with filigreed brass. Two hammers, two side-by-side triggers, and two fat barrels that looked big enough and deep enough to swallow the world.

"This here's Bessie," Winslow said. "Now, Bessie's not much of a charmer, but she's a loud little lady with two very strong opinions. Opinions which, when expressed at close range, will end just about any argument."

I curled my fingers around the shotgun's grip, feeling its weight, cradling it in both hands.

"I think I'm in love," I said. "Is she single?"

"Jenny said she's paying for whatever you want, so if you like her, you're Bessie's new steady beau."

There's something to be said for the march of progress. Back when Ecko transformed himself into a monster, gunpowder hadn't been invented yet, and bows and arrows wouldn't have put much of a chip in his heart of stone. The modern world brought new solutions to old problems.

I couldn't fool myself into letting my guard down or thinking this was going to be easy. Ecko hadn't lived this long by making dumb choices, and maneuvering him into a spot where I'd even have a *chance* to bring him down was going to take all my wits and more than a little magic. But at least now I had a shot. Two of them, actually, nestled down inside Bessie's twin barrels. They were the only shots I was going to get, so I had to make each one count.

*   *   *

Winslow set me up with everything else I needed for that night, packing it all up in an overstuffed black Adidas duffel bag. Everything except the last item in my new arsenal, riding in a Velcro sheath strapped to my ankle: a punch blade with a six-inch spike, forged from a single piece of black plastic.

"This here's composite plastic," Winslow told me, "a fiberglass blend. It don't hold an edge, so don't try to cut with it. And don't be surprised if the blade breaks off right inside the gut of the first punk you shiv with the damn thing. What it *will* do is get through a metal detector, easy peasy. Consider it a weapon of last resort."

While I was getting armed up, Jennifer led the recon charge. Most of her street dealers were college kids with beat-up second-hand rides or pizza delivery cars. Easy enough for them to cruise around Little Shawn's turf without drawing notice, taking the temperature of the street. Shawn's set wasn't hard to spot: the Playboy Killers rocked purple and gold and patrolled like an army preparing for a siege. Ready to kill and die for four measly blocks of low-rent Vegas real estate.

At the heart of Shawn's fiefdom lay the Cobalt Lounge, and

the advance scouts struck gold. Three sedans were parked out back, they reported, all of them with Illinois plates.

As I walked up the front steps of the Calles' fortress, tracked by a rooftop sniper's scope, I heard the war drums beating. Slow hip-hop bass, thumping from an amped-up Bose speaker system. In a room where the sunlight fought its way through metal slats hammered over the windows, casting dusty rays across peeling yellowed paint and stripped wooden floorboards, a folding card table bore the tools of a modern urban general: a marked-up street map, a pyramid of burner phones, and a couple of overflowing ashtrays.

Jennifer looked up from the map and whistled. I'd dressed for the occasion, in the three-piece Brunello Cucinelli suit Caitlin had bought me after my escape from prison. Midnight black and ivory, with a skinny tie and Italian wingtips so sharp they could cut glass.

"Damn, hon. Hope you're dressin' for success."

"That makes two of us. What's the prognosis?"

Gabriel tossed back a swig of beer and planted his fat thumb on a circled chunk of the map.

"Besides the Cobalt, the PKs got lookouts here, here, and here. This dump right here? That's their stash house. They got a dealer working the corner one street down, and he sends runners back and forth all day long."

"They're tense," Jennifer said, "but not as tense as they should be. I guess Angelo's got 'em convinced they're bulletproof now that they're working for Chicago."

I nodded as I surveyed the map. "Sure, that's his whole sales pitch. Join the Outfit, get rich and fat. We ready to prove him wrong?"

"Ready and willing, *ese*." Gabriel tapped the circled streets. "I just talked to Eddie Stone. We're gonna call this a co-op. Soon as you give the signal, Calles and Bishops gunships are gonna strike here and here. Hit 'em with one drive-by, then as soon as any left-overs poke their heads up—*bang*, round two."

"The stash house is a harder nut to crack," Jennifer said. "We're not even gonna try to fight our way in there. Think we'll just post some shooters front and back, and wait for the roaches to pour out once the Cobalt Lounge calls for reinforcements. Oh, and Winslow's on board. While you go in the front, the Blood Eagles are gonna be creeping into the back lot, wiring a little farewell surprise to the Outfit's cars."

I studied the marked streets, committing them to memory. Getting in was one thing. Getting out, even if I survived my impending showdown at the Cobalt Lounge, was another problem entirely. Between the cops, the Outfit, and a hornet's nest of pissed-off bangers, my getaway had to be flawless.

"How about my covering fire?" I asked.

"Here, other side of the street from the Cobalt." Gabriel pointed. "Two-story apartment building with rooftop access from a back fire escape. You're gonna have my two best deadeyes, this guy from the Fine Upstanding Crew—he used to be an Army Ranger or something, no joke—and three dudes from the Fourteen-K. Don't know how well they can shoot, but those Chinese guys get better hardware than Winslow does. Got a whole firing squad for you."

"All right," I said. "This is important, okay? Make damn sure they check their targets. There's gonna be a stampede of civilians pouring out those doors just ahead of Little Shawn's guys. Once we take control of the city, job two is getting the cops and city hall back in line. A few dead gangsters, they can turn a blind eye to. If we turn this into a massacre, though, they'll *have* to keep coming after us."

Gabriel set down his can of beer and held up his open hands. "All right, all right. You don't gotta worry about that, okay? We got it covered. Ask me, I think you're crazy, going in there alone."

"Still," Jennifer said, "if you can pull it off, that's the stuff legends are made of. Call it, sugar. What's the play?"

I looked at my watch. Almost five o'clock. In another hour,

chasing sunset, the lights of the Cobalt Lounge would flare and the doors would open to the public.

"Get everybody in position," I told her. "Let's do this."

35.

Of course, I kept an ace up my sleeve. Back at Bentley and Corman's apartment—the downstairs door still broken, but the rotting corpses carted off thanks to Caitlin's "cleaners"—I sealed my duffel bag of ordnance inside a cardboard packing box while Caitlin rummaged through Bentley's closet.

"What do you think?" she asked, stepping out into the hall. She'd slipped into Bentley's counterfeit postal-delivery outfit. It fit, though a little small on her, hugging her curves.

"I think I may have a previously undiscovered thing for women in uniforms," I told her.

She grinned, slipping her arms around my neck and pulling me into a long, familiar kiss. My tension melted away like a cube of ice on a hotplate, dissolving into a slow simmer.

"Oh, I *have* uniforms," she purred in my ear. "You should see me in jackboots. Is that the special delivery?"

I glanced back over my shoulder to the box on the kitchen table. "That's it. You up for this?"

"Are you? My part is simple enough. You're the one risking his life to gain a little face."

"More than a little," I said. "On the street, respect is everything. And if this alliance is going to survive, I need to know that when I give an order, it's going to be heard and followed. It's not just the Outfit I'm worried about. When Angelo's dead and gone, we'll still have an entire city to retake and rebuild. Lot of temptation for people to turn rogue. Lots of ways this whole project could go off the rails in a heartbeat. I'm trying to get ahead of any trouble, and position myself where I can throw some weight around if I have to."

She favored me with an amused smile. "Look at you, stepping off the sidelines. And displaying an ambitious work ethic. You could almost be a fledgling hound."

I laughed, going to pick up the box. It rested heavy in my arms, laden with the fruits of Winslow's secret stash.

"Don't worry," I said, "I'm not gunning for your job."

"Oh, I know," she said. "I was just thinking, if there was ever a vacancy...hmm. 'Princess Caitlin' has a nice ring to it, doesn't it? You never know, my father might decide to retire in ten, maybe twelve thousand years from now."

"I'll keep my schedule open."

"I might have even burned away your ridiculous streak of altruism by then."

"You know," I said, "when you're trying to corrupt someone, you probably shouldn't blatantly tell them you're doing it. Just a professional tip."

Caitlin plucked the box from my arms with one hand. With the other, she stroked her fingertips behind my ear, ruffling my hair. An electric shiver rippled down my spine.

"Darling," she said, "you are already thoroughly, deliciously corrupt. I'm just making you more efficient. So, shall we go commit a murder?"

I offered her my arm.

"When you put it that way," I said, "how can I refuse?"

* * *

The Cobalt Lounge was classier than I expected, considering it was run by a street gang called the Playboy Killers. Its name splashed the dusk in electric blue neon, the exterior built like an art deco temple from a fever dream of the forties. Brushed stainless steel jutted from the nightclub's edge like the wings on a vintage muscle car, and ropes of blue velvet cordoned a manicured walk out front. It was a spot of decadence in the heart of urban rot, and I pegged most of the clientele as local hipsters looking to mix a little frisson of danger with their twelve-dollar drinks.

I joined the line, inching toward a pair of double doors quilted in mahogany-toned leather. Out front, bouncers in tight black muscle shirts decided who made the grade and who had to keep walking, one of them giving the chosen few a once-over with a handheld metal detector before waving them inside. The only metal on me was my belt buckle; the composite plastic dagger velcroed to my ankle and the deck of cards in my hip pocket wouldn't trigger any alarms.

The rest of my gear would, and that was why I'd trusted it to Caitlin's capable hands. She turned heads as she came down the walk, putting a little extra swing in her step while she skirted the line and approached the bouncer with the clipboard.

"Package?" He held out an expectant hand. "I'll take it."

Caitlin shook her head. "Has to go to the manager. A...Mr. Shawn Mahoney? I need a signature."

"So I'll sign for it."

She tapped a stamp on the lid. "Addressee signature only. The package is insured. Sorry, I don't make the rules."

"Can you *bend* the rules? We're a little busy here, lady."

Caitlin raised her chin high. Her eyes narrowed, and she gave him an offended sniff.

"Can I bend the federal law which I swore, as a duly deputized agent of the United States Postal Service, to uphold? No, sir. I cannot and will not, and I could report you to the proper authorities for even making the suggestion."

The line wasn't getting any shorter while they argued. The bouncer sighed, waving over one of the guys at the door.

"Hey, take her to Little Shawn's office. Then walk her *out* again, okay? We don't have time for this tonight."

They brought her inside. Soon it was my turn up at bat, falling under the bouncer's scrutinizing eye. I was a little old for this crowd, but my tailored suit sent a loud and clear message: I was the kind of guy who could spring for bottle service without blinking an eye, and probably would. He nodded me through, and I held out my arms while a metal-detector wand whisked over my body. Now I was wealthy, clean, and verified safe. The bouncer held the door for me as I stepped into the heart of Little Shawn's kingdom.

I paid my twenty-dollar cover charge and wandered into an electro-swing wonderland. A rainbow of laser lights cut through the smoky dark, spinning across sweaty faces and upraised hands to the tune of high-pitched synthesizers. Dancers shimmied on a pair of raised oval stages, dressed in scraps of rave wear, their faces done up in glowing ultraviolet paint. One had her cheeks painted like a peacock, tacky plastic fairy wings strapped to her shoulder blades to complete the look, while the other had done her face like a Day of the Dead skeleton in hot-pink neon. Up ahead, Caitlin eased through the crowd at her escort's side. He carried her package, and she worked him like a tight-stringed violin, her fingertips caressing his arm and the back of his neck while she murmured in his ear. I couldn't hear anything over the music, but when he turned his head, his blush told me everything I needed to know.

So far I hadn't drawn any attention. Little Shawn knew me—we'd met at the first gathering of the New Commission—but I'd never worked with his crew. Unless the Outfit was flashing my picture around town—and they might have been—the bangers working security had no reason to recognize my face. I eased back toward a mahogany pillar at the edge of the dance floor, lifting my left foot and reaching down to idly scratch my leg. A practiced sleight. I used the harmless gesture to unstrap the thin plastic dagger and palm it, slipping it up my jacket sleeve, keeping my forearm slightly bent to hold it in place.

Just up a back hallway, past the restroom doors, Caitlin and the bouncer disappeared into a broom closet. I surveyed the room, giving her a slow twenty-count. Security was subtle—the Playboy Killers didn't go flying their colors in front of paying customers—but there was no mistaking the hard-eyed kids in bright purple kicks stationed around the outskirts of the lounge, lugging heat under their track jackets. Machine pistols, by the size of the bulges.

A bead of sweat trickled down the back of my neck as I cut across the dance floor, the press of bodies and the sweeping lights keeping the room sauna-hot. Caitlin stepped out of the broom closet just as I reached the door, looking pleased, my duffel bag slung over her shoulder. I caught the faintest glimpse of the closet as she swung the door shut. A shredded cardboard box, blood spatter, and a smiling dead man.

She passed me the duffel bag, gave me a peck on the cheek, and made her exit.

I shouldered the bag and unzipped it, mapping its contents by feel as I moved back through the crowd, heading for the bar. Rows upon rows of high-end bottles decorated mirrored shelves behind the curving chrome bar, underlit by blue LED strips like something out of a science-fiction flick. I found an open spot right in the middle and patiently waited for the bartender to finish hitting on a couple of college girls and look my way. He sauntered over, chewing on a soggy toothpick.

"Bacardi One-Fifty-One," I said. "Bring the whole bottle and a glass."

He arched an eyebrow, but he did as he was told. The amber bottle slapped down on the bar, its top fire-engine red, alongside a shot glass.

"No." I kept the bottle, but I pushed the glass back. "Bring me an Old Fashioned glass."

Looking even more dubious, he swapped out the shot glass for a much bigger one. I splashed rum into the tumbler, filling it one inch shy from the brim. I wrinkled my nose as a few droplets splashed onto the chromed surface of the bar and the odor wafted up. Bacardi 151 is named for its proof: 75.5 percent alcohol. It smells like jet fuel and tastes worse.

"You...want ice with that?" he asked me. "Or a mixer or something?"

I raised the glass to him and took a sip. The rum was a lit match burning down my throat. One sip was plenty. I put the glass back on the bar, beside my left hand, while my right stayed close to the open zipper of the duffel bag.

"Nah, I'm good. Y'know, I've been told I have a drinking problem. Can you believe that?"

He blinked, not sure what to say. I broke into a grin.

"Just messing with you. Hey, there is one thing you can do for me."

"What's that?"

"Go get your boss," I told him. "Tell Little Shawn that Daniel Faust is here, representing the New Commission, and I'm here to kill him. Then you should take the rest of the night off."

36.

The bartender scurried off, wiping his hands with a dirty towel, eyes bulging like a fish out of water. I waited. Normally I'd pass the time with a drink, but I wasn't touching the 151 again; my standards might have been low, but they still existed. The glass and the bottle sat untouched, waiting for the right moment.

The right moment came about five minutes later, when Little Shawn came out to play. He'd earned his nickname, standing about five foot three and decked out in royal purple, wearing his hair in a tight high fade. A lot of rattlesnake mean crammed into a tiny package. He'd brought a couple of his buddies with him, one with a crooked boxer's nose and the other with his eyes set in a permanent squint, like he thought he was a gunslinger from a Clint Eastwood flick. Little Shawn stepped up to the bar on my right, Crook-Nose on my left. Squint stood behind me, crowding my space, boxing me in.

I let the blaring, reeling synthesizers and thudding bass wash over me, through me, swallowing my nervous energy and making my hammering pulse a part of the music. One chance to get this right. One mistake, just one, and I wasn't walking out of here alive.

"I had to see this shit for myself," Little Shawn said to his buddies. Then he looked me up and down. "Yeah, I remember you. You were working security at the first Commission meeting. Glorified doorman. You ain't nothing but Jennifer's bitch."

"I'm moving up in the world," I told him. "Can't say the same for you, though. What'd Angelo Mancuso offer you to turn traitor? Must've been something nice."

"Oh yeah. Real nice. The world and everything in it. When you fools are all dead and gone, the PKs get all the business on the Strip. We're gonna be running this town."

I shook my head. "Yeah, because the Outfit is going to hand that kind of action to a second-rate street gang who can barely hang on to four blocks of turf. That makes all kinds of sense. Wake up, pal: you're being used for cannon fodder. And when the smoke clears, Angelo *might* give you a job shining his shoes. Hell, I can prove it."

His eyes narrowed. I could hear his mental gears clanking. Slow, rusty, but they still moved. "Yeah?"

"Yeah. Case in point: I know you've got about a dozen Outfit shooters holing up in your back room here."

"So?"

"So," I said, "you know I'm not here alone. I mean, come on, I'd have to be some kind of suicidal idiot to walk in here by myself and call you out. So obviously I've got my own hitters backing me up. Place is probably *filled* with them, just waiting for my word to open fire."

One of his eyelids twitched. He shot a look across the crowded dance floor as his shoulders tightened.

"What's your point?" he demanded.

"Point is, I don't see any of those Chicago boys in the mix. Nope, they're all chilling in the back, not lifting a finger to back your crew up. I bet you even asked, and they came up with some half-assed excuse not to get involved. Like you have to 'prove yourself' to Angelo by handling us on your own."

Another twitch. Little Shawn might be a hardcore killer, but I'd clean him out at the poker table. His lips twisted into a dull-witted scowl.

"Don't matter," he said. "Don't need their help anyway."

I looked back at Squint, who was breathing down my neck.

"Careful, pal. You spend all your time focusing on me, you're gonna miss my boy coming up behind you. Bam, game over."

He took a halting step backward, looking over his shoulder, the paranoia contagious. I was inside their heads now, right where I wanted to be.

"Yeah," I said, "figure I brought seven or eight hitters in here, somewhere in that crowd. Maybe getting closer now, closing ranks. Hey, Shawn, do you see all of your security guys out there? Any of 'em...missing?"

None of them were, of course, but spotting anyone in the maelstrom of smoke and twirling laser lights was a tall order, and the power of suggestion had filled Shawn's mind with nightmares of an ambush. He wasn't even looking at me now, lips moving as he made a silent head count. Only Crook-Nose was still giving me his undivided attention.

I'd swung the odds in my favor as best I could. It was now or never.

"Now's the part where I should probably give you one last chance to change your mind and come back to the fold, but I was talking to the guys and, well...honestly? Nobody likes you, Shawn." I turned to Crook-Nose. "Hey, you want to see a magic trick?"

"No."

I sighed. "Tough crowd."

Like I said, I was a washout when it came to elemental magic. The most I could manage, on my best day, was a tiny spark.

That said, when your index finger was casually crooked over a tumbler filled with high-octane rum—in some parts of the world, the key ingredient in a Molotov cocktail—a spark was all you needed.

The liquor ignited with a *crump* of heat and flame, and I hurled the burning rum into Crook-Nose's face. He staggered back, screaming, clutching at his eyes, and my other hand was already in the duffel, closing around Bessie's stock. The sawed-off shotgun whipped free just as Squint turned my way. One trigger yanked, one barrel boomed, and Squint's body went flying onto the dance floor. The shotgun kicked like a mule in my hand, my elbow slamming back against the bar, as the lounge erupted in screams of panic.

Shawn went for his piece, got it clear from the holster—and froze as the shotgun's double barrels pressed up against the bottom of his chin. His brow glistened with sweat.

"Listen, man, it wasn't—" he started to say.

No time. I pulled the second trigger and blew open the top of Little Shawn's skull. Bone fragments and blood spray arced through the smoky air, caught in the dazzle of laser lights. Crook-Nose came at me, his hair smoldering and face lobster-red, contorted with feral rage. The composite dagger dropped from my sleeve and into my hand. I stabbed him through the breastbone once, twice—then the blade snapped and left me with a useless nub of plastic in my fist. I tossed it onto his corpse as he hit the floor.

A gunshot winged past me, buckling the chrome bar. While the civilians stampeded for the exit, the shooters in the purple kicks struggled against the tide, trying to get a clean shot as they waded toward me. I hoisted myself onto the bar, rolling up and over, tumbling onto the other side as a burst of machine-pistol fire turned a row of bottles into a waterfall of shattered glass and vodka. I was on my belly in the splash zone, going fetal and covering my face as the wreckage poured down.

I popped up from cover just long enough to get pinned down again, ducking beneath a hail of bullets. PK shooters, six of them, had untangled themselves from the shrieking crowd at the exits. They marched toward the bar in a firing line. I gave a slow five-count, enough time for any stragglers to get out of harm's way, while I knelt down and yanked the mouth of the duffel bag open wide. I tossed the shotgun back in the bag; Bessie's job was done, for now. Then I reached for two of Winslow's presents: a pair of slender steel cylinders stamped with Cyrillic lettering, sealed at the top with ring pins. I pulled the first ring with my teeth and lobbed the cylinder over the bar, then the second.

The last goodie in my bag was an army surplus gas mask. I pulled it on and strapped it tight as the two tear-gas grenades exploded, flooding the lounge with white mist. I hefted the duffel, brushed a little broken glass from the shoulder of my three-piece suit, and went hunting.

Staying low, I snatched the bottle of 151 from the bar. The shooters were staggering, coughing, flailing shadows in the mist with hair-trigger firearms. I tossed the bottle up in the air like a target, and one obliged, firing wildly at the sudden movement until his gun clicked on empty. I snaked a card from my breast pocket and sent it flying. He crumpled to the dance floor and I stepped over his body, still crouched, eyes sharp behind the blurry lenses of my mask.

A figure stumbled from the fog, turning my way, gun swinging up in a shaky hand. I grabbed his wrist and shoved it to one side as he opened fire. Bullets raked across two of his buddies in the mist, hazy forms doing a herky-jerky dance before they dropped. I chopped the edge of my hand down on the shooter's inside elbow, buckling his arm, and swung the muzzle of the gun up toward his face. Then I hooked my finger over his and pulled the trigger for him.

Four down, two to go, and the tear gas was clearing fast. One of the shooters was down on his knees, coughing and dry-heaving, the other running for the bar—and the sink on the other side. I'd half-expected the place to flood with Outfit men by now, but the sound of stampeding feet was headed *away* from the fight. Apparently they'd decided discretion was the better part of valor. I wondered, when they made it out to the back parking lot, if they'd notice that the sentries Shawn had posted were missing. Or if they'd spot the butter-stick bricks of C-4 that Winslow's bikers had wired to the underbellies of their sedans, set to an ignition-switch trigger.

I got my answer as the floor shook under my feet, the lounge rocking from the impact of a detonation.

Strolling past the kneeling banger, I tugged a card from my breast pocket and flicked it toward him in passing. He slumped to the ground, throat cut, twitching. The last one was hunched over the bartender's sink, throwing fistfuls of water in his face. I stood behind him and reached for one of the few unbroken bottles from the mirrored shelves. Bombay Sapphire gin. Good stuff. I shrugged, then smashed it over the back of his head.

I walked back around the bar and kicked Little Shawn's body onto its back. Then I snapped a picture of what was left of his face with my burner phone and texted it to Jennifer. She'd make sure the word got out.

The mist cleared. I stood alone in the Cobalt Lounge under the spinning laser lights, the dance floor littered with corpses and fallen guns. From outside I could hear the faint echoes of screams, the crackling of flames, and the distant wail of sirens.

Time to go.

37.

My backup was already gone, the rooftop across the street vacant but evidence of their handiwork all around me: more of Little Shawn's shooters scattered along the sidewalk and out in the street, slumped over the fallen velvet ropes, cold hands still clutching their guns. The sirens came on loud and fast. No telling who would arrive first, ambulances or a SWAT team, but I wasn't taking any chances. I ripped off the gas mask and ran, darting down a back alley and turning on a side street, keeping away from the city's arteries. Losing myself in the marrow, on forgotten roads with no cameras, where nobody ever called the cops.

I navigated by memory, picturing the rumpled map on Jennifer's card table, my extraction route marked in yellow highlighter. Eventually I reached the end of the line, a lonely corner under a busted-out streetlight, and I stopped to catch my breath. I could still hear the distant sirens, wailing out against the electric dark.

Headlights flashed up ahead. A car boiled from the shadows: Caitlin's snow-white Audi Quattro. She pulled up to the curb and rolled her window down.

"I hate to say it, for fear I'll encourage similarly reckless behavior in the future," she said, "but I just spoke to Jennifer. You were right. Your social credit among the seedier denizens of our fair city has just received a considerable upgrade."

I hopped into the passenger seat. She was rolling before I even pulled my belt on, pointing her headlights away from the sirens' blare.

"Good," I said. "Hopefully now I'll get fewer people asking who I am, and more of them listening to what I have to say."

"Oh, nobody needs to ask who you are now," Caitlin batted her eyelashes, all innocence. "We all know that you're...*the guy*."

I slumped low in my seat. "Not gonna let that go anytime soon, are you?"

Caitlin tilted her head, thinking it over.

"No. Likely not."

I tried for a change of subject. "Any word from the troops? How'd we do out there?"

"Swimmingly. Everyone completed their assignments, and the 'Playboy Killers'"—she gave the slightest roll of her eyes—"don't have enough surviving members to form a bowling team. As for our guests from Chicago, most of them were taken out by the car bombs. One or two got away and are at this moment presumably running to their master with their tails between their legs."

I closed my eyes. My splinted fingers ached, my bandaged wrists burned at the slightest touch, I was going to have a nice bruise on my elbow, and my back was a mess of scrapes and pulled muscles, but I was still breathing. We'd cleared out the Outfit's foot soldiers. With the pawns down, it was time to go for the high-value pieces.

I wanted the king.

"We should get everybody together, chart out our next move—"

"What we should do," Caitlin said, "and this is Jennifer's decree, as well as mine, is scatter and lie low for the night. At this moment, the authorities—many of whom are firmly in our enemy's pocket, I remind you—are scouring the city in response to multiple shootings, an explosion, and a pile of dead bodies. You, and everyone else who participated in the festivities, need to stay well out of sight until the commotion dies down."

"We've got to strike while the iron is hot. If Angelo gets a chance to regroup—"

"*Daniel*," she said. "You are in no shape to fight. You know that. You're going to get some rest, and that's final."

I sighed. "All right. You may have a point. Drop me off on the Strip? I'll find a place to crash and we'll meet up in the morning."

"Nonsense. You're coming home with me."

I fumbled in my pocket, showing her the tiny blue amulet.

"Can't risk it. Ecko's tracking me with this, and I'm letting him, until I get the chance to lead him into an ambush. I'm not going to risk handing him your home address."

Fifteen minutes later, she led the way across the chrysanthemum-patterned carpet of the Taipei Tower's lobby. The clerk behind the front desk snapped to attention, like a napping private caught by his drill sergeant.

"Ms. Brody!" he said. "A pleasure as always. Is there anything we can, that is, do—"

Caitlin handed him the amulet, wrapped in its nest of tissue.

"Be a dear and put this amusing bauble in my safe, would you? I'll be back to pick it up in the morning."

As he scurried off, gingerly holding the prize, she looked my way. "Permanent residency has its privileges. There are three hundred and ninety-two rooms in this hotel, and superb security. If Damien Ecko wants to knock on each and every door looking for us, he's welcome to try. Now then. Shall we?"

I knew every inch of Caitlin's penthouse. The sweeping hardwood floors, the track lighting, black leather and chrome. The original Patrick Nagel painting hanging over her sofa, and the well-stocked wine rack. And she knew every inch of me. She peeled off my jacket and unbuttoned my vest, like an archaeologist carefully sweeping away sand and dust to gaze at the relic beneath. Her smooth fingers gently unhooked my cuff links, the French cuffs of my shirt tugging back to reveal strips of gauze soaked through with dark stains. She shook her head slowly, storm clouds brewing behind her eyes.

"I'm a little damaged," I told her.

"Injured," she said. "Not damaged."

Then she took me by the hand and led me into the bathroom, with its picture window overlooking the lights of the Vegas Strip and the shadowy mountains in the distance, and turned on the shower. The double showerheads pulsed down, billowing with steam, as she gingerly unwrapped my bandages. The soldering-iron burns were angry red lines marring my skin.

"You keep forgetting a very important rule. Or perhaps I haven't made it clear to you, which is my fault, but I'll expect you to remember it from now on."

I looked into her eyes. "What's that?"

One of her fingernails brushed my left wrist. Tracing the burn, like following a river on a map of hell, with a feather-light touch.

"Nobody is allowed to hurt you," Caitlin said softly, "except for me."

She held my gaze, deadly serious.

"I'll keep it in mind," I said.

We showered together, flesh to flesh under the hot spray and the steam, and then she applied ointment to my wounds and fresh, clean gauze. We lay together in her bed, under the stormy gray comforter, and listened to the rustling whisper of the air-conditioning.

"So what do you think about this?" I asked, disturbing the silence with a question. "I mean, me stepping up to the table with the New Commission."

"Are you asking me for permission?"

"No. I already made my choice. I'm asking what you think."

"What I think," Caitlin purred. "Daniel, do you know why you caught my eye in the first place?"

I shrugged. "I helped you out of a jam."

"Mm. While that certainly *helped*, no. It was how you did it. You set my tormentor in your sights because he offended you, and you destroyed him."

My thoughts drifted back to that long and terrible night. The poker game gone wrong, burning Caitlin's contract...standing in my useless circle of salt as she took slow and bloody revenge on the sorcerer who'd enslaved her.

"I think you did the honors there."

"No. I simply brought Artie Kaufman's life to its natural and inevitable conclusion. You made it possible. Then you risked your life to free that lost girl's soul—a girl you'd never even met."

"I freed her to go straight to hell," I said, the memory like ashes on my tongue.

"Damnation was Stacy's only chance of escape from a half-souled eternity of mindless torment. Her only chance for a better life, however slight, however long it might take. You were strong enough to damn her."

"Didn't feel like strength at the time. I just did what had to be done."

"Then there was Sullivan. You battled him with everything you had. And when the time came, when I *needed* to face him on my own, only then did you step aside and lay down your arms. Lauren Carmichael and her followers? Dead, and her plans in ruin, because of you. And so many others have stood in your path and fallen. You were buried in a maximum-security prison and even then, you only fought harder."

I rolled on the mattress, the feather pillow cool against my cheek as I faced her.

"Not sure what you're getting at."

"You're a man of ambition at heart—which is, frankly, arousing. But more than that...I've called you my knight in tarnished armor more than once. Teasingly, but there's a speck of truth to it. You're a warrior, Daniel. You're not happy unless you have a cause, something to fight for. I've watched you, of late. So listless, so off course—"

"I know." My fingertips brushed her bare shoulder, tracing the curve of her arm. "I burned out. I got lazy, slow. I know that. I'm trying to make a comeback."

She chuckled. "Judging from tonight, I think you're well on

your way. If you want my opinion, it's this: Jennifer's little club doesn't matter. Whether you become a lord of the underworld in Las Vegas or manage a donut shop in New Mexico, it doesn't matter. What matters is that you find a fight and a cause that's worthy of you, one that fans those flames in your heart and keeps you standing tall. Because those flames are what drew my eye in the first place."

She eased closer on the mattress, twining her arms around me. Pulling me close.

"You must remember that I am eternal, Daniel. I only see the long view. And in my vision, all this strife is simply training, like a runner preparing for a marathon. In the end, you will fight for *me*. For me, and for my prince, and for my people."

"For you," I whispered, gazing into her eyes.

She gave me a knowing smile.

38.

At Jennifer's fortress, in the fresh light of a new day, I commandeered a whiteboard. Salvaged from one of the sprawling tenement's cluttered storage rooms, an artifact from a long-shuttered schoolhouse, the dusty slate bore three names separated by stark black lines. *Angelo Mancuso.* Then *Kirmira.* Then *Damien Ecko.*

"We've got three problems," I told the leaders of the New Commission as they gathered around the card table. "These first two? They go together like a hand in a glove. The third is *my* problem first and foremost, but he's working for the Outfit, so he's on the list."

Winslow rubbed the stubble on his chin. "Obviously we gotta take Angelo out, but what's the big deal with the other two? What makes them any tougher than the rest of the shooters we knocked off last night?"

Chou Yong looked more confident every time I saw him, taking to his new responsibilities in the wake of his boss's death. Now, though, the big man coughed discreetly into a handkerchief and gave Jennifer a questioning look.

"It's all right, sugar," she told him. "Everybody here is some degree of clued-in."

"Not sure *I* am," he said. "But that man, Kirmira...he's a monster. He impersonated Shangguan Jin, our former Red Pole."

"Impersonated?" Eddie Stone, dressed like a million bucks

even at eight in the morning, looked his way. "Like, he wears disguises?"

"He...changes his shape. He's a monster."

"Horseshit," Winslow drawled.

I spread my hands. "Sorry, it's true. He's a shape-shifter."

"Oh, I *believe* you. I'm just saying it's horseshit that we have to deal with it. I can't go back to my clubhouse and tell a roomful of hard-ridin' sons of bitches that we're going up against something out of a horror movie."

"Wait till you hear about the other guy," Jennifer said.

Winslow cracked open a bottle of beer and sighed.

"Look, Faust, we all know the score, right? We know a lot of weird shit goes down in this city. But handling that, that's what people hire folks like you and Jenny for. So we don't have to deal with it. Or think about it."

"And we'll handle it," I told him, "but the bottom line is, these guys are in the mix, like it or not, and we've got to be ready for any possibility. Now this other one, Damien Ecko, he's...really old. And he has, um, some special skills—"

As I fumbled for a diplomatic way to parse "three-thousand-year-old necromancer" for a roomful of mostly non-magicians, a hammering at the door bought me a momentary respite. A Calles foot soldier hustled in, leaning close to whisper into Gabriel's ear. His boss shrugged.

"Huh. Okay, bring him on in." Gabriel looked to the rest of us. "Seems we got ourselves a special guest."

The special guest was Detective Gary Kemper, wearing his gold shield on his belt. He swaggered in like a wolf in a henhouse. From the way the room closed in around him, hard eyes on his badge, he was more like a hen in a den of wolves. I wasn't sure if his confidence was a calculated show of authority, or if he actually thought he was in charge here.

I stretched out my senses, psychic tendrils lapping at Gary's aura, just like I had done for everyone else in the room. A precautionary check to make sure we weren't facing a rakshasa in disguise. Now that I'd tasted Kirmira's scent, he wouldn't get the drop on me again. Gary was the real deal, all right. No jungle fires, no peat-moss aroma, just the barbed-wire twist of a cambion soul. Half human, half demon, and doomed never to fit in either world.

"Nice shithole you've got here," he said. "I guess crime doesn't pay after all."

"It's a fixer-upper," Jennifer told him.

Gary gazed around the room, locking eyes with each and every one of us.

"Now this is cute. You've got a regular rainbow coalition of scumbags going on here. The only missing face is Little Shawn. Oh, right, I forgot. Him and his entire crew came down with lead poisoning last night."

"You here to arrest all of us?" Gabriel asked. "Hope you brought backup, *ese*."

Needles Dominguez, the delegate from the Fine Upstanding Crew, folded his arms and stood in front of the door. "Hope he brought a lot more than that, or this bitch ain't walking out of here alive."

Gary's eyes narrowed. "Slow your roll, Tony Montana. I'm here to help. In fact, right about now, I'm the only friend you people have."

"You're gonna have to pardon our skepticism," Jennifer told him.

"Look," he said, "pretty sure you already know the word on the street, from the mayor's office on down: you're out, Mancuso is in. The brass just wants this fight *over*, before tourists start getting caught in the crossfire. Angelo's promising the moon and the stars, claiming he's already got you people beat."

"Think we just proved otherwise," I said.

"What you just did," Gary said, "was kick the hornet's nest. I've got a buddy who works in the Chicago PD, vice unit. One of his confidential informants dropped the dime on some major activity. Angelo called for backup."

"We figured he would," I said. "We're hoping to have everything wrapped up before they get here."

"You don't get it."

Gary stepped into the heart of the room, slats of light from the boarded windows drawing lines across his face.

"I'm not talking about another couple of cars, another ten or twelve goons coming our way. He called *everybody*. Every shooter on his daddy's payroll, and every thug, throat-cutter, and junkie he could scrape from the bottom of the barrel. The word's out: it's open season. And let me assure you, these people don't *care* about causing a bloodbath on Flamingo Boulevard if that's what it takes to get the job done. My bosses made a devil's pact, getting into bed with Angelo Mancuso, and they've got no damn idea what kind of a shitstorm they just unleashed."

Winslow leaned back, looking him up and down. "So what's your angle?"

"My angle," Gary told him, "is that I'm a cop. And my job, first and foremost, is protecting the citizens of Las Vegas. There's one thousand eight hundred and sixty miles between Chicago and Vegas. That's a twenty-six-hour drive. Which means we've got just a little over a day, maybe a day and a half, before Angelo's army hits town with trunks full of heavy firepower. So consider this a friendly heads-up: you've got just about that long to deal with Angelo and *make* him call off the dogs, or we're all gonna be in a world of hurt."

He approached me, pitching his voice low.

"I'm hoping that's enough incentive. In your case, though? Here's a little something extra: if you don't put a lid on this situation by the time Angelo's backup arrives, you're officially less than useless to me. And my next phone call is to the FBI."

He turned and left without another word. Nobody tried to stop him. As the door swung shut in his wake, all eyes were on me.

My eyes were on the whiteboard. Mancuso. Kirmira. Ecko. Three big problems in search of solutions.

Or maybe, just maybe, if I could find a wedge to drive between them...one solution to bring them all tumbling down.

*　　*　　*

We hit the streets. Priority one was finding Angelo Mancuso. Without his shooters backing him up, he was down to a skeleton crew—easy to take out, but harder to find than a saint in a brothel. Using the strategy room at the fortress as a call and coordination center, we dispatched the New Commission's forces across the city.

The Blood Eagles did what they were best at: ruling the roads. Packs of Winslow's bikers roved up and down the Strip, keeping their eyes peeled for cars with Illinois plates. Chou Yong's boys had the off-Strip betting action locked down; they hit the sports books and the backroom poker games, pumping their contacts for information. Angelo had a taste for the good life, and so did the gentlemen from the Inagawa-kai. The yakuza's fashion peacocks slipped into the resort scene, haunting poolside cabanas and high-end bars with their ears to the ground. Our street soldiers from the Bishops, Calles, and Crew traded their colors for civilian gear and spread across the city like white blood cells fighting an invading virus.

Jennifer and I worked the phones back at home base. By two in the afternoon, the whiteboard was a mess of scribbles, and our notes had spilled over to a pair of hastily scrounged yellow legal pads. Everyone on the streets knew somebody who knew something, a hundred leads that led to a hundred dead ends. Angelo was a ghost. All of our people were working under the same orders: observe, follow, report in.

I should have known Winslow's people would be the first to break that rule. Still, all things considered, I couldn't complain.

When the call came in, I headed over to the Sunset Garage while Jennifer hung back to cover the phones. They'd landed a fish, they said. A fish in the form of a sleek Mercedes parked around back, the sides dented all to hell and half the windows smashed out.

"My boys got a little rambunctious," Winslow said. "Took one look at the license plates and forced him off the road. Thankfully it wasn't some damn tourist, or I'd be making a whole lot of apologies right now. And I hate apologizing."

"Who was driving? Angelo?"

"Nope," Winslow said, leading me around to the back of the car. He hoisted the trunk lid and showed me their prize.

Bound and gagged, his suit scuffed and torn, the Doctor glared his angry defiance. Then Angelo's torture specialist got a look at me, and he deflated like a pinpricked balloon.

"Excuse me just a second," I said.

I walked into the garage, rummaging around the workbenches until I found what I was looking for. I came back to the trunk and held up my find. Using my hand with the splinted fingers, just to make a point.

One pull of the trigger and the cordless drill whirred to life, its diamond-tipped bit gleaming in the sunlight. The Doctor's eyes went wide.

"I'm not going to ask you any questions," I told him. "Yet."

39.

Eventually, I did ask a few questions. And he answered them.

Angelo, Kirmira, and a trio of bodyguards were holed up nice and cozy at the Medici. Top-floor suite, room 3608, with a view of the artificial lake and the dancing fountains below.

"I'm coming to pick you up," I told Jennifer, calling from the car. The Spark's engine whined as I redlined it, gunning through the late-afternoon traffic.

"I'll be ready. What's the play?"

"We take a small crew in. We go quiet: magic and sound suppressors. If we can take Angelo alive, great. If not, sucks to be him."

Jennifer snickered. "Gonna suck to be him either way, ain't it?"

"Hey, he wanted this fight. If he won't come to the front line, the front line's coming to him."

"How're we looking on plan B?" she asked.

"Working on that right now."

I hung up and made another call. Not one I was looking forward to, but I was out of options. Besides, I'd always been a proponent of fighting fire with fire.

"Thank you for calling the Blue Karma," said the heavily accented voice on the other end of the line. "Will you be placing an order for carryout or delivery?"

"This is Daniel Faust," I told him. "I need to talk to Naavarasi."

* * *

We rolled into the lobby of the Medici with a skeleton crew. Me and Jennifer in the front, Gabriel and his three best shooters—nine millimeters fitted with Dead Air silencers under their track jackets—bringing up the rear. Hitting the hotel with an army would have drawn all kinds of bad attention and handed Angelo a golden opportunity to slip away in the chaos. Instead, we'd do this quick, clean, and quiet.

We strode across the zebra-striped marble floor under the watchful eyes of cherubs in the old-world frescoes adorning the scalloped walls. Past a burbling crystal fountain, slot machines rang out along the casino floor, singing their siren song. The marble gave way to ornate Italian carpet, classy but faded with age, and a straight shot between the gaming tables to the hotel elevators.

We barely made it fifteen feet.

I knew the man who stepped into our path, an immovable object bringing our unstoppable force to a dead halt. He had a weasel's face and a vulture's eyes, his coal-black hair slicked with grease. His suit was more expensive than mine, but he either didn't care enough to get it tailored, or his tailor just didn't like him very much.

"Greenbriar," I said. "What a pleasure."

"You ain't doing this here, Dan."

"Don't know what you're talking about."

"Yeah," he said. "Yeah, you do."

Ever wonder why magicians don't just go to the casino, cast a luck spell on their dice, and break the Vegas bank? People like Greenbriar, that's why. Director of "special security" for CMC Entertainment, which owned over half the casinos on the Strip. He didn't come alone, either. Bruisers in black suits emerged from the tourist crowds, silently looming in a rough circle around our wolf pack. Half of them glinted with magical potential; the rest geared up with protective amulets and high-caliber pistols under their jackets.

"This doesn't concern you."

The scraggly mustache on Greenbriar's lip twisted as he smirked. "Doesn't *concern* me? Now, don't get me wrong, but I think you and your pals here are about to murder one of my guests. If you look up the word 'concern' in the dictionary, I'm pretty sure there's a picture of this very situation printed next to it."

"You know who that guest is, right?"

"Yeah. Now ask me if I care. The people who write my paychecks have worked very, very hard over the years to turn Las Vegas into a safe, family-friendly entertainment destination, Dan. You know how we did that? Well, among other things, we *don't* let gangsters kick in doors and shoot our guests. That's high on the list of things we don't tolerate."

"You ought to be worried about what happens when Angelo's backup rolls into town," I told him. "We care about collateral damage. They won't."

"I'll take my chances."

Greenbriar stepped closer. His men held their ground, tense, their eyes like chips of flint.

"Listen," he said, "I like you. And I owe you one for helping me out with that...situation over at the Monaco. But this ain't happening. Not here, not today, not ever. No violence on CMC Entertainment property, you dig me? Now, if you can get him off the casino grounds, hey, happy hunting. I hope you nail the bastard. But you don't wanna break this little, ah, détente we got here. You think the Chicago Mafia is bad news? CMC is worldwide, man, and they got a hundred million dollars in a bank account labeled 'payback.'"

He was right. I hated to admit it, but he was right.

Vegas was an ecosystem. A precariously balanced one at the best of times, but one constant helped to keep the peace more than anything else: my crowd didn't mess with the casinos, and the casinos didn't mess with us. Greenbriar and his crew were just there to keep everybody honest. If push ever came to shove, his corporate paymasters could snuff us all as easily as writing a check. Our deaths would be an afterthought, a line item scribbled out before an afternoon round of golf.

I held his gaze, as if I could stare him down, make him buckle by sheer force of will, but it was like throwing confetti at a wall of iron. I nodded. "Fine. Okay. You win. We'll wait until he leaves."

Greenbriar's face lit up. He reached into his breast pocket and pulled out a sheaf of glossy white slips.

"See? I knew we'd come to terms. And *these* are discount coupons for our world-famous buffet. Five dollars off your purchase, not valid during lunch and dinner rushes. It's on me, guys. Enjoy."

I took the coupons. I've got my pride, but the buffet at the Medici really was fantastic.

Besides, I was a little distracted. As I led my disheartened followers back through the lobby, through the automatic glass revolving doors and out into the sunlight, I noticed we'd sprouted a tail. A middle-aged woman, in an "I Heart Las Vegas" T-shirt and tacky, oversized plastic sunglasses. That's what she looked like anyway. My psychic tendrils, invisibly snapping at the air above her head, came away with a different picture entirely.

"Don't look back," I murmured to Jennifer, "but Kirmira's following us."

She cracked her knuckles. "Oh, good. Time for plan B?"

"Time for plan B."

* * *

Dealing with the Outfit's pet shape-shifter was one thing. Getting Angelo out of that suite and onto the street where we could take a shot at him without starting a feud with CMC was another problem altogether. Back at the fortress, I paced around the card table to work off my nervous energy.

"Angelo knows he's protected up there," I said. "He's got no reason to set one foot outside that room."

Jennifer leaned against the dirty wall, arms and ankles crossed, deep in thought.

"I'd say we pull some kinda switch, maybe disguise ourselves as room service, but Greenbriar and his critters are onto us now. We'll never get close."

"No, we've got to flush him out. Then we've got to track him, so he doesn't give us the slip." I held up my finger, stopping short. "That part we can do."

The Doctor was buried in a shallow hole in the scraggly, hard-packed ground behind the Sunset Garage. I'd kept his cell phone. His contact list was a who's who of the Chicago Outfit, including Angelo's personal line. A number simply marked "Ecko," too. Nothing I had any particular use for at the moment—I didn't need to call Damien; he knew exactly where to find me thanks to the amulet in my pocket—but I figured I'd hold on to the info just in case. I set the phone down on the map table and called Pixie on my burner.

"Little busy here, Faust. Make it snappy."

"Hey, Pix. If you have somebody's cell phone number, can you track their location?"

"On short notice?"

"Pretty short, yeah."

She sighed. "Sort of. Your phone automatically pings off cell towers when you come in range. If your target is on the move, I can use those pings to get a general direction and use the time between towers to extrapolate velocity."

"So that's a yes."

"That's a 'sort of.' I can get a rough location. If you want me to nail his location down to a five-foot radius, I need to get access to his GPS traffic. That's a little harder. Also more expensive. For you."

A rough location would be fine. We had people on the ground who could do the rest. I gave her Angelo's phone number. She gave me a price. We halfheartedly haggled for thirty seconds, agreed to the amount she knew we'd end up at in the first place, and hung up.

"Okay," Jennifer said. "We got the means to find him. Now we just gotta smoke him out."

It was a perfect problem. We couldn't get in. He didn't want to come out. We *could* go in guns blazing, but that would spark a war with CMC, a war we didn't want and couldn't survive. Nobody was crazy enough to pick that fight.

I looked back to the whiteboard and the original headers I'd marked down before the slate was covered in scribbled notes. *Angelo Mancuso. Kirmira. Damien Ecko.*

Then I smiled.

I waved Jennifer over to the map table, picked up a highlighter, and drew a fat yellow X at three points along South Las Vegas Boulevard.

"We're going to need spotters here, here, and here," I told her. "Let's put some of Winslow's guys right here on East Flamingo, near the freeway off-ramp. Lots of little spots where they can pull their bikes off to the side of the road, and come in hot if we need them."

Jennifer caught the look in my eyes and grinned. "I hear your gears turnin'. Where are we gonna be?"

I tapped the middle of the boulevard, halfway up the Strip, with the tip of the highlighter. Dabbing a streak of yellow across the Medici's man-made lake.

"In the middle of the action. Where else?"

Before we left, I took out the falcon amulet, still snug in its nest of tissue, and left it on the map table. For a couple of hours, at least, I needed a little invisibility.

40.

Under a rich amber sunset, the fountains of the Medici danced. Pillars of water surged from the glittering lake to the tune of "All That Jazz," forming spirals and arcs before splashing back down again. Jennifer and I stood at the iron railing, invisible in a herd of tourists and flashing cell-phone cameras.

The fountains were a good show, and free, a rare combination on the Strip. Still, I only had eyes for the stately resort looming over the lake, and the windows on the top floor. With the Doctor's phone in hand, I called Angelo Mancuso.

"Doc?" Angelo said. "Where the hell have you been, man? I haven't heard from you all day!"

"Sorry," I told him. "The Doctor had his license permanently revoked. Medical malpractice."

Dead silence on the line. Not even the sound of breathing.

"You had to know, after what he did to me, what he was *going* to do to me, he was kind of a priority target. Not like you are, though."

"Fuck him," Angelo said, "the guy was a creep. This doesn't change anything."

"Sure it does. You're losing men left and right, while you're sitting up there all cozy in suite thirty-six-oh-eight at the Medici."

He let out a cocky laugh. "Yeah. You found me, good for you. You think I don't know the score? You can't set foot in this place. None of your pals can either. So y'know, I think I'll just enjoy some of this room-service caviar while I wait for my backup to get here. I'll stand at the window and give a big wave while they turn you into swiss cheese."

"That's it?" I asked. "No remorse, no compassion for the fallen? You throw your allies away like they don't mean a thing, don't you? Just like you did to Damien Ecko. You promised to hand me over to him, and you never intended to follow through."

"Hey, an *extra* big 'fuck him' to *that* guy. I don't owe that skeevy old bastard a thing. You know what he is? My errand boy. My stupid, weird-ass errand boy. I'm still gonna put two bullets in the back of your head if I get half the chance, and I'm still not gonna tell him a damn thing about it."

A faint click echoed on the other end of the line.

"What...what was that?" Angelo said. "You recording this? What are you gonna do, hand it to the cops? Ain't admissible in court, genius."

"Nope, that was the third party on the line hanging up. Guess he'd heard enough."

"He?" Angelo said, his voice uncertain now.

"Damien Ecko. I called him before I called you. He didn't believe me at first, but I figured if you casually admitted to stabbing him in the back once, it wouldn't be too hard to get you to do it twice."

Silence. When he spoke again, his bluster couldn't hide the nervous tension at the edges of his voice.

"Doesn't change a thing. We didn't need his help anyway."

"It's a little more of a problem than that, Angelo. Let's see. You insulted him, you lied to him, you basically stole from him—and he's got a real hate-on for thieves, trust me on this one—oh, and there's one other important fact you should take into account."

"Yeah? What's that?"

"He's the one man in this city crazy enough to pick a fight with CMC Entertainment," I said. "You're right. We can't get you as long as you're holed up in that suite, not without bringing CMC's wrath down on us. But Ecko? He's got a bounty from two demonic courts riding on his head. He's a dead man walking with nothing to lose, and he knows it. He just doesn't *care*. If I were you, I'd get a welcoming committee together. You're about to have an unfriendly visitor."

I hung up.

Jennifer leaned forward with her hands against the railing, catching a gust of cool spray from the dancing waters. She glanced my way.

"So," she said. "Whatcha think happens next?"

"Depends. Angelo's personality is ninety percent arrogance, but he's gotta know Ecko's heavier than he looks. I'd say it's a three-way split, even odds: either he packs up and runs before Ecko gets there, he runs *when* Ecko gets there, or Ecko shows up and slaughters everybody in the room."

"I'm fine with any of those," she said.

We waited.

We didn't have to wait long, though. I was jolted from my thoughts by a tourist's gasp, a pointing finger drawing my gaze to the fast-darkening sky.

"What is that?" someone asked off to my left. "Birds?"

The swarming, churning mass in the sky over the Medici wasn't made of birds, though. Even from a distance, I knew it as soon as I laid eyes on it.

Locusts.

The furious mass swirled in the sky, packing tight like a clenched fist, then flew full-speed at a top-floor window. Cries of surprise went up from the crowd, phones zooming in to capture the moment in grainy pixels, as the locust swarm boiled into the hotel through a chunk of shattered glass.

A couple of minutes later, Pixie called. "Yeah, your target's moving. Pretty fast, too. On foot, but running."

"I am not surprised. Got a location?"

"Told you, my data isn't that fine-tuned. If you'd given me more time...hold on. Okay, got something. The target phone exited the Medici parking garage, turning right onto the boulevard. Faster now, they're probably in a vehicle."

We sprinted for my car while Jennifer made short, fast calls, relaying orders to the troops in a breathless voice.

"Looks like he turned left onto East Harmon," Pixie told me.

I racked my brain, picturing the city on my mental map. "Tell me if he turns right onto Paradise Road."

"You called it. He just did."

"The airport," I told Jennifer. "He's taking side streets to get to McCarran."

Angelo was good and scared, just how I wanted him, but I had hoped he'd try escaping town on wheels. Catching up to him and running him off the road would have been easy. Now he'd jump onto the first plane that would have him, jetting off into the night and back to the safety of his father's mansion. We couldn't let that happen.

A text message came in from an anonymous phone number. *"Terminal 3. Long-term parking."*

I drove faster.

* * *

Angelo's footsteps thudded against the faded concrete of the parking garage as he barked into his phone. "No, I don't—I don't even care if it's *coach* seating. Three tickets on a nonstop flight, why is this so hard to understand?"

I stepped out from behind a parked van, standing in his path.

Angelo had Kirmira and his buddy Sal at his side. I supposed his other bodyguards had stayed behind to cover their boss's retreat. A valiant but pointless sacrifice. The trio stopped short. Angelo hung up his phone. We stood there, facing each other across ten feet of open concrete, fluorescent tubes softly buzzing and popping above our heads. The echo of car engines growled in the distance, the garage acoustics turning them into the muffled rumbles of sleeping monsters.

"How'd you find me?" he asked.

"Help from a couple of friends. It's over, Angelo. You made your bid and you lost. Now it's time to pay the bill."

Angelo glanced to his left, then curled his lip in a cocky sneer.

"I thought you were a gambling man, Faust. Three against one? Those are lousy odds."

"The key to being a good gambler," I told him, "is doing everything you can to shift the odds in your favor. Case in point? You're flying out of town, not driving. Can't take your guns through the security checkpoint, which means you're totally unarmed right now."

My cards leaped from my hip pocket, riffling into my hand.

"I'm not."

Angelo and Sal shared a look, both of them laughing. "Is that right, magic man? You got a bad memory. I don't *need* guns to take you out."

Angelo snapped his fingers.

Kirmira buckled to the concrete. His bones creaked and snapped, his jaw elongating into a muzzle, bright orange fur sprouting from flesh stretched to the tearing point. His eyes turned a baleful yellow, glowing, as he shook off the tattered shreds of his clothes and stood tall on four paws.

"I got a tiger," Angelo said.

The five-hundred-pound Bengal, rippling with muscle and seven feet long, let out a rumbling growl.

"Correction," I told him. "You had a tiger."

Angelo squinted at me. "Huh?"

The Bengal spun, roaring as it lashed out, raking a razor-clawed paw across Sal's stomach. Blood sprayed across the concrete and he hit the ground with a high-pitched shriek, thrashing and pressing his hands to his savaged belly as a ropy strand of intestine spilled out between his fingers.

I shrugged.

"That's not your tiger."

41.

Our rout at the Medici hadn't been a total loss. I figured Kirmira would be prowling around, keeping a quiet watch from the safety of his disguises. When he followed us out of the casino, tailing us all the way back to home base, we couldn't have asked for a better opportunity.

We did exactly what he'd hoped we would do. Ignored him, as if we didn't know he was there, and went about our business.

It took a while, but eventually a frantic knock sounded at the strategy room door. Jennifer stepped over and let our guest in. One of the Calles foot soldiers, a younger kid in a yellow headband and torn jeans, looking breathless.

"Ma'am," he said. "There's trouble outside. Gunfire. We gotta get you to safety."

Jennifer and I shared a nod. We led the way, thundering up a flight of stairs and down a dusty, abandoned corridor, winding our way through the abandoned back rooms of the tenement.

"Figured the Outfit's shape-shifter was primed to start some trouble," Jennifer said, looking back over her shoulder. "Don't you worry, sugar. We got a plan for that."

"I'm in," the kid said. "What's the plan?"

"Through here. Safe room."

A door creaked on warped hinges. The room beyond hung in a murky gloom, the windows boarded over and the lights dead. We followed Jennifer inside.

"It's a sacrifice play," she said. "See, first I find a real troublemaker, somebody who's been flappin' his jaw about offering his services to Chicago as an inside man. Somebody I won't miss."

"Then what?"

I shut the door behind us, sealing us in the dark. My hand reached for the light switch.

"Then we send him outside on guard duty, all on his own, and pull all our other soldiers back. Make him a prime target."

I flicked on the light.

Plastic sheeting covered the floor of the empty room. Painter's tarp lined the walls, tacked up all around us. As the kid squinted, eyes adjusting to the light, I stepped around to stand beside Jennifer.

"Then," I said, "we pretend we don't know he's been replaced, and lead Kirmira straight into a kill room. What do you think? Will the plan work?"

The kid's eyes flared orange. He chuckled slowly, looking at the two closed doors on opposite sides of the room. Then to the plastic sheeting under our feet. His bones melted and reknitted to change the shape of his face, skin darkening, hair turning raven-black and growing out as he asserted his form.

"With respect," Kirmira said, "you have only half of a plan. You seem to have sealed yourself into a room with me and warned me of your intentions. An unwise strategy."

I shrugged. "That depends. I figured we'd play this wild-west style. Have a little showdown and see who's faster on the draw. What do you say? Are you game?"

His hands melted into tiger's paws, bristling with orange fur and killing claws.

"I am very, very fast, sir," he said.

Jennifer slid one foot to the left, steadying her stance, and beckoned to him with a curl of her fingertips.

"C'mon, then," she said. "Let's see what you got, sugar."

Kirmira leaped across the room, closing the gap between us in the blink of an eye, one paw raised high to carve out Jennifer's heart in a single lethal blow. He swooped down, claws glinting—

—and dangled in the air, letting out a strangled wheeze, as Jennifer caught him by the throat and held him aloft.

The door on the other side of the room swung wide. Kirmira's eyes bulged as a second Jennifer—the real one—strolled in and gave him a casual salute.

The Jennifer beside me wasn't Jennifer anymore. Legs and arms growing longer, more muscled, her shoulders broadening as her fingers sprouted jade-tipped claws. Her skull elongated, lips becoming a muzzle, cheeks bristling with five-inch whiskers and golden fur as her eyes glowed a vicious neon orange.

I'd seen statues of ancient Egyptian deities, goddesses with the body of a woman and the head of a lioness. Now I was standing next to one. The breath caught in my throat as Naavarasi lifted her struggling prey in the air with a single clenched hand. Kirmira kicked and squirmed, tugging at her forearm, struggling to breathe.

"To think," Naavarasi rumbled, "you actually believed this pathetic creature was one of my kin."

With his last breath, Kirmira croaked something. In Hindi, maybe. I couldn't understand the words. It sounded like a question. From the desperate, horrified look on his face, from the intensity in his dying voice, it sounded like the only question in the universe worth asking.

Naavarasi answered with a brutal twist of her hand. Kirmira's neck snapped. She tossed his lifeless body to the plastic sheets.

Seconds after hitting the floor, Kirmira's corpse began to change. His features melted like candle wax, the color draining from his skin, his bones settling and going flat as if they'd turned to cartilage, then to jelly. All that remained of the shape-shifter, nestled inside his abandoned clothes, was a frail and slug-belly-white lump of burbling tissue.

"Burn that," Naavarasi said, her tone imperious. She'd told me once that in her prime, before her realm was annexed by hell in a war that made her the last of her kind, people worshiped her as a deity. In that moment, I could understand why.

Then she shrank, the fur and fangs slipping away, her eyes fading to a gentle brown as she took on a human guise. A perfect duplicate of Kirmira stood before me now, indistinguishable from the real thing.

"This," the rakshasi queen said in Kirmira's voice, "makes two boons you owe me."

"I'm aware," I told her. "Thanks for the assist."

"I look forward to collecting."

She gathered up his clothes, leaving the flesh lump where it fell, and checked his pockets.

"I'll appraise you of their movements," Naavarasi said, "at least as much as I can without drawing suspicion. I suggest you find another means of tracking your prey once you flush them out, just in case. Or you could simply allow me to eliminate your enemies for you."

"So that's Angelo, his buddy Sal, and two or three more bodyguards. What's the going rate for a kill like that?"

She smiled with Kirmira's lips. "One boon for each life, of course. In addition to the two already owed."

"Yeah," I said, "that price is a little on the steep side. We'll handle that part ourselves."

"You're going to serve me eventually, Daniel. Why wait?"

"I'm waiting for you to tell me what your game is. You've had heavier hitters than me on your payroll, and your position in Prince Malphas's court means you could snap your fingers and recruit a dozen more. Why are you so dead set on snaring *me*?"

Naavarasi chuckled. "A lady is entitled to her secrets. Very well. I'll play my part, as requested. Don't keep me waiting. I'm liable to get...hungry."

* * *

While Sal bled out on the parking garage floor, shrieking and clutching his guts, Angelo turned and ran. He got about ten feet before headlights pinned him down, a pack of Blood Eagles rolling around the bend on tooled-up Harleys.

He ran the other way, back toward me. Toward me, Naavarasi

in her Bengal tiger form, and Jennifer, who stepped out from behind the rows of parked cars with half a dozen pistol-toting Calles at her back.

I saw it all, written on his face. The five stages of grief, except he was the dead man. Denial, anger, bargaining.

"We can—we can make a deal," he stammered.

"No," I said, "we can't."

Naavarasi took hold of Sal's throat in her mighty jaws and tore it out with one lurch of her shaggy head. She chewed the torn meat and swallowed, stepping over the corpse, her muzzle bloody.

Depression. Angelo fell to his knees on the concrete as we closed in around him. His shoulders shook and he squeezed his eyes shut.

Then acceptance.

He opened his eyes. Looked at me, like he was seeing clearly for the first time.

"It wasn't supposed to be like this," he said.

"According to who?"

His mouth hung open. He shook his head. Lost.

"My old man," Angelo said. "He always said I wouldn't amount to shit. Always said I *wasn't* shit. He said I was...I was an accident. My mom was old-school Catholic, you know. Wouldn't get an abortion. So he was stuck with me."

One of the Calles handed me his pistol. A black matte .45, heavy in my hand.

"I idolized him," Angelo told me. "I know how stupid that sounds, okay. How do you look up to a man who hates that you were even born? But I grew up in his world. He was...everything. He was all I had. And this was my shot. My one shot to prove I was worthy of his name. That I could do what he does. That I could be a man of power, like him."

His head sagged as I stood before him.

"I didn't care about this city. Or you, or the money, or...any of it. All I wanted...all I wanted was to win, and go home. And he'd go into the fridge, and he'd take out two beers. And he'd crack them open and hand me one. And he'd say, 'Son, I'm proud of you.' That's all I fucking *wanted*."

Three feet between us, but I felt closer than that. We'd both grown up in our fathers' toxic kingdoms. I'd escaped mine. Would I have ended up like him if I hadn't? Would he have ended up like me if he had?

"That's not a bad thing to want," I told him.

"I just proved he's right. I'm everything he said I am. Worthless."

"No," I said. "You fought hard. You did your best. That counts for something. And if he was worthy of you, if he was *ever* worthy of you, he would have told you so."

I thumbed back the hammer on the .45.

"Close your eyes, Angelo."

He raised his head, his eyes glistening.

"No."

Locking his gaze with mine, he reached up and put a finger to the barrel of the gun. Pushing it to the center of his forehead.

"Right here," he said. "Put it right here. And when you see him, you tell my father, you *tell* him that I went out like a man. That I faced the bullet. And I didn't flinch."

"I'll tell him," I said. "You have my word."

The pistol boomed like a cannon. Angelo's head snapped back; then he crumpled to the blood-spattered concrete.

The reverberations of the gunshot, rippling through the parking garage, faded into a rumbling echo. Then silence.

"One to go," I told Jennifer.

She nodded. "Damien Ecko."

"Let's reel him in. Tonight, all debts are paid."

42.

Bentley and Corman came in on a 9:45 flight from Orlando. By then a runner had brought the blue falcon amulet from the fortress. It rested snug in my pocket, a beacon shouting my location to Ecko every step I took.

I couldn't force Ecko to follow me, but I knew what he wanted: to hurt more of my family and friends, just like he'd done to Paolo, torturing me by proxy. And I knew if he sensed me at the airport, he'd want to know who I was meeting there.

"Thanks for coming back on short notice," I whispered to Bentley, hugging him tight as we met up in the baggage claim. "And for coming back at all. This is going to be dangerous."

"Fiddle-faddle. I've played many roles in my illustrious career, and 'bait' describes more than a few of them. Do we know if our fish is anywhere near the line?"

I had spotters for that. A handful of Jennifer's men, dressed in tourist clothes and lugging empty suitcases, prowling the concourse. My phone buzzed against my hip. As I pulled Corman into a hug, my arm around his shoulder, I turned and took a surreptitious peek at the screen.

"*Maybe him. Chairs by the AA baggage claim, behind a newspaper.*"

I glanced at the brushed steel of the baggage carousel. Couldn't make out much but a blur in the reflection, but somebody was there. Sitting alone, twenty feet from us, face buried behind the front page of the *Las Vegas Sun*. I didn't dare look closer than that, with my eyes or my magic: everything depended on Ecko believing I was in the dark.

Bentley pressed something into my palm, burning cold on an icy chain. The Black Eye. The talisman, bearing the engraving of a crudely scratched-out eye on one side, defaced hieroglyphs on the other, sent a leaden ache up my arm.

"C'mon," I said loudly as we walked past the chairs, "need to get you two out of sight. It's not safe here. You know the way to the ranch?"

"Sure, kiddo," Corman said, reciting his lines, "but I'd feel better if you were coming with us."

"Can't risk it. I've got to find Ecko. And until I do, you're safer if I'm nowhere near you."

Another text as we hit the concourse doors: *"He's following."*

"Here's where we split up," I murmured. "Drive slow and make it easy for him. I'll meet you there."

Gabriel was waiting down in the parking garage, near my rental car. I handed him the falcon amulet.

"So I gotta bring this where, exactly?"

"Everywhere," I told him. "Take a taxi somewhere, doesn't matter where, and toss it under the seat before you get out. That way it'll be moving all over town, all night long. By the time he figures out it isn't me, hopefully it'll be too late for him to do anything about it."

He gave me a dubious look. "Hopefully?"

"It's gonna be a long night."

A long night that started with a long drive. Out of the city, into the desert.

Ecko was a man long past caring for consequences. I had to get him away from civilians, away from anyone he could kill and reanimate to join his legion of the dead. I remembered the bloodless cambion back in his apartment, and his widow's warning: Ecko had stolen a semi truck. I had a good idea what kind of cargo he was hauling, too. There were still twenty or so corpses missing from that morgue in Chicago.

Emma wasn't deigning to speak with me just yet—she was a pro at nursing a grudge—but Caitlin played ambassador and relayed her approval. The Silk Ranch, still a month from its grand reopening, was the perfect place for a showdown. The remote compound, with its antique-styled buildings and rustic front gate made from artificially aged driftwood, even looked like the set of a spaghetti western.

I parked at the edge of the lot, thinking back to the last time the ranch had seen a showdown. And to Sullivan, buried—and hopefully dead—somewhere deep beneath my wheels and twenty tons of stone. Back then, renovations had just gotten started, construction equipment and pallets of drywall scattered everywhere. Now the work was down to the fine details. Fresh-laid ivory carpet adorned the floors of the main house, the welcome lounge windows decorated with frilled pink curtains. The decor fairly screamed "brothel," but then again, it was supposed to.

I wasn't alone. Jennifer scurried from room to room, dispatching a handful of Calles—the most veteran, hardened shooters she had—to their posts to watch for Ecko's arrival. While Bentley and Corman waited in a back room, Mama Margaux worked in the lounge, drawing an elaborate symbol on the carpet in glittering purple dust.

"If he sends his dead men through that front door," she told me, hunched low as she drew the sign, "cover your eyes. Gonna be one bright, beautiful flash, then a lot of falling bodies."

"Something I've always wondered," I said.

"Mm-hmm?"

"Okay, Haitian zombies aren't really *zombies*, right? I mean, they're living people who've been drugged by a neurotoxin."

Her brow furrowed with concentration. "Mm-hmm."

"So...how is it you know so much about the undead kind of zombies, too?"

Margaux stood up, dusting off her hands, and fixed me with a glare.

"Daniel, do I come to your peristyle and tell you how to hold a Kanzo and rattle the Asson?"

"Uh...I don't know what any of that is."

"That's right," she said. "You *don't*. Mind your business."

I couldn't argue with that. I made my way to the kitchen to sort my gear, the new stainless-steel appliances unplugged and still covered in protective plastic. Two fresh shells for Bessie, the sawed-off shotgun primed and ready. The Black Eye, waiting for me to put it on. And Howard Canton's top hat. I still had no idea what it was capable of, if it was capable of anything at all, but Canton's connection to both Ecko and the Enemy still taunted me. And when Ecko's dead woman attacked Bentley and Corman's apartment, there was no mistaking the sense of visceral loathing, something inside the hat reacting to the necromancer's handiwork. So I kept it close, just in case.

I would have felt even better if I had Canton's mythical wand, but then again, I wasn't going to be doing any magic with the Black Eye on. I could be powerful, or I could be invisible. Not both. And right now, I needed to be invisible.

Caitlin found me. I was still looking at the Eye, weighing it in my hand like a block of ice.

"He'll be here any minute now," she said.

"I know."

She stepped close, her fingers trailing along my arm. "It's hard, isn't it?"

"This amulet..." I shook my head. "It cuts you off from the flow of the universe. When you're a sorcerer, you feel the winds of magic *all the time*. Like the air in your lungs. Even if you're not actively using the power, you're aware of it. No, you need it. You need it to survive. Putting this thing on, it's like...jabbing needles in your ears and your eyes. All the light in the world goes out at once."

She took the amulet from my hands, her fingers light on the chain.

"Then let me be your flame," she said and clasped it around

my throat. Then she held me as my soul went deaf and blind, and my knees buckled and the breath slipped from my lungs. She held me until I could stand again, until I found my feet and curled my hands into fists.

"Now I'm invisible, just like him," I said. "Equal footing, even odds. Do something for me?"

"Name it, pet."

"When it's time to throw down with Ecko, once we get his zombies out of the way...don't help."

Caitlin arched an eyebrow. "Pardon?"

"You remember when you killed Sullivan, right outside those doors? You asked me to stay out of it. Because it was your fight. You had to do it yourself."

She nodded. "Of course."

"Well, this one's mine. I started this battle. And because I didn't finish it when I should have, people I care about got hurt. That's on me."

"You don't have to make amends for that."

I reached for the shotgun.

"It's not about making amends for the past. It's about being a better man, here and now. No more half measures, no more loose ends. Damien Ecko is my responsibility, Cait. And I'm going to live up to that responsibility by burying him right next to Sullivan."

I didn't have to wait long.

"We got movement!" came a shout from the second floor. "Headlights on the main road, coming in fast. Looks like a tractor-trailer rig."

Showtime. I strode out into the front lounge. "Mama, we good to go on our defenses?"

"Every door and every window. He can come in, but his creatures can't, not without gettin' a nasty surprise."

"Okay," I called out, "Mama and Caitlin, you're on the front line against the dead. Jennifer, you and your guys are in reserve in case any slip past. Remember, everybody: forget about head shots, that shit's for the movies. You aim for kneecaps and the spine. Immobilize them and stay clear of what's left until Mama and Cait can mop 'em up. While you're doing that, I'll be hunting Ecko."

Simple plan. He'd be focused on finding Bentley and Corman, killing them to get at me. Meanwhile, I'd be sneaking up behind him, invisible to his magic, and putting two shotgun slugs straight into his heart of stone.

"Uh," called down the Calles sentry from above, "we got a problem—"

I'd underestimated Damien Ecko one last time. One time too many.

The front doors of the lounge exploded into tinder, walls buckling, roof groaning in, as the semi slammed into the house at fifty miles an hour.

43.

The next thing I knew I was sprawled on the torn carpet, choking on dust, blinded by the halogen glare of the headlights. The semi's cab had breached the wall like a battering ram, front tires blown out and twisted at an angle, caught up on the splintered ruins of red velvet furniture. An air horn's blare pierced my ears, blotting out the world with its raw scream. Coughing, throwing an arm over my face, I scrambled to my feet and skirted the side of the cab. The front door hung wide on a twisted hinge. No driver. Just a brick tied to the gas pedal and a man's belt lashed to the steering wheel, holding the runaway truck on course.

I climbed into the cab and killed the ignition, headlights dying as the horn bleated its last. Groans of the dead filled the silence. A horde of them, shambling, crawling, clambering in over the wreckage of the wall and the useless, shattered wards.

Caitlin shot past me, enraged, grabbing one of the creatures from the edge of the pack by its throat and its wrist. She wrenched it around, hard, the corpse's arm tearing free with a twist of dry red sinew. "Go," she barked, her mouth lined with shark's teeth. "We can handle this. Find Ecko."

Margaux darted by on the other side of the truck. In the corner of my eye, she was different. Taller, leaner, garbed in a purple suit that wasn't there when I looked straight at her. Streamers of black light trailed behind her, following her outstretched fingers. A corpse lurched toward her, arms reaching out for the kill. Her fingers snapped, punctuating a burst of guttural Creole, and the dead man's chest exploded.

I ran for the back door. Bursting out into the desert night, heart pounding. Crouched low and cradling the shotgun in my hand. With the Black Eye around my neck, the gun was my only weapon. The cards in my pocket were only cards. Canton's top hat, perched ridiculously on my head, was only a hat. But just like I couldn't track Ecko, he couldn't track me.

We were two snipers, pursuing each other across the ruins of a battlefield by the pale moonlight. Sight, sound, and gut instinct. That was all we had.

I crept around the building's edge, keeping to the shadows, eyes squinted against the dark as I stared at the outbuildings. No swinging doors, no telltale hints. He was out there, somewhere close, watching while his minions laid siege.

A glimmer of movement caught my eye. The tail of a coat in the cold night breeze as its owner ducked around a corner. I held my breath, counted to three, then jogged across the open, dry ground between the two buildings. I crouched low on the other side, keeping my ears perked.

Then I saw him. Ecko strode out into the open, his back turned to me as he watched the battle unfold at the broken wall. He didn't know he was being hunted. I emerged from cover, slow and easy, and inched up behind him.

No last words, no cute patter. I'd get close—close enough to be certain, since two shells were all I had—and blast him straight to hell.

I closed in. Ten feet. Then seven. Then five. I took one more step, raising the shotgun, taking aim—

—and he spun with blistering speed, slapping the gun from my hands. It clattered to the dirt and I hit the ground a second later, Ecko's open palm smashing into my chest like a pair of brass knuckles. I felt a rib crack, my breath jarred from my lungs, the top hat falling from my head and rolling to the side as I landed hard on my back.

"Interesting technique, shielding yourself from me like that." Ecko tapped one of his ears. "I heard you breathing from twenty feet away."

I ripped the amulet from my throat and hurled it away. The universe came flooding back in, the winds of magic roiling around us like a gathering storm, singing their sweet siren song. I could breathe again. My cards leaped into my outstretched hand.

Ecko's foot came slamming down. I cried out as my splinted fingers snapped, cards scattering everywhere. He kept my hand pinned under his foot, regarding me with an amused smile. His other foot kicked the shotgun away, out of my flailing reach.

"I have walked the Earth for over three thousand years, Mr. Faust. And you genuinely thought you could challenge me? Your insolence infuriates me more than your deeds. You're an upstart with no respect for history." He glanced at the fallen hat and laughed. "Oh my, is that...is that *Canton's* hat? Good old Canton the Magnificent. You thought that would help, did you? Once again, you only know a sliver of the story. Just enough knowledge to get you in trouble."

"What's the connection," I grunted through gritted teeth. "Tell me."

"Oh, just another would-be champion looking to end my life. I faced him in...mm, want to say fifty-six? Fifty-seven? Good music back then. Anyway, I killed him. Too bad you couldn't find his wand. Now *that* was a powerful relic. With that you might have had a chance. The hat...is just a hat. Sorry."

He crouched beside me, one shoe planted on my broken fingers, grinding his heel down.

"You don't have the power to defeat me," he said, amused. "You never did. You never could. I am the chosen servant of the King of Worms, Mr. Faust. His acolyte, his emissary. And now...now I'll show you that power firsthand."

He raised one hand high above his head, fingers hooked into claws as he spat an incantation in a twisting tongue. A spell, a prayer, a ritual call to the dark. I struggled, helpless as thunder rippled across the desert flats. The gathering storm clouds, blotting out the stars, rumbled in answer to his words. His voice rose to a crescendo and then...

Nothing.

He blinked, tilting his head at me.

"Apparently, the king doesn't feel like indulging me tonight."

"Your gods abandoned you," I croaked. "Maybe he has too."

"Magic isn't an exact science. That's all right. We can do this the old-fashioned way."

Ecko straddled my chest, dead weight pressing down, and wrapped his fingers around my throat.

I flailed against him, pulling at his forearms, clawing at his wrists, but it was useless. He was made of concrete, and I was made of flesh and blood. Flesh turning purple under his squeezing hands, choking the life from my body. I'd done everything wrong. I'd gambled, I'd lost, and now my friends would pay the price. Spots blossomed in my fading sight as my breath failed, my pulse jackhammering in my ears while my heart raced to the bursting point.

In the corner of my eye I saw the shotgun, too far, impossible to reach. On the other side, Canton's top hat, fallen and useless in the dirt.

"*He was a stage magician in the forties,*" Carolyn Saunders had told me. "*Mostly forgotten today. Also, quite the skilled occultist. He concealed his affinity for* real *magic behind his sleight of hand. I believe you know a thing or two about that.*"

"*I'm not the first guy to work that angle,*" I had said.

Canton's wand. Truth and lies. A chip of Houdini's bone inlaid on one tip, and on the other, a chip from Djehutimesu, Ecko's first teacher. My mind raced back to Chicago, my dinner with Halima Khoury.

"*Hmm. Interesting. Something just occurred to me.*"

I remembered pausing, my pita halfway to my mouth. "What?"

"He was a bit of a trickster, they say. An illusionist, with a scoundrel's reputation but essentially a good heart."

Ecko's voice slithered into my ear, jarring me from my reverie. "Give up, Mr. Faust." His fingers clenched tighter around my throat. "It's over. No hope, no salvation, not for the likes of you. All is lost. *Accept* it."

And then I was back in the cave, out in the desert wastes. Sipping tea with the Mourner of the Red Rocks.

"You will come to a point where all is lost, where your foe's fingers are wrapped around your throat. In that moment, as your last breath escapes you, remember one thing: a question. This question. Ask yourself, 'Where would you hide it?'"

Ecko froze. He stared down at me.

"Why..." he asked, suddenly uncertain. "Why are you *smiling*?"

"Because," I wheezed, spending my last breath on the words, "we're all alike. Stage magicians. We try to be innovators, but we've all got the same fondness for the same old corny, classic tricks. Guess you could call it...respect for history."

My hand plunged into Canton's top hat. And kept going. Past the inner brim, which melted under my fingertips. And farther still. To a cold and airless void beyond, swallowing my arm halfway up to the elbow.

Something narrow and hard, a long, thin cylinder, floated against my outstretched palm. Gently pressed against my fingers by a cold and spectral hand. Passing on the torch.

"Now watch me pull a rabbit out of this fucking hat."

Violet light exploded from the hat as I drew out Canton's wand, a blast of raw power that threw Ecko like a toy, slamming him to the dirt. Wheezing for breath, I shoved myself up on my elbows and scrambled back. The wand pulsed in my hand. Mahogany, adorned with caps of ivory bone, a stylish tool from a stylish age.

Not Canton's wand. My wand now.

I got to my feet. And I knew what to do. The wand sang in my inner ear, a song of lies and truth, and both ached to play their parts.

For a moment, I was back at the start of this mess. Across the street from Larry's World of Liquor, weaving a simple spell while the Delaney brothers babbled at me. I'd caught a sense, in that moment, of something greater than myself. A glimpse of the legacy I'd inherited, the chain of sorcery stretching back through showmen and philosophers, through warlocks and heretics, all the way back to the first shamans in the first caves, discovering the magic of fire. I felt them all, felt myself standing at the end of their lineage, and I had wondered if they saw me, too.

Now I felt them again. Saw them, their ghostly visages ringing the clearing like gossamer mist. And as their silver eyes turned to face me as one, I knew the answer to my question.

I put on Canton's hat, then picked up the gun. Wand in my left hand, shotgun in my right.

A fog washed in over the desert sand. An impossible fog, pea-soup thick and cloaking the world in swirling white. Ecko staggered to his feet, shaking his head to clear it.

"Faust," he bellowed, "come out! Come out and face me!"

I twirled the wand in my fingertips. I knew, instinctively, which end was which.

"Face yourself first," I said. And with a slash of the ivory tip, I ripped away his illusions.

44.

The dapper, dusty old man was gone. In his place stood a rotting horror, a desiccated corpse wound in filthy, gore-encrusted bandages. Ecko's jaw dropped on a broken hinge as he clutched at his body, at the amulets bristling under parched and sewn-up skin.

"Take a good look," I told him and drew upon the air. Mercury billowed from the wand's tip in a silver stream, hanging in space, blossoming to offer a smooth, shiny reflection.

Ecko saw himself, the true face he'd concealed for centuries, and screamed.

I darted around him, slashing the air, mercury streaks blooming in every direction. Mirrors confronting him everywhere he turned, forcing him to see his own decay, the depth of the corruption he'd hidden for so long. He bellowed from a raspy, sand-dry throat, emaciated hands flailing wildly.

It was a distraction. Just enough to let me slip up behind him and press both barrels of the shotgun to his back.

"This is for my friends," I told him and squeezed both triggers.

Ecko's chest exploded as the slugs tore through him, withered meat and chunks of stone and broken amulets flying across the dirt. He fell to his knees, let out one last, agonized hiss, then collapsed onto his face.

The mercury mirrors dissolved in puffs of silver smoke. The impossible fog cleared away, leaving nothing behind. Nothing but me and a dead man. I stood over Ecko's corpse, catching my breath. Feeling the wand tingle against my hand, a comforting and dangerous caress.

"Is it finished?" Caitlin asked, standing behind me.

She looked like she'd just run a marathon. She, and Jennifer, and Mama Margaux. The three of them gasping for breath, spattered in a few buckets' worth of blood, but none of it theirs.

"It's finished," I told them. "Ecko's zombies?"

"Last one keeled over just as I was about to send it packin'," Margaux panted. "You saved us about...five seconds of work. Try a little harder next time."

"I'll make an effort."

We walked away, side by side. Jennifer squinted at me.

"You need to take that hat off."

"This hat is worth a million dollars," I told her. "And it just saved my life."

"Yeah, but it looks ridiculous on you. Cait, back me up here."

"You need to take the hat off," Caitlin said.

"The hat stays."

"Let him wear the hat if he wants," Margaux said. "Just not if he's going to be seen with any of us in public. But in private, he can wear what he likes. After all, I hear he's...*the guy*."

I grimaced. "Not you too."

It felt good hearing my friends laugh, and laughing along with them. Laughter means you're alive and breathing. Laughter means you've got something to feel good about, something to feel thankful for. And we had plenty of that to go around.

We'd just fought a war together. And we won.

* * *

The war wasn't really over, of course. Not yet.

Five black SUVs, Explorers with tinted windows, rolled out of Las Vegas on I-15 North, aiming for Salt Lake City. And then, on to Chicago.

We hit the outskirts of the city on a cold, starless night. Halloween weather, and the lush lawns of Dominic Mancuso's mansion were blanketed in orange and scarlet leaves. The sentries on the house's wrap-around porch squinted as a heavy fog drifted over the grass, blotting out the world.

Then bursts of machine-pistol fire, muffled by sound suppressors, dropped them where they stood.

The front doors of the mansion blew open, locks powdered by a breaching slug, and the foyer flooded with men in black. An Outfit hitter ate a hail of bullets, tumbling over the second-floor balcony and crashing to the marble floor below. Another took the stairs down, rolling and collapsing in a bloody heap. The New Commission's finest fanned out, going loud now. Gunfire and screams echoed through the house as they cleaned out Mancuso's soldiers one room at a time.

And I led the way, with my wand in one hand and a silenced nine-millimeter in the other. A general commanding my troops.

Double doors at the top of the stairs thundered open. Koschei the Deathless strode forth, cracking his knuckles in anticipation. He paused, curious, as my men cleared the way for a new arrival. Caitlin. She stepped into the house and smiled sweetly.

"So," she said, "about that rematch."

I could understand his hesitation. She wasn't wearing an evening gown this time. She'd opted for something more utilitarian: a sturdy pair of overalls and a surgeon's plastic full-face visor.

And the newly bought tool in her hands, a cordless forty-volt Black and Decker chainsaw.

The saw revved to life, the toothy blade whirring and eager to slice. I left Koschei in Caitlin's capable hands. A small entourage followed me into the back warrens of the house, hunting down the man at the top of the pyramid.

I found Dominic in his office. He reached into his desk. I saw the flash of a gun just before my pistol barked, putting a hole in his shoulder. His piece thumped to the carpet as he clutched his wound.

"Fight's over," I told him. "You lost."

He jumped up from his chair, pressing his back to the wall.

"Don't do this. Don't, just—look, anything you want. I've got money, drugs, anything you want, name it—"

"I was thinking, 'you, dead.' Can I have that?"

The old man threw himself to the carpet. Down on his knees, his forehead to the floor as he whimpered and begged. I had expected rage, defiance, anything but this.

"Please, we can make a *deal*," he said.

"Your son said the same thing."

He froze, looking up at me. "My...son?"

I nodded to the man on my left. He tossed a burlap sack to the floor.

Dominic pulled back the folds. Just far enough to see his son's severed head inside. A faint, strangled cry rose from the back of his throat. His trembling fingertips stroked Angelo's hair.

"Hell of a thing," I said, "discovering you do care about your son after all, *after* you sent him to die."

"Please," he whined, "I'll call it off. I'll call everything off, just let me go. I'll do whatever you want."

I shook my head. I couldn't keep the disgust from my face.

"You know the saddest part?" I asked. "All he wanted was a little love. Have a beer with him. Tell him you were proud of him, *once*. That's all you had to do. But I'll tell you one thing: when the time came? He didn't beg, didn't cry, not like you. He stared down the bullet. He wanted you to know that."

I aimed my pistol right between his eyes.

"I want you to know it, too. Because Angelo was twice the man you'll ever be. *Despite* you."

In his final moments, Dominic swallowed hard and mustered his last tattered scraps of defiance.

"This doesn't change anything. We're just one family. The Outfit is bigger than the Mancusos, lots bigger. And when the other families hear about what you did—"

"They'll do *nothing*," I said. "Because we're proving, here, tonight, that we can reach out and destroy anyone who stands in our way. We can get at you in your homes. In your *beds*. And nothing can stop us."

Dominic's lip trembled as his gaze dropped, staring down the barrel of the gun.

"So tell me something, Dominic," I said. "I was just thinking about our last conversation, at the Willowbrook. Tell me...do you think I'm a man of power now?"

I didn't give him a chance to answer. I didn't care. I shot him dead and walked away, my entourage at my back.

Caitlin had an entourage of her own down in the foyer, working feverishly to beat the clock. Two were mopping the gore from her surgical mask and unclogging the chainsaw. The rest were sealing Priority Mail boxes with heavy tape. Fifteen in all, each addressed to a different nonexistent address in a different state. Once they were mailed out, first thing in the morning, the various chunks of Koschei's dismembered body would find a permanent home in dead-letter offices all across the country.

"Do you think it'll work?" I asked her.

She wiped her hands on her blood-drenched overalls. "Either that, or we'll end up with fifteen tiny Koscheis. So...I choose to believe it will work, yes."

I put my arm around her waist and pulled her close.

"Let's go home."

* * *

No rest for the wicked. I had a full list of errands to attend to as soon as we got back to a welcoming Vegas sunrise.

First and foremost, hunting for a new apartment. Caitlin had promised to go looking at a few prospects with me that afternoon. My down payment secured, courtesy of a small loan.

A loan, not a gift. I wouldn't take her charity. But I was about to start a brand-new job, and money wouldn't be a problem.

I had a meeting to attend. A meeting in a rented conference room at the Flamenco, behind closed doors and two layers of armed security, at a long slate table with high-backed leather chairs. The luminaries of the Vegas underworld all in attendance, securing their claims as the heads of the New Commission.

And me, taking the seat at Jennifer's right hand.

I held up the bottle of Veuve Clicquot from Larry's World of Liquor. It had been sitting in Bentley and Corman's refrigerator, waiting for the right time. That felt like now.

"Brought a little something," I said. "How about a toast to a job well done?"

"Fairy piss," Winslow grumbled, holding up his own bottle. "I'll stick with my Bud."

Everyone else was game, and the cork popped and the champagne poured. A quiet celebration, a toast to our survival and another day in the game. I raised my glass high.

"To the future," I said. "May it be bright and shining, as rich and pure as solid gold."

I gazed across the table, meeting every eye, and smiled.

"Because we're going to steal it."

Epilogue

T he Play lay open on a desk of polished glass, scattered tarot cards all around it. The leather-bound tome was a treasure trove. A reliquary of a blasphemous faith that seethed with sealed power. Seals that had obediently shattered, one by one, surrendering their gifts to their rightful owner.

Until now.

Act Five, Scene One, read the page before him. *The Thief is taken away to face torment and death at the hands of the False Warden.*

The pages beyond it stuck fast as though they'd been glued together.

The Enemy hunched over his desk, flickering, his body an electric shadow. His pearly teeth clenched in frustration. Then he swirled away, gusting through the corporate halls of Northlight Tower like a cyclone of black smoke. He found Ms. Fleiss in the blue glow of the situation room, standing behind a team of technicians with her arms folded and her lips pursed. A dozen monitors siphoned data from all over the globe, sniffing for trigger phrases, listening for connections.

"My lord," she said, turning and bowing her head. "He...escaped me. I'm sorry."

"*How?*" he demanded. "I was assured that this Faust was nothing but a common street mage. A penny conjurer. How has he escaped your grasp *twice?*"

"It won't happen again."

"That isn't an answer."

"Marcel is back from Rome. I've put him in the waiting room."

He paused. As he wavered, thinking, his outline looked like a stop-motion sketch brought to life. Vague scratchy lines of white chalk on black construction paper.

"Then let's secure our investment. And don't think for a second that this discussion is over."

As they strode into the waiting room, the young receptionist primly stood and left without a word. Only Marcel Deschamps remained, the Frenchman rising from a beechwood bench, offering a cocky smile.

"I'm back, with gifts," he said, offering them a bundle wrapped in jade silk. Fleiss took it from him and unwrapped it, holding the contents out for the Enemy's inspection. His blurry-negative head nodded once. She wrapped the bundle back up again and set it on the reception desk.

"So," Marcel said, "where's the next score? Paris? New York? Keep crossing my palm with silver and I'm your man. You know there's not a prize on this planet I can't take."

"I'm aware," the Enemy said. "Alas, you won't be leaving for the foreseeable future."

"No jobs yet? That's fine, I have a room in town. I can wait a few days."

"You won't be leaving this building," Fleiss told him. She faced him as the Enemy circled around slowly, getting behind him. Marcel frowned.

"We have a problem," the Enemy said. "I was...mistaken when I reported that Daniel Faust was deceased. He has yet to face his appointed doom."

Marcel shrugged, uneasy. "So let's find the guy. I'll help."

"That's the problem. If you die before we can hunt down Faust, you'll take the title of the Thief with you. Reincarnating on some far-flung parallel world, where it could take eons to find you again. And preventing me from unlocking the powers of the Fifth Act. I'm so close now, Marcel. So close to returning to my full strength. I can *taste* it."

"Hey, I'm not going to die anytime soon," Marcel said with a nervous laugh. "You know me, I'm careful."

"You're a cat burglar who likes to climb skyscrapers, drive Italian sports cars at high speed, and drink to excess," Fleiss said, inching closer. "That's a risk we can't afford to take. So you'll stay here, as our guest, until Faust is neutralized."

"You can't keep me here against my will," Marcel said, turning. "That's a load of—"

He froze as Fleiss's fingertips rested on his temples. She moved in, her body pressed to his, their lips inches apart. Then her master closed in against his back. His ethereal photonegative body tingled against Marcel like static electricity. A shadowy hand stroked the nape of Marcel's neck, another running along his arm. Intimate. Almost arousing. Marcel had been in a threesome once, in Belize, that had started much like this.

Then Fleiss opened her mouth and a prehensile, gnarled tongue spilled out, leaving a trail of slime as it lapped along Marcel's cheek.

"You would have been the greatest cat burglar of all time," the Enemy cooed into his ear, his voice hypnotic. "If it hadn't been for the accident."

"What...what accident?" Marcel stammered, paralyzed between them.

"You remember. You were five. Your mother was drunk. She was usually drunk. It was Christmas Eve."

Marcel nodded, his head jerking. "My parents were fighting, shouting. She...she was going to drive us to a motel for the night. My father took her keys away. He threw them in a snowbank, so she couldn't find them until she sobered up. How did you know about—"

"No," Fleiss whispered, "he didn't. He put them in a bowl by the door."

"He put them in a bowl by the door," Marcel echoed.

"And you and your mother got in the car," the Enemy purred, his hands roving over Marcel's flesh. "Do you remember now?"

Marcel tried to shake his head, but he still stammered. "I-I remember. We got in the car."

"Yes. Yes. And she slid on a patch of black ice. And you hit a delivery truck head-on."

Marcel tumbled to the waiting-room rug. Confused, he looked down at himself.

At the lump of scar tissue at one shoulder, where his left arm used to be. At the stump of his right wrist. At the way his tailored slacks fell short at the nubs of his knees, where the surgeons had amputated both of his legs when he was five years old.

He looked across the lobby to one mirrored wall. To his disfigured face, the web of scar tissue marring his emaciated neck, and howled in animal terror.

The Enemy's pearly teeth bared a Cheshire smile.

"There. Now you won't be able to endanger yourself *or* escape. A perfect solution." He paused. "Also, the shrapnel severed your vocal cords."

Marcel's horrified shrieks became a faint, whisper-soft wheeze.

"Much better. Ms. Fleiss, please find a place to put Mr. Deschamps until we need him again."

Fleiss hefted the struggling, broken man over her shoulder like a sack of groceries.

"Oh, and do make sure he's comfortable," the Enemy added. "After all, there's no need to be *cruel* about this."

"As you command, my lord."

"Then come back around, and we'll discuss our strategy for dealing with Daniel Faust."

"I...do have something that might help."

The shadowy head tilted. "Oh?"

"I caught a glimpse inside his mind just before he escaped. I know how he thinks and what he cares about more than anything else. If we want to draw him out, there's only one way to do it: go after his friends, his family. I don't know their names...but I saw their faces."

The Cheshire smile grew larger. "Excellent. Bring in a sketch artist."

He flowed through the shifting halls of his empire, to the darkness of his office. The only light in his inner sanctum glowed from a laptop screen. He clicked open an instant messaging program and typed out a quick message to one of his servants.

"*Progress on finding the Scribe or the Paladin? Also, looking for information on a target named Daniel Faust. Magician, human, last known location Las Vegas. High priority. Attaching a partial dossier.*"

*   *   *

Another laptop sat on another table in a dark and smoky room, pinging as the Enemy's message came in. A snake curled around the computer, sinuous, banded with scarlet and yellow scales. Jade-painted nails rapped out a quick response.

"*Unfamiliar with this Faust person, but will do some research. Still no progress finding the other targets.*"

"*Redouble your efforts,*" came the response. "*This is urgent.*"

Naavarasi chuckled. She reached to one side, scooping a handful of rogan josh from a bowl with her left hand and dropping a gobbet of meat down her throat. She swallowed it whole, without chewing, before wiping her fingertips on a cloth napkin and typing her reply.

"*Of course, my lord. I live to serve you.*"

Off to her right, a cockroach skittered over a discarded paperback. *The Killing Floor* by Carolyn Saunders. And in the background of her screen, the last email she'd sent still sat in her archive: "*Daniel. Care for some inspirational reading? — A Friend.*"

A fresh window popped up on her screen. "*Everything is in place, Mistress,*" it read. "*Initiate next stage of the plan?*"

Naavarasi gazed across her blood-soaked restaurant, her little slice of hell, and smiled.

"*Initiate.*"

Afterword

What a topsy-turvy, wild year it's been. Writing, the launch of the Harmony Black series, writing, discussions about a possible Faust television show, moving house, writing...at this point I'm not entirely sure *how* to take a day off anymore, but that's okay. Totally worth it. And now that my publishing schedule has more or less smoothed out (and the Revanche Cycle came to an end with this year's release of *Queen of the Night*, the fourth and final chapter), I can pretty much guarantee you won't be waiting an entire year for another full-length Faust novel. Which is good, because there's a lot going on. Plans in motion.

Gotta take a second to give a shout-out to my awesome team: thanks to Kira Rubenthaler for editing, James T. Egan for cover design, Adam Verner's top-notch audiobook voicework, and the assistance of the always-reliable Maggie Faid. And thank *you* for reading! I hope to see you again in 2017, when Daniel Faust will learn a dangerous lesson: seizing power is hard enough, but keeping it...well, that can be murder.

Want to get the advance scoop on new books and projects? Head over to http://www.craigschaeferbooks.com/mailing-list/ and hop onto my mailing list. Once-a-month newsletters, zero spam. Want to reach out? You can find me on Facebook at http://www.facebook.com/CraigSchaeferBooks, on Twitter as @craig_schaefer, or just drop me an email at craig@craigschaeferbooks.com.